THE ABALONE UKULELE

An historical novel set in 1913 Shanghai, where four cultures are about to collide: China, Korea, Japan, and the US. The point of collision is three tons of Japanese gold ingots meant to undermine an already collapsing China.

THE ABALONE UKULELE

A TALE OF FAR EASTERN INTRIGUE

R. L. Crossland

THESPRING

Washington, DC

Library of Congress Control Number: 2021907791
ISBN 978-1-7359378-1-6 (alk. paper)
ISBN 978-1-7359378-7-8 (hardcover)

THESPRING is an imprint of New Academia Publishing

New Academia Publishing
4401-A Connecticut Ave. NW #236, Washington DC 20008
info@newacademia.com - www.newacademia.com

Dedicated to the American and Korean combatants who
participated in Operation Dark Moon (1951-1953)
during the Korean War,
and the stalwarts of the New York Naval Militia
(1889-present)

CONTENTS

NOTE ON ROMANIZATION

All Chinese words and names employed use the pinyin romanization system with the exception of the names of historical figures, and major geographic locations in Wade-Giles romanization which are as they would have appeared on charts of the era, and Chinese words that have been adopted into the English language and romanized randomly.

All Korean words and names employed use the Revised Romanization of Korean 2000 with the exception of the names of historical figures, and major geographic locations which would have appeared on charts in the first half of the 20th Century using the McCune-Reischauer romanization system and Korean words that have been adopted into the English language and romanized randomly.

*'Twas like a Maelstrom, with a notch, that nearer, every day,
kept narrowing its boiling wheel.*
—Emily Dickinson

PART I

YI'S STORY

Seven times down, up eight
—Korean proverb

Map of 1911-13 China and Korea
© R. L. Crossland 2020, Artwork by "RenflowerGrapx (Maria Gandolfo)"

CHAPTER ONE

Tientsin, China, 1893 – file Alpha, folder one

Sergeant Go scuttled across the bow of the junk *Jilseong* and found his officer, Korean Army Captain Jung-hee Yi, prone on the foredeck. He was scanning the waterfront with those ungainly, expensive night field glasses of his.

Yi said nothing and Go knew what that meant. He was searching each lantern-illuminated face on the pier for some hint of special attention.

No suggestions, no indications, no apparent threat.

"Everyone pictures emissaries as clad in silk, wearing ceremonial daggers. If they only knew how much time we expended these days ankle-deep in ox manure," the heavy-shouldered captain confided.

Sergeant Go squatted next to him, looked thoughtfully at his own mucky feet, and chuckled. Then he stifled a cough. Taking the night glasses, he panned full circle, watching for that single aggressive movement from any unexpected quarter. The advantage to the outsized front lenses of the night glasses was they collected more light facilitating better defined images.

He caught the eye of each of the two courier detail lookouts and waited for them to acknowledge. He studied the junk's captain who overlooked the helmsman and his five crewmen as they stood ready to handle lines.

"It's diplomats they associate with manure, not couriers," Go rasped with a snort of derision. "Not much we can do. Not feeding the oxen for two weeks before a jaunt just won't work.

Several of Yi's men were rigging the derrick that would lift the oxen out of *Jilseong*'s hold in belly slings. The derrick wasn't large enough to swing them over the side safely. The Korean junk's narrow beam required the oxen to be first deposited on deck, and only then, moved to the pier. The tribute silver was equally heavy and would follow the same route.

Yi's methodical planning had assured the junk made landfall and passed the Dagu Forts by dusk. He always consulted the *I Ching*, the *Confucian Classic of Changes*, studiously thinking through the six variables to each successive operational challenge. And then addressing the six options each variable generated. It was his duty. His beliefs required he achieve his potential and honor the ancestors always.

They'd doused their sails and then surged up the Hai River to the piston rhythm of the auxiliary steam engine. A series of four pagodas marked a river more sinuous than a dragon's back.

Now, the third pagoda loomed dead ahead marking the terminus of the boat segment of their journey. On either side of the river lay the dimly lit structures known as the "Long Storehouses." It was 100 li from the Forts to the walled inner city of Tientsin. They were at the 85 li mark.

"I miss the old procession deliveries, all the rippling banners, the bells and gongs. They were festive affairs." Sergeant Go mused. "On the other hand, those Porro prism glasses make it so a man can pluck the shadow off a silhouette."

Annually Korea paid China tribute in silver, copper, ginseng, and other goods valued at about 30,000 tael. A *tael* was 1.2 ounces of silver frequently fashioned into boat-shaped ingots, *sycee*, of different denominations. When paid in silver exclusively, the total yearly silver shipment weighed eighteen tons.

Yi was ten years younger than Go. They and their men, were part of the organization that made those payments in several installments. Korea paid tribute and in return, China agreed to safeguard Korea and remain out of its internal affairs.

Yi nodded. He knew Sergeant Go played the simple soldier, but his contemplative sergeant knew there was nothing simple about courier duty — even in the procession days. Go was always analyzing the next step, the step after that, and projecting prioritized options.

Yi could make out the pier now. Behind it was a ramshackle warren of sheds, shacks, and *godowns* that spread left and then up the river. A floating hedge of junks rafted one and two-deep opened to receive *Jilseong* which trebled their size. The junks weren't pickets, rather residential and bumboat squatters at sufferance. They maintained their unofficial night anchorages pointed upriver for a small fee as long as they kept confidences and didn't interfere with important commerce. The junk-curtain flapped to one side, just enough to allow the Korean junk to tie up.

The oak double-timbered junk rode low in the water. He still feared grounding on a river shoal, even pier side.

The weight of *Jilseong*'s cargo was significant, when added to the weight of the English-built boiler and triple-expansion engine which were confined in steel-lined compartments. In a couple years, he planned to replace that engine with a British steam-turbine engine. The prime and secondary steering stations were inconspicuously sandbagged in a web of tarred line. The builders had fashioned an armored (and uncomfortably compressing) "crib" below deck to shelter the crew and courier detail. A similar crib cradled the silver.

The junk's speed under steam guaranteed few ships could catch her, but her draft made grounding on a river shoal an ever-present danger.

This was Tientsin, gateway to Peking, one of several unheralded points of delivery, an upriver port of the Hai River. The city's borders encompassed the three foreign concessions of Britain, France and Japan, and the ancient walled inner city. Other foreigners, Russians, Germans, Austro-Hungarians, Italians, Belgians, Americans, and Koreans, walked its streets without attracting attention.

Within minutes they tied up the ramp, to Sergeant Go's monosyllabic commands. Single syllables did not betray accents.

When *Jilseong*'s crew was done, Sergeant Go stomped on the deck three times and the remaining sixteen men of the courier detail filed on deck to offload cargo.

The night was cool, yet every man's tunic was soaked in sweat. Several of the detail – their carbines wrapped in rolls of cloth like bedrolls — took positions behind crates and baskets. None wore uniforms.

"Ready to offload sacks of 'iron ore'?" Yi asked.

Go bristled, though not because he was the elder. Yi realized he'd unconsciously struck a nerve. Officers attended to grand concepts; noncommissioned officers like Go made things happen. They were *always* ready to address the practical.

Oxen, unlike horses, grew restive if they had to stand in one place for long. They needed to be loaded with the silver in the staging area ashore quickly and moved quickly. Loading the oxen's massive arching packframes on a swaying deck risked capsizing the junk.

"Does the sun go down at sunset? Does snow ever blanket Mount Baektu's peak?" Sergeant Go answered, raising one eyebrow. "You have a gift for these new ways, and more tricks than a shaman. Still there are things you have to learn, and I, cousin, am here to suggest them. Let's not get ahead of ourselves. We're both plowing new furrows in uneasy times."

"I wouldn't doubt there was a shaman somewhere in your bloodline," Go added almost resentfully.

Yi knew the readiness question was wrong the moment he'd asked it, though he was anxious to move the evolution along. Who in his position wouldn't be?

Sergeant Go, a distant relation, gave his stocky captain hints how to be a good officer when no one was looking. Sergeant Go was steady, reliable, and circumspect. Yi was *muban*, the military officer caste of Korean of the yangban aristocracy. He had passed the exams required to take his commission.

Go's family had once been yangban, too, but three successive generations of his family had failed to pass the civil or military examinations. This failure relegated his family by law to the next lower class, the *jungin*. He had served with great merit to achieve his present position. He galled at the slightest suggestion of incompetency in his current role. Whatever Go's issue, Yi knew it wasn't with him personally.

Then too, Yi had overheard a discussion between Go and one of the men. Evidently Go was not happy with shamans, healers, or fortune-tellers this week.

Go was as lean and tough as whipcord, nevertheless Yi wondered if his health, or the health of some other member of his family, was failing. Yi was struck by the thought Go had seen a shaman recently.

Yi wanted to ask, to assure him that he was an excellent soldier.

He wanted to tell Go that three generations of scholarly failure meant nothing in the real world. Yet, Yi couldn't cross the line, it would only make things worse. "Always the ancestors," Yi sighed feeling obliged to reveal his personal demons and trying to end the exchange. "Oh, a mythical bear who became a woman and mother of the Korean nation is in the Yi bloodline surely. But no shamans we admit to. Can't a man ever be alone and free of the ancestors? "

Go having made his point, smiled avuncularly, and returned to the oxen.

Points of transition were particularly vulnerable to ambush, he knew, and needed to be addressed smartly. The time constraints on unloading added to the general tension.

After a rough crossing, Go imagined the oxen would be relieved to place their hooves on a stable surface. Below, they had been chained and bolted into position. Oxen were inclined to bunch up, and stampede, even in a confined space. Their combined weight, if they were allowed unrestrained movement, was capable of capsizing the junk. That was a risk, even tied to the pier.

Right away he saw a problem. The lead ox baulked at descending the ramp.

Sergeant Go strode quickly to the first ox and adjusted its blindfold downward. Oxen could only be led across a ramp like this one blindfolded.

The mess created by the bowel-vacating oxen below had coated feet and hooves with ordure. The first drover, a new man, had concentrated on his beast's footing, not the position of its blindfold.

Yi caught Go's attention and made a hand gesture signaling "well-done." Let all our problems be so easily resolved, thought Yi, skimming his drover's switch along the junk's rail.

Moments later, his men were leading the remaining seven oxen from the heavy-timbered junk to a small staging area.

As the last blindfolded ox was led down the ramp, Yi was reminded that male oxen were invariably castrated. It made them steady and reliable. All their oxen were, in fact, males; male oxen were larger and could carry larger loads.

Debarkation had required concentration on the ramp. Now in the gloom, Yi could dog-trot to the eight oxen and pack-frames ashore and focus his efforts there.

"Strong and docile," one of his men observed reading Yi's mind. "Thankfully, we've been allowed to remain strong and decidedly un-docile."

The lead drover, Corporal Mun, was organizing the staging area and gave Yi a crisp, almost imperceptible, nod of the head.

"Oxen at the back, ox packframes, left; ordnance sacks center; the two 'ceramics' *jiges*, right. Don't even think of dropping those 'ceramics,' brothers. Keep them well clear of those heavy-hooved beasts back there" the corporal susurrated as each detail member deposited a portion of the cargo.

He looked directly at Yi, accompanying that last caution with a brief flare of his eyes.

Each ox packframe resembled the picturesque Camel Back Bridge in Peking. The pack-frames were designed to straddle an ox at its midsection. Beside the frames, sacks of iron ore tailings stacked in groups of five concealed the silver tael. Yi's men, experienced drovers, quickly cinched on the arched pack-frames and loaded the sacks.

Ordnance included extra carbines and ammo, and curved, single-bladed swords, in straw-stuffed sacks.

These jiges were A-frame man-packs designed to carry an innovative item Yi had recently introduced to the detail's organizational gear.

The ox-train floated soundlessly through the alleys and along the footpaths, hastening down a series of narrow alleys and footpaths that would have proved impassable by ox cart. The ox-train moved along the bank gradually angling northward. These oxen didn't respond to voice commands. Instead they responded to a code of whacks on their haunches by way of a switch. The occasional lowing attracted no attention.

Oxen transport was a mode that traced both sides of the Yellow Sea with ubiquity. The courier detail set course to a prearranged livestock pen with sheds and a walled paddock on the outskirts of Tientsin.

They arrived at the paddock a few hours later. The stonewalled enclosure looked tired and its mortar had degenerated to light grit. Its first course had been built finger-tip-to-shoulder high using mortar and stone. Later, another course, the same height, had fortified the paddock with the same materials, plus timber posts and shoring.

Once there, the men bivouacked behind the shed, upwind of the aromatic manure and human night soil pile that was the pen's owner's greatest source of revenue. The pen didn't attract casual onlookers. Its value lay in its seclusion and its stench.

Yi always watched the oxen consume the waiting feed and water with care. A portion of the water went to his men and allowed Yi to clean up and assumed a courtlier appearance, the appearance of a man of resource and experience.

As dawn broke, Yi set off to meet the representative of the Chinese empress by crossing a bridge, and taking a ferry, into the walled inner city to announce the time and place of delivery. A heavily-laden ox-train could never have negotiated the walled city's narrow streets, and it would be ripe for ambush.

His orders were to exchange bona fides, to provide the intricate points of turnover, and to supply the rendezvous point. Then he was to keep away from the silver until well after dark, then slip back unseen to the livestock pen. The next day – if all went well – he'd lead the Chinese counterparts to the tribute.

The tael, all washed free of iron ore tailings and manure splatter, would be primly stacked in a nearby godown, ready for counting and acceptance at noon the next day.

The meeting went well. His counterparts appeared forthright.

His hours of coordination with the Chinese finished, Yi considered the next eight hours his own.

At twilight, he sauntered into a *changsan* house, a gaming establishment, he knew well.

The emissaries of the *Qing* dowager empress had in the preceding year agreed to take possession of the tael tribute in Tientsin and a few other places on the Empire's eastern border. Tientsin was Yi's favorite.

This particular changsan house, just outside the walls of the inner city, presented an explosion of color and gilded mythological depictions. Many of the images replicated figures in Korean myth, with only minor differences. The building was also peppered with lanterns of all sizes, dimensions, and design. The owner promised to introduce gaslight soon.

He recognized some faces — more of the women than the men — and not others.

Most of the establishment's women were well-known entertainers and courtesans.

There was a smattering of European faces. He'd never formally met a European, and wouldn't have been able to understand their languages at any event. Travel outside of Korea was rigidly regulated. The primary threats to tribute delivery, he'd learned from his superiors, were rogue Chinese and Korean elements. Then came European filibusters. Finally, there was the distant threat of unsanctioned political elements from Russia or Japan.

Korea's national security had been spun for ages like a child's pinwheel by incursions from China, Russia, and Japan.

China had attempted several times to conquer Korea, but found those adventures too costly. Korea, like China, was fashioned from several kingdoms. From the outset, Korea was protected by the natural fortifications of an extremely mountainous peninsula. The empire and the feisty kingdom came to a mutually beneficial agreement; Korea could remain independent for a price.

For some time now, China had held Russia and Japan at bay, in return for tribute payments.

He searched the well-appointed gaming room with about twenty chattering Chinese men and women. Two thirds of the crowd were very loud. One third were raving with success, a third were muttering with loss. The final third was whispering and holding very, very still, lest they draw the attention of the warring gods of fortune.

On the periphery, a few well-dressed, polite men with broken noses and facial scars provided drinks and maintained decorum.

Yi at once searched for Liqin, a comely Chinese-Korean half-caste woman who lived in the Korean quarter. She spoke Korean, though felt no obligation to observe the customary and cumbersome Korean proprieties between single men and single women involving introductions, station, and chaperones.

"Yi-nim…" she started with a Korean honorific that no one there understood. She had burst out of nowhere.

He laughed at her formality.

She fluttered her eyes dramatically and continued, "…you grace us once again with your eminence.

"So, my gallant friend from across the Yellow Sea has not forgotten, this poor little girl so all alone in this strange land after all?"

He stammered, not able to generate an appropriate retort. She was rarely alone, she wasn't poor, and she was hardly a forlorn "little" girl, but a grown, worldly woman.

Liqin's skin was smooth and white as alabaster. She could trifle with words, kittenish looks, and the bric-a-brac of gambling, for hours. Changsan, or "long three," was a term for a good cast in a game using dominoes. She was a "Changsan courtesan," an entertainer schooled in music, literature, poetry, and games of skill or chance. She hosted gambling parties.

She led a glamorous night life, yet found Yi's life exciting and hers wearisome in comparison. If he was that interesting, Yi thought, why was it she could reduce him to a tongue-tied dolt in public and a single-minded lover in private?

Liqin maintained lodgings in Tientsin's Korean colony, close to the changsan house, but not in a room over it.

He touched her silk-covered side briefly and let his hand trace her outline downward. She was svelte, even so flaunted the curves of a full-figured dancer. Tonight, the establishment was filling up fast.

She excited him the way gambling did. He felt uneasy about the future and the risk, and the reaffirmation of luck at gambling was a comfort. Luck was an avowal that the gods favored him, and her attention also seemed verification. A man favored with dice and women could fare no differently in battle, and his luck as a gambler with her by his side was uncanny.

Yi wasn't as happy with his soldierly status as she was. Yet she never let it slip with others that he was a Korean military officer.

He chafed at the courier service's mechanical nature. Everything must go according to form. He wasn't satisfied; despite Sergeant Ko's compliments, he believed he owed his position more to his education and potential, than his competency.

In Confucian society, tradition and knowing one's role were central. One's personal preferences meant nothing at all, yet what *was his role?*

A beefy drunk confronted him in one of the many Chinese dialects Yi didn't understand, but he did catch the word "foreigner." Yi carried a knife, but he waited patiently for one of the men on the periphery to escort the drunk away.

"I'm glad you don't have bound feet," Yi whispered to her and flicked his chin briefly toward a bejeweled matriarch across from them.

"I am changsan. I sing, I play the lyre, and best of all, I dance..." She swiveled her hips slowly against him. Her professional name, "Liqin," he knew, meant "beautiful, stringed instrument,

"...though I'm told my talented feet are not my best feature," She added with a downcast look of false humility.

Korea's power was also declining. He could see that both countries were locked in a mutual Confucian stranglehold that kept their cultures in suspended animation while the outside world was changing rapidly. Did duty to the ancestors mean valuing form over substance?

He cast the dominoes and scored a "long three." The growing crowd cheered. Liqin cheered the loudest.

He was winning, yet it was as if he were vaulting from stepping stone to stepping stone across a familiar stream and realized midstream the stones had been replaced. The new ones were unstable and misshapen.

For the moment, he felt strong, lucky, and favored by the gods.

The lights seemed brighter, the noise greater, and the smoke thicker.

Next to them, a wealthy crone with a hairdo with intertwined ivory carvings smoked a pipe. Yi recognized the sickly-sweet smell of opium. Liqin followed his glance. She turned and said something into his ear. He shook his head, indicating he couldn't hear her. She repeated, "decadence," and that surprised him.

Yi assumed her hostility was to the Chinese class structure. Korea's hierarchy was disturbingly similar, yet opium had made few inroads there. As a military officer he automatically held a high position in that hierarchy, he too was an aristocrat.

In China and in Korea, those who found their way to positions of power were placed there by cultural habit only, or academic merit. The ability to take exams on the classics lacked appropriate merit when foreigners, in China at least, could wrest cities out from under rulers. Korea feared the same predatory practices by China, Russia, and Japan.

Liqin rested her palms in the center of his chest as if to push him away, then pulled him toward her. "You have won yourself a night of pleasure."

The role of Korean warriors now was almost ornamental. He felt that every time he returned to Korea, the country seemed more tired and listless.

In China, he observed Westerners with firearms of increasing complexity. Why weren't Korean soldiers universally armed and trained to match the Westerners, or even the Japanese? Yi had made that effort within the limits of his authority.

The Japanese appeared to absorb the Western ways of making war without difficulty. What could the Japanese do that Koreans couldn't as well?

He had introduced new ways, still he knew they weren't enough.

Yi's night wore on and his luck held. In celebration, they moved on to her lodgings.

There they often talked of his travels elsewhere. He seemed to have a hypnotizing effect over her and as long as he kept talking, she kept stroking and undulating. He found this to be an exciting advantage and played it for all it was worth.

It was no secret that she was the favorite of a doddering Japanese embassy official who paid for her lodgings, yet she was enthralled by a Korean junior officer no one knew.

She posed questions in their pillow talk: "You carry gifts to our empress. I don't believe you. How can one man handle bandits? Do you carry these gifts in your sedan chair? Are they objects of great beauty, great antiquity or great value?"

"They are small things, woman's things, tweezers, a thimble, a ladle. Things I could wrap in a sow's ear."

Liqin made a *moue*.

"As for bandits, I cut them into little bits and then eat the pieces marinated in vinegary red pepper sauce over barley" he'd growl archly.

The last question, too, after lovemaking was always the same: "When will I see you again?" That was a question he never once answered.

They made love until an hour beyond midnight, and he timed these visits to have him back to his men several hours before dawn.

He returned to their camp in the stonewalled paddock five hours before dawn, checked the three sentries, and lay down on his thin quilt.

Sergeant Go, next to him, awoke, but said nothing.

Three shots, almost simultaneous, awakened Yi. His men – in little more than undergarments — were grabbing their carbines and foot-gear and scrambling to their stations on the stonewall perimeter.

Someone was picking off their three sentries, Yi concluded and bellowed. "Get those ceramics flying!"

Using an ember from the firepit, Corporal Mun lit the slow-match pigtail on several Byzantine grenades and lofted them at, and beyond, the closing raiders. Slow match did not leave a trail of sparks back to its point of origin.

The grenades were fist-sized, stoppered jugs of naphtha. Koreans were the best ceramicists in Asia. They could fashion the best ceramics, and in this instance the most frangible incendiary grenades. These projectiles with their sticky liquid contents had doomed several attackers, now easily identifiable as Japanese naval infantrymen, to a fiery death. Yi recognized the distinctive flat hats and leggings.

The naval infantrymens' screams and the sound of gunfire had driven several oxen to rip free their hobbles, smash their stocks, and charge through the paddock.

His men were reluctantly shooting the remaining oxen to fill the holes in their stonewalled perimeter. His men rushed to their positions on the wall, defending themselves with devastating accuracy using Gewehr 88 carbines, a weapon he had also introduced to the courier service. They donned their clothes and equipment. They didn't wait for orders.

His men took up their positions matter-of-factly. Yi wondered if they had more faith in their leadership than warranted.

The incendiary grenades had not only driven off the initial threat, they now back-lit what would be the next wave.

"That first attack was a probe, they're preparing. Expect this next wave will be serious."

He composed himself. "If you haven't noticed we're outnumbered, but we can see them and they can't see us."

Corporal Mun scurried back to Yi and Go with what was left of the night field glasses and placed them carefully at Yi's feet. The left front lens had been destroyed by a bullet and now two Porro prisms tumbled into the dirt. Yi concluded his senior sentry had detected movement outside the wall with them, too late to raise the alarm.

Go snatched the damaged glasses and peered through the remaining lens tube.

"Imperial Japanese naval infantry battalion."

"How many?" Yi asked.

"I figure they're sixty-men if they hold to the British model.

They're carrying Murata bolt-action single-shot rifles. Expect two machine-guns and two mountain guns, if they're holding to the British model. The usual practice is one battalion, drawn from the crew of one cruiser. I figure there's a Japanese cruiser somewhere in sight of the Dagu Forts."

During the procession years, Go had studied the military and naval forces who visited China's treaty ports to perfect Korean courier tactics, though no one anticipated tribute-thieving attacks by a formal, foreign military force.

As if on cue a machinegun began to chatter.

Outside their perimeter, Yi saw several running silhouettes rushing forward with a crew-served weapon. No random banditry here. This was a set-piece battle between a covert tribute detail and an intruding military force, no locals involved. No one had anticipated a pitched battle with a trained, disciplined, well-armed adversary. This was a precursor to war, an effort to drive a wedge between Korea and China. He hoped this was a very small military operation, yet it was too brazen, too loud. Were their attackers confident no one would come to aid the tribute detail? Why?

Everyone hugged the walls as the gun dappled the south wall.

The paddock's walls were only as tall as the shoulders of his tallest man. Yi wished the walls were two-thirds taller and crenelated. Fortunately, Sergeant Go had had them break away stones for firing-steps and to provide firing loops.

The machinegun stuttered and stopped.

"I think it's a Hotchkiss gun and not feeding correctly. They're positioned far too close." Go laughed and tossed a Byzantine grenade to mark it.

"South wall, aim at the crew of that gun. We can do something with that error.'

Go seemed to take forever with the execution follow-up to that command, "Fire!"

The machinegun went silent.

There was a spontaneous cheer.

"Quiet," Sergeant Go ordered.

Later, in the time it took a man to walk a casual li, a momentous boom and shower of broken rock shattered the stillness.

"It took them a while to figure what to do next," Sergeant Go contributed.

Five more thumps punched a "V" out of the west wall. One of his Koreans was clearly dead, the other, hit by flying rock, was crawling with a smashed leg toward the east wall. Their single mountain gun had been sited beyond carbine range and Byzantine grenade illumination.

Yi waited and stared into the dark until his eyes hurt. The damaged, now one-lensed night glasses had their limits.

The Japanese battalion was positioning just out of range in a double line abreast.

About four-to-one odds, he calculated putting his faith in the broken night glasses. *This isn't over yet.* He knew his Koreans held a slight advantage as defenders, especially firing more modern weapons with five-round clips. Then too, they had a wall, albeit a deteriorating wall, protecting them.

Their Gewehr carbines did not have range of the Japanese Murata, but this was low-light fighting and the Japanese had decided to move too quickly. A Gewehr could create terrible carnage. It was capable of firing a bullet through two or three men at a time. That was why concentration of men was rare on modern battlefields.

The Japanese error was they had breached the wall at one point only. *He would exploit that error.*

"Sergeant, have a few men from the east and the north walls form a line about ten paces behind the breach in the wall. The men on the south wall keep up a steady fire. Only have two or three men on the west wall fire, and less frequently. Once the Japanese are a calabash toss from the west wall, then the west wall defenders can open up. We want the breached west wall to be extremely appealing."

Go gave Yi a perfunctory smile.

"Hear that?" Sergeant Go yelled affirming his captain's order to the Korean survivors.

The two double-sections comprising the Japanese battalion began to move toward the west wall and two against the south wall. Each double-section began a "leapfrogging" approach to its assigned wall.

This maneuver was executed in turns; one section of each double-section would make a short rush forward and fall prone protected by cover fire from the other section. Then, in reciprocation, the covering section would then rush forward and drop, covered by the prior rushing section. This rush-and-drop maneuver was repeated a half-dozen times. The Japanese were covering open ground, yet Yi's men had only brief moments to pick out silhouettes and shoot.

Yi looked at the north wall. The ground sloped away from that wall and the sheds were at the base of that wall. It would be the hardest to attack.

"Hold fire," Go ordered. "Swords placed where you can reach them."

He paused, "Breach line, hold, hold your fire, hold. Try to cut down two with one shot if you can when they plunge through."

The leapfrogging had stopped, this time at a kneeling, not prone, position, as the Japanese lines were brought up even.

The kneeling Japanese weren't firing at all, just gasping for breath and anticipating what would come next.

His men on the walls were going through five-round clips with a slow, grim precision. He could see Japanese naval infantrymen falling.

Shortly, they'd released a volley that marked a new phase in their attack.

"Back-light them, now," Go yelled. Mun and another Korean lobbed eight naphtha grenades behind the approaching Japanese battalion."

Avoiding the embers of two firepits in the stock pen, and the grenade stations, Yi moved to the south wall, the unbreached wall.

The Japanese fired a volley to put his men's heads down. Yi heard the word "*yosh*" roared in unison from the Japanese line and guessed it meant a belated "let it begin."

Yi experienced a *frisson*. What right had they to make this show of elan? It was his Koreans who were outnumbered. It was they who held their positions unflinchingly.

Suddenly, the remnants of the two sections flung themselves forward in a bayonet charge.

The two-sections attacking the south wall wavered. They had advanced the longer distance and realized they stood little chance of any of them making it to that wall. Once at the wall they could sling arms or go over with only one hand free. Either way, they were highly exposed. Yi heard a Japanese command, and the south wall Japanese sections swerved to the west wall.

"We're going to let a few through the breach," Go yelled to the six-man line.

"South wall defenders take care of any stragglers from that first bunch with cold steel as they come over your wall. Keep your eyes on the other walls. Only the breach line can shoot targets within the paddock walls. We don't want to shoot each other.

"The rest of you on the perimeter, aim and fire as fast as you can. You can fire at any of them outside the wall or on it."

Go, running down his mental list, came to the key tactical considerations. "*Breach firing line, don't fire into the breach in the wall as fast as you can.*"

He could hear the rattle of the charging Japanese force.

The Japanese would be through the breach any moment. Already it was difficult for them to hear Go's commands.

Go gave one last instruction, "Volley fire on your own, not on my command. Just count to 'three' between volleys. Keep your shots headed down your personal alley. No use wasting bullets on already dead Japanese having a hard time falling down. They can't shoot through their front line, however we can. Count your shots. After five shots *you must slip in another clip, smooth and steady.*"

The first image through the breach was a lethal reach of bayonets that looked like the spread claws of a tiger.

All four Japanese naval infantry sections hit the breach in the wall at once and jammed. They chanted, "banzai!" with a cadence reminiscent of men hauling on a rope line.

The breach line issued its welcome. Yi was surprised to hear them counting aloud between volleys. They were smacking the breach as coolly as a clerk stamping papers.

The carnage began. Some Japanese had been let through, enough to let the others jam. The dead in the jammed breach did not fall immediately, but were held in place by those in front and behind them. Their non-commissioned officers, oblivious to the trap, were pushing from behind.

The breach line kept firing volley after volley. The shredded bodies offered no protection to the men back twos and threes behind them. That was the terrible lethality of the Gewehr, and the Murata in return, but the Koreans were spread out and the Japanese had impulsively allowed themselves to be channeled. The bodies eventually formed a slope and Yi saw a few Japanese infantrymen bounding up the slope and landing at the feet of the Korean breach line only to be shot when they landed.

The Japanese began boosting themselves up beyond the edges of the breach, though shallow side shots from Yi's perimeter marksmen were dropping multiple targets, too.

Other Japanese attempted to scale the walls of the paddock only to be cut down as they straddled the wall crests or tumbled over.

Yi found himself engaged by two shrieking Japanese and discarded the night glasses. They felt compelled to seek mutual protection and Yi continuously weaving right and left, found it easy to lead each into the other's way. Their long Murata rifles augmented by equally cumbersome bayonets were no match for his close-quarters sword work honed by generations of tradition.

He found the working half of the night glasses, undented and undaunted, crushed beneath the feet of one of his assailants. The Byzantine grenades had stopped burning, even so Yi counted only five Japanese men staggering back to the origin of the second assault.

Sergeant Go's left arm had been pierced by a bayonet, however he'd checked the bleeding. Yi, Go, and eight other Koreans had survived.

Clandestine missions were a form of gambling. Participants either won in a big way or he lost in a big way. Yi believed they had won, yet wasn't sure. Time would tell.

"Well, done, sir. You coaxed the Sons of Nippon through their own private entrance." Go's commands had been crisp and perfectly executed, still he looked thoroughly drained.

"Thank you, Sergeant Go. Kindly have the men even out their ammunition and have their wounds attended to. How's our situation on water?" "Compliment the men on their cool heads and deadly skills," he said over-loudly, hoping the words wouldn't come out with a breathless quality.

Go waved his hand from his mouth toward their men and mimicked an orator delivering a great address. Go was signaling the praise must come directly from Yi, for maximum effect.

In the darkness, Yi smiled his pride in his troops and wondered if he looked as worn and shaken as Go and they did. He realized they couldn't see his face. He must say something more. *Smiling in the dark was useless.*

He picked up the badly battered night glasses and waved them high.

"You have fought a battle that will be remembered for ten thousand years. A few against the many. You were as strong as the rocks on our coast that withstand crashing waves and typhoons. You were like the Cheju's Dragon Head Rock off Cheju Island, defiant and unbowed. You were not just like a massive stone, you were living breathing dragons. By the gods, you spit five-round clip fire," Yi pronounced with finality and pride.

"*Mansei!*" his men chorused. Ten thousand years.

The paddock was quiet for an hour, though it was still several hours until dawn.

Together Go and he inspected the perimeter and had a scout search the sheds to the north.

Go paced back and forth along the east wall until, Yi thought, he'd worn a groove at its base.

CHAPTER TWO

Tientsin, China, 1893

"Captain, they're back," Corporal Mun whispered.

"How can they be back?" We killed almost all of them.

Yi shook his head. He must have fallen asleep.

He could hear voices in the distance, then the roar of mountain guns and the detonation of their 42mm shells. He looked over the wall and could see the silhouettes of what had to be either the other half of the first battalion, or a whole new battalion of Imperial naval infantrymen.

Could the first battalion had traveled light leaving behind two of their crew served weapons and attacked with reckless overconfidence?

This new group or new battalion – which meant a second cruiser off-shore or that the first cruiser had carried more naval infantrymen than routine — had the benefit of the first's experience.

Yi's men had plugged the original breach with stacked Japanese bodies.

Mun was depressingly buoyant as he passed out the remaining ammunition.

"Any possibility we're the kind of dragons who can sprout wings?"

Seizing this tribute shipment had been the object of significant planning.

He studied a new breach in the south wall.

Sergeant Go yelling new orders to the men, turned to Yi and hissed more than whispered, "You over-clever young fool, you had to have led them here."

Three thumps in succession and another three thumps left a third breach in the south wall.

"No, I couldn't have…" he said turning to Go.

Had he?

He had been trained how to shake off surveillance – double-backs, clothing changes, in one door out another, reading reflections, the whole list. He observed the protocols. To find them, an aggressor would have had to put a regiment ashore to sweep this coast on such short notice. He suspected he may have triggered the timing of a trap laid with the cooperation of corrupt Chinese. Well, Japan had been threatening war with China with greater belligerent moves every day. It had a continuing presence in the treaty ports including Tientsin and could spring a trap quickly.

Duty-bound to protect or deliver the silver, his courier detail would die in place.

He had failed. Only minutes remained before they were overrun.

All the members of the courier detail knew a sufficiently large, determined organization could steal the silver, if that organization were determined to pay the price. Well, today's price in men would be dear for Imperial Japan, but likely worth the cost of driving a wedge between Korea and China.

A final six thumps and a fourth breach ventilated the paddock's walls. The walls looked like an oval of decayed teeth.

Mun looked north. "Those sheds are afire. Now, we're the ones who are back-lit!"

Yi looked at Go. "I didn't lead them here. They must have had an informant, a Chinese official or Japanese spy or both. They could guess the how, but not the when! With sufficient manpower they determined the where."

Grabbing his sword and reloading his carbine breathlessly, he added. "The Japanese simply saturated this section of coast with naval infantry once they had the when."

The meeting with his Chinese counterpart might have set things in motion.

Ko then flicked the butt of his carbine faster than lizard's tongue, across the back of Yi's head.

Yi's last conscious thought that morning was *the world has changed* forever.

Four men in Japanese uniforms stood around him. One held a Nambu pistol to his head.

"Captain Yi, your service to the Kingdom of Korea, if you will, is hereby terminated," one said in Mandarin and laughed. One of the other officers laughed as well. "You've left your post for an assignation with a woman. That woman was the agent of a not unfriendly nation, Imperial Japan, soon to be your country's big brother. You were in a position of responsibility and trust. You failed your country."

The speaker chuckled over the solemnity of his own words. Why did he have to convince Yi of anything? They had him.

Yi agreed. He felt the air leaving his chest and a choking sensation in his throat. They were correct. Perhaps he had betrayed his country, carelessly and unknowingly. Sergeant Go had saved his life and he hated him for it.

He guessed he was in the back room of a shop in commercial building somewhere on the west bank of the Hai.

Japan and China were going to war, now or shortly. Korea's status would change forever. These men must have set the trap.

He had been neither steady, nor reliable. He had diverted his attention for the company of a beautiful woman. *No wonder they castrated male oxen.*

He hadn't been followed; he was certain. His visit to her had triggered a major sweep of Tientsin's wayfaring sites by Japanese intelligence, the *Kempeitai.*

"All, but two, of your courier detail are dead." The second Japanese officer continued, again in Mandarin.

Me and who else? Did it matter?

"I'll bet each of my men cost you four to one, or better." Yi interrupted. All four men shifted postures.

The second officer walloped Yi, tipping him over tied to his chair.

He had squandered the lives of eighteen men and a fortune in silver. All dead and he'd only suffered a bump on the head. No one would believe he'd survived by luck, but rather by betrayal. Sergeant Go's act was a gift, a curse, and a debt invoice.

His ancestors must be wringing their hands over his disgrace and already turned their backs upon him.

Unless he could erase this catastrophic dishonor, Yi Jung-hee was destined to become a disinherited ghost and walking cenotaph to eighteen righteous ghosts.

"We will circulate the tale of your disgraceful conduct. We'll let it be known that a Korean meeting your description was spreading silver around Tientsin at gambling parties and spending on courtesans. It won't be you, simply someone who looks like you.

"You cannot return to Korea. I hereby sentence you to exile forever, or until you can find friends like us to smuggle you back into Korea." The second Japanese officer seemed to enjoy his part.

Yi strained to control his breathing, and his body's other reactions to fear and disgrace. He must listen more carefully than he'd ever listened to any conversation — in what might be a foreshortened life.

Yi knew he was blinking too fast. He willed himself not to blink at all, and his eyes came up with a compromise.

The second Japanese officer stopped to let the import of his words sink in.

The third Japanese officer spoke in Korean. "Seven times down, get up eight. We always have hope. You just need new friends."

The Korean proverb, repeated in different forms throughout Asia, could mean many things. Normally, it served as a reminder of the Korean virtue of persistence. Yi realized this whole conversation was scripted, a prepared presentation. They had his consignment of silver taels, and they had his reputation, still they wanted something more than their own amusement.

"Seven times down, up eight. In a way, you can still recover from all this. We are offering you a job in the Japanese intelligence service. We suggest, as a gambling man, that you bet on Japan. Time has passed by Korea and China. Their days as independent countries will soon be over. It won't be long before they cease to exist at all," the Korean-speaking officer counseled.

A chance to start over meant starting over under their control. Yi was surprised at how quickly everything became clear to him.

He was of no use to anyone he cared about. He had been knocked down. Whether he had been knocked down "seven times" or just this once didn't matter. Anything to buy time, or in a few minutes his throat would be cut. *Nunji*. His salvation lay in nunji, eye measure.

To them this was just a drill in anticipation of turning future Korean officers, a no-cost trial conversion of little consequence.

"No." They'd expect him to refuse initially. Nunji was the art of making high-stakes decisions on intuition. Korea survived among its aggressive neighbors of China, Russia, and Japan on little more. Who better to sway Koreans than one of their kind?

The unspeaking fourth Japanese officer drew and cocked his pistol.

"One more time — you have nowhere to go. You can die now or work for the Japanese intelligence service."

Trussed up, but physically more powerful than any one of them, Yi raged inwardly.

"No."

The Korean-speaking officer nodded to the one with the pistol.

"On what terms?" Yi reversed abruptly in faltering Korean.

Seven times down, up eight.

"Our terms are what we choose them to be, and you'll be grateful if we say you're grateful. No more Korean royal livery for you, no more officer status, no more respected family privileges, of that, we can assure you."

Liqin gave him seaman's papers and a letter of recommendation to a Japanese ship in the harbor. She touched his upper arm wordlessly. This was a contrived affront to break his spirit further, another insult, he realized.

The Japanese officers had dismissed him so quickly, he realized, because they didn't really care what he decided This was still another insult. He would be hunted by agents of the Chinese empress and his countrymen for the lost tribute. Women like Liqin were all they needed to keep men like him in line wherever he was sent.

That night as he stood on a pier holding his papers and looking at the *Nagasaki Maru*, a passing sailor gave him a studied look.

They intend to destroy my country, my heritage, and want me to help them.

Yi's head was swimming. His brain was generating and rejecting frantic ideas steeped in retribution and redemption. It was as if he were trying to ignite sand with a cascade of sparks scraped from flint on steel.

"I will find a way exact a revenge beyond what has been visited upon my country, and me." He seethed.

Bold words, whispered cravenly.

"Brother, you're not considering a Japanese ship?" a sailor said in Korean. "They'll treat a Korean like pig dung. My ship makes the run to the Land of the Golden Mountain. The captain has the face of a pale monkey, even so he's fair and pays regularly. Another Korean is on the ship, too, which will make three of us. The Western barbarians can't tell us from the Chinese. To them, we're all the same."

Yi had failed his country, and now he would fail Japan's docility test. He was not going turn the key on his own cell. Koreans were not tractable.

He looked at Yi closely. "What were you whispering just now? There was something in your face. If you sign on the American ship don't show that face ever. It will scare them."

"Just muttering." Yi said staring at the placid harbor.

He hadn't met the half-caste courtesan by accident. Coming together with her wasn't a matter of *umyong,* "luck," "fortune," or "fate."

Yi had been looking at the world through a gambler's eyes. All luck, good or bad, was simply the roll of the dice. For now, he must treat it all as gambler's bad luck.

He had believed umyong was smiling on him at the time. Wasn't that what gambling was? A way of testing the favor of the gods?

Yi laughed at himself, he'd been too wrapped up in cleverness. He'd studied everything through the cold lenses of his night glasses, except himself. He had been used and betrayed despite his training and lineage. His fondness for women and gambling had made it easy for them.

He knew precious metals. Knowledge of their properties and security had been his family's profession. Now they had become his failing and disgrace. Those skills could still be his deliverance. He'd learned one profession. He'd have to learn one, maybe many others. He'd need to learn many new things to achieve retribution of the kind he contemplated.

That disgrace was a debt to Korea that he must satisfy.

The Korean sailor's reaction made Yi realize he was a dangerous man.

He was a dangerous man and he would make himself a patient man.

Yi joined his new friend in climbing aboard the American ship.

CHAPTER THREE

The Inside Passage: Alaska-bound, 1898

In the moonlight, Assistant Cook Yi could see the side-wheeler's wake bubble up in its peculiar double pattern of white turbulence against black water. Yi was cutting up fish while fending off an agitated colony of Bonaparte's gulls perched two levels above the main deck. The cook had sent him topside with a cutting board to do the work. As wide as he was tall, Yi slashed at the filets with the same level of angry intensity he applied to all his tasks. The noise of the gulls barely carried above the commotion created by three times as many passengers as the ship could handle.

He worked by the light of a hurricane lantern with a hooded reflector. The wick he kept low and its illumination he confined to the fish and his hands with a wet canvas rag. If he were discovered by the passengers, they'd be all over him for uncooked tidbits. Here, above eye level and in a not easily accessed nook, he derived some pleasure from seeing and not be being seen.

Yi was working as a steward, cook's assistant, and launderer. One of the Six Companies headquartered in San Francisco had found him this job. Each company served as both an agent and guardian for Chinese sojourners to the Land of the Golden Mountain. This company specialized in seafarers, stewards, and cooks.

Yi hoped someday to be a miner. He had lost a fortune and if he was to atone, he needed to find a fortune. He looked around the ship and was surprised at the percentage of passengers who had no intention of actually working in the gold fields. Some sold devices of various sorts to mine more efficiently, to protect the miner from the elements, and to make the miner more comfortable. Some devices were clever, some foolish. Other equipment was intended to help provide services — cooking, laundry, entertainment, carpentry, or transportation — at prices that wouldn't have been tolerated in San Francisco.

An odd assortment of useful and harebrained machinery, warm clothing, and vacuum-canned foods were stored in the ship's hold. All these hangers-on on board considered themselves merchants. In Yi's country, merchants were barely tolerated and severely regulated. Merchants were disruptive. They were confined to certain sections of a town or village, and not allowed to come and go freely.

In his homeland, social order was all important. One must know one's place in society. Merchants valued money more than order. A merchant with too much money might think to challenge one of the yangban, the aristocrats. Yi chuckled to himself. Once he had been one of those aristocrats, a *muban*, a member of the warrior class, and now he was a cook.

In the dark, the ship darted between skeins of fog. Barrel-chested Yi coughed from time to time as the smoke from the boiler fires joined that of the sailors' numerous cheroots, cigarettes, and pipes. Voices would grow loud in one part of the ship as they faded in another. His hands moved quickly and without hesitation as he filleted the fish.

Below him on the stern railing stood three men, a young man, and two noticeably older men. The combined radiance of the hot smokestack tips, the faint glow of the fixed stern light, and the water-reflected moonlight, gave Yi a view of vivid clarity.

The youngest man, not yet in his twenties, was a tall, gangly man in a red and black plaid jacket Yi had heard described as a "mackinaw." The three stood with their boot heels on the lower rail just within the stern railing. Three sets of boots, one set of seaman's gumboots like Yi's worn by the man in the mackinaw, and two sets of hobnail boots worn by the older men.

The oldest of the three men, a portly man with white hair, had the gangly man in the mackinaw engaged in conversation. The other — in a frockcoat — had his arms crossed sullenly, his feet now braced on the deck in defiance.

The lee stern rail of the main deck wasn't comfortable. Cargo was stacked everywhere on every deck. Yi knew that particular section of main deck was especially cold, wet, besieged with stack gas, and downwind of the horses and the few mules. Men sprawled everywhere else — too sick or too hungry to go about their business — while attempting to sleep. With the wind dead on the bow, that main deck section of stern was calm and isolated for the moment. The side-wheeler had been a ferry; her shipyard had never intended her for the open ocean. At some point, the Inside Passage would be too much for her.

Yi didn't plan to stick with her for long. He shared a desire for gold, common to all the old ferry's passengers.

He remembered seeing the man in the red and black mackinaw earlier on the cruise. That gangly man had come aboard as part of a larger group of five, perhaps six, whose mannerisms and general similarity of appearance made him believe they were related by blood. They had all worn seaman's gumboots with the same mark branded into the top edge of each boot. In addition, they shared a muscular heaviness of shoulder and a way of folding their necks forward that combined to lend them a birdlike look.

Not songbirds, he thought. No, birds of prey. They were all tall men with large hands that reminded him of skillets. Otherwise, as a group they were quiet and unremarkable beyond an air of surliness that discouraged small talk.

For the transit, the ferry now had bunks built four-tiers high from rough lumber, though still that wasn't enough for the number of gold-mad passengers. When they reached Skagway, the lumber would be stripped out and sold as dressed lumber.

Serving the passengers breakfast took seven hours, and to serve them all supper another seven. They had no midday meal. Now, well into the evening meal, the glow of a discarded cigarette arched away from the main "promenade" and into the night waves like a falling star.

With a deft gesture, the gangly man in the mackinaw moved his hand across the white-haired man's throat in two swift motions. The older man, the portly man, spasmed and then slumped to the rail. When the sullen man in the frock coat made a cry, the lanky man's hand slashed again. The man in the frock coat, too, slumped forward, and the man in the mackinaw held him up. The young man seemed to pat one, then the other, consolingly. No, Yi realized, he was emptying their pockets. Then the young man tipped the first, then the other, backward over the rail.

Of the three sets of boots, only one set of the gumboots remained.

The young man looked around, and Yi drew back into the shadows. He realized that in the space of mere seconds, the young man in the mackinaw had cut the throats of the two older men, robbed them, and pitched them over the stern rail into the water.

The young man smiled strangely, and the smile beamed in Yi's direction. The other men Yi had seen with the young man before flowed toward their companion out of nowhere, paused, and then they too smiled. They clapped shoulders.

Yi guessed the two older men's bunks would be stripped of anything valuable – their luggage identified and divided.

Was Yi sure what he'd seen? Had he really seen anything at all? There'd be more dead men, and lost men, before the side-wheeler found its way to Skagway. He knew the meaning of the two deft movements across the throat. A knife? A razor? Everyone had one or two of those.

Yi had seen similar work in Tientsin. The rumor was that no lawmen did civilization's duty in Alaska, and if you needed to do something about a crime, you had to do it yourself or rely on a miners' committee.

On this ship, Yi was known as "Snowfall," a nickname that derived from his halting description of his ability to keep a kitchen. It would be "clean, white, like snow from sky." He knew the nickname was a joke, however he also knew the joking name suggested a degree of acceptance. His experience was pretty much the same back in San Francisco, China, and, even, Korea. During the past five years, he had become adept at staying alive. Humor was as useful as an edged weapon when it came to survival. Humor could turn a foreigner into a non-threatening fellow traveler. Acceptance meant continued existence. He'd need to collect many more such markers before he'd dare to rock this vessel by reporting a double murder.

Yi looked into the wake again and saw only paddlewheel turbulence.

If the two men were astern of the ship in the water, they weren't flailing to keep themselves afloat. The water was cold, though immersion alone wouldn't result in death without a struggle. A cry for help on the way to the Klondike was a waste of breath.

Yi looked again, and the young man in the mackinaw jacket was being hugged under the arm of one of his group. Yes, this had a "family" aspect to it. The young man was supported. Then the group of men disappeared into the interior of the ship.

The situation was like one of those riddles the Zen monks used to explain life. This, however, was a riddle about death. A man's throat is cut and he falls overboard without a sound, did he ever exist?

Yi had already jumped ship, with Six Companies approval, from a creaky coastal steamer, *Ning Chow*. It has been sold to Western buyers to exploit the huge demand to get to the goldfields. He had no friends among the crew of this ship. This new ship was no improvement, still Yi needed to keep his eye on his goal.

"Even if the sky falls on you, there is a hole that you can escape from." Yi had recited the proverb to himself every day since he had lost the tael shipment in China.

Yi had been a man of action once, a man who guarded fortunes in silver and gold, yet on this side of the Pacific, he felt frail and inconsequential.

He inquired about the group in the galley and the senior steward shook his head. The senior steward was a patient man. "Them? The family name is Spuyten, I guess. The old man's just bought liquor for everyone. A real swell, he is. Them five behind him with the long arms are his bullying brood."

Sure enough, the passengers were becoming louder. The oldest of the six men was waving his arms in flourishes. His smile was so great it almost didn't fit on his face. He was the loudest and happiest of them all. He was a hale fellow and every passenger's best friend. A beaming, wide smile with good teeth, and even dimples, draped across his face like bunting. A man of great personal charm, Yi thought, a man whose smile was contagious.

Everyone ate standing up and on the move. At mealtime, the galley spaces could accommodate only a small fraction of the boat's passengers.

The Spuyten brothers had divided themselves within the "dining salon." Three seemed as happy as their father, though the other two were more withdrawn.

"I was a first mate on my last ship, and I'll be captain and owner of my next one after I return from the goldfields. Listen to me now! The name's Spuyten, and you'll hear that name again. I go by 'Hellfire' Spuyten.

"See those fellows there, and there? They're my boys, Giles, Cornelius, Diderick, Bram, and Elias. I picked them names out myself. Good names, always good for a first impression. Ha, old-country, butter-wouldn't-melt-in-their-mouths names — they're just as regular fellows as you'd want to meet. They've been trained to achieve high station in this here world. Can't say as I know anything about the next world."

Hellfire's eyes sparkled. "We'll be the first to the goldfields. We'll have our stake. Or we'll find someone who'll let us share theirs," he said with a broad wink. "Where there's a will, we get our way. We're seafaring men, up to battling men and nature. The world's either wolves or sheep, and we're wolves." Hellfire looked around with irrepressible charm and a boyish smile.

"A-yuh, a-yuh. I'll drink to that," yelled a voice from the back of the space. "We'll all be tycoons and captains of industry and transportation when we get back."

"How are you at battling geology? You ain't there yet," bellowed an unconvinced traveler. "Still I'll drink your liquor."

The head steward turned to Yi. "Keep away from them. They's the Spuyten crowd. Heard of the old man long before the Stampede. Hellfire Spuyten was a 'bucko' mate and a hard driver. He's probably killed or crippled a couple dozen men out beyond the sight of any jetty or jury."

"Another round for everyone, steward!" yelled old man Spuyten, doing a little jig.

"That Spuyten fella, he's a great fella. Salt of the earth," chimed in a man swirling his whiskey around in an enameled cup.

"It'll cost you three times what the last crate of whiskey cost," said the steward to Hellfire. "We're dipping into supplies for Skagway."

The elder Spuyten impishly spilled gold pieces onto the galley counter. "No need to fret, steward. Nothing's too good for my new friends."

The steward turned to Yi and kept his voice low. "Yeah, he's a sport. Just watch your back, your throat, and your money, around the likes of that family."

Spuyten's collecting his own acceptance markers, Yi thought.

The steward turned so only Yi could see his lips. "We carry all sorts. Dreamy men with more money than brains, men who sing 'hallelujah' on seeing a roaring campfire and go giddy at the prospect of a great adventure, and then nightmarish men who skulk just outside of the light of the campfire and drool over the opportunity to separate men and their treasure beyond the reach of law. Spuyten's that sort, I venture. Keep well clear of him because he's not just a predator, he's an addlebrained predator. He's killed more cooks than anything. Gets it into his head they're trying to poison him. He's tossed a few over the side and he's simply executed others."

The steward met Yi's eyes. "You're a Chinaman and that's a kind of disadvantage. Like all bullies, Spuyten wants his prey to have some sort of disadvantage. I've seen some of the sourdoughs coming back, and they look nothing like the ones you see here. Red rims around their eyes, and you see them sleeping standing up," the steward added. "Wolves and sheep, eh?"

The steward glanced briefly Hellfire's way. "That might be insulting wolves. I'd steer well clear of that lot, Snowfall, my Chi-nee shipmate. Hellfire Spuyten is a down-on-his luck schooner's mate known for smashing crewmen's heads with blocks and tossing them over the side on a whim. He's soaring like a buzzard in an updraft tonight. Higher than any mountain in Alaska one night, then lower than a clam's belly the next.

"His mate's ticket is in jeopardy. I'd say Hellfire's got a dangerous turn of mind and he's desperate," the steward concluded. "The one you asked about in the red plaid coat — that's Elias. Word is Hellfire's celebratin' something he did today."

Schooled in the muban traditions, Yi knew about death. The two bodies would float vertically for a while as they exsanguinated. Then their heavy boots would tug them downward once their clothing soaked up the seawater and released the few captured pockets of resistant gas and air.

The swells grew, and so did the wind. Many of the passengers didn't leave their bunks. Those who did whiled away their time leaning over the rail — losing what little food they'd taken in. A side-wheeler ferry wasn't built for the Inside Passage, still this was late summer and men had fortunes to be made.

Two days later, Yi watched the weary passengers and their awkward cargo leave the ship at Skagway, departing from the superstructure of the side-wheeler. Only the beginnings of wharves had yet been constructed, and each passenger's cargo had to be lightered ashore at outlandish rates. The passengers screamed insults at the lightermen, but paid up nonetheless. The race to the Klondike was on, and the current wisdom was the best claims would go to the early arrivals.

Yi wanted to jump ship again, though he had to be cautious. He was a foreigner here and knew all too well what a foreigner's life had been worth in China, still he took confidence in his skill at *nunji*, eye-measure, a particularly Korean survival skill, and perhaps an opportunity would present itself.

"Hey, Hop Sing, you speakee English?" called out a lighterman.

Every third Westerner in these waters addressed anyone they thought was a Chinaman as "Hop Sing." Yi didn't take offense. The error was frequently useful.

"I speakee."

"You want job? You without a queue, yeah you. You built solid, like ox. You want a job shifting cargo?" The lighterman followed with his job offer showing not the least hesitation.

Yi stomached his excitement. This was a negotiation of terms.

"A coolie is strong, coolie never rests, right? You make big money. We only lighter when the tide is high. You make extra at low tide lugging cargo through the mud, too. I'm an old China hand. I've done Tin-sin, Shag-eye, and Yoko-hammer," the man told him.

The lighterman named a wage. "A gold eagle on it, Hop Sing. The name is Noble, like the liquor."

A flying fish tattoo winged across the back of the lighterman's right hand, and a dragon undulated across the back of the other. Yi watched the lighterman. He was grabbing boxes and sacks as he spoke and he seemed to control the movements of two other boats nearby. He was a man of influence and leadership — Yi's nunji, his ability to work on instinct, told him so.

The lighterman was a boatman with Asian experience.

"My name Yi. Need boots, leather boots."

Noble seemed to make a mental calculation. "Boots. Hop Sing Yi need leather boots with hobnails, and golden eagle. Hop Sing Yi work hard, right?"

"Work plenty hard."

Though Yi smiled, he did so sparingly. If past experience was any measure, smiling was never going to become a habit.

Yi was coiling line when an old man came up to the part of Skagway's waterfront that Noble claimed as his headquarters. "How'dy do? My name's Coffin. Some folks call me Whitey, but not to my face."

"Pleased to meet you, Coffin. I go by Noble."

"Charlie or Cyrus?"

"Neither. Just Noble will do on this miserably muddy beach." Noble fanned his arm shoreward.

Yi had heard the joking question more than once. "Charlie Noble" was a sailor's nickname for a stovepipe. "Cyrus Noble" was a popular bourbon whiskey with San Francisco origins. The lighterman didn't have time for humor. All too soon, the weather was going to turn cold.

"You're a seaman, right? Can you splice?"

"Can I splice?" Noble looked sidelong at Coffin. "Short splice, long splice, eye splice, and end splice."

"Any splice that'll run through a block." Coffin rolled his boot toe in the mud.

"That'd be a long splice. Toughest of the lot to do. Takes time. How many?"

Coffin pointed to numerous coils of manila line. "All these coils of manila line into one long line."

Noble whistled. Outfitters normally sold stampeders a standard 200-foot length of line. "Many, many long splices. You rigging a sailing ship or something?"

"A very long breeches buoy."

Noble leaned his head to one side and looked hard at Coffin. "I hear you right?"

"A sort of vertical breeches buoy from the Scales to Chilkoot Summit. It'll need a canvas basket, but no leg holes."

"That's over on the Dyea Trail. I shoulda gone there. Skagway's got too many galoots." Noble paused. "I have a palm that'll handle sail canvas. You have blocks…what you landsmen call pulleys?"

Coffin beamed. "More than enough. They don't weigh much and multiply the strength of a man's arm. I knew there'd be a use for block and tackle."

"You set on sheerlegs for this contraption of your'n?"

"Already cut and nearly in place. Just east of the Mountie station on Chilkoot Summit."

"Mr. Coffin, this is one of my lightermen, name of Yi. He's Chinese." Noble was mistaken on that last point, but Yi wasn't concerned. Most people had heard of China, few here had heard of Korea.

Coffin looked Yi over and nodded approval, though his eyes didn't quite focus on Yi as a human being. Yi wondered if his semi-invisibility as an Asian here was good or bad. He knew Westerners found communicating with him difficult, so they tended to pretend he just wasn't there. They didn't realize he understood English several notches higher than he could speak it.

"Yi, shift Mr. Coffin's coils of line under the tarp with the pack-frames and hand trucks."

Noble and his flying fish tattoo maintained a cordial alliance with Captain William Moore, one of Skagway's men of influence. Noble led his lightermen fairly and efficiently. True to his word, he found Yi a pair of hobnail boots and he showed him how to splice. With his experience hauling tribute to destinations in China, Yi knew he could occasionally come up with a trick that made the lightermen's work easier.

Yi's work lightering lasted until one Saturday night, when Noble — half-drunk — was maneuvered into a fight with one of Soapy Smith's men and then shot dead. Soapy Smith, who ran the rackets in Skagway, wanted control of all sources of revenue on the waterfront, and lighterage was an ever-growing business. Smith wasn't as ethical as Captain William Moore. Noble had been right, Yi thought. He should have moved to the adjoining port of Dyea.

Once again, a man who had befriended Yi had met a bad end. *Every grave has an excuse.*

This was a Korean proverb that Yi found himself remembering bitterly, and too frequently.

During his days in San Francisco, Yi had learned to stay clear of Western drinking establishments. He was aware of the friction between the Chinese and Westerners there. Since he was neither, he felt no reason to become involved. In Alaska, the situation seemed different. For the most part, everyone was a foreigner, and nature's dangers were so close. Nature was enemy enough, and a rational man didn't go out of his way to cultivate additional enemies.

With the death of Noble, Yi found a job in a laundry run by a widow. Here, as in San Francisco, he was a "celestial" and in San Francisco, the local Chinese had developed reputations as launderers.

At the laundry, Yi fell in with a Tlingit Indian of the Chilkoot Tribe. The Chilkoot, Klukwan or "Kluk," had run afoul of his chief's rules on backpacking gear and was now doing penance as a launderer. The Chilkoots regarded Chilkoot Pass as their monopoly and they were aggressive businessmen. Not even Soapy Smith dared cross the Chilkoots.

The trail through Chilkoot Pass was theirs and no other tribe could engage in packing without their permission. The Chilkoots provided competent packing services to miners at prices they fixed among themselves. They held fast to those fees. In addition, the chief demanded one dollar per head for every white man passing through the Chilkoot Pass, and got it. Kluk hadn't abided by the rules and now endured his "sentence."

Walking home one night to his pigeonhole, his sleeping refuge in the crawlspace below the laundry, Yi came upon several Westerners attacking Kluk in a Skagway backstreet. Chilkoots were sturdy. They could pack loads two and three times the weight most Westerners could handle, nevertheless this fight was three on one. Yi knew, Chilkoots were men, and no man was indestructible. Others were watching, and who knew what their interest was in all this. Robberies, brawls, and shootings were daily occurrences in Skagway.

Yi could fathom no reason for them beating Klukwan. Ultimately this was Skagway, and a reason wasn't necessary. They were drunk, and he was available. Likely, they didn't know he was a member of the Chilkoot tribe or understand that tribe's significance. The Alaskan territory had other tribes.

Yi had seen mobs in Korea and in China. Though those countries placed an emphasis on harmony, sometimes groups found harmony in disharmony. Americans, he had decided, frequently found harmony in disharmony.

Yi hesitated. A mob could quickly pick up steam simply on the premise of engaging outsiders. He expected no one to intervene on his behalf, and he realized his mouth was dry. Yet he had no time to think. He had been a defender once, a warrior.

Yi struck one stampeder, using a stylized punch with his knuckles level, and then whirled and backhanded away the second. The stampeder crumpled with a broken jaw.

"Kluk, not time to do fighting with *cheechakoes!*"

Yi grabbed Kluk roughly and bellowed at him in *Hangugo* as if lecturing him. No one understood, for some reason this new man on the scene, Yi — an Asian or a Chilkoot perhaps — was castigating their victim, and that victim was the focus of the lecture. The stampeders were drunk and confused. Apparently, someone had presumed to take their place disciplining this arrogant Indian.

The man's action didn't seem right, and so they focused on the intruder. The second stampeder took a swing at Yi. Yi grabbed his wrist, lifted him into a fireman's carry, and released him into the third stampeder. Korean soldiers daily practiced *ssireum*, traditional Korean wrestling. Yi almost enjoyed himself, yet kept in mind the matter of harmony. Creating disharmony wasn't Korean.

An unexpected fourth man rushed Yi, who clasped the backside of the fourth man's trousers with one hand and pulled him into his hip. He popped this fourth man into the air with his hip, landing him on his back in the mud. Yi fell with the fourth man and on top of him, bringing his hip into the man's groin. The fourth man cursed, but didn't attempt to get up when Yi did.

Yi then grabbed Kluk and continued to shake and berate him. He seemed to be in control of the troublesome Indian. The other watchers lost interest and wandered off. He hustled Klukwan off to a quiet alley, during which time Kluk attempted to punch Yi several times. Yi, however, parried his punches easily.

Yi ached in unexpected places. His nose was bleeding, out of alignment and sensitive to the touch. Yi quickly reset it before the swelling could lock it out of alignment for good. Disharmony was never a positive, even physical disharmony.

Yi tasted blood running down the back of his throat and one knee was stiffening up. Being a defender, a warrior again, was good.

The next day, Kluk said nothing about the brawl. He didn't talk much, though he eventually told Yi he was quitting the laundry and going back to packing miners' gear up the Chilkoot Trail to the Yukon River headwaters.

The Chilkoot chief concluded Kluk's punishment risked conflict with potential Cheechako customers. No good could come from Kluk living in dangerous proximity to the stampeders, so the chief welcomed Klukwan back onto the tribal grounds and into the tribal business.

Yi, too, had tired of laundry work that brought him no closer to the gold he sought. When Kluk invited him into the tribal backlands, Yi followed and was offered a job as a packer. Klukwan introduced him as "Skookum" Yi. *Skookum* meant strong. Strength had meaning to a tribe known for just that. Yi, too, began packing miners up through Chilkoot Pass to the headwaters. The work reminded him of the times he had packed the Chinese tael tribute on a jige, a Korean A-frame pack-board, over the Jangbaek Range to China. He had taken one of two basic routes of smuggling tribute into China, the mountains on foot or the Yellow Sea by boat.

Yi's life seemed to be coming full circle. He was a Korean, a mountaineer from "the land on end." Climbing the Chilkoot's Golden Stairs bore a haunting similarity to climbing the Jangbaek Range.

Among the Chilkoots now, Yi put all his effort into what Noble would have called "learning the ropes." He also set out to learn the numbers.

The Chilkoot Trail, from Dyea to Lake Lindeman, the first of the lakes at the headwater of the Yukon River, was 33 miles in length.

A stampeder was required to have 1,150 pounds of food to enter Canada. The Canadian authorities had determined the Yukon couldn't feed the anticipated number of stampeders. Each stampeder needed another 850 pounds of equipment to cross the border at Chilkoot Pass into the Canadian Yukon, the site of the goldfields. The average cheechako, or Alaskan greenhorn, could carry 50 to 75 pounds; occasionally, a very fit cheechako could carry 100 pounds on his back.

Frequently, the requirement meant 40 trips for a cheechako, if he could do it, at a cost of three months' time. Winter travel with a sled was easier; summer travel in the mud was more difficult. The packing rate varied accordingly. By the fall of 1897, the Chilkoot Trail was clogged with tens of thousands of stampeders and their gear.

Before long, Yi the newcomer was doing time-weight-distance problems in his head.

The tribe tolerated no inroads by other would-be entrepreneurs on the Chilkoot Trail. The trail was their power base. They controlled it zealously. They had been packing goods up and down the trail for 200 years before the gold rush.

Packing was part of their culture; a Chilkoot man could carry 150, 200, and even 250 pounds of equipment using a tumpline, a strap, over the forehead or sometimes the chest, or both. Chilkoots also acted as trackers, towing loaded canoes up the Taiya River, also with a tumpline.

The Chilkoots would negotiate a rate per pound, walk ten yards, get offered a better rate and drop their packs.

If a Chilkoot fell by the wayside on the trail, no Chilkoot would stop to give that Chilkoot assistance. No other Inside Passage tribe was nearly as stoic.

Yi often wondered if the Koreans and the Chilkoots were related.

Trudging up a mountain with a pack was routine for Yi, nevertheless the Chilkoots' shrewd understanding of the interrelation of weight, distance, and climate conditions to come up with a market rate was something new. As a Korean soldier and an aristocrat, Yi had had little contact with the merchant class or market economics. The muban class shunned contact with businessmen. Business was demeaning.

As a tribute courier, Yi was more sensitive to the effect precious metals had on the outside world, still as a muban he had never had to haggle for anything. Haggling was disharmonious. Perhaps if Yi had grown up in the community just outside the gate of a Chinese city on the Silk Route, he would have felt more at home in town, but he had grown up spending his time in mountain garrisons or traveling quickly through the countryside. That was not to say he'd never seen haggling in Korean markets or drawn conclusions on how those techniques might be employed.

Now, as a ward of the Chilkoot tribe, he was obliged to haggle and to know the market price per pound to the minute. He also found hardening his neck muscles to the strain of two-inch moosehide tumplines necessary.

Yi toiled weeks learning to be a packer. The port of Dyea was wilder than anything he had seen in the largest cities of China or Korea. The cheechakoes had no concept of the task they had undertaken. The trail edges were piled with discarded equipment, inappropriate equipment, or equipment too heavy to make the ascent. Some equipment was discarded to lighten loads. Here and there roamed starving, abandoned pack animals.

Some stampeders broke down and quit the minute their supplies were piled on the beach. Others, after many trips to Chilkoot Pass, stepped to the side of the trail and began to cry. Some committed suicide. Others were found farther from the trail. Yi observed victims of various afflictions: physical or financial exhaustion, broken bones, smallpox, spinal meningitis, scurvy, or exposure. At least the Chilkoot Trail wasn't as heavily littered with dead pack animals as Dead Horse Pass on the trail from Skagway, which also led to the Yukon River headwaters.

Farther still off the trail were the corpses of stampeders calculatingly murdered by stampede predators...and those murdered by their partners in the heat of a moment.

Supplies had to be watched, even in Dyea, until they were piled under the muzzle of the Mounties' Maxim gun at Chilkoot Pass. The goldfields lay in Canada's Klondike district. Mountie posts were established on the trails leading from Skagway and Dyea to assure miners arrived in Canada with the required supplies. Mounties watched over approved supply caches, one ton per miner, at initial staging points such as the Scales. Moving food and equipment from the Scales to the headwaters of the Yukon was not an undertaking for one man, or to be performed in a single run. Once through the Chilkoot Pass, theft diminished though hardly disappeared.

The circumstances would only get worse when the temperatures plunged below zero. Many men would die, thought Yi, though not so many Chilkoots, and none hopefully from the Land of Morning Calm.

CHAPTER FOUR

Yi always felt strange during the periodic "shape-up" for packers at the trailhead near the Taiya River. The mountains and climate were familiar, yet the noise, chaos and impatience were not.

Yi believed he violated the harmony of Skagway and Dyea just by being different, by being Korean. He strove to counteract that, to please, to get along. He noted that Skagway, and now Dyea, took no note of his effort, nor did it attempt to promote his personal harmony. *Gibun*, harmony, was a broad horizontal concept, and America seemed to glory more in the disharmony of narrow, vertical spikes than in peaceful horizontals. Perhaps, now was the time to ally with a narrow, vertical spike and abandon broad horizontal lines.

In the middle of all this particular hubbub, Yi noticed one man, the white-haired old man who had asked him to splice all that rope, who carried the banner of "being different" to soaring heights. That man thrived on disharmony of thought and deed.

"Shalom alaikum," the stampeder said, stepping forward to greet Yi. The man was lean as a willow reed and had a slight eye twitch. Yi looked at him impassively though immediately recognizing him. The man had a longish white moustache that drooped below his chin. He took off his hat to inspect Yi more closely, and Yi noted his head was bald and ringed with tufts of white hair.

"I know you Chilkoot Indians to be Tlingits and Tlingits are one of the Lost Tribes of Israel and want to keep that a secret, but you can't fool Ephraim Coffin."

Yi knew he wasn't an Indian, and Coffin should have remembered so, too. Noble had told Coffin as much. Coffin was still deceived and might be a complete fool. Coffin talked on, though the rest Yi couldn't follow. He sniffed dangerous disharmony, then concluded he needed a disharmonious ally.

The gimlet-eyed Yankee pointed to Yi and invited him to look over his own gear. Coffin described what each bit of equipment was for. Coffin's supplies were complete and well-researched. He possessed a smattering of tools reduced in size and frequently merged with another tool to reduce space and weight. One item looked like a whipsaw, yet was in pieces. Yi realized that though Coffin might be off the mark in big things, in little things he was fastidious and invariably correct. *Moreover, he had provisions for two.*

Yi noted that Coffin was rawboned and fit; his clothing was well-broken-in and appropriate for Alaska. Coffin frequently consulted the sky and his pocket watch. His eyes scanned the mountainside constantly.

"I had a partner when I left New Hampshire — Portsmouth, New Hampshire, to be precise," Coffin offered without being asked, "but he got hisself shot three nights ago over a shell game in Skagway. That's what the word is."

Yi nodded. "Noble die, likewise. No good, travel trail alone."

Coffin continued. "I'm a mechanic. I don't see much value in lingerin' 'bout Skagway, and only a little bit more value in Dyea. Had a Stockbridge Indian work for me when I had a bicycle shop back there in the Granite State, when I wasn't applying mechanical principles of a larger magnitude. Indians are good workers when they have a chance and motivation."

Yi wasn't sure he'd heard the last words right. They seemed to have too many syllables.

"First rate workmen. It seems to me the theme of these two adjoining towns is parasitical. I could hire you as a packer, but I think you might do better. I need a new partner. How's 'bout a 70/30 split, my favor, seeing I'm providing the provisions? Hate to be overly pushy, still time's a-wasting, and those who don't press on will rot or die. We ain't going to be traveling just now, but we are going to be enterprising."

"I have provision," Yi replied, looking stubborn. "Okay 65/35 split, favor me. Partner, you-me?"

Yi had never heard the term "parasitical," and he assumed it was not complimentary. He held no warm feelings for Skagway either. He had no opinion of Dyea, except it wasn't close enough to the gold.

"Skagway's no good for anyone," continued the older man. "Colonel Soapy will clean you out if you linger. This town's like a big stirred-up anthill ruled by a miners' committee that's just a front for Smith. The town has too many single-minded men and double-action revolvers. My former partner was all too fond of shell games and fast women. They found gunpowder around the wound in the back of his shirt and lady's face powder on the front."

"He gamble? Overmuch?" Yi responded, not expecting a reply. "Women. Gambling. No good, too much mix. I know." He assumed a faraway look and seemed to forget his potential partner. Women and gambling were familiar ground.

Coffin appeared to collect his thoughts. "Skagway and Dyea's full of men who want to get to the Klondike first. Now I sure don't want to get to the goldfields last, yet I'm not so certain something isn't to be gained by moving ahead slowly and taking note of those who've tried to go first and failed. Only this Skagway is poison. Need to get up to the Yukon headwaters before spring."

Yi nodded. Packing, after each hike up, he'd collected abandoned supplies and clothing he scavenged on the route back. Some he sold in Dyea. Smaller, more valuable items he sold in Skagway. Sometimes he picked up the same items twice. Some he cached. He was prospering and collected gold coins, despite the fact he hadn't seen a single gold nugget. Gold could take him back to Korea, and gold might redeem him.

Coffin had all the necessary supplies.

Yi had to admit that Coffin was prepared.

"Even got coffee from 'Frisco and butter from Wisconsin in vacuum-packed tins," Coffin pronounced with great satisfaction. "I advocate wool clothing. It's good wet and in all weather."

Yi noticed that Coffin hadn't explained every item in his kit. He had a sack of strange items he described as "my own inventions."

"A 70/30 split?" Coffin offered again.

"No, 65/35. You have bad memory. Next time you forget I will remember 30/70 split, my favor. You bring own goods to the Scales. Put up marker pole and cache our supplies. We start from there," Yi said forcefully.

Coffin raised his eyes to heaven. He threw out his hand with a show of reluctance.

At that, Coffin cemented the deal with a shake and a hug, then whispered, "Liked you better as a Chinee. You picked up all these sharp habits dealin' and associatin' with the Lost Tribes, I 'spect.

"Lost tribes? Ancestors of Skookum Yi, never lost. All names may be found on shrine since the Silla dynasty," Yi argued. "Skookum Yi lost to them, maybe."

Yi realized his name would never appear on that shrine, and his heavy shoulders slumped.

"You pack a bit more and I'll hoist a few more weeks. When the snows come, we're off to the lakes and the headwaters. They'll be building tramways in due time and this hoist'll be just 'nother gimcrack. Get one of them duck canvas parkas. Chilkoots will know where."

"Hey look, there's that foreign Indian and that addled ol' Yankee," said a side stander with a snicker. He was wrapped in a blanket and wearing a derby. "They've been working a hoist up to the pass,"

Coffin had erected the hoist two weeks earlier and was charging by the pound to lift material from the Scales to the pass. Yi had started helping him. Several other men had joined Coffin in the venture. This was the steepest section of the Chilkoot Trail, referred to as the Golden Stairs. Going up the Stairs cost, too. It was a toll staircase. The men charging the toll didn't seem to mind Coffin's hoist, which was 50 yards to the east

"Gentlemen, if your packer chooses to up your fee or you just want to get more of your goods up faster, E. Coffin & Associates can help you for two cents a pound."

The line to the Golden Stairs was stalled, even at this early hour.

"Hey, Whitey, o-o-ooh excuse me, Mr. White Knight, what you got in your bag we ain't seen already?" harangued a beefy, bearded man with boots that laced up over the calf. "It's your own invention, am I right?"

Yi had gotten used to this. Coffin had brought a sack full of pulleys and other items of interest, gadgets. His gadgets were "inventions," some useful and some simply clever in execution. Many of the Skagway regulars had taken to calling Coffin "White Knight" for his uncanny resemblance, Yi learned, to the Tenniel rendering of that character in *Through the Looking Glass*, an ancient classic of the West. Someone had shown Yi a picture from that book.

"You'll all want to borrow my whipsaw when we reach Lake Lindeman. The planks aren't just going to make theyselves, ar' they?"

"Ah, we'll get our lumber someplace," the bearded man said.

"Could slow you down, brothers," Coffin argued. "First into Dawson is going to get first pick of claims."

Coffin had the whipsaw's sections out and was starting to assemble them. Yi was impatient, nonetheless the line wasn't moving. "I'll let you use my whipsaw at a reasonable price."

Yi stooped to help Coffin. When he looked up, he found six men he had seen before. One yelled, "Look, some of the teeth are bent the wrong way. This old fool don't know nothin'."

One of the six long-armed men picked up a piece of the saw. "Heh, the White Knight's got a worthless piece of junk he's gonna haul all the way to Dawson."

"Better put that down, chum," Coffin said almost casually. Yi watched him. This was another side of Coffin.

The man in the mackinaw jacket bridled a second, then acted as if he were ignoring Coffin. The other four mimicked his posture.

In a flash, Coffin swept away the feet of the man in the mackinaw, swinging a shovel like a nightstick, ankle high. He doubled the man over by poking the shovel handle into his stomach.

Disharmony, thought Yi. Yi recognized the man in the mackinaw as the straight-razor murderer on the side-wheeler.

"Maybe you didn't hear me, there bein' five a-you and you payin' more attention to impressin' each other than anyone else," Coffin exclaimed. "Put that down, chum."

"That's my brother," one of the other five men said and lunged forward. Coffin pole-axed him with the shovel. Stampeders were crowding around. As they did, three of the men dragged away the two fallen men. The sixth man, "Hellfire" Spuyten, just stood staring at Coffin.

"Nice work, White Knight, could use you as a ship's officer," the elder Spuyten pronounced.

Coffin knew, Yi gathered, that he wasn't being complimented.

"The real test, of course, is when not so many folks are around," Spuyten added as an afterthought. "Wolves and sheep, wolves and sheep, you know."

The name "Spuyten" carried with it an undercurrent from the crowd. Yi knew that name from the side-wheeler. This was the Spuyten clan, a father and five brothers, with long arms, necks that folded forward, and hands like snowshoes.

The snows came in late October. To some, they spelled the beginning of hardship and to others they signified greater mobility.

Coffin had sold his breeches buoy hoist to four stampeders whom he trained and trusted would make a go of it. He shared the profit with Yi as agreed.

"You, Whi'-'nigh'..." Yi started.

Coffin winced.

"...you have family?

"No patience for that. I have a lot to teach, even so my kids would to be born full grown."

"I have family, mother and father in *Josun*. Never see again. Must believe I'm dead, "Yi said and paused. "Better, I think."

Earlier in the day, Yi had caught himself addressing Coffin as *"hyungnim,"* older brother.

At the Scales, two Mounties gruffly looked over their gear.

They needed a year's provisions to cross the border and they satisfied that requirement. To Yi, the Mounties looked skeptical. They judged an old man and a Chinaman, however well-equipped, as ill-suited for the Yukon.

In a Mounty's eyes, all cheechakoes looked ill-suited for the Yukon.

Yi and Coffin cached their supplies with Mountie approval at Chilkoot Pass. They waited another month to begin the second part of the Chilkoot Trail. Coffin wanted to hear what problems early stampeders would have getting to Lake Lindeman. In late November, they alternated pulling sled-loads from Chilkoot Pass to Lake Lindeman, one of the two lakes that comprised the Yukon River headwaters. Their first load included the tent. The tent would remain heated and serve as a refuge at the end of each trek.

One watched the Chilkoot Pass cache and tent while the other dragged or carried a load. The work was slow, still downhill for the laden portion of the circuit, and not as slow as it had been carrying loads from Dyea to Chilkoot Pass. The worst part would be the long periods of darkness and the extreme temperatures.

Storms from time to time brought the cycle to a halt because the trails virtually disappeared.

On the downhill run to Deep Lake with the first load of supplies, just as they descended into the tree line once again, Coffin gestured Yi well off the trail and they set up a makeshift camp. "We need to plant a trove for a rainy day," he said.

Coffin seemed to be looking for something. He appeared selective about where they built their fire. Eventually, he found the place he was looking for and built a reflector fire at the base of a ledge.

The next morning, Coffin dropped an empty coffee tin and an empty butter tin in the snow and began digging under where the fire had been. Soon, a narrow hole had formed amid the ashes.

"Well, Skookum, we have our supply cache at Chilkoot Pass. It's protected by the Mounties and marked by a pole. I think this is the time and place to set up our rainy-day money cache. We've done pretty well so far, you an' me, contrariwise our luck could change. Nature and men can turn ag'in us."

Coffin pulled a belt from beneath his parka, a money belt and it jingled. Yi had seen these before when stampeders had paid him off for packing. Yi didn't accept paper money and apparently neither did Coffin.

"I'll put half of my coinage into the cans and you should, too, partner."

Yi pondered the risk. He was aware of a confidence game that required placing money, money mingled with that of a partner, with a third party or in a safe place. All along the ascent to Chilkoot Pass were rigged games involving shells and thimbles, some coupled with a warm tent and shots of liquor. The mayor of Skagway, Soapy Smith, was a confidence man. Yi knew that confidence games thrived where men gathered, men who dreamed of quick wealth.

"Here, my money," Yi stated impassively.

They did no accounting, however Yi believed Coffin had been successful with his breeches buoy hoist.

"We're at 75/25, right?" Coffin said brightly.

"Sure, 30/70, my favor maybe," Yi said glumly and tried to work a Korean abacus in his head, a *juban* in Korean. It was a wearying tease.

"No, that's completely and cussedly wrong," Coffin said, as if talking to himself. "I'm just made contrary. What you cache stays your'n. Fair's fair, and you been a valuable steel counterweight to this here skirring, expedition'ry machine. Put your coins in one tin and I'll put my coins in t'other. If anything happens to me, the contents of both are your'n. And whatever we make from here on out is half your'n. You been one solid packer-sledge-tracker. "

"Remember these rocks and those trees. The trees may come down. Thousands of stampeders have been coming, and wood will be cut. All anyone will notice is someone built a fire here."

They dropped the first tin in the hole, then covered it with stones. Then they dropped in the second tin and covered it with a flat rock and a layer of soil. The second can contained coins and a hammerless pistol with an owl head engraved on the grips. The cache was for emergencies. Most emergencies could be addressed with cash, though not all.

Yi wondered how much he would miss the money. What disturbed him was what might Coffin do to him to keep all the money? This was hard country for a man alone.

At times, Yi wondered if he really cared anymore. The packer's roulette wheel ruled, and all directions were equally distasteful. Gambling had cast him from his former world and appeared determined to haunt him in this new one as well.

Coffin was always cheery and helpful to those around him. He was forever thinking of means to make moving food and equipment more efficient, even so his advice wasn't always welcome or well received by others.

The heavy snowfall at Chilkoot Pass slowed them down. Each time Coffin or Yi returned for one more portion of their gear, they found their cache several feet deeper in snow. They had erected a marker pole, but had no idea how long the pole would remain above the snow level.

They had no margin for error. On more than one instance, Yi found stampeders curled in the snow with their knees up and their forearms frozen in front of their faces.

On some occasions, he helped men disoriented by the cold and crippled by frostbite, hoping others might do the same for him.

CHAPTER FIVE

Coffin began to measure off a "saw-pit" beyond their camp at Lake Lindeman, at Lake Bennett, the next lake down the line to the Yukon River.

A saw-pit was really a scaffold that allowed two men to work a whipsaw with one man several feet above the man holding the other end. Coffin thawed the frozen ground within the area designated for the pit by building fires. A month later, he had the saw-pit working.

His original whipsaw, "his own invention," didn't work. Irrepressible, he managed to buy another from two stampeders who'd had enough and were heading back to Dyea.

At first, Yi thought that Coffin was indiscriminate in his choice of friends. He had a good word for everyone. He continually allowed newcomers to Lake Lindeman, and later to Lake Bennett, to share their tent until they could set up their own.

Eventually, Yi realized that the friendliness was not a bad idea. In treks back and forth to the Chilkoot Pass cache, a packer would repeatedly cross paths with the same men. Having those other men in your debt couldn't hurt. Yi grew to realize that Coffin chose men carefully when it came to saw rental and boat building, and by then Coffin had accumulated a circle of acquaintances who regarded Coffin, and even Yi, with favor and trust. When a single error could cost a man his life, his network of acquaintances could help a man survive, at least…to his second error.

Coffin directly, and Yi indirectly, were collecting markers of acceptance.

Yi found himself addressing Coffin in Korean as *hyung*, "older brother" with regularity. Coffin was a man of limitless theories. He didn't mind that his own people regarded him as strange, he enjoyed it. Rare was the day he didn't float an idea before a stranger challenging that stranger to find its weakness. Coffin's brain was a knife forever looking for whetstones.

Yi also realized Coffin's bluff affability had a false aspect to it, an element of self-interest. This falseness was all the more unsettling when Yi realized how often he had seen that same affability in everyday life in Korea, China, and San Francisco.

Why did he find it so unsettling here in the Yukon?

Yi seemed to sleepwalk, dragging his sled to the Chilkoot Pass supply cache and back. Then they made a second major move from Lake Lindeman to Lake Bennett. Each length was a numbing exercise in drudgery.

Survival, though, was a matter of method and preparation. Yi always carried several candles and food. With a fire, he could boil water and fend off dehydration in the middle of drifts of water in its frozen, fluffy form. The Chilkoots had warned him not to allow himself to sweat. Sweat turned to ice. Wearing layers of clothing that you could peel off was better than wearing the heavy fur coats favored by the worst-advised cheechakoes.

Packers paced themselves so they didn't overheat and begin to sweat. Though everyone was in a rush to get to the goldfields, no one could make it down the 500-mile Yukon River run until the ice broke up. That wouldn't occur until May or June.

When Yi dragged his sled to Chilkoot Pass, Coffin stayed behind. They assisted each other according to their plan, yet days would go by when they couldn't be mutually supportive.

Yi kept in contact with the Chilkoot packers, and with Klukwan in particular. If Coffin could be affable, he could, too. A man must draw his lessons where he might. He must collect markers of acceptance.

On one trek, Yi noticed a strange drift alongside the trail. He stopped to investigate and uncovered a stampeder's frozen body. The stampeder's gear was gone.

Yi looked into the frozen man's face for answers. Two dark slashes, nearly parallel, along the left side of this neck told Yi that death had been quick.

Spuyten handiwork?

Stealing could reduce the months needed to move supplies to the Yukon headwaters. Though the Mounties exercised strict control, here beyond Chilkoot Pass no one was weighing or tracking the supplies of individual stampeders.

Yi notified a Mountie at Chilkoot Pass and continued his endless treks. Sometimes, Yi wondered if he'd ever had a life beyond the Chilkoot Trail. The snow in Chilkoot Pass was 60 feet deep. He had to dig to find their supplies.

At Lake Bennett, Coffin's inventiveness, or more truly, his logistical genius became clear. At their newly-erected sawpit, they leased out Coffin's two whipsaws; payment was several gold pieces and a few planks. Before long, they had accumulated a pile of lumber, albeit green, and a moose-hide pouch of gold coins. They watched a dozen cheechakoes fashion boats and eventually hired two boat builders.

"We won't build on speculation," the boat builders insisted. "Cash up front. We built whitehalls in New York."

A whitehall was an elegant two position rowboat with a wine-glass cross section.

"This is rough work and bigger boats, admittedly the principles are nigh-on the same."

Coffin smiled. "That seems fair enough. Build them like you built your own boat. I've got block and tackle. We can use logs to roll them down to the ice."

The two new boatwrights nodded. "And we're through when the ice breaks up."

"Sure enough. You get paid for every boat you put on the ice," Coffin confirmed.

Coffin could talk with a pipe clinched between his teeth. "We need to wait, get the hang of it, and still head down the river when the ice breaks up. I hear we'll face rapids and bad eddies. The first boats will show us where all the little Scylla-houettes and Charyb-dishers be. Well, don't suppose classical allusions have meaning to a Chinese."

So now he was Chinese again, Yi thought.

Yi had known mountain rivers. On several occasions he had navigated the Yalu and the Tumen Rivers. He could guess what frigid-water pitfalls lay in store.

"Don't absolutely know that these 'boatwrights' know what they're doing, on the other hand I seen my share of boats in Portsmouth. The boat doesn't need to be pretty, just get us there. We'll know soon enough if they understand their trade."

Coffin puffed on his pipe. "Still, we have no guarantee any stampeder will make it to Dawson."

Their camp had a good view of the river. They kept their sawpit in back, out of sight. Then Coffin and Yi framed and planked their boat with their stock of green lumber. Yi knew sampan construction, and these boats were similar.

"We'll rest a couple days. That river doesn't like us foreigners. We're going to need our full strength."

Yi nodded.

They came in one night as if they owned the tents at Lake Bennett. Yi recognized them instantly, the long arms, big hands, and folded necks...the Spuytens. The six Spuytens encircled them with a casualness that left Yi looking for a shovel or hatchet.

"We know boats and ships. How much for that boat?" Hellfire Spuyten demanded. "I'll give you a good price for it. Looks like it can carry a few tons and it has enough rocker in the bottom to maneuver rapids. Builder knew how to apply pitch. Is the builder a Yankee or a Columbia River hand?"

"Yankee handiwork," Coffin said. "That's our boat, not for sale."

"Well, then this other one must be available. Looks like the same folks built it."

"Been sold already, to several of those fellows in those tents over there," Coffin lied. "All the boats 'round here already have owners. 'Course you're welcome to find the owners and dicker."

"Well, this one's still here. You can sell it again. I'll better their price."

Yi watched as men began to pour out of their tents. Soon a larger group encircled the Spuyten clan. Coffin had been wise to gather allies, Yi reminded himself. In the goldfields it might be — how did the cheechakos put it — "cut the cards," but here, now, there would be no intimidation of Coffin and Yi by strangers.

"The best way would be to offer these other fellas a price for their boats." Coffin made a vague motion toward the men in the outside circle. "This other boat is no longer mine to sell."

"And we do have a miners' committee here," one of the boat owners bluffed.

Hellfire Spuyten's face darkened. "You know, I like that boat." His finger pointed to the first boat, Coffin's boat. "My heart's set on it. Well, boys, seems no boat buyin's goin' on here."

Hellfire's eyes sparkled likes stars in the Arctic firmament.

April should have heralded milder weather, it didn't. Yi made trips from Lake Bennett back to Lake Lindeman for the last of their supplies while Coffin supervised the boat building. Yi used the rest period to hunt for fresh meat. He fashioned a fire-hardened sapling and attempted to track rabbits.

Evenings on Lake Lindeman, Yi made a habit of climbing into the scaffolding of the sawpit and looking at the stars. The constellations were the same as they had been in Korea and China. He learned that the constellation he knew as *Jilseong*, the Stepping Stones, was called the Big Dipper by Westerners. Of course, frequently, he could see nothing in the sky at all.

As May passed, the excitement of the cheechakoes grew. Everyone knew the ice was going to free up and the 500 riverine miles to Dawson would be open. Men came to Coffin for his block and tackle to drag their finished boats to a favorable starting position. Next up was going to be a race to Dawson through several sets of rapids and then down the river.

On May 29, 1898, the ice broke up on Lake Bennett and the first wave of boats hurried downriver. Ankle-deep in snow, Coffin looked at Yi. "Let's wait a day. Let two more waves find all the Scylla-houettes and Charybd-dishers. We'll be a tad late as they mark the rough spots with their wreckage."

Yi had no idea exactly what those words signified, still he had lived long enough to understand the need for caution, and Coffin had been right at every turn so far. They had both prospered without setting foot in a goldfield.

One night in late May as Yi stood balancing himself on a log strut in the sawpit at the headwater of the Yukon River, he heard soft bootless steps behind him and then felt himself thrown from the scaffolding. He heard himself inhale and then heard nothing at all.

When Yi came to, he couldn't move his arms or legs. He just listened.

"This is our saw now, old man, and it will do our bidding," Hellfire ranted. Yi knew that voice by now. "We have your money belt an' we figure you must have a sack of gold coins 'round here too. You ever seen them music hall magicians saw a lady in half?

"We're going to charge you that sack of coins just for participating. Know this, still and all we're going to find it anyway. That redskin packer of your'n is dead and most everybody's left.

"Where's the rest of the coins?" The voice belonged to one of the sons, Yi assumed.

"Why should I tell you? You're going to kill me anyway." Coffin was a hard man in his own way, Yi realized with admiration.

"Yeah, well, tell us quick and we'll cut you in half quick," Hellfire yelled, drawing chuckles from his sons.

"The old geezer's dead. If the redskin isn't dead, he had no pulse, and I jabbed him with my knife like to test 'im. His back mus' have broken good," said one of the Spuyten brothers. Yi guessed he was Elias, the one who wore a mackinaw.

"We got our boat now. Told you I liked the look of them boats. Well, in Dawson we're going to stake a claim or become indispensable to someone who has one," Hellfire summarized.

Coffin would invent no more, and the Spuytens had again followed their philosophy that divided humanity into wolves and sheep.

No one but a gravely injured Skookum Yi was left to mourn Coffin. The former denizens of the camp were hurtling down the Yukon River. Those cheechakoes feeding into Lake Bennett now had other things on their minds.

A Mountie found Coffin's dismembered body. Yi had no way of telling if his back was broken, though he was still breathing.

After weeks of rest at the Mountie's hut, Yi was able to travel again. His strong, thick body had absorbed the impact.

Yi collected the cached coins, including Coffin's contribution, a sack of gold coins about the size of an ostrich egg. He realized he had options.

Hyungnim, doo mannapshida. (I will see you again, honored older brother), Yi thought to himself sorrowfully.

Men seeking raw gold were willing to pay minted gold for services that helped them get to the goldfields. So confident were they of success that mundane tasks, such as packing and laundering, were well rewarded. Yi wasn't exactly wealthy now, even so he could take some time to think about the future. Until this moment, his whole life had been a simple matter of flight and survival.

In life, Coffin had been a good man. The lighterman with the flying fish tattoo, Noble, had been a good man. Sergeant Go and the others had been good men. Yi was tired of being dogged by dead good men. Life had shown him too many dead good men. The time had come for life to show him a few dead bad men, he thought. He didn't know that many, yet a few in particular came to mind.

The Korean word *gibun* rolled around in his mind. He believed in harmony. His culture worked on the principle. Yi's life had now touched five countries: Korea, China, Japan, the United States, and Canada. If he was to ever again experience personal harmony, certain disharmonies needed to be cast out and harmony restored.

On the low end of the social scale in a foreign country, he had subsisted in invisibility. Invisibility was a characteristic some men sought and others had thrust upon them. Ultimately, he owed Korea several tons of silver tael sycee. He owed several dead men for their patience and kindness. He would be patient. The evil he planned to fight would cross his path. He wouldn't have to look for it.

The targets of his retribution would be repaid with a just and terrible interest. The objects of his restitution would be afforded means and opportunity.

He had learned from cultures that valued harmony and cultures that valued disharmony

Yi hoped the ancestors would be pleased with his progress, regardless, he meant to turn his anger into action.

CHAPTER SIX

Yerba Buena Cove, San Francisco, 1899

Flat on his back, looking between surrounding men's legs and other ships, Gizzard Spuyten could make out a gas-lit string of waterfront saloons, cafes, billiard parlors, barber shops, and chandleries. The new ferry terminal was somewhere off in the fog, with the bustle of arrivals and departures indicated by surging waves of unidentifiable sound.

Even now, before the false light that preceded dawn, men and women were leaning against the gaslights, the closest a few hundred yards away. Each gaslight cut its own sepia-tinted corona through the cool, damp night.

A large man loped along the road that paralleled the pier, giving what seemed to be a lecture to an invisible class, judging from his manner and intensity. Farther down the frontage road, a fiddler played for coins.

Overall, the scene gave Gizzard little pleasure.

A sinuous Chinese girl in black-silk pajamas with elaborate red and gold embroidery had boarded the tired schooner earlier and called out to him in words that sounded like someone tapping a crystal glass with the blunt edge of a knife. The only word he understood was his name. She'd beckoned him up the ladder out of the roundhouse with an urgent wave to the main deck, and then disappeared. Was she an admirer? Had someone sent him a treat? Gizzard didn't know where she'd gone, or for that matter, where the rest of the crew had disappeared to.

He knew now that she had been a lure, and the few remaining crew members had been threatened or bribed off the schooner. When he'd walked toward where he'd last seen the seductive Chinese girl, seven men, who looked Chinese, plunged from the schooner's rigging like a crashing rogue wave, landing so violently that he hadn't a moment to think. Six of those men formed a half-circle that backed him against the mainmast and swept his legs from under him. The largest man stood apart from the others, facing Gizzard.

Gizzard could now hear the shrill laughter of women and the faint, tinny sound of an out-of-tune upright piano. He had trouble telling exactly where the sounds came from. Saloons marked the waterfront like the dark keys on a piano keyboard. *Ashore,* he thought to himself. *I should be over there — ashore, not here.*

A sailor with his girl, who appeared to be his senior by ten years at least, spun around a gaslight and tossed the fiddler a coin.

Gizzard lay on the unpainted deck of a floating firetrap. The ship was two days back from Skagway, and the Yukon Gold Rush, with a fortune in gold dust. He wished, despite the tawdry allure of this waterfront, that he were somewhere else. This tired, battered ship had once been yellow, a Pacific Northwest island ferry that had outlived its usefulness. The sheen of the deck condensation caught the red of Gizzard's long-handle underwear, cut by the two vertical lines of his suspenders. Though never a cautious man, he wore a belt also. The belt held an empty knife sheath. The knife — which was no longer there — was the inspiration for his nickname, "Gizzard."

"Iffin I don't like 'em, I cuts them right up the gizzard" was the oft-recounted Gizzard observation. He didn't much care for anyone other than his father and four brothers, who were equally cutthroat, and he didn't really care that much for them either. So, he had done his share of ripping human beings "up the gizzard" in his 30 or so years.

The double barrels of his shotgun had been broken at its stock and the rounds ejected across the slippery deck. His wrist had been broken as well when his knife was taken. He still possessed a straight razor in his gumboot. Contrary to his immediate impulse, he decided he'd keep that there until his odds improved.

Paw Spuyten, "Hellfire" Spuyten, had ordered him to guard the gold, and he had failed. Hellfire Spuyten and Gizzard's brothers, Cornelius, Diderick, Bram, and Elias, had other matters to attend to that night. The schooner-ferry belonged to his family. These Chinamen had no right to be here.

Six men now stood surrounding Gizzard, and the seventh stepped forward and loomed over him. Some of the attackers wore pajamas. Some wore woolen attire; some wore denim. All wore hats of Western manufacture: bowlers, watch caps, and even a broad-brimmed hat with a Montana peak. Three of them wore queues down their backs, the customary, long, braided pigtail that to Gizzard signified one more useless quirk of a race too strange and upside down to bother with.

Two of his captors wore black jackets with full sleeves. One black jacket glistened like the deck. The seventh man, built wide and square, wore a peacoat. That small detail bothered Gizzard, though he didn't know why. The wide, square man looked somehow different from the rest, physically more powerful — yet he too had almond-shaped eyes and high cheekbones.

One of the men in black jackets turned to the seventh man, "We got poetic justice, eh, boss?"

Gizzard *had heard* the phrase before, though it flashed through his mind without triggering an example.

"Poetic" was a term he associated with the weak and effeminate. And "justice" stood out as a designation he regarded with equal disdain. It, too, he associated with the weak and effeminate. He had never given either term more than a minute's thought in his life. Now that phrase seemed to hang there, annoyingly, just beyond his comprehension.

To Gizzard, they all looked pretty much the same, albeit some more dangerous than others. Perhaps the hawkish arch to the bridge of the seventh man's nose had added some sense of distinction. Just another Chinaman, however, Gizzard mused. Though Gizzard did note this man wore Slater mining boots that laced nearly to his knees. Those boots had been popular in the Yukon, except the only Chinaman he had come across in the Yukon was long dead, he remembered with a repressed smile. Still, the man did look familiar.

All seven had to be Chinamen, and under different circumstances, he might have tormented them for his amusement. He wondered if he could study their faces and remember them, to even the score later on. Gizzard was a big man, over six feet tall and well over 200 pounds. He was taller than each of the seven men. He was heavier than most of the Asians, yet he couldn't say if he outweighed the man in the peacoat.

He gave up that idea as fast as it came to him. To even the score later, he needed to survive, and that meant he had to focus on the present.

The faces of each of the seven Asian men wore the marks of hard lives endured. Among all eight men on deck, the seven Asians and Gizzard Spuyten, they could have constructed a whole ninth man from their combined scar tissue, broken bones, and lost parts. Two or three of the attackers bore looks of dangerous irrationality.

"These gentlemen beside me are member of society, society much like Brotherhood of Mason. Chinee kind," the man in the peacoat stated in even tones, addressing Gizzard and scanning the seawall.

Their spokesman's English was marred by missing articles, mismatched plurals, and the consonant difficulties of the Far East, still Spuyten's sense of survival was going to bring him right to the head of the class this evening in terms of attention. This seventh man was the Asians' leader. Gizzard again thought something was familiar about him, however he put the idea aside. He'd never had more than a three-word conversation with any Chinaman.

Their leader's right eyebrow arched in irony. "We lift up the downcast, comfort the oppressed, and when we can, we step on snake. Not sure America Masons give as much thought to snake."

The seventh man might have been joking, yet did he convey just a suggestion of anger in his tone, or was that only sarcasm? "Mostly we make our livings as cooks. That's why we carry hatchets or cleavers...yes, for cooking."

"Yeah, cooks and washerwomen, and privy cleaners. You don't amount to much of nothing, do you people? You get disrespectin' with me and you'll answer to me an' every Spuyten this side of the Rockies. What are you a-jabberin' about, John Chinaman? Ain't none of you is Masons."

Yes, Gizzard concluded, the seventh Asian was making some

sort of joke at his expense. Damn Chinaman. Many of San Francisco's Chinese residents considered themselves sojourners and had little time or the patience to learn English. Few but the Jook-sing, the American-born Chinese, could speak bona fide English, however the seventh man didn't speak in the cadence of a Jook-sing. Gizzard noted he could tell a joke in English. That level of fluency and confidence made Gizzard feel uneasy. All but one of the Asian men carried a cleaver or a hatchet, even the one with only a single hand. Another with a split eyebrow and puffy eyelid carried a hammerless revolver with a medium-length barrel. Gizzard suspected the man was blind in his marred eye.

They must belong to *Tongs*, Gizzard decided. He had heard of Tongs: Chinese gangs in America. In China, they were called *Triads*. He'd heard the coolies could be tough, though had never believed it. If he had, he thought, he might not have pushed so many around. Gizzard would've liked to rally a bunch of sandlotters with pick handles, or the crew of his father's new ship, to show these heathen Chinese something about intimidation. His sandlotters would have been a match for the intruders.

These Chinamen had struck the shotgun from Gizzard's hand with the back edges of their cleavers and hatchets and unloaded it. For good measure, they'd given him a few smacks on the head with the flat sides of their hatchets.

Surprisingly he was still alive, Gizzard thought, with an apprehensive sense of superiority. Damned coolies never got it right. They should've killed him without hesitation. How tough could short men be? They didn't have it. Soon enough Pa and his brothers would help him straighten these highbinders out. Paw would have every McCullum & Spuyten crew — from the new partnership — running down these heathen wharf rats like the wrath of God. No one crossed the family of his paw, "Hellfire" Spuyten.

Gizzard could hear the fiddler on the frontage road sawing away at Macy and Hays's "Gold Will Buy 'Most Anything,' But A True Girl's Heart" with real intensity, or maybe the blood was just flowing faster through his ears. A sucker's song, but suckers made life easy for people like him.

"We have count twenty sacks of gold dust. The other half come soon? When? What boat?"

"Now jus' what makes you think I'm a-gonna tell you that, Johnny Chinaman? You some big boss of the order of scullery maids and washerwomen hereabouts?" Gizzard laughed.

"No tell? Well, we not take everything you have." The seventh Asian emphasized the word "everything," which made Gizzard uneasy. This man was being too open with his intentions; he was too confident.

"How far you think can swim with gold dust?" the Chinaman asked. "My friend here, they gamble, you savvy? *Fan tan, pai gow,* what you call poker. You swim from here to pier with sack. They bet on it. You bet how much can swim with. You must swim fast when you're in the water, savvy? Man with revolver — that would be me — will shoot at you on count of ten. I will count in English, being fair."

Gizzard leaned aside and spat.

"You measure gold you think you can swim with. Put in moose-hide sack."

Gizzard was trying to do the multiplication. He knew the value of a sack of gold dust, though not the weight. "I'll take a whole sack."

The seventh Asian shook his head. "Whole sack is 50 pounds. No good. Too much. No man can swim with 50 pounds anything."

"I can toss around a 50-pound sack like a crab apple."

"No good. Here is drinking-liquor shot glass to put gold in bag. I count ten. You spill gold dust, we smash other wrist, savvy?

Gizzard splashed a number of glasses of gold dust into the sack. The Chinaman with one sagging eyelid counted to ten and pulled on the drawstring of the partially filled sack.

"Wear boots. Can't jump into harbor without protecting feet," the seventh Asian cautioned.

"Mighty considerate," Gizzard hissed.

Gizzard had on the same gumboots he'd worn in the goldfields. Of course, he hadn't done any panning. Panning was too slow for his tastes. He and his brothers found other ways of collecting gold.

If he kept his boots, he kept his razor. That meant a chance for quick retaliation.

Gizzard's eyes were on the gold. The thought of swimming without the gold was never a consideration. He couldn't go back to his father and brothers with only a portion of the gold, nevertheless with resilient slyness he realized he could live well off a portion of the gold. If this was all that was left, he'd keep it for himself and hightail it. His brothers would be angry about the loss of gold and his disappearance. Despite any duty he owed them, Gizzard Spuyten had to look out for himself. In any event, his father and brothers would have to find him first.

The Chinamen fashioned straps from rope for one moose-hide bag and slipped them over his shoulders like a knapsack. Gizzard spat again, this time at the feet of the Chinaman with the cauliflower ear. The man seemed to take the gesture impassively, handed the hammerless revolver to the seventh Asian, and then suddenly punched Gizzard in a strange, straight-armed manner about a hand above the navel. The blow wasn't exactly the wallop that had made the heavyweight Fitzsimmons famous, but it caused Gizzard to drop like a sash weight.

"One-two-three…" the leader began.

As Gizzard rose unsteadily, the group toppled him headfirst over the rail. His boots filled up with air. He struggled to get rid of his boots and keep the knapsack on. He bobbed up once to peel off his footwear, and in doing so, lost his razor. His arms were still in the knapsack straps. One boot floated off, the other filled with water, and eventually he turned upright, frantically treading in the harbor.

Gizzard sank, sending up a stream of bubbles. The stream tapered off as his head cleared, and he realized that twenty pounds of gold was too much to swim with. Still he could walk submerged along the bottom if he could figure out which way the pier was. Underwater, an inky dark closed in on him. He released another group of bubbles, his last.

Onboard, the marauders' leader, Skookum Yi, wiped his brow.

One of his gang on the pier held a pocket watch. An explosion of bubbles erupted about ten feet from the pier, and then the night was quiet, but for the fiddler's tune and the lapping of water against the pilings.

The triad member with the watch yelled out the time and distance from the pier. "Fifteen seconds, 30 feet!" Grumbling rose up among the men.

"His rope straps probably made releasing sack too difficult," one speculated.

"Making him keep boots on altered results," suggested another glumly. One Eye, who had a superstitious bent, guffawed. "Gizzard Spuyten not let go of the gold. He never could. Spirits of men he kill to get it, they keep him underwater."

"The bastard probably murdered two men for every pound of gold he had in that moose-hide sack," said Yi. And that was counting Gizzard alone. The number of men the entire Spuyten family had killed was well beyond count. Yi rubbed a finger along the gunwale with impatience. The Spuyten family's time would come.

He put the hammerless revolver back in its holster. He had never intended to fire it to start Gizzard's swim. A shot would have attracted too much attention.

Yi wiped his face and looked into the water. His upbringing had taught him to repress anger, except in debts of honor, and even then, the emotion rarely rose to the surface with any heat. Yi knew in Japan this emotional repression was called *haragei* or the "belly art" and greatly esteemed. The ability was certainly admired among warriors and leaders in Korea as well.

Gizzard Spuyten, his father, and brothers had preyed upon many. They had amassed this fortune in the Yukon gold fields, bullying miners, killing them, or robbing them of the supplies necessary for survival and leaving them for dead. One of their victims had been Yi's mining partner, a man whom Yi had loved like… an eccentric older brother.

"No chance. Tried to take more gold than he could swim with," Yi said in English to himself, or maybe to Gizzard's ghost. He drew air through his teeth. "He couldn't think, see anything else. No chance."

In the water below, one gumboot bobbed upside down between the ship and the distant pier.

"Not a Chinaman's chance," Yi said with an arched eyebrow, again in English. The phrase had no real meaning, nor conveyed irony, except in English. Where the Asian man came from, and he was no Chinaman, Chinamen had enjoyed an abundance of chances for centuries. Only on this side of the Pacific was life hopeless for a Chinaman.

He gave brief thought to the rest of Gizzard's associates, the Spuyten boys — "Hellfire" Spuyten and sons. Yi wouldn't waste his life chasing them, though if they crossed his path, that was another matter. Yi believe in karma, and over the last six years he had tempered his impulsivity, his violent streak. This was one debt of honor that he continued to stomach, a debt to the man whom he had regarded as an older brother.

The other debt of honor, less personal, he owed was to the people of Korea. This obligation was a far greater burden and far harder to set right. To square that commitment, he would have to take on the Empire of Japan.

"Not a Chinaman's chance," he repeated. He pictured the old man in his mind for a moment, then flexed his fingers momentarily into fists. This was as close as he'd come to a show of emotion.

Yi buttoned his peacoat, exhaled slowly, and stood up straight, looking westward. The others in the gang had fled the schooner minutes before. Yi gave a long, dark sigh, for he well understood the concept of poetic justice. Sometimes he felt as if he carried what his countrymen called "a dark, five-league fog" with him. He felt little for Gizzard Spuyten's fate, other than an incomplete sense of retribution. Full retribution might come in time, but it had to be accompanied by his restitution of several tons of precious metal, silver preferably, but gold would do.

PART II

THE LANDING PARTY

*Whatever happens, we have got
the Maxim gun, and they have not.*
– Hilaire Belloc

CHAPTER SEVEN

Woosung, China, 1911

Several rounds of ineffective fire disturbed the dirt just in front of Naval Lieutenant Elswell's landing party. The flying dirt was followed by the sharp reports at the slow pace of bolt-action rifle fire. Sharpshooters?

Seaman Hobson, one small cog in that landing party as part of the Gatling gun detail, wasn't sure.

Experience told him to focus on the larger picture.

No one was asking for his opinion. He wasn't going to get caught up in every piffling threat in a situation beset by a thousand threats. "Can I return fire?" asked Krafts, a first-class petty officer, eagerly un-slinging his Krag-Jorgenson M1903 and cartridge belt and adjusting the sling around the outside of his elbow. Krafts was from Tennessee and a dead shot, at least according to his own frequently offered estimation.

Attempting to size up the situation, Lieutenant Elswell responded in the negative.

Around them, the military formations looked like tin soldiers deployed on a sick child's counterpane, Seaman Hobson thought.

As part of *USS Rainbow*'s landing party under Elswell's leadership, Hobson's job was both to serve as a naval light infantryman, and to man the landing party's Gatling gun. The seaman watched the different forces, each a colored patch, converging on wharfs, warehouses, and most importantly the cable station. Men streamed down alleys, bridle paths, and oxcart ruts. Innumerable creeks and ridges impeded movement. To Hobson, the gently rolling coastal plain around this troubled village, just downriver from China's most significant port, Shanghai, looked every bit like a tired quilt. They were there to protect an American cable station in the village of Woosung.

Two patches of color had spilled out of *USS Rainbow*, a former station and distillery ship, now a troopship, and had the two patches crunched forward with machine-like efficiency across the beach. The larger patch was all khaki and bristled with black steel, the Marine patch. The smaller patch, Hobson's patch, was Navy undress blue with a lower border of khaki leggings and the occasional glistening of brass above its two-wheeled gun carriage.

Other patches that didn't belong to the two landing party patches were there, as Elswell had put it, "...primarily, one, to seize or destroy the cable station — two, to fend off or destroy the landing party — or three, to loot. Of course, some of these groups might be helpful and plan to do the opposite of one, two, and three."

Krafts grumbled when he saw the small group that had peppered their position withdraw. It moved down the slope toward the waterfront.

Hobson touched his cartridge belt for reassurance. *Tongmeng-hui? A warlord's battalion?*

The appearance of machine-like efficiency came at the cost of hours of drill, and it conferred a psychological edge on the battlefield. To third parties, the maneuver gave the impression of engine-like application of maximum force with minimal effort.

Moreover, the drill instilled a sense of routine and familiarity to its participants — loading, aiming, and firing in unison — as it became second nature.

Here in the East, the West was known for its wondrous machines. Could the West, however, turn its men into unstoppable machines? Maybe, Hobson mused, all too aware at the moment of his own mortality. He had observed in the past that these wheeling-flanking-countermarching formations were particularly chilling to those who hadn't seen tactics executed by the numbers, and he hoped his past observations in peacetime would hold true today.

We foreign devils, he mused, *with our strange and colorful attire, in our tight formations, and with our deliberate movements, are bound to intimidate any route-step gaggle of warlord conscripts and jail sweepings.*

China was in disarray. The Qing dynasty — or Manchu dynasty as it was known to some — had collapsed. A stunned China found itself immobilized by a leadership vacuum. Hobson's officers wondered who would prevail.

Many splinter groups hoped to join with the Tongmenghui, one of the early Nationalist secret societies.

China was a big machine itself, Hobson thought, *but none of that machine's gears were connecting right now and many of its pulleys, springs, and flywheels were tearing it apart. Yet, in Korea, he remembered, China had been regarded with a begrudging reverence. Too many languages, dialects, factions, clans, and sects.*

USS Rainbow was cruising the coast to "observe" conditions that might affect the safety of Americans in Shanghai, Zang, Nanjing, Xiamen, Shantou, Qingdao, and Dagu. China was in turmoil though that shouldn't have an unsettling influence on Americans or their interests. Americans, many believed, were bringing something good, the twentieth century, to a long-decaying country — and their positive contribution should not be impeded.

Woosung had now been the scene of rioting and looting for a month. *USS Rainbow* carried on it a Marine Expeditionary Force sent to do what it could to ensure stability and protect American interests. The unit was to engage in "demonstrations" naval shorthand for "demonstrations of force." Woosung guarded the waterway to Shanghai. The local government had been deposed, still the new government's composition was unclear and no new national government was in place. There was word of an uprising in Wuchang. Imperial China was unraveling faster than the revolutionaries could handle. They had taken the Woosung forts and the Woosung arsenal already. If Woosung could be held by the rebels, hope remained that the confusing coalition of forces could take Shanghai. Woosung was now threatened by the advance of a nearby warlord, General Zang. Chief "Uncle Billy" Gillingham, leader of the Gatling gun detail and Hobson's boss, had said as much. *Uncle Billy knew China.*

Chief Gillingham read books, could write Chinese characters, and wore a frogged silk Chinese shirt with a mandarin collar as a makeshift smoking jacket in the chiefs' locker. He was known as "Uncle Billy" though never addressed that way.

The cable station was the expatriate lifeline to the home country. To whomever won, the message was to be clear: Don't harm
Americans or American business interests, and keep away from cable stations. Hobson wasn't entirely comfortable with the concept,
yet a threat or two in this part of the world brought stability, and
with it a semblance of peace. Not that China at this point in her
history could approach anything resembling sustainable peace. It
could attempt superficial peace and hope superficial peace would
grow into something more.

Hobson watched the large Marine patch tear off a platoon,
which double-timed up the oxcart ruts to array themselves as a
blocking force. This patch was all khaki, saddle-soaped leather,
whip-cord, rifle barrels, and campaign hats. Another Marine platoon tore off and floated across the wharves and godowns. A third
had established a protective perimeter around the foreign quarter.
Hobson noted that a particular torn patch of khaki, Marines, had
assumed defensive positions, then magically dissipated. Tin soldiers on a counterpane rarely established defensive positions. Marines were all about maneuver and engagement, though too, they
were capable of blending into the scenery and defending. The wind
changed, and he caught the stench of human excrement used lo-
cally as fertilizer. He wiped down the hopper on his brass Gatling
gun with a polish-soaked rag. The naval landing party, including
Seaman Hobson and the heavy weapons, a Gatling gun and several field guns, had been positioned here in reserve, in the event
the local warlord brought up his own field guns. The Navy-blue
patch with the khaki lower edge would be moved at endgame. Perhaps "counterpane" was the wrong image. The moves and counter-
moves made it appear more like an undulating chessboard.

A ragged popping indicated looters were again approaching
the godowns. A few demoralized groups of soldiers, wearing remnants of Qing livery, receded before them. Some godowns smoldered from previous riots, while others showed the ravages of earlier depredations. Hobson was well aware of the utter squalor in
which China's lowest classes subsisted and how they viewed chaos
as a desperate opportunity.

Looters had no particular political philosophy. On the other
hand, they might be the dupes of an organization with a political

agenda. Hungry and lacking prospects for any decent future, they were easily manipulated pawns of the program of more powerful individuals.

On two adjoining rises to the east of the village were the two colored patches that worried Hobson. On one hill was a large, speckled, butternut patch, likely the Tongmenghui, and affiliated elements of the New Army. Both groups were rising factions in China. Only a small portion of their force was uniformed. Several speckled butternut rectangles broke off from the main patch and descended from a hilltop toward the port.

If the Tongmenghui, or any other democracy-oriented faction wanted to control China, a victory against foreign intercessionists might give them the time and credibility they needed to establish themselves. The Tongmenghui, Lieutenant Elswell had said, were great believers in symbolism.

First, he said, they believed they must expel the Qings, then they must curb the foreign powers, and only then could they restore economic and moral strength to China. "Darn, they have the order wrong," opined the lieutenant. "Pick fights with the foreign powers last. Now the Qing dynasty is nearly gone, they would do best to restore economic and moral strength first. China, as far as the world is concerned, ran last in both attributes. Right now, they have an open-door policy toward foreigners. They locked out the West for centuries, and look where it got them. Now they don't have the leverage to go back."

Hobson thought the lieutenant favored the Tongmenghui from an intellectual standpoint and at a distance. Today, however, once within the range of their small arms, the Americans would extend the Tongmenghui no courtesies.

Chief Gillingham, who led the Gatling gun detail, ominously pointed to the other hill. On it was a blue-gray or perhaps Prussian-blue patch, General Zang's men, beyond the range of USS Rainbow's six-pound cannons. The way General Zang's forces were arrayed indicated they too, like the Americans, had field guns.

The looters below in the village were no match for the Marines. Two volleys down each alley and they were gone.

The Tongmenghui and its affiliates advanced with more heart, and the looters returned to the outer confines of the port complex with renewed enthusiasm. The blue-gray patch stood fast while the speckled butternut patch moved forward. Were they moving in unison? Hobson couldn't tell, but he estimated that the Chinese under arms outnumbered the Expeditionary Force about ten to one. Rotten odds. From what he could tell, the Expeditionary Force planned to advance on sheer guts. This was a demonstration, and they were going to demonstrate the meaning of "dire consequences."

If the Tongmenghui advanced, however, their own casualty rates would be horrific. Why might the Tongmenghui advance without field guns? Hobson questioned. *The Qing dynasty was collapsing and the Tongmenghui forces were confident that destiny was on their side.*

As long as the blue-gray patch didn't move, the naval landing party's field guns didn't move.

The Marines up ahead — between Elswell's landing party and General Zang's men — picked off the looters only as they advanced. The Tongmenghui's composition wasn't clear. The looters were confused, too, and didn't advance.

"Look at that leathahneck run!" called out Chief Gillingham. "The winged feet of a young Apollo."

A Marine messenger sprinted up to the Gatling gun, wide eyed, breathless, and hatless. His eyes darted across twenty degrees of arc.

"Navy Lieutenant Elswell?"

"Over here, messenger, you have word for me?"

"Major's compliments, "The Marine runner gasped, "Major's compliments, a sizeable force of what he takes are Tongmenghui are moving to the West. The major requests the presence of the Gatling gun for the defense of the foreign quarter, sir. The squad behind me will guide your party."

The messenger gave Elswell a piece of paper and had him sign another.

Minutes later, a Marine squad of fewer than a dozen, moving far more slowly than the runner, waved the gun crew forward.

"Chief, here's your escort, and these are your guides," Lieutenant Elswell called out, looking up at General Zang's field guns. They hadn't moved.

"Krafts, make sho-ah we got them all," Chief Gillingham responded. Krafts called the muster: Ryder, Weishar, Jefferson, Santos, Dellett, Ivorsen, Greenberg, Olsen, LaPierre, and Hobson, the junior man. Each man wore a watch cap, blue jumper, watch sweater, a blue uniform trousers with khaki leggings, and a khaki cartridge belt.

"Foh'd, the coffee mill detail…"

Ivorsen snickered at Gillingham's usage. Any man-powered machine in the Navy that had a wheel on it anywhere eventually found itself referred to as a "coffee mill."

"…guide on them leathahnecks. Keep an eye out for shahpshootehs, pitfalls, mud, and that peculiah type of fertilizeh."

"Coffee mill, it be," muttered LaPierre not too loudly. "My grandpapa took fire from one of these consarned machines during the War Between the States. We might as well be shootin' coffee beans. There's better ordnance. Hope we don't meet up with any."

"Which war was that, Rebel?" Jefferson, a sizeable black man with glasses, asked without heat. The nickname "coffee mill," Hobson knew, had been assigned to the Gatling gun by none less than Honest Abe himself, the crew had been told in training. The Model 1871 Long Gatling Gun with Bruce feed was a marvel, though cumbersome at a dead run, down alleys with surfaces that seemed to change every hundred yards from mud to cobblestone to wood plank and back again.

Newer versions of the gun were available, but *USS Rainbow* had been sent to the Far East as a tender. Now, as a troopship, her magazine was an expedient collection of other ships' castoffs. The coffee mill's ammunition was not interchangeable with that of the 1903 Springfields that the Marines were using or the Krag-Jorgensons of the sailors who manned it.

"…man the drag…mahch."

"March" was a euphemism.

"Field guns and Gatling guns were always moved at double-time. Hobson wondered if that was a tactical necessity or the Navy's philosophical attitude toward landing parties. He remembered an instructor putting it this way: "War on land is an alien environment for sailors. Move quickly and keep it brief. Overwhelm the landsmen through technical knowledge, energy, and efficiency. Then, be done and be gone."

Naval landing parties were capable of taking apart their guns, manhandling them over walls, through tunnels, across chasms, and then reassembling them to fire on key points well inland. No one knew how to use mechanical advantage — block and tackle, levers, parbuckles, sheerlegs, rollers — like sailors.

The Marine squad moved more slowly than the messenger, yet far too fast for a party dragging a Gatling gun on a light landing carriage connected to a limber, with Bruce feed trays, eight boxes of ammunition, and encumbered by the party members' slung Krag-Jorgensons. The coffee mill detail kept them in sight, though when they entered the village, its alleys narrowed. The Marine squad could easily negotiate corners, where the coffee mill had to be pivoted. The Marines could weave through the makeshift barricades of overturned handcarts where the coffee mill detail had to clear them away.

"Invented by a dentist," observed Gillingham. "Those fellahs are mastehs at inflicting pain."

Ryder guffawed and caught a tongue-lashing from Gillingham.

"'Uncle Billy' is getting a mite testy," Ryder whispered under his breath.

They made a turn to the left, saw two dead Marines from the squad, and heard ricochets. The Marine squad leader knew one way back to the Foreign Quarter and had just realized that a key alley was too narrow for the coffee mill. He doubled back, cussing, and the coffee mill detail had to reverse. The Marines and sailors attempted to find a route parallel to the too-narrow alley. The trouble was the alleys were not arranged as a grid of right-angle intersections. The coffee mill detail crossed a bull's-head intersection just as a large party in schoolboy uniforms, still another possible Tongmenghui affiliate, dog-trotted up to form the front line.

"Pah-ty, wheel about, commence fire," Gillingham said.

The way a man might order eggs for breakfast, Hobson thought to himself. Gillingham might wear a silk bathrobe, still he didn't rattle. Hobson noted Uncle Billy limped on his left side and his left eyelid drooped. He had been that way for as long as Hobson had known him.

Ivorsen dropped with a bullet through his forehead. Jefferson tossed the man's lifeless body inside a dwelling through a curtained window to retrieve later…maybe.

Santos took a round loading the Bruce feed tray. Loading was hazardous. The newer model Gatling guns had armored shields in front; this older model did not. The trouble with a Gatling gun was its weight, its unmanageability, and the fact the crews were largely exposed, especially when loading. Four men were needed to fire a Gatling gun. The others fired their bolt-action Krag-Jorgensons. Krag-Jorgensons were efficient, yet the coffee mill detail was using outdated smoking-powder cartridges.

About half the Tongmenghui were armed with Arisaka Type 30 6.5mm or 1904 Mauser 7.9mm rifles that fired smokeless rounds. In toe-to-toe street fighting, smokeless or smoking made little difference.

As the Americans turned each new corner, Hobson could hear women screaming anew. A woman's scream was the accepted warning system worldwide. A woman screamed, and men knew to rush forward to protect, or to scurry for cover.

The Tongmenghui forces, though buttressed by an element of the New Army, were uncertain and ill disciplined. Their army was *too* new. They surged toward the coffee mill, and suffered the immediate loss of eight men, half wearing butternut. Their losses caused them to fall back and disperse. Both sides had little cover, on the other hand the coffee mill detail had a superior rate of fire and the chilling aspect of an alien contraption that spit flame without noticeable pause.

"Where's them gawmed gyrenes?" Gillingham didn't raise his voice. The Marines hadn't seen the coffee mill detail, already falling behind them, reverse before engaging the Chinese factions. "Detail, fix bayern-nets."

A Gatling gun could address whatever was directly ahead of it, unfortunately it needed to be protected on all sides.

"Hobson, you ah Asiatic as they come. Find them gawmed gyrenes. Or find the gawmed Foreign Quarter, t'either one, don't mattah. Take Dellett with you."

"Aye, Chief. Find them, them gawmed gyrenes and in the process lose Dellett."

Dellett was not amused.

Hobson wondered if he was selected because he was the most junior man and the most expendable. Unlike the majority of the crew, he had lived in Asia before donning a uniform. He pondered telling him that this was China, not Japan or Korea, but thought better of it. Maybe he did have a slight edge.

Perhaps the choice of Hobson was because he was striking for promotion to quartermaster third class. Quartermasters were navigators. Technically, Hobson reminded himself, quartermasters were navigators at sea.

He was known for his dark eyes, black hair, and high cheekbones, and his ability to "think in Asian." Because he spoke Japanese and Korean, Gillingham believed, Hobson had insight into the Asian thought process. Gillingham was himself an old China hand, but Hobson was better able to put himself into Asian shoes.

Ultimately, he could find his way around their towns and villages.

They dogtrotted to where Hobson had last seen the Marines. They'd been told a squad of Marines would guide them to where they could best support the main body of Marines. Trouble was the Marines had lost them, found them, lost them again, and now the gun crew was isolated. Hobson kept close to the alley walls and under the overhanging eaves and balconies. He heard fire down another alley.

China, Japan, and Korea, to Hobson, had vast differences, though most Americans wouldn't know it. Everything in Woosung was more elaborate and more colorful than in Korea or Japan. China was the Middle Kingdom, the center of all civilization. Few buildings in Japan were painted, and few buildings in Korea had balconies.

On the other hand, in all three countries, markets were positioned outside the gates of large cities. Letting strangers, whatever their goods, inside the main city was too dangerous. In all three countries, the streets were narrow, crowded, and mazelike. In European countries, house numbers were consecutive and could help you figure out where you were. Not in China, Japan, or Korea. In the Far East, villages were divided into districts, neighborhoods, sectors, and, ultimately houses. House numbers were assigned in order of construction within a sector.

Meanwhile, Dellett was looking for loot. He was always on the hunt for loot, which kept him alert at all times. A fellow looking for loot also wanted to bring that loot back home, or what use was the loot? Dellett was not one to take undue risks.

"There they are!" Dellett said, poking a pocket watch into his jumper pocket. Whose watch had that been, Hobson wondered.

"Lost them!"

"Well, you slipknot, don't lose them again," Hobson scolded. Chasing these particular Marines with the coffee mill seemed futile.

The coffee mill detail caught up. "A group in butternut and mufti is rallying behind us," one of the gun crew in back of them called out.

"Hobson, you got your choice. Get us to the Foreign Quarter or saltwater," Chief Gillingham ordered, unflustered.

A Tongmenghui round caught Dellett right where he had tucked the watch.

Hobson dragged Dellett's body to the side of the alley, covered it with a pile of baskets, and again took the lead position.

Dellett paid attention to the wrong things, Hobson thought.

"Sou'southwest is that way," Hobson said, looking up at the sun. He felt overextended.

"Yeah, we knew that," grumbled Jefferson, catching up.

The drag line and the coffee mill weren't far behind.

Due south meant saltwater. The two men led the coffee mill a quarter mile farther, until all the roads were cobblestone. Hobson looked for planked alleys, which indicated wharves. The women's screams stopped. They were approaching a commercial waterfront and habitation had thinned out.

Wharves meant proximity to water and the ability to signal USS *Rainbow* for withdrawal, if it came to that. A position like that might also mean taking a stand with their backs to the water.

CHAPTER EIGHT

Hobson looked back and could see six men left moving the coffee mill. Four men were required to operate the old dinosaur. "Chief, I think the best route is toward that T-intersection," Hobson said. "I smell saltwater."

Hobson ran ahead to the T-intersection and looked right and left. To the right he saw 60 feet of planking jutting out toward open water. What lay to his left was uncertain.

"Bluejackets, here, here. Over here," summoned a wide, square Asian man. "I speak English. They call me, Yi. 'Skookum' Yi."

The fellow wore a dark-gray tweed wool suit, a straw hat, and a silk bowtie embroidered with red-crowned cranes. Pince-nez glasses poked out of his jacket pocket, and a gold chain ran from his lapel buttonhole to the spectacles. He had beckoned with the barrel of a hammerless revolver. Hammerless revolvers didn't catch on clothing, Hobson mused, and were designed to be concealed beneath a suit jacket. *Classy finery, draped over a mass of muscle.*

Behind the wide man signaling, across the left arm of the T, were handcarts piled with crates. The crates must have contained something that made them a bulletproof barrier. Behind them were a dozen men in Qing livery, their heads wrapped in skull-tight turbans, each with a single bandolier draped diagonally across his chest. One handcart was moved to let the Americans through.

Hobson recalled that the Qing Dynasty had collapsed, and if these troops were genuine Manchu, they could not be regarded with confidence. The Tongmenghui forces and General Zang's men were normally the enemies of Qing dynasty, and traditionally no question would have been raised as to whom these dozen liveried men would fight, except the dynasty no longer existed. Today, the Americans had no means to tell which way these men might pivot.

Chief Gillingham ran forward and scanned the arms of the T. "What we have heyah is the 'Lady or the Tigah.'"

Despite the warmth of Yi's greeting, Hobson didn't trust him. He couldn't take his eyes off the men in Qing livery. He noticed they didn't wear braided queues. Maybe the practice was to jam queues into turbans?

On the edge of the Qing formation was an attractive Asian woman in threadbare pajamas and an apron who talked casually with a "Qing" noncommissioned officer. Her hair was wrapped in a nurse's dignity that gave her a Sphinx-like appearance.

Her bearing was stately, too stately for a peasant woman or tattered volunteer nurse.

Something about her told Hobson that like the man in the gray tweed, she was not Chinese.

Something was "off," on the other hand Hobson didn't have the time to study all the interlocking parts. He could conceive of too many potential threats, and now they found themselves in a corner.

Chief Gillingham decided to split the difference. He angled the coffee mill diagonally across the intersection, tucking just into the right arm of the T. They might be firing into the Tongmenghui only, but if the coffee mill detail took fire from the men in Qing livery, Gillingham would be able to rapidly shift fire.

"Stuff them Bruce feed trays and keep them stuffed," Chief Gillingham growled.

The Bruce feeds were thin vertical trays that gravity fed into the coffee mill. Each reloading left the loader dangerously exposed. During training, some wag had suggested loaders be outfitted with armor like one of Mark Twain's medieval knights in his novel about a time-traveling Connecticut Yankee.

At 200 yards, another group, in blue-gray uniforms this time, came forward shoulder to shoulder from one side of the alley to the other, bayonets out...General Zang's men. Their front rank didn't kneel nor did it stop. Zang was planning to charge with the expectation that numbers would carry the day. Perhaps any other maneuver would be too complicated.

Jefferson swung the tongue of the coffee mill carriage so the coffee mill was aimed nearly straight down the main alley, parallel to the seawall and at a right angle to the pier. The gun could still be returned to diagonal. Jefferson set a wooden barrel as an improvised aiming stake to assure the coffee mill didn't swing into the Qing soldiers…inadvertently.

Greenberg worked the crank and Krafts traversed the coffee mill from side to side, raking the main alley and causing blue uniforms to crumple as if a scythe were reaping stalks of wheat. Despite gaping holes in their ranks, the Tongmenghui kept coming and firing. Hobson could no longer see the Qing soldiers. The Tongmenghui and General Zang's men probably didn't know the Qing-liveried soldiers were on their flank. Hobson had no idea who would end up shooting at whom, and he foresaw no opportunities for clarification.

"Hobson, you're a quahtermaster strikeh, right? You know scivvy-waving?"

"Aye, Chief, born to it, part of my rate. I know semaphore like I know how to roll and stopper."

"Don't get smaht. Get out a signal to the ship or any launch you see."

The steam launch always had a quartermaster assigned to read signals. *USS Rainbow* was barely visible. Of course, the steam launch had to be in sight, Hobson thought, which qualified the viability of that course of action.

In the distance, back up the peninsula, Hobson could hear the occasional dry cough of another unknown machine gun. It coughed fire at a faster rate than the coffee mill.

Hobson could see the launch. He signaled "r-u-r-u-r-u-r" to get their attention, unsettlingly the launch was held at bay by the other gun and wouldn't approach the wharf. He puzzled over the word "Maxim" in its return message. Where had any faction of celestials picked up a Maxim gun? No one in the entire United States Navy had a Maxim gun.

The steam launch remained offshore, out of range. Hobson returned to the coffee mill and yelled above the din, "No boat. They have to stand off. Somewhere behind the Tongmenghui and Zang, someone's firing a Maxim."

"A Maxim?" Gillingham showed no reaction.

Ryder took two rounds to the body as he loaded for Krafts. Then Krafts took a round to the upper chest and started crawling.

Gillingham knew their fight was over. "Wounded, crawl to daylight and into the water. Find something that floats."

Weischar took a round into the upper leg that broke the bone. The muscle in his upper leg shortened its length like a collapsing telescope.

Gillingham was wounded. Blood streamed down his double-breasted jacket.

"Hobson, over here." Chief Gillingham beckoned. "We're going to have to wheel the coffee mill off the pier into the drink. These heathens can't take her. Lagan it. Then swim for the ship."

LaPierre and Hobson exchanged glances. LaPierre, a boatswain mate, found some line and tied it off to some splintered wood, improvising a lagan buoy.

Every other bluejacket in the coffee mill detail was down or dead. The Qing soldiers had disappeared.

Hobson grabbed the coffee mill carriage tongue and began pulling. Others pushed. Gillingham, with one hand to his chest, kept turning the crank though the barrel was depressed.

They arrived at the pier.

"All hands, over the side."

Time stopped. Chief Gillingham detached the crank handle and lobbed it off shore. He turned his back to their attackers to tip the coffee mill over the side.

That act at that moment etched into Hobson's mind like an engraving. Uncle Billy was dying. He could have stopped earlier, facing the enemy, knowing that his duty was done. Later, *USS Rainbow*'s human puffer fish who congregated around the scuttlebutt might interpret bullets in his dead back as a significant clue to his detail's failure.

Yes, Hobson thought, well those small-minded sailors could go wear ice-skates in hell. Uncle Billy had still pressed on, exposing his back to the enemy.

The pier had a lip, stubbornly they manhandled the coffee mill over.

Uncle Billy took a final round and tumbled into the harbor with nary a splash.

Hobson stood halfway down the pier. Everyone else was gone.

Time seemed to grind to a stop. He had worshipped Uncle Billy.

Hobson could see General Zang's men breaking ranks and running for him and him alone.

Behind them, in the armpit of the T, he noted the wharf building had steel bars across all windows and steel reinforcing around all doors and windows. Painted in English above one massive door were the words "Jinsen Steam Navigation." Painted on the steel door below was a house flag with a crane, a red-crowned crane. "Jinsen" was another name for "*Chemulp'o*" or "Incheon"…in Korea. The red-crowned crane symbolized luck, longevity, and fidelity, throughout Asia.

Well, they had found saltwater and Woosung's foreign quarter.

Hobson stepped off the pier and took a long breath just as a bullet grazed his shoulder.

The water was as dark and thick as scullery waste. Hobson could hear firing and thought he felt a hot, spent slug drop against his ear. The firing intensified, then stopped. Clearly, General Zang's men and a good number of Tongmenghui had decided to unify to kill Seaman Hobson. Today Zang's men and the Tongmenghui were friends. Tomorrow?

In his submerged and oxygen-starved condition, Hobson's disoriented imagination visualized a blue, khaki, butternut, and gray-blue blizzard of quilt patches. The patches floated downward like snowflakes, sometimes joining in mysterious alliances, and then quietly separating. Hobson vowed never to rest beneath the folds of a checked counterpane again.

Hobson stayed down as long as he could. He tried to find a piling, but was totally disoriented. His lungs were going to burst. He stuck his arms into the bottom mud to his elbows to keep himself from bobbing upward.

His hand found something heavy and he clutched the heavy object in futile hope.

It must be part of the coffee mill and therefore must be preserved. His foot struck a piling and though now inverted, he clamped to the piling for dear life to keep from surfacing.

His lungs could hold out no more.

He came up, head upright again, under the pier next to Green-berg and LaPierre, who were clutching an unconscious Weischar. Hobson saw no sign of Chief Gillingham. Their uniforms, once Navy blue, were now a pathetic, wet-rat gray.

The firing above them was deafening and seemed to surge and wane like surf.

Then it stopped.

"Hey, gobs, you gobs can come out now, wherever, wherever you are."

Gawmed gyrenes, Hobson thought. That had been Uncle Billy's expression.

Someone dropped a line and LaPierre rigged some bighted variation of a bowline to haul those in the water up, even the badly wounded.

Hobson could hardly stand. He still clutched something heavy in his hand and wasn't ready to release a means of self-defense. He had lost blood, and the six or more different kinds of shell casings that covered the pier made walking difficult. The dead bodies and puddles of blood made the footing tricky. On the pier were six very alive Marines. "Thought we lost you." A Marine with two chevrons spit a streak of tobacco juice.

Hobson could feel the anger boiling up in him and his shoulder aching. He still clutched the heavy object in his hand. It could do damage.

"Lucky these guys found you," the corporal stated with little enthusiasm. The other Marines turned away.

"These guys?" Hobson echoed. "This passel of late-for-supper gawmed gyrenes?"

They ignored him while the corporal explained what he thought had happened. "The warlord…"

"General Zang?"

"Don't know him personally, whatever his name is. The war-lord fired on the Tongmenghui and everyone decided to withdraw, best I can tell."

So, Hobson concluded, after using the Tongmenghui to help him clear away the US Navy gun crew, and taking severe loses himself, Zang turned on the Tongmenghui to begin narrowing the array of potential competitors.

"Hey, the celestials are withdrawing," the approaching steam launch's coxswain called out. "You must have chewed them up with that ol' Gatling."

Standing in front of Jinsen Steam Navigation was the wide, square man in the woolen suit and about a dozen men in Qing livery. Their faces were gray with powder, and they were covered with blood spatter. Hobson studied them as he felt the energy flowing out of his body. They'd been dressed like Qing soldiers, yet weren't Qing soldiers. Hobson realized queues hadn't been what triggered his suspicion. He just knew Yi's men weren't Chinese.

A pile of Tongmenghui and Zang's troops lay just beyond where Hobson and Gillingham had tipped in the coffee mill. The "Qing soldiers" fighting both Zang's men and the Tongmenghui must have opened up at that point.

Rough exchanges took place between the Marines, the launch crew, and the landing party survivors. Hobson worked his way over to the Qing liveried soldiers. He was soggy and exhausted, though he was starting to grasp the larger picture.

"*Annyong hashimnikga, hyungnim,*" Hobson said, standing directly behind one "Qing" soldier. "*Ije gun nassumnikga?*" Good day, elder brother, is it over?

"*Ne, annyong hashimnida. gun nassumnida,*" the "Qing soldier" said, turning to Hobson and then working his jaw in surprise, trying to get his response back down his throat." Yes, good day, now it is," he had answered Hobson in Korean.

The liveried soldiers weren't Qing, simply a false flag private army of Jinsen Steam Navigation.

Lieutenant Elswell's third point had been that some groups on the battlefield other than *USS Rainbow*'s two landing parties were there "to loot," and he had allowed, others might be there to prevent looting. The Jinsen Steam Navigation men were there to prevent looting. They were protecting the warehouse with the barred windows.

Hobson turned quickly, stumbled several yards to the stocky man in the gray tweed suit, and spoke in English. "Mighty peculiar weapons. What exactly are those, you figure?" Hobson didn't address a particular figure. The weapon looked like a rifle for a giant, with a large disk about the size of a handcart wheel mounted horizontally near its rear sight. The Qing-liveried men had several of the unfamiliar guns.

"What are these?" Yi said in heavily accented English, matter-of-factly. "These are Lewis guns, light machine guns, still in development stage. Designed in your country. At 12 kilograms, they are lighter than the Vickers or the Maxim guns. And of course, they can run rings around a Gatling."

He shook his head ruefully. "We couldn't fire until you were off the pier. You will remember you rejected our invitation of safety."

"Was that your Maxim we were hearing behind the Tongmeng-hui and General Zang's men?" Hobson asked.

"Yes, that was our Maxim. We purchase what weapons become available. Their orders were to keep any group that came this way from retreating. We had no way of communicating this. I realize now those orders were overly broad. Naval flags meant nothing to that detachment. Your launch never took direct fire, but damage was done. I apologize."

"*Ping gye opd nun mu dom opd da.*" Hobson quoted the Korean proverb: No grave is without an excuse.

The man's eyes drifted down to Hobson's full hand and he turned away. What was that clump of muddy metal Hobson held?

The Asiatic Fleet was at the far end of the United States military's logistical train. It would be a long time before *USS Rainbow* ever saw a Lewis gun. The Gatling gun had chewed up the two celestial bands, but the Lewis guns and one Maxim gun had chewed the bands up worse. Perhaps somewhere the USN had a Maxim, but not here, on this ill-starred day in Woosung.

"Hobson, I'm going to let you bleed a bit more, let all that Chinese harbor scum ooze out," advised Culper, the hospital apprentice in the steam launch. "You landing party fids gots too much piss and vinegar anyhow." Midway down Culper's shoulder was an embroidered red cross.

"Thanks, Culper. You are jus' all compassion."

Fids? Flashes of heat lightning flared behind Hobson's eyes, still no storm had been noted in the day's weather.

Culper began droning on about the differences between Eastern and Western medicine. "Basically, in the East it's about needles that are solid and in the West it's about needles that are hollow."

Hobson wondered if Culper was nervous or the idle chatter was meant to calm everyone in the boat. "Nothing more dangerous than a hospital apprentice with a sharp instrument," said Hobson concealing his ire.

Culper's eyes were searching for less obvious wounds. "Don't even come close to a quartermaster with a signal book. What's that thing in your hand?"

It was black, heavy, and shaped like the sole of a sandal or maybe a toy boat. It had several smaller Chinese characters under a large character for "courage" engraved on the surface of what was probably its top.

"Is that tarnished silver? Some kind of ingot? By the way, Chief Gillingham didn't make it," Culper added. "Poor ol' Uncle Billy."

Hobson observed that certain sailors delighted in conveying bad news. Such a sense of *schadenfreude* — pleasure at someone else's bad luck — reinforced their own sense that they were either street smart...or lucky...or immortal. Hobson's father had taught him that word.

What had been General Zang's objective? What had been the Tongmenghui's objective? Were they after the cable station or were they interested in silver?

Hobson realized he felt Billy's loss deeply. Uncle Billy had found a way to live with one foot in the West as an American sailor and one foot in the Far East writing Chinese calligraphy with a brush. Hobson had been fond of Uncle Billy, and now wondered if he had just seen a sign. Was his own hope of living a life reconciling the best of the West and East futile?

"Yeah, well, Culper, why don't you just go...?" Hobson never finished the sentence but instead faded into unconsciousness, dropping the fifty tael *sycee* into the bottom boards.

"Imagine that, a silver ingot just lying around that wharf like a lost penny," the hospital apprentice, Culper, confided to Paymaster McCorkran. "Must be quite a few shipped through that wharf if they could afford to lose an ingot from time to time."

USS Rainbow's skipper caught wind of the "silver toy boat" and tucked it away before Paymaster McCorkran could get his talons into it. The skipper hoped those seventy-five ounces of silver would serve as the ship's war artifact, a trophy, until eventually *USS Rainbow* was turned over to the wreckers.

CHAPTER NINE

USS Pluto, Huangpu Moorings, Shanghai, April 1913

As Hobson ripped off his undress blues and hurriedly examined his dress blues for lint and Irish pennants, he heard striking of the ship's bell on the quarterdeck. The watch-keeper on the quarterdeck struck "da-ding, da-ding, ding" in the second dogwatch, 6:30 p.m. "Liberty," Hobson mouthed silently. Liberty ashore, and a rendezvous with a ukulele.

Each ring of the watch-keeper's bell recorded a turn of the sandglass since commencement of the watch. The sandglass was turned every half-hour. Few crewmen carried pocket watches. The vessel's chronometer rarely left the captain's cabin, and so timekeeping was a matter of audible signals.

Timekeeping was important to Hobson because he was a navigator, or quartermaster. Timekeeping allowed Hobson to fix his ship's longitude. Few navies allowed their enlisted men to learn the mysteries of navigation — a matter of control. The United States Navy was one of the exceptions. Hobson plotted the ship's course using a compass and the sun and stars, then factoring in the influences of wind, tide, and current. In the shipboard division of labor, Hobson's job was to address problems of time and space.

Hobson finished supper and donned his flat hat, carefully aligning its tally band, which read "*USS Pluto*," the name of his new ship. He wasn't sure whether or not he missed *USS Rainbow*. There, he'd been a seaman striking for the quartermaster rate or specialty. He'd since been promoted. Now, he was a naval petty officer, a non-commissioned officer.

He and his messmates hoisted the table to the overhead, stow-ing it until the next meal. Each night they used several light falls, block and tackle, to raise the planked table to the overhead.

Hobson double-timed to the portside ladder. At each port-of-call, a small launch was moved from its cradle high up in the ship, and, using various falls and assemblies, slung over the side. A lad-der arrangement was assembled and rigged to allow crew mem-bers to descend into the launch. This process was one of the many everyday mechanical wonders that defined Hobson's life at sea.

Naval seamanship, at its heart, was, as his shipmate Benjamin "Washboard" Harte put it, "a matter of understanding the applica-tions of l-l-leverage and m-m-achineration."

Washboard was one of the two other crewmen from his watch who descended the ladder and dropped into the liberty launch as the Shanghai drizzle worked its way into their wool melton uni-forms. Washboard was a yeoman striker who had grown up in Phil-adelphia on the fringes of the Mainline. He had five older brothers, and his father had been an owlish judge who had read books by the peck.

From his father, Washboard had inherited the habit of observ-ing people as groups. Had fortune favored Washboard with a more-sedate disposition, he might have studied at a conservatory and been a percussionist. Fortune had not done so, however, so he just tapped his pudgy fingers on anything available, playing the washboard. He was at war with the letters "m" and "p." His habit-ual stammer of those particular letters gave a percussionary trill to every statement.

Dropping just behind him on the launch was Aloysius "Harp" O'Grady, the son of a Brooklyn bank teller. Harp's nose no longer had a bridge. He knew everything a man ought to know, and some that wasn't known, about J.P. Morgan and Diamond Jim Brady, and no one could separate Harp from the contents of his money belt. Someday, he was going to take a job with a railroad, and the world had better watch out. He had sent away for a shorthand cor-respondence course and had had someone show him how to use an abacus. "Ships and trains, ships and trains, take an interest in one or t'other, an' count your gains."

Harp, a boatswain's mate, had boxed in smokers and carried his arms proudly away from his body. Like Washboard and Hobson, Harp wore tailor-mades, but Harp also wore an additional chevron. The bell-bottoms on his trousers flared a full yard in circumference.

The light rain continued as their launch headed shoreward, and the wet paving stones and ribbon-like trolley tracks glistened under multicolored harbor lights.

As the small white boat arrived at the landing, the liberty-men vaulted onto the Fleet landing. Each sailor began a different journey that wended its own way down a network of alleys through Shanghai, eventually leading to the Lane of Lingering Joy. Now that USS Pluto had been in Shanghai for over a month, evening liberty had fallen into a routine. In port, they stood one-in-five watches — one evening aboard, the next four they could take ashore — and so Hobson could leave the ship at the same time in the evening for several days in a row.

As he separated from the others, Hobson passed a somber Chinaman in a Western suit holding a pail and shaking it.

Hobson couldn't tell if the man's discomfort arose from his new-looking shoes or a social ailment he opposed, for on the pail he shook was written "The Anti-Kidnapping Society" in English and Chinese characters. The local merchants had started the organization in 1912, when China's burgeoning bandit population had begun to focus on the lucrative practice. Hobson tossed two bits into the pail. The man with the pail moved his head in a barely perceptible bow.

Shanghai in particular had experienced a rash of kidnappings during the last year, and the expatriates had decided to do something about it. Both colonials and prosperous Chinese were targets of gang kidnappings. Hobson knew his naval status made him an unlikely prospect. Sailors were too impoverished, too far from family, and too closely aligned with thunderous retribution to make good kidnapping prospects. Hobson's navy was the hard and powerful navy that Teddy Roosevelt had built. Sailors, American or otherwise, made poor prospects for kidnappers.

Yet Shanghai was Shanghai, and even sailors kept a weather eye out. Kidnapping was a brazen act: heavy-handed and well suited for Shanghai. "If God lets Shanghai endure, he owes an apology to Sodom and Gomorrah," one missionary had observed. And if it weren't kidnappers, something else might well be occurring, equally repugnant. These were restive times and ever-bolder banditry flowed throughout China like a rising tide.

Across the street were two Americans on horseback, wearing hats with flat broad brims and Montana peaks. Part-time troopers of the Shanghai Volunteer Corps, they impassively surveyed the street. A warlord might attempt to take Shanghai, despite the knowledge the foreign concessions wouldn't back down without a fight.

Hobson dodged a jinrikisha and two rough-looking French sailors with their pompomed hats. The navies of six countries were in port.

The shorter of the two Shanghai Volunteer Corps horsemen eyed the lean, hollow-cheeked swabbie with contempt. Not lost on the well-fed businessman/part-time cavalryman was that this sailor looked and walked like a cowboy, nor that the sailor dealt daily with Shanghai's dangerous elements at closer quarters.

The Anti-Kidnapping Society and the Shanghai Volunteer Corps reminded Hobson that Shanghai was just a freewheeling convergence of cultures perched on — as one of his chiefs had put it — "a volcano of humanity." Unconsciously, Hobson unbuttoned his cuffs and folded them back to show embroidered dragons with red and gold flowing from their mouths like lava.

As he walked with a belligerent roll, he occasionally caught sight of Washboard and Harp — sometimes ahead of him and sometimes steaming abreast, on parallel courses — their hats cocked forward like gun batteries.

Every evening, Hobson passed Gold-tooth Kiang's pawnshop and admired a nicely crafted koa-and-mahogany ukulele, inlaid with abalone shell.

Hobson studied the tiny shop's massive awning shutters and heavy oak and wrought iron front door and wondered why a second-hand goods shop was laid out like a vest-pocket blockhouse.

The pawnshop used the ideograph for the Chinese chess piece *pao*, the artillery piece, as its logo. Hobson chuckled. Apparently to encourage Occidental as well as Oriental patronage, Kiang had hired someone with a command of English to paint his bilingual sign, a Chinese chessboard had no direct counterpart to a knight's pawn. Instead, the Chinese piece closest to that position, the pawn positioned in front of the pao, had been substituted to achieve the tortured pun. The sign painter — perhaps paid by the letter — had emblazoned below the Chinese ideogram, the words "The Red-Queen's-Knight's PawnShop." No Occidental would forget that name. Elsewhere in the shop it had been shortened to the "Red-Knight's Pawnshop."

Many Chinese characters were incorporated in Korean and Japanese writing. With the benefit of reasonable fluency in Korean and Japanese, Hobson chuckled at the creative translation. A symbolic attempt had been made to have warrior "pawn" replace the verb for secured lending. Unfortunately, Chinese chess pieces and European chess pieces didn't exactly match, however ten to fifteen minutes' careful explanation would bring home the punchline to this intercultural joke.

The ukulele had been pledged as security to cover a loan to a German merchant sailor, and according to custom, it should not have been on display in the window. The shop's manager, the tall "Gold-tooth" Kiang, however, had decided the instrument would attract business and had placed it there. Hobson checked it daily. If the German merchant sailor didn't redeem it by Monday — that beauty would be up for sale on Monday. Kiang had quoted Hobson a price that Hobson thought eminently reasonable.

Except that Hobson couldn't afford that price. He really had no way to pay for it, nevertheless he still checked on it daily. He hoped for a legacy from some forgotten uncle, enhanced by a speedy postal delivery, or any manner of other impossible miracles.

"Ukulele for sale?" the dark-haired sailor asked each time he passed.

"No for sale. Come back one week, make cheap price, you pay Mex or greenback. 'Cept if someone buys first."

Gold-tooth Kiang always said a week, though Hobson had determined that it was a day less than a full week by a few hours and confirmed that the ukulele would come up for sale on Monday by reading the slip upside down as Kiang waved it at him. The date was the only group of characters on the slip that he could read with certainty.

As Hobson walked away, he watched a younger Chinese man

with a limp, approach with his hands tucked into the cuffs of a dull-gray workman's tunic, as if they were a muff. The younger man smiled in a respectful way with his eyes downcast, and Hobson realized the young man was smiling at Gold-tooth Kiang, not at him.

Hobson then trudged to Madam Guan's; an establishment affectionately known to *USS Pluto's* crew as the "Lesser Shanghai Indian Club & Garter Society." In addition to the expected selling points of any singsong house, it had two rowing machines, a set of Indian clubs, twelve hardcover books, nearly a hundred dime novels, a phonograph, ten copies of the Police Gazette, a pool table, and several tables for acey-deucy.

China gave Hobson a strange feeling. He had been brought up in Japan and Korea, mostly Korea. In both countries, China was accorded great cultural respect. The level of a man's education in Japan or Korea was measured by the number of Chinese characters he could read. Each country had its phonetic alphabet or alphabets, yet had absorbed Chinese characters. Buddhism and Confucianism had both come to Japan and Korea through China. Many other cultural legacies had come to Japan and Korea through China. The *judo* that Hobson had learned as a sport owed a debt to China's Shaolin priests.

Hobson felt like an English schoolboy visiting Rome or Athens. In the western Pacific, ancient China always seemed to exist at a more exalted level, in the same way ancient Rome and ancient Greece did in Europe. In this part of the world, China seemed to have addressed every human experience first.

What had the ancient Chinese to say about kidnapping epidemics and recreational bordellos?

Hobson rounded a corner and found himself on a converging course with four merchant sailors, walking two by two. The one in the front closest to the curb wore a visored hat. His shoulders were heavy and his neck folded forward.

Behind them were two *jinrikisha* runners sprawled unconscious on the cobblestone, tangled in the double-shafts of their two wheeled carts. The fold-up tops of their jinrikishas were torn. Clearly the runners had been paid off with abuse, rather than specie.

Hobson might have had room to pass, though evidently these sons of guns intended to force Hobson into the gutter, which was wet and filled with horse dung, courtesy of the Shanghai Volunteer Corps. If Hobson and the merchant sailors each kept their paces, the approaching sailors all would converge abreast of the horse droppings damming the gutter.

"Give way, give way, gob," one of the four shouted. They quickened their paces, and Hobson did, too.

Hobson feigned stepping aside, then plunged between the four men. He might have stepped aside, but for the laid-out jinrikisha runners. In that moment, dreadnought grit and John Brown-like wrath converged in Hobson.

The man with the visored cap and double-breasted jacket, a ship's officer, grabbed Hobson around the neck with hands that put Hobson in mind of canned hams. The merchant officer's eyes were as opaque as oxblood marbles, though the corners of his mouth curled upward with menace.

The man was about six inches taller. Hobson brought his forearms up below his assailant's elbows, breaking the strength of the hold. He twisted his body 90 degrees so his right shoulder and right hip were at the man's chest and groin.

Hobson hooked his right arm behind the officer's neck, grabbed the sailor's right coat sleeve with his left hand and then slammed his hip into the man's groin. He spiraled counterclockwise and the man's feet went skyward, knocking the men nearest him aside. The officer hit the twelve-o'-clock position before plunging downward.

The merchant officer slammed into the paving stones on his back with his right cuff still clinched upward in Hobson's hand. The man's arm was absolutely straight and Hobson was holding the man's wrist to his jumper.

As a missionary's son, Hobson had been taught to turn the other cheek, however as a Caucasian in strange surroundings, even his father had permitted him a compromise. His father had allowed his son to learn judo, Jigoro Kano's new self-defense sport, in Japan and later in Korea. Kano's sport, judo, literally meant "giving way," or "gentle way." As a member of the growing American Fleet, Hobson had drifted wide of his father's hopes. "Giving way" or "gentle" were not exactly the bywords of a fighting force.

"Knock seven bells out of him, boys! Make'm chime!" the ship's officer on the paving stones demanded of his three confederates.

Hobson saw the gleam of brass knuckles flash from one of his attackers' pockets.

"Belay that," Hobson warned. "Mr. Slipknot here of the merchant service has issued a faulty rudder command. I'd caution you keep those knuckledusters stowed. It'll go better for him."

The seaman with the brass knuckles kept on coming. "Such a pretty sailor-suit, gob."

Hobson broke the merchant officer's arm at the elbow with an audible snap and an even more audible scream. With a slowly revolving motion, he changed his position. The injured man slid around with Hobson to keep his arm from hurting more.

Hobson wasn't letting any of the three men get behind him. "I can wriggle his elbow some more and that elbow will take a powerful long time to heal. Backwater all, savvy?"

The ship's officer yelped each time Hobson shook his damaged arm.

"Yeah, backwater all, aye," said one of the remaining three.

"So, you take a walk that way, and I'll let Mr. Tackline brush hisself off. If he gets mouthy, I'll think of something else to break." Hobson's face was expressionless as he glanced behind him. "And I think you forgot to pay those 'rickshaw runners. Just drop some coins on them right there."

The men emptied their pockets and strode off sidelong, apparently not sure of how their leader would take it and if they might later be held accountable.

But the officer nodded compliance, and they moved off.

Hobson put pressure on the broken arm. "What ship you off, Mr. Tackline?"

"Third mate. *Qilin Cathay*," the officer muttered. "You'll remember that name soon enough. You will remember that, and the name of Spuyten. Cornelius Spuyten. 'Fightin' Spuyten, to some."

"Fightin' Spuyten, huh? Rhymes, don't it? That's clever, mighty clever name. You may not be used to my naval way of speakin'."

Need to keep them where I can see them. Need to keep them off-balance anyway I can.

A lecture would be the best way to keep them from regrouping.

"'Tackline' is a stretch of line marking a gap in a flag hoist. It's six feet of line with no flag. E-ssent-ial-ly, a tackline is six feet of nothin'. Thought that about fit you to a 'T' — six feet of nothin'."

Hobson wrinkled his brow. "As for remembering you, well, that may be, but first read the tally on my cap, *USS Pluto*. Got that?"

He picked up his flat hat that had been knocked off when he'd thrown Cornelius Spuyten.

"And I'll just wait for you to make good that promise. While we're all remembering, you might make sure not to forget the USS part means 'property of the United States Navy,' too. I'll spell it for you, if y'like?"

He heard a reluctant grunt or two.

"Go to hell, gob."

"Also, Mr. Tackline, you should be watching where you step. Seems you've got horse deposits all over the back of your nice pilot cloth coat. High quality stuff, I must say, even so, warm this time of year. Those Shanghai Volunteer Corps horses are well cared for. Not your run-of-the-mill horse deposits."

Hobson narrowed his eyes. "Some days I'm not sure who I'm fightin' and who I'm protectin'. Today, I felt like protectin' every-one 'cepting leastwise you and your messmates."

Not quite done yet, Hobson added, "I wouldn't continue reach-in' for whatever you've tucked in your boot with your good arm. I'd view it as a good reason to put your face in them road apples."

Fightin' Spuyten inched sideways, crab-like, along the curb. He had hit the cobbled surface hard.

"It's all about leverage..." Hobson mused, brushing off his hat. "...and 'machineration.'" He started to walk away, then turned. "You don't want me to look back and see you. Now I am going to make sure those coins deposited over by those two cold-cocked coolies don't wonder away.

"Don't you be here when I come back.

"I'm going to count to ten. I can do it in Japanese, if you'd like."

As Hobson climbed the steps, several working girls called out. It was early in the evening, and the pace wouldn't pick up until the gaslights glowed in earnest.

Not far down the street, he noticed a Packard idling, attended by a thickset Mongolian stylishly dressed in a Western suit with spats. Hobson guessed the man's nationality by his pallor. The Mongolian was leaning against the Packard with an aura of proprietorship. "Who's that out there?" Hobson called to no one in particular.

A husky girl strolled to his side. She had a rosebud mouth and long eyelashes that lent her a certain look of feline wisdom. "That man, he is Mongolian. Name is Khan. He is General Zang's driver, his bodyguard sometimes. He borrows Mongolian from Three Harmonies Society. General Zang big man in country villages, not big man in Shanghai."

Hobson caught his breath. This was warlord Zang from Woosung, whose men had exacted their toll on the coffee mill detail.

The woman's fitted silk pajamas wrapped around her like a second skin with favorable effect. She had an overhanging cutwater and a proportionately counterbalancing beam. With her hair up arranged in a Western style, she looked like a ship's figurehead in silk pantaloons.

"My name is Clementine," the pretty Chinese temptress offered with a wink. "Not real name. I like American song. Silly, happy song, nice name. Everyone remembers name."

"Why does he leave the engine idling?"

"Don't know. I think he is mean man, dangerous man," Clementine answered.

"Madam Guan doesn't make you walk around in herring boxes, does she?"

"Maybe if customer asks." She made a moue. "Two more years contract on the Lane of Lingering Joy. Then I have a dowry. My family could buy small piece more land in a village far northwest of Shanghai."

Hobson nodded. Her present situation was hardly honorable, nonetheless the fact it benefited her family and herself was honorable in Confucian terms. That all transpired far from her village made the circumstances satisfactory.

She giggled, holding one ivory hand over her mouth. "Driver Khan thinks may split fancy pants working the hand starter crank. He rather spend General Zang's money on gas than his own money on trouser repair."

Her comment brought tittering among the other first-floor sitting-room girls.

On the top floor, Madam Guan maintained a beer garden. Washboard and Harp were already there with a couple of Guan's girls. Hobson climbed the steep steps to the rooftop watering hole and paid for a bottle of beer. Sitting with a few of his messmates, he took off his shoes, leaned back in his chair and wrapped his toes around the wrought ironwork, while looking down at the street. From his aerie, Hobson studied the Packard and its driver.

"I think a p-p-picnic would be the thing, a p-p-icnic on Sunday out at —" Washboard paused to draw a breath. "— the arched bridge among the willows beyond the Shanghai-Hangchow rail line. The problem is our gal-dern logistics."

Logistics, Hobson, pondered. Logistics.

No one had the money to hire a car and the spot was beyond jinrikisha range. So, for the time being they'd have no picnic, unless Hobson could come up with a plan. He planned things. He fixed things. He accepted the challenge with a nod. "Sometimes I think you two gobs give me too much credit. If I'm so good at transportation and navigation, why do I do so much walking?"

"Because that's what sailors do ashore, when they're not getting into trouble," Harp pronounced with a sigh.

"We could take a tram," Hobson offered.

"Naw, we gotta do something m-m-memorable," Washboard stated with finality.

Just before midnight when Hobson walked back to the ship, the Packard and its driver were gone.

He came aboard *USS Pluto* just as a sleepy-eyed watch-stander set a peg in the last position of the log board, signifying eight bells in the First Watch, midnight.

In the next few days Hobson was going to apply himself to problem of picnic logistics. He realized the difficulty was primarily one of picnic finance.

CHAPTER TEN

The next morning, *USS Pluto*'s crew stood ready in their dungarees, many with capsized Fighting Bob Evans hats that would never again be white. Some, those most exposed to coat dust, wore
goggles they had finagled from aviation stores and bandanas ban-
dit-like over their noses and mouths. It was one of those rare occasions in port, Hobson realized, that the general public saw US Navy
sailors in something other than their dress uniforms. The sky was
as dark as their moods.

Hobson surveyed the decks from *USS Pluto*'s charthouse.

Periodically, *USS Pluto* shifted to the coal quay to keep its bunkers filled to the maximum. Coaling was a dirty, backbreaking ritu-
al of the 1913 Navy. Aboard *USS Rainbow*, taking on coal had been
an intense, periodic task. Aboard *USS Pluto*, taking on and distrib-
uting coal was unending. The fleet had once sailed under clouds of
white sail, now colliers with their coal grit, steam, and smoke, were
the harbinger of a darker future. They were black-hulled pariahs.

Hobson skimmed his fingers across a handrail layered with decades of paint.

Both were large, tired vessels that had never been designed as
naval warships, however who owed their membership in the United States Navy to the rapid naval expansion brought on by the
Spanish-American War. *USS Rainbow*, with a displacement of 4,400
tons, was a troopship or floating barracks. She was a British-built
merchant ship converted by the Navy in 1898 to a distilling and
station ship for Philippine service.

His newest old ship, *USS* Pluto, with a displacement of 4,800
tons, was a collier, one of the fuel suppliers for the fleet. She,

too, was a merchant ship purchased for service during the Spanish-American War in this instance to haul coal.

By contrast, Dewey's flagship, *USS Olympia*, had a displacement of 5,900 tons and USS Baltimore had a displacement of 4,400 tons. While cruisers — warships — devoted space to big guns and the crews to man them, colliers — auxiliaries — devoted themselves exclusively to the transportation and storage of coal. That was the collier perspective, the perspective of an auxiliary.

The warship perspective had evolved differently. With its inhabitants packed in such close quarters, a ship could be an unhealthy environment, and therefore cleanliness was king. White uniforms were a means to a larger goal. Dirty white uniforms indicated a dirty white ship. They were the canaries in a mineshaft.

On average, warships packed crews ten times greater than merchant ships comparable in tonnage. With guns, magazines, communications, and related machinery, warships had to be ready to go where the conflicts were, not just follow the trade routes. So, they had been designed for a greater degree of self-sufficiency. The upshot was white uniforms, pristine holystoned decks, and glistening white hulls to ensure a high degree of hygiene. Coal was the anti-Christ. The stacks were at war with the decks. Coaling was the most despised periodic task. Coalpassers drew extra pay to offset the sweat and squalor of their duties, and colliers were the pariahs of the fleet.

Coaling in port, Hobson knew, was easier than coaling afloat. In port — as the ship was today — the heaviest work was handled by the pier-side local coal loaders — coolies. All *USS Pluto*'s crew had to do was receive the flow from the barges and even out the bunkering. Coaling afloat was *USS Pluto*'s work. Afloat, the coal had to be taken by buckets or baskets out of *USS Pluto*'s bunkers and hauled by lines over to a warship. A bucket of coal weighed about 150 pounds. Afloat, coaling was done under the unblinking eye of a stopwatch.

Friction always existed between the pier-side coalmen and the ship's crews. This wasn't helped by the shore facilities' inclination to stretch their coal with dirt that didn't burn well or keep the pressure up in the boilers.

As bad as coaling was, though, the task wasn't as bad as stoking. Temperatures in the fire rooms could reach 150 to 175 degrees. Coalpassers drew a few dollars extra pay a month, though they were never clean and had to walk through special passageways so as not to soil the decks.

A fully-laden steamship had an operating radius limited by fuel, unlike a sailing ship, whose operating radius was limited by its food and water supply. Weight was a further concern because the coal bunkers constantly required leveling out. Even distribution within the ship kept the ship on an even keel.

"Eyes aloft!" called Harp on deck of the *USS Pluto*.

It had begun to rain. Coal dust collected in rivulets down the decks. For once, the stacks weren't at war with the decks; the bunkers were. Soaked by the sudden downpour, the crew's denim uniforms looked slimy and smudged.

"Belay coaling," the chief in charge bellowed. "The first lieutenant says this stuff ain't anthracite, and it's got a high sulfur content. We store it wet, and that creates a risk of spontiferous combustiality, or terms such-like. We might all burst into flame afore I — as my mother always predicted — go to hell in a handbasket or was it a coal bucket? She were a hard woman."

A warship was in trouble if it ran low on coal at sea in a typhoon. In turbulent times, colliers were a necessary evil, forbidden to rest.

CHAPTER ELEVEN

USS Pluto, Huangpu Moorings, April 1913

Tuesday, the night, after the abortive coaling and an exhausting next day of taking on coal and bunkering, the liberty launch was slow in pulling away. A sheave in a block in the fall that lowered the steam launch failed, and a new one had to be substituted. Every waiting sailor understood the failure, and would have been capable of effecting this minor mechanical repair. Since the incident at Woosung in 1911, Hobson had been promoted a grade to petty officer third class. He took charge, sent a few of the libertymen to retrieve tools and parts, and in short order. The sheave was replaced, though Hobson's evening liberty was delayed.

At long last, Hobson approached Red-Knight's Pawnshop, falling in behind a group of sailors of the Imperial Japanese Navy and a familiar young Chinaman in the customary gray long tunic worn by shop clerks. The young clerk had a standard route from the Old Chinese City to the part of Hongkou District that Hobson visited regularly.

Hobson understood most of the Japanese sailors' conversation, nonetheless in Shanghai he was under direct orders not to speak Japanese to anyone. Japanese speakers in the US Fleet were extremely rare. His gift would draw attention, suspicion, and quite possibly a fatal accident. His talents might someday give his country an edge, for now those language skills were being kept under wraps.

Hobson had mixed feelings about the Japanese Navy. He had grown up with young Japanese men much like the ones in front of him. He liked Japanese individually, however in groups he felt their behavior could take on a darker aspect. Stellar with kites and paper-folding, these men were also masters of the most brutal forms of military oppression. Their country possessed a grimly efficient and oppressive intelligence network, the Kempeitai.

Korea, Hobson's second home, had suffered the worst Japan could offer. The Japanese regarded the Koreans as backward sub-humans and treated them as obstacles to progress, tolerated as long as useful, though liquidated as a matter of course.

Discussing with them the differences between the newly-built Japanese navy and the US Navy would have been interesting. However, Hobson thought, these were representatives of a country that wouldn't explain the disappearance of his parents in Korea. Japan had brought untold sorrow to the Land of Morning Calm and the White-clothed People.

The Japanese sailors took a left turn, and Hobson found himself dogging the steps of the Chinese civilian in the long gray tunic.

While trailing the man, he unconsciously fell into step. He shook his head. He was walking down a cobblestone alley behind a civilian, a random stranger, and he still felt compelled to fall into step. His annoyance was brief; the man's limp was hard to replicate, and he fell out of step. That, too, unsettled him.

Twice more Hobson found himself unconsciously trying to imitate the limp. He could not. A limp was essentially a sort of mistiming in physical machinery, occurring when a joint lost its full range of motion. This limp didn't work that way. It was more of an imbalance. The man in the gray tunic defied Hobson's understanding of human locomotion.

It wasn't a limp, so much as a tottering motion.

Human physical operation was a matter of leverage and "machineration." As a sailor, Hobson was a student of both.

He and the Totterer shared a destination, a pawnshop.

Madam Guan's, Lane of Lingering Joy, International Settlement, April 1913

"Harp, how's a pawnshop owner make his money?" Hobson asked, attempting to sound bored as he ran his fingers across the acey-deucy table at Madam Guan's.

Five years older than he was, Harp had made a round-the-world cruise. Like Hobson, Harp was a man of the world.

Harp paused for a moment to tamp his smoke. With one battered hand, he began sketching with his pipe. "A pawnshop's a kind of bank. The pawnshop and banks make money by lending money and charging interest. You gotta put up something as coh-lat-ter-roll — if you skip, they can sell it and get their money back. The collateral is worth more than they lent you and the interest together, so they win coming and going. Some jewelers do the same thing. They lend you money on your jewels and figure out the interest. In fact, pawnbrokers often double as jewelers. Lots of these guys just calculate a fee for a certain amount of money for a certain amount of time. Same as interest, really."

Hobson remembered that the English part of Kiang's sign read, "Diamonds, gold, and jewelry."

"Without pawning anything, you could just buy the jewels, right?"

"Yes-s-s-s," Harp hadn't thought of that until this point. "Here in Shanghai, money doesn't have to be in greenbacks or Mex, Jewels are more negotiable than most currencies in troubled times. Jewels are a way of consolidating your savings into a small, portable packet you could tuck in your jumper pocket if you were 'on the lam.'"

As Hobson knew, US Navy sailors in Shanghai were paid in either American greenbacks or Mexican silver pieces. In Shanghai, "Mex" was the preferred medium of exchange.

"So, if you're a jewelry shop or a pawnshop, how do you increase — what do you call it — your cash/jewel inventory, what you lend out or sell?"

"In theory it should all be nearly in equilibrium. What's pledged and not redeemed can be sold for more than the value of the loan. Sometimes they experience a sudden surge in demand. Might need deliveries to keep up your cash inventory. Or you might increase your gold and jewelry stock, to turn it into cash to lend out. Well, a bank uses an armed coach or armored motorcar."

Harp scratched his ear. "Never thought much 'bout it. Don't know what a jewelry or pawnshop uses. Probably bring it in little bit at a time, in-con-spicuous-like. Several deliveries over time, maybe. Any delivery, of course, would be a king's ransom by sailor's standards."

"And that delivery..." Hobson observed, "...perhaps silver coins and unmounted jewels, might be a daily occurrence in a busy, well-run pawnshop?"

Harp leaned back in his chair, clearly ready to sum up his pontification. "Hobson, if you ever save any money, I'd recommend you invest it in ships or trains. I know for a fact Commodore Vanderbilt never owned no pawnshop."

That evening, Hobson walked by the pawnshop as he had done every day that week. Again, he inquired about the abalone ukulele. The following evening, he observed the Packard, its engine running and its Mongolian driver waiting patiently. That same evening the young Chinaman with the gray tunic and the respectful smile tottered past Hobson as Hobson left the pawnshop on his way to the Lane of Lingering Joy."

This was a pattern that played out daily. Was there a connection between the Packard and the Totterer?

Hobson would see the armored Packard in various places – side streets most often with its motor-running — on his route from ship to the pawnshop and to Madam Quan's. Was someone trying to habituate the neighborhood to this strange practice? Would the car eventually become an accepted, and therefore unnoticed, presence in Hongkou?

Later that evening, Hobson showed up at Madam Guan's.

"Maybe the warlord, General Zang, has a girlfriend on this street?" Hobson asked Clementine when he ran into her again outside Madam Guan's.

"No warlord, he no come. No girlfriend here on Lane of Lingering Joy. He no like Lane of Lingering Joy, he big time fancy-man. Maybe driver has girlfriend on street, but not warlord," she reported. "Warlord likes entertainers down Bubbling Well Road. Classy girls. Top drawer. Expensive girls."

In her breathless way, Clementine sounded sure of herself. Husky Clementine's gaze was steady and her jaw set. Hobson liked the manner in which she postured in the doorway — a professional skill, yet inviting just the same. Wind chimes played a tune in one of the windows up above.

Hobson absentmindedly bounded up three sets of interior stairs to the beer garden.

A few minutes after he sat down and had ordered a beer, Harp, Washboard, and Clementine joined him. As was the men's habit, they rested their stocking feet on the wrought iron railing and looked down upon a street scene framed by two potted bamboo plants. The beer garden on the roof was always the quietest spot in the establishment. Small talk, wind chimes, and distant and tinny ragtime tunes from the Victrola had a soothing effect. Then also, no one wanted to start a brawl that left a brawler or two crumpled facedown at street level.

A pool table and a tired, tabletop, hand-cranked gramophone occupied the largest room on the second story. The second story was where the brawls usually started. Some said a pool cue gave an American sailor a sense of invincibility. Single stick and bayonet drills were regular physical training events aboard ship. Boxing smokers were a fleet-wide activity. In too many ports, a sailor's uniform made him an easily identified target, and the locals always outnumbered the sailors. The manly art of self-defense was a day-to-day concern, not merely a pastime. The US Navy had not forgotten the *USS Baltimore* incident, in which two sailors were stabbed to death and eighteen were injured outside a bar in Valparaiso, Chile. Not everyone liked the world's newest global power.

The Lane of Lingering Joy was merely an alley lined with balconies and drying laundry. Foot traffic abounded, despite the fact the idling Packard had to treat the lane as a one-way street.

Clementine was a fount of information on ships' movements. "A British light cruiser is coming in Sunday. A Japanese destroyer comes in Monday. Austro-Hungarian training ship will be in Monday. Big time week, next week." Her livelihood depended on keeping current. She could tell you the paydays for each navy represented on battleship row.

Of course, many others made a business of monitoring the coming and going of foreigners and their money.

In the street below, three men staggered out of a basement walkup and acknowledged the warlord's driver with easy familiarity. Hobson observed the three with interest. They were friends of the driver, however not retainers of the warlord. The three didn't have the glazed-eye look one might expect of those emerging from such an establishment. Hobson wondered if their staggering was for the benefit of casual onlookers.

"Unregistered opium den. No more registered dens allowed in Shanghai," Washboard observed.

"None?" Harp was the most experienced Asia hand. "Can't see the locals a-holdin' to that one."

"No new ones. No new opium dens in Shanghai. New law."

To the others, Hobson might appear distracted. "Say, if we got a car Friday night, where could we put it where it wouldn't be noticed until Sunday?"

No one seemed to have an answer. Clementine left for a moment, her hips swinging hypnotically, and returned with the same suggestive grace. "Madam Guan say Jimmy Lu will let you put a car in his godown, quarter-mile from fleet landing, for forty-five Mex dollars."

Everyone was studying Hobson. Wasn't this the way of sailors, dreaming grand dreams with empty pockets? It was unlikely, Hobson thought, they could launch this picnic affair without some ready cash. Ready money, in his experience, was the product of criminal activity, or cooption of criminal activity. Fortunately, he had a plan. He had made observations.

One of the crew whistled; for forty-five bucks, they might as well hire a driver or get a squadron of jinrikishas.

"I'm offering fifteen," Hobson countered.

"Where we going to get fifteen?" grumbled Washboard, who had just squandered a week's pay playing pool against an Italian sailor. This particular Italian sailor, having a pencil-line moustache and a jacket with a nipped waist, had started all thumbs, however his skills increased as the bets went up. Washboard speculated wanly that his progress in mastering a cue had been one of those profit-motive miracles.

"Leave the 25 to me," Hobson said thoughtfully, still slightly outside of the conversation.

Hobson put his shoes back on, left Madam Guan's for 45 minutes, and returned. Harp and Washboard looked at each other knowingly. Hobson did nothing on impulse; something was up.

Hobson huddled with Clementine, Harp, and Washboard in a corner of the beer garden.

Hobson had studied Clementine when she wasn't looking. She would do. She would do nicely. He knew equally that he wouldn't have the money if his plan, centered on the Red Knight's Pawn-shop, failed.

When he left later that night, the Packard and its driver were gone.

Hobson returned to the ship before eight bells in the First Watch.

Wednesday, Hobson had been on liberty less than half-an-hour be-fore the recall siren on *USS Pluto* sounded, the white cross on a dark blue field, special code flag was hoisted to the yard. It meant general recall. All liberty had been cancelled. General recalls were an annoying reality. Warships, even auxiliaries like colliers, might be called to sortie on a moment's notice.

The rumor going around was of a warlord's force moving on Shanghai, however the story proved to be another false alarm. Still, bandit activity was on the rise in the outer areas, and the tension between the Yuan Nationalists and Anti-Yuan Nationalists might soon boil over.

Hobson turned over what remained of his last visit to the pay-master to Washboard.

With it, Washboard planned to buy a generous hamper of pic-nic chow before Sunday.

After the recall stand down, most of his shipmates had raced over to the Lane of Lingering Joy in jinrikishas. Hobson's liberty plans were every bit as urgent, even so he had to pick up something first and confirm a few things. His habit was to complete tasks quickly, contrariwise he knew that he didn't want to execute this chore too early.

He didn't walk by the Red Knight's Pawnshop this time, in-stead went straight to the Lane of Lingering Joy.

He removed his neckerchief from beneath his expansive blue collar with the white piping. Then he coiled a roll of pennies into the cloth's center and hefted the weighted neckerchief in his hand. Most Asiatic Station sailors routinely wound something heavy in their neckerchiefs for defensive measures. Now Hobson winced as he flicked the bound roll into the palm of his hand. Plans could go awry. Every sailor knew that.

He looked up to Madam Guan's beer garden. It was dark,

though he could make out Clementine's shapely silhouette just above.

The Packard was where he expected it to be, on the route between the Huangpu River and the Red Knight's Pawnshop. Its windows were constructed from multiple laminations of glass, which made its windows both impossible to roll down and "bulletproof." Close up, the heavy windows were intimidating. The purpose of the steel venetian blinds and small knife-rest gun-ports was more apparent. As usual, the Packard's engine was running. Apparently, no one sat inside. Hobson tried to open the door, and found it was locked.

He turned and recognized the man he'd trailed: the young Chinaman of the respectful smiles, the Totterer. Hobson was pleased he wouldn't need his neckerchief and its formidable roll of pennies. He put the heavy scarf back around his neck.

On Thursday, Harp and Hobson, dropped by the Red Knight's Pawnshop.

"Gold-tooth, let me talk to the owner of this shop," Hobson gushed as the only other customer was leaving. This was no time for conversation over a cup of tea.

Harp studied the Red Knight's Pawnshop's door and shutters. Just inside was a second door constructed of glass with a glass transom.

"What for? Ukulele not available yet. Five more days."

"It's private."

Gold-tooth looked bored.

Hobson could smell burning incense. A shop full of pledged curios needed a single cheery scent to mask the many dead-broke scents.

"You talk to me manager. Savvy? You want much big loan? Plan maybe put up battleship for security, sailor-boy?"

Harp rolled his eyes. Gold-tooth had dealt with too many sailor-boys.

"Let me talk to the owner. I'm serious. You have a problem," Hobson persisted.

"He not here. He never here. He has much businesses all over place."

Hobson could see they were getting nowhere.

"Where can we talk?"

Kiang studied Hobson and then Harp. "Back there." He point-ed to a long curtain that ran clear across the back of the shop. He moved in that direction and was the first through it.

Hobson and Harp followed. Once through the opening, they re-alized Kiang had picked up a Webley revolver. They were looking down its muzzle.

Harp raised his hands first. Hobson followed.

"You're going to be robbed," Hobson started and added, "...not by us."

"Me?" Gold-tooth pointed to himself. "Who? Pawn shop? When?"

"Just let us talk to the owner" Harp said eying him with a cheery smile.

"I manager here. That good enough for Yankee sailor-boy. You talk to me."

Gold-tooth wasn't going to let them get anywhere near the owner. His job, understandably, was to screen the owner from day-to-day headaches.

"This shop and your daily messenger are going to get hit when he delivers the dobie and baubles Friday near closing time, or pos-sibly, Saturday night. You've been building up your available Mex to lend the crews of all those ships coming in this week.

Harp nodded to three large safes in the back area behind the curtain. Their doors were closed now, however when the Totterer stepped into the shop the largest one would be opened quickly, the one reserved for loans to fleet sailors.

Gold-tooth's eyes were attentive. "How you know?"

"I'm trying to help you! I don't want my ukulele damaged." Hobson appealed to Kiang's view of the world. Self-interest was something he could understand. Hobson realized his investment in this affair had risen several moral pegs above an obsessive desire for an easily stowed musical instrument.

"I take care of. If tip true, I give you reward," Kiang smiled re-vealing his gold tooth.

"Don't know about a reward, though if they use a car, I'd like use of the keys and the car for a couple days." Hobson interjected.

"These bullyboys are going to have guns. Something fancy, bet on it. I've watched these men. They're bad men, not triad men maybe, just bad men."

If they had access to a six-cylinder armored Packard, it seemed likely all their hardware would be top drawer, Hobson had concluded. He had a mental checklist of what he had to tell Gold-tooth, to his own surprise the keys weren't high on the list.

"You'll need some gunman yourself, and a plan," he blurted. "You'll need a diversion maybe. Otherwise you or your messenger is going to get shot."

He reached for the final consideration, "I can help you. I get shot at for a living. Even shoot back some times. Your delivery man must be coached, and he'll need a bolt-hole when the shooting starts."

Hobson had never contemplated robbery, even so he was an experienced leader. He'd stood on the bridge of ships studying other leaders' thought processes. Identify the three or four pivotal concerns, plan for them, train for them, and expect unidentified, disruptive problems to pop up.

"I am manager. I take care. This my job. You go now," Kiang pronounced abruptly.

"I don't think you fully understand," Hobson persisted.

"I take care of." Gold-tooth had stopped listening.

"I've seen these fellows watching your messenger." Hobson pleaded.

"You go now."

Hobson knew he'd failed. He and Harp were being dismissed.

On Friday, three days before ukulele day, Hobson cornered Harp as they stood in line for the noon meal. "Draw leggings, a pistol belt, and a baton from the master-at-arms. We have shore patrol duty tonight, maybe tomorrow tonight."

"Two nights straight? I just had shore patrol. Didn't see that on the watch bill yesterday." Harp gave Hobson a dejected look.

"We're going to observe, and somehow foil, a robbery."

"Red Knight's Pawnshop?"

"Yes, I'm not sure Gold-tooth Kiang's up to this."

"I'm not sure I'm up to diverting a broadside from four local gentlemen hefting heavy ordnance…with a billy club."

"Okay, Harp, you don't have to use the billy club."

Hobson didn't like bringing Harp into this. What was he leading him into?

On a far corner about halfway between the fleet landing and the pawnshop, Hobson spotted Clementine. The road was in the International Settlement and one of the few more than the width of two oxcarts wide. The road's paving blocks were still slick from the early afternoon rain.

Her face was smudged with coal dust, braids curled around her ears, and she wore a patched threadbare shift topped by a shapeless vest. Her papoose-pack looked as if it might contain a baby, except he knew it carried various gradations of firecracker, large rockets, and a box of kitchen matches.

To communicate with the Totterer under fire they needed someone who spoke the Wu dialect to give short sharp commands. Something told Hobson, Clementine was very capable in that department. Harp and he came no closer to her.

Well beyond her was the Totterer and not far behind him trailed the largest of the Packard driver's three new friends. Clementine and he had discussed his plan and he knew she had seen the three men and the driver together more than once in the last week.

Hobson felt uneasy about her participation too, despite the fact she was a natural fit. No one else could scout unnoticed, obtain the necessary pyrotechnics, and communicate in the right language.

Hobson realized he was fond of her. He had asked for her help reluctantly and if she declined, he knew the project was dead in the water. He was surprised by her buoyant response, "You say, Goldtooth offer reward?" Clementine said with disturbing enthusiasm. It dawned on him she was – not unattractively — a risktaker with ambitions.

Suddenly the Packard whipped by Hobson and Harp. Its doors flung open and two of the driver's friends, helped jam the Totterer into the backseat. The speed of their maneuver impressed Hobson. He had to remind himself he was in the kidnapping capital of China.

Something about the Totterer seemed different, however Hobson couldn't put his finger on it.

Clementine stopped and casually leaned against a building. He imagined her cooing to her imaginary baby. Once the Packard was out of sight, she began striding toward the pawnshop just around the next bend in the road.

Soon Hobson could see the pawnshop, and Clementine beyond the shop and on the opposite side of the street. The shop was open for business, though devoid of customers.

Harp shook Hobson's shoulder.

"Hear that?" Harper called out, his blood up. "They're turning around. Here they come."

Hobson had thought they'd fall in behind the Totterer as he entered the shop. No, they wanted more physical control of his person for some reason.

The Packard swerved pinning the shop's immense door open, and plugging the pawnshop's entryway like the cork that sealed a ship-in-a-bottle.

Hobson and Harp adjusted their vantage point so they had a good view of the small space between the car and the pawnshop's entryway. Three men wielding Broomhandle Mauser pistols burst out of the car into the shop thrusting the Totterer as a shield before them.

Had Gold-tooth taken his advice? Where was his diversion?

Some of the Packard's blinds were shut. Hobson couldn't see through the thick glass of the car's windshield, but he assumed the General's driver was still at the wheel.

Now a fireworks diversion wouldn't work; it was too late and there was nowhere for the Totterer to duck for safety.

He had put Harp and Clementine in danger for nothing.

"No! No! No!" he muttered turning to Harp. He waved Clementine away.

A single volley of shotgun fire roared from the back of the shop shattering the transom above the entryway and sending shards into the street. A cloud of dust blossomed atop of the Packard as the trajectory of broken glass, detritus, and spent shot, hit armor.

There was a yell. It sounded like an order, but was unintelligible on the street.

Then a few semi-automatic pistol shots, then a second volley of shotgun fire. and then an extended silence.

Were the three bully-boys dead? Hobson feared most there'd be a fourth casualty.

Five Shanghai Municipal Policemen poured out of a nearby store with riot guns, and aimed them blindly at the driver's position of the armored car. The door opened. The General's driver, his arms raised, had elected to take his chances with the police rather than with the General.

"I gotta get up to see, I gotta see," whispered Harp excitedly. Both of them realized they were lying on their stomachs. They'd dropped when the pawnshop's transom had been shattered by a ragged five-gun buckshot salute.

"Though maybe we ought to wait another minute," Harp added remembering he wore one more chevron than Hobson.

"Can we be of assistance?" Harp as senior petty officer inquired twirling his baton with an air of magnanimity.

The car had been moved and a police officer waved Harp and Hobson into the shop.

Where was the Totterer? Had he survived? There were four safes now, not three. The newest addition lay on its side to the right of the entrance with its door ajar. Small arms fire couldn't have toppled a safe.

The five Shanghai Municipal Police officers had constructed a barricade behind the curtain to the three safes. No one could have survived their fire, though their first diversionary volley had been high and shot out the transom. Several of them were looking down at the fourth safe.

"Policemen, these good sailor-boys I talk about. Hobson, was his plan my boss approved."

Hobson was confused, "My plan?"

Gold-tooth pointed to the transom, caught his breath, and began to explain:

"Number one, you say we need gunman. We used Shanghai police – these men here. They bring many riot guns loaded with buckshot."

Gold-tooth's eyes shone wide and bright.

"Number two, you say we need diversion. First shots were aimed first at robbers, yet really fired above heads. This was a diversion so my man Kang could go to bolt hole, to safe placed on side."

The police officers shuffled impatiently, most understood English. Hobson chalked them up as the ultimate heroes here.

"Number three, Kang dropped to ground, crawled into this new safe 'under repair' and kicked out jack holding door open. We rehearsed many times. He had bolt hole and was prepared, just like sailor-boy Hobson said do."

A somewhat dazed Kang, not the Totterer, squirmed out of the fourth safe.

The real Totterer was standing behind Gold-tooth in a Western suit. He stepped forward with a well-balanced movement, comfortably and upright. The Totterer no longer wore silver coins and jewels bound to the inside of one leg with sparadrapum. He handed Hobson a set of car door keys which Hobson gathered had been taken form the General's driver. Hobson noticed the resemblance between Gold-tooth and the man for the first time. He was just as tall as Gold-tooth when he walked upright. The robbers wanted this man as a shield and a hostage. Gold-tooth would have had difficulty not cooperating with their demands if they'd entered the pawnshop totally unexpected.

The Totterer's identity had not been something Gold-tooth would divulge to anyone, least of all, a random Yankee sailor-boy.

"The starter button is near the steering column. Remember it's a button not a switch," advised Gold-tooth's son, the young Chinaman of the respectful smiles, offered.

The seat of the General's driver's pants had never been in jeopardy. The Packard didn't use a hand crank starter.

His father looked tired and relieved.

On Sunday, one day before ukulele day, Harp, Washboard, Hobson, Clementine, and a couple of Clementine's girlfriends, drove out to the arched bridge and the willow tree in the Packard. They had felt compelled to remove the armored side windows to allow for ventilation. They also had to push aside four 1896 Broomhandle Mausers and a couple sticks of dynamite – which gave Hobson and Harp pause — to jam the wicker picnic basket into the rear of the car.

The car was extremely heavy and they made sure to steer clear of mud.

Hobson had received a very generous tip from Gold-tooth and would receive a sizable "finder's fee" when he returned the warlord's car that evening. The warlord, one General Zang, would have to find a new driver.

Washboard read aloud from *The Shanghai Evening Post and Mercury*, noting the Packard's driver "and three of his confederates from the Three Harmonies Society had attempted to hold up a pawnshop."

Had the hold-up been sanctioned by the Three Harmonies Society?

Gold-tooth Kiang paid Hobson a handsome reward. All the planners, Harp, Washboard, and Hobson received cuts. Clementine used her portion of the picnic group's revenues — her "consulting fee" — to buy herself out of Madam Guan's contract "in the wind and dust," early. Clementine now had a dowry. Hobson realized he would miss her company on the rooftop terrace. He now freely admitted to himself that he liked Clementine.

The Shanghai newspapers noted three men had been killed in a shootout with the Shanghai Municipal Police. The newspapers never mentioned the curious name of the pawnshop.

At the arched bridge by the willow tree, the planners were joined by more *USS Pluto* sailors. These additional participants and their girlfriends hadn't been part of Hobson's fundraising endeavor.

There, the partiers played a slow-pitch softball game. Only the girls were allowed to pitch, and anything as undignified as running was done by the sailors. Washboard tapped away at the bridge with the wrong end of a bat just to hear the sound. Harp decked one drunk gunner's mate when he began to annoy one of the girls.

All in all, the day was successful, thought Hobson. They seemed to have three times as much beer as anyone had expected, the food was plentiful, and one sailor had even described the picnic as "fancy."

Hobson played the ukulele. It wouldn't be his legally until the next day.

The ukulele was beautifully constructed, inlaid with nacrescent abalone shell, and nearly sailor-proof. Washboard accompanied him on his namesake instrument in several syncopated interpretations. Though Washboard desperately wanted them to take a try at the "Maple Leaf Rag," Hobson suggested a ukulele didn't have the requisite range, and they'd better stick to "Alexander's Ragtime Band."

The three sailors, Hobson, Harp, and Washboard, had difficulty negotiating the ladder as they climbed from the liberty launch. Up above the quarterdeck, the watch-standers feared they might have to deal with an incident of a disciplinary nature. Staggering libertymen in groups were prone to pranks. Fortunately, the three were aboard by eight bells in the First Watch, and in their hammocks before the watch was fully relieved.

Shanghai was a volcano of humanity, always on the verge of a major eruption, and continually releasing minor flows. Occasionally, the volcano flowed silver, though silver often intermixed with blood.

Ultimately, as Washboard would have put it, pulling off this special picnic was "all a matter of leverage and m-m-machineration."

The Monday evening after "ukulele day," Hobson had the duty and had to stay aboard the ship as part of the watch.

Tuesday evening, at the Fleet landing, Hobson noticed a wide, square Asian wearing pince-nez glasses seated in the back of a Marmon touring car. The man looked vaguely familiar, yet Hobson couldn't place him, and in any event, this wasn't an evening for strenuous concentration. Hobson thought he had seen the man in the Red-Knight's Pawnshop when he had picked up the ukulele, though if someone was driven about in a Marmon, he thought, pawnshops were an unnecessary part of the car owner's life. Perhaps Hobson had seen the Asian fellow somewhere else.

General Zang's finder's fee was waiting for Hobson and would be split four ways. Hobson returned the extra pistols and the dynamite. Clementine confided the word on the street was the general's former chauffeur and the Three Harmonies Society were in Zang's bad graces.

Uncle Billy's image flashed through Hobson's mind for no apparent reason.

CHAPTER TWELVE

Madam Guan's, International Settlement, Shanghai, April 1913

Harp greeted Hobson in the sitting room of the Lesser Shanghai Indian Club & Garter Society with a smile as broad as a piano keyboard. Hobson could hear odd, unidentifiable music different from the usual at Madam Guan's. It sounded like a cross between organ music and a wind-up music box.

Per usual, a few merchant seamen were present in the sitting room. Madam Guan's establishment didn't confine its services exclusively to the United States Navy. Madam Guan had to serve a broader market because the US fleet shifted its attention several months a year to the Philippines. She also welcomed the patronage of the British Royal Navy, the American Merchant Marine, and British Mercantile Marine.

Hobson scanned the room. "Well, you look happy as a clam. Some railroad heiress taking you to the Shanghai Race Club?"

Harp was irrepressible. "It's a great day. Got hold of a San Francisco newspaper. Gunboat Smyth KO-ed Bombardier Billy Wells in New York. I've got evidence."

"Hey, let me see that newspaper," grumbled a merchant seaman with forearms like the pistons on a yard tug. He was wearing a denim flat cap and the newly-introduced 'bib overalls.'

"Can't let you have it," Harp bubbled. "It's evidence."

"Gunboat" had been heavyweight champion of the Pacific Fleet before turning professional and had been a sparring partner for the controversial Jack "Galveston Giant" Johnson, the first black man to win the world heavyweight championship.

"So, you can collect on your bet?" Hobson asked.

"Plan to collect as soon as the flagship's blackgang shows up. Didn't I tell you? 'Take an interest in ships an' trains, one or 't'other, an' count your gains.'"

"A 'gunboat' is a boat, not a ship."

Hobson suspected the blackgang, the coal-begrimed portion of the crew who worked below decks on a ship's engines, boilers, and propulsion machinery, would avoid Harp for the next few weeks.

Hobson couldn't identify the source of the music. "Say, Harp, what's that noise?"

Harp executed a whirl with an imaginary dancer. "Madam Guan just got herself a Polyphon."

"Polyphon?"

"That's Latin, or maybe Greek," a British sailor with a shock of white hair announced with gravity. Hobson remembered the man's name was Miller. "It means blooming big music box in an oak cabinet or such-like."

Miller rubbed his white beard that matched the sailor's beard on his pack of cigarettes in every aspect but color, and pointed to a large walnut cabinet that resembled a grandfather clock.

Harp's eyes twinkled. "It is a clockmaker's dream. They've jammed a band into a cabinet. Put different metal discs in it and they play different tunes. Guan's got discs here for 'Peg o' My Heart,' 'You Made Me Love You,' 'Moonlight Bay,' 'Waiting for the Robert E. Lee,' 'My Melancholy Baby,' 'When Irish Eyes Are Smiling,' 'Ballin' the Jack,' 'Danny Boy,' 'Sweethearts,' and 'The Memphis Blues.'"

"Well, the selection's nowt so good, but it soun's good," Miller conceded, "'but 'afta put a coin in, or no music. The Krauts make 'em. Saw the *Kaiser Barbarossa* once — that battleship — looked like a clockwork tinplate toy. Germans should stick to music."

"'The Memphis Blues' on a machine," mocked a hard-bitten seaman from the McCollum & Spuyten Line, who nudged a shipmate with a less-than-gentle elbow.

Hobson was impressed with the Polyphon.

Harp grinned. "Gonna be tough keeping the girls topside with this down here. The auguries are auspicious," he added, reading the horoscope section from one of Shanghai's English language newspapers.

"'Auguries,' that's Latin, or maybe Greek, also," the burly British tar chorused with gravity. "I know 'tain't German. You want good ship names, you have to go to Latin, or maybe Greek, mythology. Gives 'em class. Posh, init?"

"Harp, that newspaper's months old."

Miller tilted his head forward and looked out of the tops of his eyes at Harp. "Don't mind my askin' but how did yer do yer navigatin' and noon sextan' sightin's, if yer always livin' a month in arrears? Did yeh use bird entrails in their stead?"

"I've been wo-manicipated..." Clementine uttered with tipsy gravity. She had paid off her contract, Hobson knew. She now helped out with the bookwork until she could plan her next step. Going back to her family was off the table and talk of a dowry had ceased. Her family had contracted her out and then succumbed to cholera.

Hobson admired her well-tailored, deep-burgundy, side-buttoned tunic, though apparently, she had misplaced her pants. The tunic's cuffs and edging were gold, and its black frogging and mandarin collar were partially undone. Clementine occasionally wore Western clothing, but not lately.

Hobson had been drinking, too. Logically, because they both were suffering from the same chemical imbalance, their conditions should have cancelled each other out, yet from a communications standpoint, the chemical imbalance only made talk between the two more difficult.

"...and the great President Abraham Lincoln did it. Several Abraham Lincolns, in fact, in pictures on American banknotes, along with banknotes picturing President..."

She seemed to realize she couldn't pronounce the man's first name.

"...Grant." Her rudder was clearly jammed and she was looping, both verbally and physically.

Hobson, no less impaired, felt the urge to guide and protect her. "Free, free at last."

"Quartermaster Hobson, as a free wo-mancipated woman, I ask that you navigate me to my berth topside...upstairs...that place up those stairs."

Clementine had never been quite so gracious. She was flicking a still-sealed bottle of Cyrus Noble bourbon around like a silk and rice paper fan. Her stock was up, as was her temperature and pulse.

Her room was barely large enough for its single brass bed. This was a sailor's scivvy house, not a gilt-edge bordello. Clementine shared a bathroom on that floor with ten other girls, and their guests. Her room also contained a small bureau, a chamber pot, and a mirror. On the bureau was a pearl and silk electric lamp, a bowl of fruit, a bottle of boiled water, an incense burner, and a cigarette box. Clementine bounced on the creaky bed. She swirled a sheet around herself and reversed her comb so the prongs shot upward.

"No more scratchy beards and drunk, grabby men. No more visit to nurse and China women looking down nose at 'sea-sister.' No more pushed aside by changsan or storytelling girls who look on sea-sisters as no better than flower-smoke-room girls. No more wind and dust."

Ladies who worked the waterfront trade, or sought out any foreigners, were known as "sea-sisters." Changsan were entertainers whose affections could be and frequently were bought. Storytelling girls — lesser entertainers — and "flower-smoke-room" (opium den) girls were all prostitutes who dwelt in the world of "wind and dust." Clementine had expressed the status of each in descending order.

"Free at last. See? I am Liberty. I have seen Liberty woman on American coins."

On American coins perhaps, though not Hobson's coins. Hobson and the rest of the Asiatic Fleet were paid in Mexican silver.

"Maybe you're the Indian rather than Liberty," Hobson jibed. Indians were featured on most new US coins. US coins were rare in Shanghai.

She scowled and attempted to look dangerous. "I don't think Indians ever free. Always attacking or being attacked. No time to think of free."

She pushed Hobson over the footboard railing and landed on top of him, crouching on all fours.

"Yes, definitely more like an Indian. She-who-pounces-by-moonlight," he wheezed. Hobson's head was swirling in a sour-mash bourbon whirlpool. Beer, not bourbon, was his preference.

"Ha, you must never ridicule Clementine, never. She is symbol of Liberty."

Hobson's thoughts seemed to drift and swirl about like fishing net floats in a strong current, one barely connected to the next yet accelerating away from the net caster. "Okay. Well I'm 'on liberty,' and the best I can tell, liberty is on me. We should be able to negotiate something here."

She smiled owlishly. "For you only, Mr. Quartermaster Sailor. Today everyone and everything is free."

She flicked off her side-buttoned tunic with a flourish.

Hobson pulled his weighted-neckerchief over his head with a reciprocal grand gesture. "Well then, we shall take liberties. I will be free with you and you will be free with me."

Husky Clementine took his thirteen-button trousers and jumper off expertly. She was experienced enough to dispense with undoing all the buttons. Then her mood changed, and she burrowed under his arm.

"Still row? Wrestle, too? That nice."

In the past, Hobson had shifted and stoked coal. He rowed on USS Pluto's cutter in competition. His team had won the Jade Rooster trophy. He had judo-wrestled as a boy in Japan and Korea before joining the Navy, and that, too, had molded his physique. Shanghai pictured American sailors as tall and lean, and Hobson fit the mold. During moments like these, she marveled at the circumference of his forearms.

He was about to answer when he heard her snoring. The snoring was feminine, though snoring all the same.

Then he, too, fell asleep.

He awoke to feel her hands working their way from the center of his chest downward. She was discarding her camisole and shorts. His shorts and undershirt had disappeared. A slow, rubbing movement commenced, a more forceful gripping movement, and then a tsk-tsking that was, he thought, totally insincere.

A small candle flickered in an enameled cup, and next to it, two joss sticks smoldered in a small glass bottle.

"You may not take liberties. I forbid it," she said, and then with a feline movement straddled him.

Clementine had an "athletic" build. A farm girl, she was slim at the waist, however too broad at the shoulders to fully qualify as a Gibson girl and too tall to qualify as a Chinese calendar girl. She had the breasts of a Gibson Girl and the angelic face of the girl on a Chinese "My Dear" tobacco brand cigarette card.

The Lesser Shanghai Indian Club & Garter Society catered to the Western seaman's trade, and Madam Guan carefully eyed the ads featuring Western women in Western newspapers. Her contract girls had to meet certain standards. In return, she had them inspected and cared for by doctors trained in the West.

In Chinese judgment, the girls of the establishment would be considered ungraceful and insufficiently submissive in demeanor. No Chinese women with bound feet worked in this establishment.

Hobson was glad the practice hadn't found its way to Korea or Japan. The women in Korea were kept behind walls, and the women of Japan hid demurely behind parasols, however neither were crippled in the name of beauty. It occurred to him that high-button shoes and corsets, too, were a form of hobbling, but hobbling was not crippling.

Clementine looked down at him and she clasped his hands to her hips. She rose and fell like the prow of a dory heading into the beach — as if the dory's bow was rearing then plunging with each successive undulation. She rose to meet each successive swell and then slid gently down the reverse. Then the dory hit the breakers, accelerating and becoming unstable in the plunging, tumultuous surf. The dory quivered at each crest, and then plowed downward with the surge.

Hobson closed his eyes, and her soft cries reminded him of seabirds.

He rolled her under him and capsized the dory. They clung together tightly as they rolled sideways in the undertow by the high watermark. They changed position several times while waves of sensation broke over them, and they found themselves at the berm line among rolls of seaweed that resembled sheets and a quilt.

He ran his palm down her cheek and she locked his hand between her cheek and shoulder.

Not once had he noticed the metallic creaking of the bed. Some time passed before he regained focus. Only then did he hear the creaking of many beds, the sound of a bamboo flute from the next building, and ongoing unintelligible banter between the women on the front balconies and the men in the street.

Hobson looked at the pressed-tin ceiling.

"I like the sound of your giggling," he said.

"Like that you like," she responded.

He couldn't tell if he liked the brass bed or not. It creaked, but so did every bed in the Madam Guan's creaked. Keeping a secret at Madam Guan's was difficult. It had been a long time since Hobson had actually slept in a bed. Madam Guan's didn't encourage long-term guest occupancy. He could remember his berth on the schooner of his missionary parents. Aboard *USS Rainbow* and now *USS Pluto*, he slung a hammock every night and took it down every morning. He washed his clothes in a bucket and ate his meals from a table lowered from the overhead on rope line. Hobson had never had his own room and couldn't reasonably expect one in the Navy, ever.

Clementine's room was windowless, and of course, not really her room at all. It was her room for as long as Madam Guan let her stay there.

Hobson smiled. It struck him that her double entendres were a happy sign of intelligence and adaptability.

PART III

THE BOARDING PARTY

The desire of gold is not for gold. It is for the means of freedom and benefit.
-Ralph Waldo Emerson

CHAPTER THIRTEEN

Several days later, as Hobson left the fleet landing on his way to the Madam Guan's, another man fell into his stride, a powerful, square-built Asian with pince-nez glasses and a silk bowtie embroidered with red-crowned cranes. The man wore a suit with vest and pocket watch. The day was bright and full of promise. Hobson dodged men wearing yokes draped with baskets, who reminded him of walking scales of justice. Laundry fluttered above him like sun-bleached flag hoists. Young children interwove the straight courses of their elders, playing games of flight and pursuit.

The man certainly seemed familiar. Was he the man with the pince-nez glasses in the Marmon and the man in the pawnshop when Hobson was handed the reward?

Do I know this man, from before...?

Now at last, as they moved together through the bustling crowd, the man spoke to him. "I am called Yi. Years ago, some of your countrymen knew me as Skookum Yi. You and I have been drawn together twice by set-piece battles, one involving a field gun. Umyong. Excuse me, I am a great believer in umyong."

Hobson was puzzled. Umyong was the Korean word for "fate" or "fortune." The Red-Queen's Knight's Pawnshop's logo was pao, the Chinese character for the artillery piece. When was the other meeting? He searched the man's face. He was Korean, that Hobson knew for sure from his physique, his pronunciation, and his use of the Korean word "umyong."

As if reading his mind, the man suggested, "'Woosung.' At the Red-Crowned Crane wharf, then the pawnshop here..."

The word "Woosung" gave Hobson a *frisson*. Uncle Billy. *Gill-*

ingham's Last Stand. A Gatling gun wasn't strictly an artillery piece, though neither, for that matter, was an actual pao a chess piece.

Hobson slipped into Hangugo, the Korean language. The man with the glasses didn't blink. A prosperous man of affairs, he spoke to Hobson using the Korean usages of an equal. Korean and Japanese were hierarchical languages. A man's relative station in life dictated his choice of words in addressing another. Among Korean or Japanese speakers, advanced age or responsibility required that you use one "language" and a junior might use an entirely different "language." The man felt a kinship for Hobson.

Hobson thought for a moment. "'Red-crowned crane' and 'Red-Queen's-Knight's Pawnshop' are word-play on an Asian image, sort of a pun, aren't they? 'Pawn' is easy. It has two meanings in English, 'foot soldier' and 'loan secured by valuable item.'"

The Korean looked embarrassed, yet kept walking.

"Red is red, right? A red queen would wear a 'red crown,' wouldn't she? And the move of a pao is one of flight, same as European horse head piece, er, knight, and just like the movement of a crane. The Red-Crowned Crane migrates among the countries of Korea, China, and Japan," Yi explained. "A poor joke. I've been hammering away at English for fifteen years and various Chinese dialects even longer. Sometimes I find myself reaching a bit too far to find humor in life. American Sailor Hobson, I think we will rapidly understand each other. Clever men of honor such as we are rare. Men of honor who consider just retribution are rarer still. We are, I think, most rare indeed."

This extraordinary man smiled at Hobson with hesitation. "May I invite you to lunch? Nothing fancy, you might say. Ham grilled over charcoal. Dirt floors, *maekgoli*. A cantina of sorts."

Maekgoli was traditional Korean rice liquor served hot.

Hobson returned the smile. He'd not had Korean food for a long time, and hadn't expected to find any in Shanghai.

"We can take my Marmon. These are unhappy times in Korea," Yi added, not inviting a response.

Yi gave a brief wave, and the Marmon and its driver pulled up behind them. It had been floating behind them all along.

The Korean restaurant owner was deferential to Yi. Not that it mattered, since little difference existed between the best seat in the establishment and the worst. They were in the old Japanese quarter in the Hongkou District above Suzhou Creek.

The vault was about the size of six horse stalls and open to the street. After hours, and in bad weather, it could be sealed off from the street with wooden panels. On this day, the collection of portable charcoal grills kept the cavern-like eating place warm. The patrons were all males, though that wasn't unusual. Maekgoli was not — Hobson would have been cautious in telling Clementine — a drink for women. The vault was sooty, yet inviting.

They wrapped the grilled ham in lettuce leaves and served it along with side dishes smelling strongly of garlic.

Yi's gaze periodically drifted out to the street, but he seemed at home in this working-class eatery. No one else other than he and Hobson wore Western attire, nor did anyone seem to pay attention to the American sailor or his host in Western gentleman's clothing.

"It has been too long since I've had *jeyug bokgeum*. Far too long. I like Chinese food, even so Korean food holds memories. So, what is your connection to the pawnshop?" Hobson asked.

"The shop is mine. I own it."

"And the wharf in Woosung?"

"It is mine too, not exclusively. I have partners."

"The shop must do well. That Marmon catches the eye."

"Well, my primary enterprise is cooperage."

"Cooperage. Yes, cooperage." The word took a while to sink in. Yi was in the barrel business. Barrels were ubiquitous containers in shipping; solidly constructed, they could be moved rapidly, and didn't allow easy inspection of their contents.

"Blue-light import-export?" asked Hobson

Yi didn't understand. "Blue lighting" was an old maritime term for smuggling.

The Korean held up his hand to signal the need for a pause. "It might be better to describe me as a financier, a banker. An insurrectionist banker." He turned his chair to face the street. "I transport furs and precious metals without causing disruption."

"Opium?"

Yi looked disappointed. "I established my business for a purpose. Opium is a product that kills purpose. My purpose and opium can't co-exist. I'm not out to destroy the opium trade in China, nor will I have a hand in it. If it shows up in places I protect, I will fight it."

Seconds later, a commotion began at the entrance to the vault. Four Chinese men burst into the eatery, turning over chairs and proceeding directly to Yi's table. Burly in build, battered in appearance, they made a dramatic entrance.

The leader, a Chinaman with a dark complexion, spoke harshly and defiantly to the American. "I am called Persimmon, family name Ma. You will remember my name and the name of the Three Harmonies Society. Hobson, you took my superior's car without permission, and for that, you must be punished. The Three Harmonies Society has determined this must be so."

One of the others with his back to Yi's table delivered a speech of similar length in Chinese. He couldn't see any weapons, though he kept his eyes on their hands. He recognized one Chinese word, the word for persimmon. He had to shift mental gears. That was the man's nickname, not a proper Chinese name, rather one related to his reputation and character, and bestowed by his triad boss or General Zang. He was saying this action was endorsed by "his superior" in the Three Harmonies Society.

Odd, Hobson thought. Zang had paid him a finder's fee for the car. He concluded that Persimmon still had a cleaver to grind, and his triad did, too. He had foiled their robbery.

Instilling fear was an art form, and drama was a component.

As a Westerner, Hobson's first mental image of the word "persimmon" was that of a fruit, a sweet, tangy fruit. The image was a silly one, frivolous, a girl's name.

That fruit, however, grew from a tree. The name was a play on images. In China, and in Korea, the persimmon tree was known as a hardwood that carpenters found difficult to work. It could be used for furniture though was more often found in simpler items like pool cues. Persimmon's superior had a gift for black humor. People first visualized the persimmon fruit that could be "sweet," and too late they confronted a thug who resembled a hard wood that would not conform easily to productive enterprises..

Perhaps finding a tough who spoke English had not been easy — broken English surely, but English nevertheless. The English-speaking Chinaman's sinister appearance was capped by a droopy, scarred left eyelid. Hobson realized this oration was a verdict. All that remained was his execution.

Persimmon wood was characterized by dark serpentine veins. The image left Hobson with a sense of constricting darkness.

Hobson looked at Yi with disappointment. He had fallen into an open hatchway, and he had no idea how far he was going to fall…

Yi rose and tucked his glasses into his jacket breast pocket. To Hobson, he appeared larger somehow. His mouth and jaw seemed tauter, his shoulders wider. "This is my establishment, and I will not have it dishonored. Whatever your business, it must be taken outside. You are not aware that I do commerce with the Three Harmonies Society and from time to time pay amply for its protection. That protection includes the protection of my reputation. No blood can be spilled here." He responded in English.

Persimmon looked surprised, though the warning language seemed sensible. Hobson hadn't heard the Three Harmonies Society's interests extended into the old Japanese quarter. Business was business. Executions of non-triad members on the premises jeopardized a source of revenue. Oddly Persimmon hadn't done his homework before disrupting a Three Harmonies protected establishment. Yi's announcement made sense, though Persimmon showed no embarrassment or sign of altering his course.

Two of the Chinese men grabbed Hobson and attempted to drag him out into the street. Hobson rotated, his arms flung outward, swinging them at full length and knocking the men who held them into the surrounding tables. He shook himself to be sure he was completely free. Release seemed too easy, until he realized Koreans behind him had intervened.

Both hatchet men lay as crumpled paper on the dirt floor, struck down by a flurry of improvised clubs. The other men in the vault were standing and holding canes or short sticks. Yi's clientele had intervened.

The other two triad members had bound over a line of wheelbarrows and were running down the street. Several Korean men were chasing them. The wheelbarrows were of Chinese design and manufacture, wooden and flat. Hobson wondered where they had come from. They hadn't been present when he'd arrived. They showed a barrier-like order in their disarray.

"You did me great commercial favor in protecting the Red-Knight's Pawnshop," said Yi. "Foiling a robbery was simply forgivable behavior by a foreigner, yet would have cost a Chinese his life. Taking the Packard car, even temporarily, was a challenge to the triad lieutenant's authority. You have embarrassed him. His boss paid you a reward for its return. I'm sure the lieutenant—perhaps Persimmon himself—was made to re-pay that 'reward.' Persimmon, it appears, is determined to correct the embarrassment."

He observed Hobson, seeming to muse over such behavior on the American sailor's part.

"Foiling a crime is one thing, but embarrassing a boss is another. I had word of this potential threat when I invited you here. It is true I have dealt with the Three Harmonies Society, but not for protection. Today, this establishment was protected by Koreans, and I don't believe the other two triad men will make it back to the Old Chinese City. For the time being, I think you need to plan your visits ashore with great care." Yi handed Hobson a gun. "Hold this for me, would you?"

The revolver was an Owl Head, owing to the image engraved on its grips. This model was "a hammerless." With it, came a box of bullets and a small holster that looked much like a money belt and that could be worn under a jumper. The holster was several inches wide and secured by two straps. The outer pouches were waxed harness leather, while the inside was cotton duck. One pouch had been tailored to the outline of a hammerless pistol.

The best money belts were waterproofed so their owners could wear them when they washed down under a pump. Life was different when every day a sailor had to secure all his worldly possessions in a seabag, a ditty bag, or a bucket.

"I will tell you, nephew, when I need it back. The trouble with the Three Harmonies Society is they attack in numbers."

The patrons returned to the vault, as if confrontations were an everyday affair. The bodies were removed, and the meal continued. Hobson could feel the maekgoli taking effect and the revolver felt large and conspicuous on his waist under his jumper.

Yi was not to be deterred from his business. "As I said, I'm a banker of sorts, and I have a proposition for you. It is also a proposition to the United States Navy. I started guarding silver, however this is a matter of, how shall I say it, 'expropriating' gold."

"Gold? Really? I'm in the immature diamond business myself," Hobson responded doubtfully, looking at the coal dust under his fingernails. "One of USS Pluto's human carbuncles, that's me."

Yi chose to ignore the quip. Hobson also realized that he had never been an experienced maekgoli drinker. "I need to speak to the captain of the captains, to the Navy general," Yi said.

Hobson saw no need to correct his terminology. "Well, Mr. Yi, I'll try to help you. Of course, I can't say I swing much weight in larger naval circles. On the other hand, my experience has been that sailors at all levels seem to show an interest in gold."

Hobson noted the lines in Yi's face and the look of exhaustion, and regretted his flippancy. Yi may have been well-heeled, but he wore the weight of responsibility, too.

The Korean shook Hobson's hand in a vise-like grip and laughed.

In Asia, a laugh could indicate humor, happiness, intense embarrassment, or discomfort.

"Discretion is all I ask. Discretion. The futures of many are at stake."

Hobson decided not to have another cup of maekgoli.

"Yes, seonbae," Hobson replied in the Korean style. Seonbae meant "a senior, an upperclassman, a mentor." A mentor's words required careful attention, though they could be disobeyed, he recalled.

Yi's next inquiry surprised him. "How do you buy an insurrection?"

Hobson puzzled over the question. "Buy? You mean instigate with money? Can't be easy. What's to keep folks from taking the money and running? Part of wars is staying alive and money is a great way of working your way out to the 'egress,' as P. T. Barnum put it. Money applied the wrong way, to my way of thinking, encourages people to want to survive for themselves, not die for a cause."

Yi listened attentively. "Wars are expensive and wasteful. Arms are expensive. How do you make sure they get to the right people with the right motivation? And who can you trust? Professionals probably, but what if a country has precious few military professionals inside or out?"

"Maybe you just toss seed piles of money around and hope the seed piles fall on fertile ground," Hobson responded, raising his palm.

"Even then, how do you recognize fertile ground?" Yi puzzled.

Hobson had no idea, though anyone who had set foot in Korea toyed with the concept of insurrection.

"If you need to reach me, leave a note with the broker at the Red-Knight's Pawnshop," Yi instructed. "Stay on your ship for a few days. I won't know for a while if a boss, a lieutenant, or someone else in the Three Harmonies Society still wants his revenge."

Days later, Hobson, Washboard, and Harp looked for the vault where Hobson had eaten grilled ham. All they found was a locked storage space filled with burlap sacks and wheelbarrows.

Mr. Yi seemed to have a way of making things of substance appear and disappear.

The United States Navy was bi-chromatic, Hobson thought as he lay in his hammock.

The Navy made getting up in the morning and in the middle of the night easy. Moreover, if you knew what the temperature was outside, you knew what the official fashion dictates were.

Nearly everything Hobson possessed was one of two colors. His seabag was white, his hammock was white, and his ditty bag was white. Some sailors went so far as to get their galvanized buckets enameled white ashore. His bucket was an issued item. He washed and shaved out of it. He did his laundry out of it. When he changed ships, he took it with him, along with his hammock.

When it was cold, he wore blue uniforms, his dress blues or working blues, and often a peacoat and flat-hat that were blue.

The ships varied from the scheme, yet were bi-chromatic, too: either gray stateside, or white in the Asiatic Fleet.

All of China, by contrast, was like an explosion in a paint factory. Perhaps to sailors, that heightened the appeal. Hobson preferred Japan and its more subtle color schemes.

Korea, he thought, rested somewhere in between, though now, under the Japanese, Korea was being stripped or bleached of all color.

Hobson was summoned by Wheelwright, his commanding officer. Handsome, strong-jawed, clean-shaven, and straight-backed, he was also a commanding officer of integrity and discretion.

"This is a-way over my level of authority," Wheelwright said. "No confusing coal and gold. This Skookum Yi's proposal could result in an international incident." He looked at Hobson without appearing to see him, despite the fact Hobson knew Wheelwright saw him perfectly well. Before Draper was the rarely seen "official business" Wheelwright.

"Well, we'll fasten this project with one round-turn to that professor of ciphers, smoke screens, and false-moustache cards sharpery," Wheelwright added. "No telling how the Grand Poohbahs inside the Office of Naval Intelligence enveloped within the Bureau of Navigation will regard a foreign businessman's request to see the admiral."

Hobson guessed the "cardsharp" was Lieutenant (Junior Grade) Draper, with whom he and Wheelwright had dealt before.

Hobson had seen the crinkled commission, jammed in one of the lower drawers of the battered roll-top desk before him, reading," Lieutenant Junior Grade Stuyvesant Van Rensselaer Draper, III, New York Naval Militia." Most people just call him "Draper" or "the professor." He was about it, when it came to collecting and interpreting naval intelligence in the disintegrating Empire of China and the growing Empire of Japan. He was responsible for both empires, although Japan took priority.

The sweep of his office in a garret cubbyhole nestled under the mansard roof of the Tokyo Embassy Annex was not commensurate with the expanse of space and range of knowledge for which he was accountable. His other work spaces, Hobson recalled, were a horse-stall-sized shared stateroom aboard *USS Saratoga*, the station ship in Shanghai.

He was the Office of Naval Intelligence representative for (L), the code letter for Tokyo. His cubbyhole was a testament to overwork and disorder brought upon by the complexity of interpretation and the sheer breadth of his duties. His emotional life had been rolling, pitching, and yawing like a wherry caught in a weir. He'd sought an exotic challenge and had found one.

Hobson knew Wheelwright and Draper were at opposing ends of the officer spectrum. Wheelwright was a crisp officer of the line from the Naval Academy, destined for admiral. Draper was a rumpled naval militia officer, destined to toil unnoticed among the cobwebbed piles of ship blueprints, crop reports, and foreign message traffic.

Strangely, Hobson thought to himself, the two officers got along famously.

CHAPTER FOURTEEN

Admiral's Quarters, USS Saratoga, Shanghai, May 1913

Draper had cleared an audience with the admiral, and it had spurred a staff meeting on "expropriating gold."

Admiral Simeon "Ol' Blue Flame" Bulkley, commander of the Asiatic Fleet, had as a senior officer sailed with Dewey into Manilla Bay. He made clear that he loathed the subject matter and questioned the wisdom of Yi's project, though he called a staff meeting anyway.

Draper saw the proposal as a rare opportunity for the Navy to check Japanese expansion.

Personally, his analytical work was extremely important, but he secretly hungered for a more physical aspect to his service. His chief responsibility was collecting intelligence on Japanese ship-building and gunnery technology. He could read Japanese characters, *kanji, hiragana, and katagana.*

The Battle of Tsushima had shown that Japan had blossomed from a backward feudal empire to one of the world's top industrial powers in the space of a few decades. Britain's once overwhelming inventory of wooden warships had been rendered obsolete and Japan no longer looked to Britain to build its warships. Japan was building them itself. Japan had far-ranging ambitions. Theodore Roosevelt had initiated planning for war with Japan at the Naval War College in War Plan Orange. Naval warfare required more advanced planning than most forms of warfare. If Draper mis-reported the size and range of Japanese guns, or the quality of Japanese steel, war with Japan could be lost before it started.

Yi's project to buy America, and Asia, time by slowing Japan's unsubtle grabs for China, allowed China a chance to stabilize and reorganize.

Draper understood balancing this immediate project and monitoring Japanese ship design might be complementary, disturbingly their competing demands could make his life the tenth ring of Hell. He'd volunteered for a naval militia commission, so be it.

Eight senior officers sat around a green-baize covered table, including the Asiatic Station's paymaster, who held the rank of commander. Two ancient chief petty officers stood in readiness.

Draper watched Hobson sit, seeming uncomfortable in a chair against the wall beyond the foot of the table.

Skookum Yi sat in an adjoining stateroom. If he felt anxious, he wasn't showing it.

Draper believed himself to be as prepared as time had permitted, however there was a vulnerability to being the most junior officer in the room. These were the Eight Olympians of Asiatic Station.

Admiral Bulkley was in the habit of releasing lightning bolts. That was clear.

Was Hobson a heroic demi-god?

Where did that leave him? Draper pondered about his own station. Was he some sort of junior god? He decided he was a lesser god, Triton, messenger of the seas. That would do. After all, he was only in his thirties.

Known as "Ol' Blue Flame" for his verbal style, the admiral was rarely at a loss for words, which were always rich in the tones of patrician Philadelphia. As for Yi, the admiral wanted no direct, unaccompanied contact with any local civilian without official status, indeed with anyone who wished to entice him or his men with gold.

Chinese warlords were continually attempting to compromise those with the ability to place ordnance on a target. This had the appearance of a potential bribe, and the admiral had survived forty years naval service by knowing shoal waters when he saw them.

"Theft of Japanese specie is, of course, illegal," said Paymaster McCorkran, "utterly contrary to regulations — 'The Rocks & Shoals,' all of it. Nothing we should be doing. Here in China, in Japan, in America, anywhere." He fidgeted, gently tapping his fingers on his pomaded hair and its axe-stroke center part. A distinct aroma enveloped Paymaster McCorkran. Draper suspected the man used oilskin wax to keep his hair and moustache in place.

"Yes, of course," the admiral said in irritation. "The Bible also says some things about theft, and coveting, too, I recall. Thank you for reminding us, paymaster. The Japanese are pouring kerosene on the Chinese fire. A fire that they, in part, started. If we can instead dampen that fire without attention, well, so much the better. The Nationalists are becoming unruly. We don't know that they'll change things for the better around here, or make things worse, but slow-going in this political fog is probably the best thing for all concerned."

The paymaster's eyes darted around the room, though the rest of him maintained the absolute stillness of a pierhead rat caught in the light.

Draper had landed in Japan for several reasons. The first reason was he had tired of academia and he wanted to help his country make its mark on the global stage. The second reason was to duck the advances of a professor's daughter in New York, while reason three was to avoid a duel.

Reasons two and three were connected. A colleague hadn't taken kindly to Draper's peer review of his piece on Virgil's metaphors, or the fact Draper was the focus of the amorous daughter's attentions. Draper wasn't afraid of losing the duel. He was afraid of winning the duel. He was a Renaissance man, albeit one who wore half-glasses, yet one who could line up the sights of a pistol with reliable result. Taking things one step further, he could see himself in jail without good reading light, getting unwanted pies from the professor's daughter.

Draper glanced over at Hobson, who wrinkled his nose twice like a rat, clearly sharing Draper's impression.

Of course, in China, and in Yi's own Korea, Draper knew, rats held a higher standing than in the West. Despite the rat's reputation for trickery and stealth, Asians tended to respect the creature for the intelligence it displayed in locating, acquiring, and hoarding its booty. The first animal in the Asian zodiac, rats were revered for their persistence, ambition, and humility.

Or perhaps their appearance of humility.

Well, Paymaster McCorkran, Hobson, and he, intended to remain as dutifully still as possible. Like any intelligent and industrious rat, Draper thought contrarily compelled to break the stillness. Silence meant acquiescence and eventual failure, as he saw it. He felt forced to describe the effect of the gold on Chinese and world economics in his role as representative of the Office of Naval Intelligence.

"If I may point out the subtle significance of what is going to happen…" In his presentation, he used phrases like "bimetal economy," "gold standard," and "Gresham's Law." When he described gold coins replacing a bushel of wheat in ancient Babylonia, the eyes of the men in the room began to glaze over. Reading his staff's drifting attention, he summarized, "To exploit Chinese instability, Japan is willing to let gold leave its country."

Admiral Bulkley was being unusually patient. "Mr. Draper, I'll need to write a report at some point. Perhaps you could give me a paragraph that the Navy Department will understand at a glance."

"Well sir, we think…" Draper was being recklessly plural, he knew, especially since he comprised the entire Japanese/China desk of the Office of Naval Intelligence.

"The Empire of Japan wants to wreck the new Nationalist currency, the yuan. They want the Chinese to dump all their yuan in favor of yen. They are going to set an artificial exchange rate that is generous. Japanese banks in China are going to play up the magnitude of their holdings in gold and play on the uncertainty of anything not backed by visible, palpable gold. These same ingots are going to be photographed in the vaults in successive Japanese banks."

"Ha, gold as a comfort when the future's uncertain. Bet that gold just stays in the banks, if the government collapses," Admiral Bulkley interjected. "Darn, still another reason to avoid a currency collapse."

"Yes sir," Draper continued. "Once Ma and Pa Celestial have their savings in yen, they get a good rate, solidly backed by an apparently stable foreign government. No one knows what to make of the Nationalists. Clearly, they don't control all, or even a significant part, of China yet. As a result, Ma and Pa Celestial are going to take a favorable view of most Japanese conduct. They are going to lean toward a continuing presence of Japan in China."

The admiral rubbed his chin with the back of his hand. "This is some of that ol' Sun fellow's thinking, isn't it?"

"Sun Tzu? Don't think he ever addressed this form of warfare directly, though it is consistent with his teachings."

Draper felt a relief in knowing the admiral was a quick study and read more than the message traffic and coastal pilots. The author of *The Art of War*, Sun Tzu had lived in the sixth century B.C. His observations on unconventional stratagems were well-known in Asia.

"No torpedoes or exploding shells here, though ingots can cause damage, too," Admiral Bulkley said gruffly. "I want the United States Navy's touch in this matter to be lighter than sea smoke." He glanced around the table.

Had the admiral bought into the concept?

Draper must have stared because for a moment the admiral's eye caught his and Draper knew.

He'd heard that many naval officers and petty officers had a sense of destiny. They shared the belief that at some moment in time they would be called upon make some small unrecognized decision that would change the course in history.

Yi's gambit would garner no one a medal or an ounce of recognition. More likely it would result in inestimable deaths, and a devastating sweep of discharges, disruption, and disgrace.

Its shear audacity and scope appealed to Simeon Bulkley's sense of purpose.

"Let me see." The patrician flag officer frowned in contemplation, and then continued. "Your informant tells us the gold is on *IJS Kurama*. The Japanese will either need to come alongside the piers and offload under guard — that's the way I'd do it — or lighter it ashore. Then they'll take the gold, about a ton or two, rumor is, using heavy-duty carts, two or three carts likely, to the bank. Three weeks, you say — the gold comes in three weeks."

"Two to three tons, that's what the scuttlebutt is." Draper didn't reveal his sources. "It will come in crates of gold bullion, or kegs of gold coins or ingots."

"Sturdy kegs will be easier to move on or off ship and up and over piers and seawalls," offered Chief Backer. "Rolling several hundred pounds is far easier than manhandling crates, up and down, up and down."

Paymaster McCorkran could no longer remain still. "We can divert the gold from the ship at the pier or at a mooring, when it comes to shore, or on shore, or at the Yokohama Specie Bank. The problem as I see it, Admiral, is time. Whenever I've escorted payrolls to the ships I've always thought if I had a bit more time on a payroll run I could…"

Draper noted Paymaster McCorkran pause and visibly decide not to complete his sentence. Draper suspected what McCorkran had begun to say would cast him in a bad light.

Draper had mixed feelings about the paymaster as an ally, albeit Draper was feeling lonely. The admiral didn't seem to be overly enthusiastic about his plan. Draper realized he had never helped formulate an operational plan before.

"Most of this little monetary excursion will be in plain view of the entire city of Shanghai, surely in sight of the Bund, and will be quite time-consuming," Paymaster McCorkran said. "Seizing control of the shipment and transferring it to a location under our control will take time. Two Japanese ships are in the harbor, and they can put a considerable number of men ashore under arms in a short period of time."

The admiral frowned. "Paymaster, if we take control of the gold, can you find us a discreet place to store it on short notice?"

"Yes, sir, the problem is whoever stores it will know that it's Japanese gold. They're gonna see them Nip marks all over any ingots, bullion, or coins, just like our marks are all over our bullion and coins. Hard to keep people's mouths shut."

Paymaster McCorkran was no ally, Draper concluded. He wanted all this to go away.

Ebulliently the paymaster went on. "Sir, might we find a less official way of storing all this loot? And I don't know much about sea law, but does prize money enter any of this, since this gold will be taken by 'naval force of arms'"?

The admiral regarded the paymaster with ever-narrowing eyes. "I guess I'll have to read up again on the Treaty of Paris and its provisions relating to prize money. You can go back to your accounts now. Payday will be here before you know it."

Embarrassed, the paymaster left the room.

"Prize money?" the admiral repeated, looked at the overhead so everyone left in the room knew the question didn't really require an answer. No one was ever sure if the admiral was humorless or his brand of humor was at some superior level of subtlety.

He looked closely at everyone present. "The details of our plan will not leave this room. Clear? Mr. Draper?" he said, dubiously glancing Draper's way.

"Yes, sir," Draper said. "However, in one regard, Paymaster McCorkran is certainly right. Time is our enemy. Loading and unloading two to three tons of gold is time-consuming and the fastest ways to do that are also conspicuous, and easily foiled. Derricks, donkey rigs, booms, parbuckles..."

"Sirs?" Chief Boatswain's Mate Blybecker raised his massive, calloused hand like a schoolboy. All Blybecker's career he had been handling, diverting, juggling, and disposing of cargo. The chief boatswain's mate felt practicality was the essence of his rating, and therefore, he no doubt felt obligated to speak. "Why not simply stow the loot under a tarpaulin somewhere and come back when it darn well suits us?"

"Bookmark the gold in plain sight, so to speak?" Draper said.

Hobson met Draper's eyes and smiled. Apparently, a similar line of thought had crossed his mind.

"Here in Asia, fans are employed by women to signal coyness," the admiral observed, "however in America, magicians use them with equal effectiveness to make things disappear." Again, he looked around at all the men at the table.

"There's Point A, and there's Point B. We will wrest the gold between Point A and Point B. I will look to each of you to suggest diversions, distractions, and silk fans."

Everyone in the room understood the developing plan. This had now become a matter of magic: a folding fan or two, and some clever sleight-of-hand. Better yet, the concept was now comfortably American.

Draper pondered how often and how widely the art of larceny was discussed in the Navy, both above and below decks. The subject was only broached as an intellectual exercise, of course.

At the same time, Hobson extended that thought to wonder how much government loose change Paymaster McCorkran had diverted to his own use in his career.

The fifty-tael sycee, the boat-shaped silver ingot, on *USS Rainbow* surely didn't look like the one he had recovered two years before at Woosung. He had held that odd silver ingot in his hand and it was not an object whose details he'd ever forget. Someone on *USS Rainbow* had swapped it for a lead replica.

Draper looked over his notes. Almost everyone had left the staff meeting; only he and Hobson were left. Everything had been addressed. The devil was now in the details.

Admiral Bulkley scanned the room, training a piercing eye on Hobson and Draper. He scowled in their general direction. "Make no mistake about it. This port just oozes skullduggery, and my orders are to keep a lid on the bubbling Japanese kettle. So, we're going to engage by nefarious means. If you get caught, well, we're going to consider you a disgrace to the United States Navy. To the world you will be a disgrace, a despicable grand larceny disgrace. Between us, you will be a disgrace for getting caught."

He was telling Draper and Hobson what to do and at the same time telling them they were going to take the fall if caught.

"One other thing, not one ounce of that Nippon gold can land in any permanent way on Chinese soil, and no American is going to derive any financial benefit from that gold. That clear? And, Mr. Draper, keep that polyglot quartermaster…" He nodded at Hobson. "…whom you seem to be forever borrowing at will from *USS Pluto* — from screwing this up. Quartermaster Third Class Hobson, keep this militia intelligence officer from screwing this up. If I hold this command after your court martials, I might see fit to pardon you two, but it's a good bet I will have been consigned to the brig, or forcibly retired by that point."

Later that day, Yi met with the admiral in his stateroom. Draper and Hobson sat in on the meeting though both kept their mouths closed.

In the middle of Yi's describing the scheme, the admiral interrupted his visitor. "To be blunt, I can't take and keep some other country's gold in peacetime. It will open a Pandora's box for the United States Navy."

Yi sat quietly for a moment. He kept his hands and glasses in his lap. Draper was confident what Yi would say next.

"I had hoped the gold would be used to benefit the people of Korea," Yi said softly, yet with dignity.

The admiral didn't respond immediately. Draper knew the man had no orders with respect to Korea. Korea was a sensitive subject. Teddy Roosevelt had been awarded the Nobel Peace Prize for negotiations in which Korea had been a featured topic. Several years earlier, the US Secretary of War had come to a tacit agreement with the Japanese that approved Japan's sovereignty over Korea in return for its pledge not to interfere with American interests in the Philippine Islands.

Yi sat upright and waited for the admiral to respond.

Japan wasn't Spain, a country the US had quickly and handily defeated in the Pacific fifteen years earlier. That said, Draper also knew the admiral had orders to closely watch the Japanese Navy and discreetly contain its efforts when possible.

"Three tons of gold. How can I be sure this money won't be used for 'bad purposes' or against the interests of the United States?"

Yi thought for a moment. "I will store it in the United States or I will store it in a location where Americans can exercise control over it."

"Didn't some Frenchman say, 'Behind every great fortune is a great crime?' How can I be sure of your intentions?" Admiral Bulkley scanned Yi's face, looking for answers, yet Draper knew he'd have better luck studying the face of one of those wooden statues in front of a cigar store.

Draper leaned forward. He hadn't expected this turn in the conversation.

Then Yi blinked. "I'm not so sure anyone can say that I maintain a great personal fortune, but I can say that my story starts with a great crime, and that I was one of its victims. Fortunes have flowed through my fingers. I intend to put the gold in a safe place. Or perhaps several places. I need to fully think this out. Korean insurrectionists are training in Hawaii, the American Midwest, and in Manchuria."

"And you will let me know where that place is?"

"Better than that, I will show your representative where that place is and why Americans will be in a position to seize it if I act inappropriately. Or if I act in an untrustworthy manner, that is, against American interests."

"What would keep you from moving it after it ends up in this repository?" The admiral placed one palm on the table for emphasis.

"Only my word. What would keep you from seizing it and using it against American interests?"

"Only my word." The admiral leaned back and looked at his cuff braid. He was treading in dangerous territory. "We are then equal in our discomfort. And who do you propose my representative should be?"

"Lieutenant Draper or Petty Officer Hobson. They are the most knowledgeable about the intricacies of this affair, however that's a choice for you to make. The journey to the repository will be dangerous. I will trust your judgment."

Ol' Blue Flame shaped his beard with his knuckles. Draper imagined he wasn't sure he cared who got the gold out of here, as long as the Japanese didn't get it back.

The admiral's words slowed. "What's to keep you from giving the gold back to the Japanese for a finder's fee?" He seemed to have come to a decision.

Yi sat quietly. "I'm Korean. My country has been called 'the Hermit Kingdom' by some for its remote location and its old-fashioned attitudes. Japan has used Korea's isolation to its advantage. The Japanese managed to overthrow our monarchy through subterfuge. My people have few modern weapons and little experience in organizing themselves for modern war. Japan is grinding my people into dust and stripping my country of its resources. They're giving our cities Japanese names, forcing us to abandon our language, and seeking to eradicate our culture."

Yi moved one shoulder and then the other as if slinging on the straps of a heavily-laden jige. "I wish to underwrite a rebellion. My greatest fear is not doing that correctly. By infusion of gold I may create false hope and cause a great loss of life. That is my responsibility, not yours. I don't want this to turn into an embarrassment for your country, or a tragedy for mine. I've given considerable thought into how that gold can be used to help rather than harm."

"I think I understand what you're saying," Admiral Bulkley said and then nodded toward Yi and waited for him to continue.

"Admiral, I will further the interests of Japan when it is possible for you and me to take a horse-drawn sleigh ride through Hell. Insurrections are expensive propositions. Governments can exist on credit. Filibusters must pay cash on the barrelhead. If you want to throw out an occupying army, you need another country to support you, either overtly or clandestinely. Three countries have always shown an interest in Korea: China, Russia, and Japan. Japan has administered knockout blows to China and Russia. No other country is any longer interested in or capable of helping us." Yi sighed.

"So that's the situation," Bulkley conceded.

"Admiral, it is possible we can put this shipment of ingots and my personal fortune into Korea, and not change Japan's course the width of a strand of silk."

"So why do it?"

"Perhaps I do so to appease my ancestors," Yi said with a fatalistic grin. "Perhaps I do so because I failed my country before and have a debt to pay. In any event, I cannot let the heritage of Korea be erased from the surface of the earth."

Draper believed him. Hobson didn't move for a long while and then nodded.

The admiral shook Yi's hand and the meeting was over.

CHAPTER FIFTEEN

Shanghai Moorings east of Suzhou Creek, Huangpu River,
May 1913

The effort was to be what the Navy called "a cutting-out expedition," and a few of the key players had mustered the cutting-out party. The vessel to be "cut out" was a steam launch.

The Red-Crowned Crane Plan, as it was being called began as Hobson, Draper, and Chief Blybecker, commenced watching the Japanese cruiser *IJS Kurama*'s steam launch for a period of four days. Dark rings showed around Draper's eyes as he removed his half-glasses and picked up a pair of binoculars. When he put them down, his free hand continually fiddled with the watch fob in his pocket. He was the lone intelligence officer assigned to the Asiatic Fleet. Draper knew while he was shepherding this operation in Shanghai, information on Japanese battleship technology was accumulating on his desk in Tokyo.

Draper studied each inch of the Japanese ship for the fourth time.

The plan was good. Nothing could go wrong, he had assured the admiral. Something always went wrong. This was a complex project entirely executed by mortals.

The two watched from upstream on *USS Saratoga's* Bund-side bridge-wing. Plans named for exotic wildlife had been popular since the Civil War's successful Anaconda Plan. After consulting several ships' masters-at-arms, Draper had figured the Japanese guard would be ten men and an officer. Hobson estimated that two tons of cargo would drop the waterline of the steam launch significantly, three tons more so, and he noted the Japanese had reconstructed the sides of the launch to give it greater freeboard.

Hobson had suggested that Draper pay the harbormaster to put the Japanese on a specific mooring. Hobson's suggestion had worked and Draper could imagine the Japanese consternation.

On the fourth night, Japanese sailors in landing party rig climbed into the steam launch at two in the morning.

"Dry run, open bushels of coal," observed Hobson, yawning and looking into the telescope. "Launch isn't riding low enough in the water. I've been counting strakes above the waterline. Two tons and eleven men is 6,000 pounds displacement. Three tons and its about 8,000 pounds. They don't have that tonight. She's showing too much freeboard, though I think they're about ready."

The launch that left *IJS Kurama* swanned its way east of Suzhou Creek and turned between finger piers two and three near the Japanese consulate. A steam tractor towing six steel-reinforced carts rolled up. Sailors of the Imperial Japanese Navy loaded the bushels of coal, unloaded the bushels of coal, covered them with tarps, milled about the pier, and then re-embarked the steam launch.

Hobson swept his telescope back toward the ship. "The Japanese have crew on the deck of *IJS Kurama* observing, as well as they can in the dark. From their postures I'm sure they lost sight of the launch when it turned into the pier. *Very good.* I'm positive a guard will be set for the gold-bearing carts. The trip to the bank isn't that far, even so the sons of Nippon are leaving nothing to chance," Hobson concluded, collapsing his telescope.

The Japanese were going to offload at their fleet landing, cart the gold across the Garden Bridge, and head to the Yokohama Specie Bank to make a night deposit.

Their rehearsal was flawless and a wonder to behold.

Two nights later, the Japanese executed their actual undertaking in earnest.

Draper remained on *USS Saratoga*, and Hobson had positioned himself on the finger pier complex adjoining the IJN fleet landing.

Naval Lieutenant Higashi, the duty officer on *IJS Kurama*, followed the white-hulled steam launch with his binoculars. With the extra weight, the steam launch pushed its way through the water rather than over it.

IJS *Kurama*'s captain had wanted a berth at one of the deep-water piers, yet instead they were nearly out of sight of their fleet landing, which was nestled among a series of finger piers in the area of the old towpath that led through Hongkou.

The steam launch's white hull glided quietly through the night water. Its hull grew increasingly difficult to discern, but its running lights told any interested observers where it was and which way it was headed. Wisely, the Japanese had chosen a moonless night to execute their well-rehearsed plan.

As the launch approached the finger piers, it was obscured for a second by motor junk activity. The launch was to turn in toward the Bund between the second and third finger piers. Higashi knew just where the Imperial Japanese Navy's fleet landing was by the yellow-white-yellow lights stretched between the two finger piers. As long as the launch was headed toward those lights, all was well. Higashi was reasonably sure it was doing just that. Three sailing junks raised their sails like three geishas opening their fans. The result was a floating triptych.

Lieutenant Higashi saw unexpected flames ahead of where he had last seen the launch. *Had it originated from the watch shack that overlooked the fleet landing?* He looked carefully and the yellow-white-yellow string of lights floated from right to left and back again above the fire. He could now hear an angry crowd, but couldn't see the launch or its lights. He called down to a watch-stander, who made the appropriate notation in the log.

The Japanese duty officer cocked his head. He thought he heard the drone of pumps and the sound of water from hoses, and then remembered the conflagration. He entered that into the log also.

Hobson, Harp, and Washboard were part of the boarding party comprised of over two dozen men, a mixture of Yi's Koreans and USS *Pluto*'s collier crew. An equal sized group of USS *Rainbow*'s men floated in reserve on sampans downriver. All were dressed in denim. The Navy men wore stevedore jackets, rather than their usual jumpers of denim material. As a group, they wore a mix of dark flat caps, bandanas, skullcaps, and conical hats of rattan, and had smeared their faces with grease and coal dust. Hobson smiled at the rattan sunhats. They were the same as he'd seen in Korea and Japan, differing only slightly in shape and weave.

The detail waited in sampans just outboard of a rust-streaked tugboat. Above them were more American sailors and expatriate Koreans dressed similarly. All communications — English, Korean, or Wu dialect — had to be in words of one syllable. A single syllable passed too quickly to connect with any particular language. No future identification could be made by language. A mistake, and retribution would be severe. That retribution would come from Japan.

In any event, that anyone could hear their exchanges was unlikely, because Yi, using several of the touts who served the American fleet landing, had arranged for a Chinese mob to attack the Imperial Japanese landing watch-shack, set it alight, and stay to watch the fire. The soaring flames and the din of the mob sounded like a collision between a brass band and cats in heat.

The Japanese steam launch approached gingerly. The joint Korean-American boarding party — above the Japanese on the two adjoining piers — tightened a cable until it was just a few inches above the water surface in the gap between finger piers one and two. At the same time, the yellow-white-yellow lights strung over the gap between these finger piers went out and an identical string of yellow-white-yellow lights went on between finger piers two and three. The cable caused the launch to slide gently toward the second newly illuminated opening.

A large junk slid from its position masking one pier opening and closing another, its sails up and luffing. In flapping its sails, the junk masked the real Imperial Navy fleet landing between the piers and unmasking a false fleet landing. Two other junks did the same, completely obscuring the real landing with a triptych of fully battened sails.

Within that second opening bobbed a decoy fleet landing, a small darkened river tug with a crane on the right, and a group of sampans nestled on the left.

Hobson looked toward the heavily laden tug. In the tumult, the Japanese coxswain wasn't likely to grasp the subtle difference in the waterfront. He had room enough to tie up. The spot was tight, even so this was a cocky Japanese coxswain.

Wearing a gray newsboy's flat cap, his face smeared with coal dust, Hobson wondered if the launch coxswain considered why the shore patrol had allowed these boats to gather around the Japanese fleet landing. He tucked his corncob pipe into his waistband and found himself shifting his weight from one foot to the other in readiness. Other members of the cutting out boarding party were doing the same.

He choked down the urge to make small talk. One casual sentence could compromise them.

The launch coxswain wiped his eyes, made an adjustment in course, and steamed unknowing into the maelstrom. As no doubt planned, the *IJS Kurama's* quartermaster on the launch attempted to alert the Imperial Navy shore patrol of the arrival of the ingots with *IJS Kurama's* masthead lights, except the shore patrol had its hands full with the angry crowd and the fire.

Generally, a crowd pays to watch drama, Hobson thought to himself. *This crowd had been paid to generate drama.*

The Japanese couldn't understand the reason for the attack, and now a tractor with steel-reinforced carts rolled right into the middle of the riot, and the crowd rose to the task of overturning the carts. The Japanese coxswain found the commotion around the shack confusing, and the lights on the pier above him made seeing what was going on difficult.

A truckload of Sikhs from the Shanghai Municipal Police arrived and began cutting a swath with their *lathi*. The crowd began to throw firecrackers.

Surprisingly large firecrackers, Hobson thought as he resisted the urge to wipe his brow with its carefully applied coal dust.

IJS Kurama's agitated duty officer could hear what he believed to be shots and explosions ashore. The officer couldn't raise the Imperial Navy shore patrol or the launch with flashing lights. He sent the duty messenger for the senior officer of the landing party detachment. He had the duty messenger find the chief boatswain and direct him to begin lowering boats.

From his vantage point on a finger pier, Hobson could see everything.

The gold-laden Japanese steam launch went toward the false landing and hit the now submerged cable draped between the piers. The launch turned sideways and its props fouled the cable.

Two webs of grappling lines shot out from the piers and clawed at the seats and gunwales of the steam launch.

Hobson saw Chief Machinist Mate Phipps blow a whistle and the portable dewatering pumps focused their hoses on the crew and passengers of the steam launch. The hoses and pumps, normally used aboard American ships to drain water in emergencies, were now drenching the steam launch.

A Japanese officer brandished his revolver, to no avail. In seconds, the force of spray from three converging streams of water washed him overboard. One by one, the passengers and crew of the steam launch were pushed over the gunwales by the hose streams.

Soon, only one Imperial Japanese Navy sailor was left, a chief who was built about five feet high and five feet wide. He had wrapped himself around the boiler and was keeping his weight low. The launch was beginning to swamp and a grappling line parted. If the launch foundered, the equivalent of three million US dollars in gold was going to the bottom of the harbor and all of Shanghai would soon be diving into the Huangpu River.

Hobson had to admire the Japanese chief petty officer's tenacity. The launch was filling up, in Hobson's view, *like a galvanized bathtub on Saturday night.*

Hobson flipped open the cover flap of his pistol holster. His 1911 was all the rage in the Philippines and easily identifiable as an American-made sidearm with stopping power. He knew things could go wrong quickly.

A new ensign in engineering, Ensign Hays, realized that unless the boarding party did something about the Japanese chief petty officer, the launch would sink, and the gold with it. Worse still, three hoses focused on a boiler couldn't bring good results.

Hays jumped from the pier to the launch, breaking both ankles. He staggered and then struck the chief twice with a wrench.

Then the boiler burst.

CHAPTER SIXTEEN

The explosion on the Japanese launch brought the firecracker pops to a deafening crescendo and reinvigorated the Chinese mob onshore.

Hobson watched the crowd surge back. Several policemen and Japanese shore patrolmen found themselves pushed into the harbor. The swimming policemen focused their eyes upward and ignored rescuing boatmen. As a group, Hobson concluded, they found treading water preferable to engaging the incendiary crowd ashore.

Hobson had left *USS Saratoga* earlier dressed in anonymous working denim and positioned himself on a critical pier.

Had the officials looked behind them, they would have seen several dozen men in wet denim scrambling up cargo nets using cranes to swing barrels to an age-worn tugboat.

The ensign and the chief had disappeared. Twisted metal and a large hole in the hull could be seen where the boiler had been, but the grappling lines held. The Japanese steam launch was safely secured to the hip of the old tug. The crew of the tug was rapidly jettisoning ballast to counterbalance the weight of the newly loaded barrels.

Aboard *USS Saratoga*, Draper could see *IJS Kurama*'s duty officer's head shaking slightly, as if he thought he was seeing double.

Draper knew the brief appearance of two fleet landings had the Japanese officer confused.

The duty officer closed his eyes and then seemed relieved to see the lights of one fleet landing only. Much bustling was going on around the junk with its sail up, however the duty officer un-doubtedly had other things on his mind as he called away another landing party and sounded the siren. A more heavily armed party of sailors was away at last, and in the distance, Draper could see another detachment joining them from another Imperial Japanese warship.

Draper wondered if the duty officer had been schooled in steam rather than sail. If he had been schooled in sail, he would have no-ticed the light wind tonight couldn't be filling the junk's sails. The junk's sails provided concealment, rather than propulsion.

Not that he, as an intelligence officer, knew much about the dif-ference, though the greater value of basic training in sail for officers was an argument he frequently heard and now certainly agreed with.

Landing parties from two Japanese ships descended upon the fin-ger piers within a half-hour. By then, Hobson had watched the Ko-rean-American cutting out party sever the grappling lines using axes. The steam launch settled to the bottom quickly.

As the Japanese landing parties arrived, flames flared from the Imperial Japanese Navy's fleet landing shack. Hobson saw the Jap-anese armed sailors on one boat attempt to stand and move for-ward to view the excitement. Their NCOs growled and the men resumed their benches.

With surprising precision, fishing junks rescued each of the surviving launch passengers and crew. The junks proceeded in a disorienting manner downriver and eventually deposited the Japa-nese launch's surviving crew on the opposite shore of the Huangpu River among the silk and cotton mills of Pudong.

The men were far from the International Settlement. The Japa-nese sailors would take hours, perhaps days, to find their way back to the Imperial Japanese Navy fleet landing in Shanghai

The Japanese naval force landed and secured the razed watch shack. Japanese boats moved up and down the harbor in search of their lost steam launch.

By dawn, the fleet landing was crowded with Japanese sailors and a supplementary force of sailors with backpacks and rifles. The Imperial Navy had several divers down, yet no one was quite sure where their launch had been attacked. Searchers eventually found a few hats with *IJS Kurama* tallies and a boat hook drifting near finger pier three, but no launch, no guard detail — and no gold.

The river tug, its running lights doused, steamed downriver, leaving a trail of heavy black smoke as Hobson and its crew evened out the distribution of ballast and heavy barrels.

Climbing the ladder to the tug's wheelhouse, Hobson spotted an Asian woman, her face obscured with coal dust and in tattered workman's attire. She never walked back to examine the tarped cargo or share scuttlebutt. She had "presence" and Hobson assumed she was the owner's representative.

With no moon, its stack's smoke couldn't actually be seen, but it obscured the tug from every craft that attempted to follow it. This was just as well, because at a discreet distance on either side of the tug were two weaving steam tugs identically configured with cranes to confuse or divert pursuers. Then upon a prearranged signal all three tugs split up. Two of the tugs headed all the way to the Yangtze, one then headed upriver and the other downriver. The third tucked into the shelter of a wharf in Woosung.

There, inspection by Hobson and an officer from *USS Rainbow*, revealed each less than ten-gallon cask was still sealed and intact, all but one. Somehow during the course of the evening, one cask had caved in at one end. Its lid had come loose and a few ingots, perhaps as few as two, were missing.

Hobson considered it an acceptable loss. So many men were juggling so much cargo, with minimal communication, in the dark.

Inconsequential, small potatoes.

That was his hope, but where were the missing ingots?

In the next months, Japanese military intelligence, the Kempeitai, descended upon Shanghai in force. Several triads were singled out for special attention, yet in the end the investigations only resulted in a higher than ordinary homicide rate. Shanghai Municipal Police statisticians noted an upsurge in deaths of Chinese and Japanese men between the ages of 16 and 40.

As Yi sat at his roll-top desk in his wharf office in Woosung, his face showed no expression at all. This was the first day he could remember that his karmic debts and his karmic credits had begun to approach equilibrium. As a man of the world, he realistically didn't expect that status to last. He felt numb, and couldn't savor the moment.

Draper was sure some compromising disclosure would work itself adrift of the US Asiatic Fleet, except no one in the fleet seemed entirely sure what they had pulled off. No one, to his knowledge, had actually seen any gold. US sailors hadn't themselves benefited, so what was there to brag about? Moreover, Admiral Bulkley, "Ol' Blue Flame," had taken the time to leave certain burning impressions upon them.

The US participants had seen members of the Imperial Japanese Navy. They knew that they risked danger from that quarter and that dictated silence. Then too, this unknown group of Asians had been working alongside them. Triad hatchet men? Danger from that quarter also dictated silence. Better to tell some other story you knew about, like the one about the lookout who had washed overboard.

Among the admiral's staff, the consensus was that the Red-Crowned Crane plan had been a success. All that remained was for the crane to migrate.

For the moment, China had been saved from economic disaster. The Japanese hadn't flooded Shanghai with gold to undermine the value of the Chinese yuan. The value of the savings of Ma and Pa Celestial would not plummet. The Kempeitai and the Shanghai triads might take to be squaring off against each other looking for the lost gold.

The staff's consensus was the maneuver had gone smoothly, though Draper instead of relaxing, felt his anxiety grow. Was he losing his grip?

He'd studied Greek tragedy and knew success attracted discord. They'd sabotaged a grand plan, barely sidestepped an international incident, and tossed a fortune to the winds.

They had done what they considered right, however in doing so, had they opened Pandora's box?

CHAPTER SEVENTEEN

Nanking Road, Shanghai, May 1913

Hobson was feeling cheery on this day. The operation had gone smoothly.

"So, Washboard, Harp, anyone see *my little almond parfait*?"

"What's a PAR-fay?" Harp responded. A stroll down the Nanking Road always left him skeptical and in the mood for particulars. If he was to be a railroad tycoon, he needed to get into the habit of attending to details.

"One of them new French ice cream parlor extravaganzas. Lots of swirling whipped cream and sweet stuff." Hobson said with a pedantic swirl of his hand.

"*Almond* parfait?" Harp countered. "With you it's always been a question of whether you're partial to nuts or just maybe plain nuts."

"L-l-look," Washboard said, pointing to a commotion several blocks down the Bund.

And there they were, Clementine and several girls dressed in modern Western splendor, marching in support of the new parliamentary democracy. This was a formation of fallen women with Clementine, dressed as Miss Liberty, front and dead center. She had a torch, and by her side instead of a book of laws was a Chinese abacus, a *suanpan*.

Harp looked over. "Washboard's been drilling them for a week. You figure they can present arms and execute a countermarch?"

"Not sure what the appropriate 'present arms' for ladies of the evening might be," commented Hobson. "Wouldn't 'present charms' be more appropriate? Are people supposed to hear ruffles and flourishes or see them? Whatever they present, I think it's safe to approach."

Most of the people watching the strange procession barely noticed the two dozen women were dressed in straw hats, shirtwaists, long skirts, and blue stockings. To those who did know, their apparel was one small harbinger of victory for a new China.

Clementine had seen the rotogravures of the Great White Fleet's parade through Melbourne. Hobson had shown her a cruisebook published to commemorate the global circumnavigation. He had never guessed that the photographs had made such an impression.

Clementine smiled like an almond-eyed Mona Lisa.

"You sailors are all going to hell," bellowed one hatchet-faced dowager in a large hat tied on with a scarf. She appeared to be from a Yangtze River mission. "You and your lady friends, your floozies, are…"

"Well, happy Beatitudes, to you, too, ma'am."

"…going to hell, right quick. You boys come over here, lose your way, and start dressing up your fallen women and disporting them as if they were paragons of womanhood."

Hobson, Harp, and Washboard ignored the lady missionary. The parade advanced, though Shanghai barely acknowledged its existence. Nothing, malevolent or benign caused the Shanghai boilers to alter their pressure settings.

"It's like they're loading the Ark, but dozen by dozen instead of two by two," Harp observed. And, Land of Goshen, they've forgotten the males completely!

Hobson, of course, was the son of lay missionaries. Different missionaries, he thought, with different hopes and aspirations, and insights.

Hobson wondered what tidal wave of rising expectations he had unleashed when he'd encouraged Clementine to buy out her contract.

When could happiness be wrong?

PART IV

THE LAGANING DETAIL

*An inch of time is an inch of gold, but you can't buy
that inch of time with an inch of gold.*
—Chinese proverb

CHAPTER EIGHTEEN

Lane of Lingering Joy, International Settlement, Shanghai,
May 1913

Hobson had just dropped Clementine off at Madam Guan's where she justified her continued food and board as a bookkeeper.

"It's time for you to come with us, seonbae." The term was extremely polite, yet he knew he had no choice. He thought he remembered them from the pork barbecue vault and the violent incident with Persimmon Ma.

He hadn't been up to the Red-Knight's Pawnshop in a while. He had thought that for him, the gold heist was over.

These men whisked him to wharf in Woosung, driving a familiar Marmon.

"Try these on," said the tallest Korean, perhaps their leader.

He pointed to two piles. One displayed the clothes of a Chinese laborer: a pajama bottom and top, with a blue vest. The other showed a Western suit, a shirt with celluloid collar, a tie, and a bowler hat.

"A Chinese laborer, I can understand, but a Western professional man? What profession?"

The tall man didn't respond at first, and then said with a shrug, "Some profession that won't attract attention where you're going."

"Korea?" Hobson could think of no other place where being a Westerner, yet not a member of the United States Navy, mattered. The idea was unsettling. Back to Korea again? He wasn't afraid of going there. He was afraid, instead, that, if given a rifle, he might be inclined to fight for their liberation, and he'd likely never come back. Such a move would be desertion, abandonment of friends, and the betrayal of a commitment.

One of the Koreans was losing patience with him, and handed him the clothes of a Chinese laborer. Hobson found a set that fit.

He became even more confused when the four men hustled him to the river, the Huangpu, and put him aboard a 60-foot junk.

A block-like man emerged from the shadows. "Good evening, *hubae*. We start up Yangtze tonight. You sleep there." He pointed to an empty spot inboard of the ship's painted eyes.

"For the next few days, you must not speak to anyone but me, and even then, outside the hearing of others. We are moving the ingots. Admiral Bulkley gave me a choice. I had to choose who'd be 'the admiral's representative' between you and Lieutenant Junior Grade Draper. I chose you. When we are through, you will understand why."

Yi wore the mandarin-collared gown of a successful Chinese businessman, the attire of a junk owner.

Around them, the Chinese crew readied the junk for departure.

Hobson was both relieved and disturbed. He wasn't being encouraged to desert. However, Korea lay to the east and the head of the Yangtze lay to the west. How would Korean insurrectionists benefit from gold hidden somewhere in eastern China along the Yangtze? If the gold stayed in China, it remained a potential threat to the Chinese economy and helped no one he had bargained to help. Admiral Bulkley had insisted the gold not be set down on Chinese soil. His head was being spun in two diametrically opposite directions. To evade the Japanese, was Yi exercising some strange combination of the complementary forces of yin and yang?

Hobson found a quiet place on deck where he could see more, blocked off all thought of the future or past, and just observed the present. The time had arrived to spirit the Japanese gold out of Woosung and away from Shanghai.

Hobson had been a deck seaman with the landing party at Woosung, though now he was an exalted quartermaster third class petty officer and had developed the quartermaster's lofty view of the world. Quartermasters stood watch on the bridge. They served as lookouts, made log entries of everything from course alterations to weather observations to loading of unusual cargo, read the charts, cared for the navigational equipment, were responsible for all signaling. They also kept track of the ship's boats away and boats recovered, and kept their ships from colliding with all manner of hazards. They observed, they measured, they recorded, they advised. If all the officers came down with food poisoning, it was a good bet the quartermasters could navigate their ships from point A to point B. Quartermasters were a ship's eyes and memory.

As the junk left Shanghai and proceeded up the Yangtze, Hobson fell unconsciously into his quartermaster habits. He'd keep no formal records, nevertheless make mental record of everything. After all, he was the admiral's representative.

Leaving Shanghai, Yi's junk was surrounded by many other watercraft. Hobson kept track of the blue-and-white striped sails of the Chinese River Police boats, nicknamed "fast crabs" because of the speed they could achieve under oars. Yi's junk was nowhere near as colorful. Hobson couldn't detect so much as a dab of paint on its hull, however this wasn't unusual. Nor did it fly pennants of any kind, though it did carry small disk-shaped plaques ornamented with meaningful characters. Its sails had once been the color of a tangerine, but now were little more than a dingy off-white and festooned with patches of mildew.

The fast crabs shuttled about the river, often appearing to move sideways through the current to inspect cargos of market goods and fish, silk cocoons and rice, seeking out contraband cargos of opium and salt. Hobson wondered if a country whose government had collapsed could still have contraband and where exactly any collected custom duties went.

Initially, the land they passed onshore was flat, only occasionally rising into little lumps that served as cemeteries. In China, prime real estate went to one's ancestors. The little lumps hid wild hare and river deer. When Yi's junk passed too close to a bank, it flushed out bouquets of pheasants and coveys of bamboo partridge.

Each day as they sailed upriver, the Yangtze's boat traffic thinned further. Finally, they reached a point where the current cancelled all forward movement, and the captain steered his junk to a village on the water's North China bank.

There, they retained a crew of 40-plus "trackers" to begin the long effort of towing the junk upriver. In other parts of the world, the work of trackers was accomplished by horse, oxen, or steam tractor, China however held tightly to its traditions.

The trackers attached a towing line to the foremast and looped harnesses over their shoulders that merged bamboo fiber into the single towing line. A helmsman remained at the stern while a half-dozen coolies worked a sweep forward that exercised far greater control in keeping the junk parallel to the shoreline. A towed sampan bobbed in the junk's wake, and Yi, owner of both, observed the entire panorama from the sampan with boyish glee.

The trackers' harnesses could be released, for every tracker lived in fear of being dragged backward off the riverbank into the current, and tangled in a rat's nest of lines and harnesses.

Hobson watched from onboard as the onshore trackers pulled the boat in a column of twos to the beat of a drum. The lead tracker called out, "Ayah, ayah!" Sometimes, the trackers' weight was thrust so far forward their heads seemed to levitate just a foot above the trail. Careful footing was everything, Hobson knew, and the trails beside the river were often mere notches or footholds carved by a thousand toes.

Each night, the junk was brought close to shore and secured just off the bank by heavy poles laced across triangular webs of taut lines.

Hobson watched without success for the occasional US Navy gunboat. The Yangtze was the unofficial boundary between North China and South China. To the north, they ate grain, primarily wheat, barley, and millet, and to the south they ate rice.

As the Yangtze narrowed in the following days, the current increased. Eventually, once the Gorges revealed themselves in the distance, Hobson caught Yi, now back aboard the junk, singing to himself in Korean — the song about hiking in the mountains, a song of sadness, of leg-weary travel and travail. This was the first of the Three Gorges, which rose up in sharp contrast to the flat topography of Shanghai that had originally been little more than mudflats, and river silt. The sheer-sided gorges had been carved from majestic striated rock formations and trimmed with evergreens.

Hobson understood Yi was reminded of Korea, also known for its breathtaking mountainous terrain.

"My heart pumps through veins of silver and gold," Yi said,

almost giddily. "I've guarded metals, traded in them, gambled metals, and lost them. I even tried to prospect for metals, unsuccessfully, in North America." He paused as if to recall another refrain of the song. "'No man hears the words gold or silver without suddenly holding his breath.' My family's reputation was tied to gold and silver. These days, my work concerns gold. In my youth, it was about silver." The powerfully built Korean shook his head. "Did you know that all the gold ever touched by man from the beginning of time could be carried in one or two tea clippers, leaving room for additional cargo?"

"It is easy to cut, shape, and draw into threads. It hardly corrodes. Silver tarnishes quickly, gold slowly and little."

Yi's face darkened; his mood had changed. "To Japan, gold can clinch its destiny in the East. It can validate Japan's quick assimilation of the ways of the West and it can be used to implement the techniques of war described by Sun Tzu."

Hobson knew better than to interrupt. Yi didn't strike him as a man to divulge confidences, so this was a rare moment.

"Gold to the United States means vindication of its sense of manifest destiny, yet in this instance the United States is not seeking gold. No, it is only attempting to foil Japan's equally held sense of destiny."

Hobson listened carefully.

"To Korea, gold is synonymous with the Koreans' cry of *mansei*. The world interprets that cry as 'freedom,' though it really means 'ten-thousand years.' We chant Korea will endure for ten-thousand years because we believe Korea will endure as its own land. Gold to me means hope for my country, and the return of my honor."

Hobson knew the old Korean song Yi had been singing about hiking in the mountains and whistled a few bars. He wondered what chords might do as an accompaniment on his abalone-inlaid ukulele.

"I talk too much sometimes," Yi said. "Sometimes it's simply about umyong, fate and fortune, a subject only the ancestors can properly access."

Onshore, the Gorges rose up magnificently before them like the opened jaws of three dragons.

Hobson had held gold, but only in coins. He'd only touched a fifty-dollar gold piece twice. His existence was confined to paydays performed with Mexican silver, which quickly tarnished when exposed to the sulfur in coal dust.

The junk encountered rapids with increasing frequency. Rapids presented steering difficulties for the lumbering junk and were frequently coupled onshore with rough, rocky terrain and narrow footpaths for their trackers. US Navy gunboats did not patrol above the rapids at Three Gorges, however Hobson had heard that was going to change.

He had seen many Chinese watercolors of soaring rock promontories with clinging, cascading plant life, graphic attempts at recording river expeditions like this one. No steam tractor could have negotiated these gorges. Hobson might have enjoyed the trip if not for the risks and the secrecy.

The gorges made him uneasy. Korea had had its bandits, and so did China. He had clambered into the holds and seen the rice buckets. He didn't bother to lift one, because he knew couldn't. Gold was one of the world's heaviest elements. A bucket filled with gold would weigh almost twice as much as a bucket of lead.

Junks were compartmentalized up and down, just like modern steel warships. Yi's junk was vertically divided into three chambers.

Since the collapse of the Qing Empire, bandits had become a part of the Chinese landscape, yet they weren't Hobson's only fear. Japan wanted its gold back and had maintained a spy network throughout China for decades. By now, they could expect Japan was offering a generous finder's fee for the recovery of the ingots through that spy network.

Hobson noticed that Yi, too, looked backward periodically.

He remembered there were two ingots unaccounted for and that unknown left him uneasy. Perhaps they lay at the bottom of the Huangpu River.

Another junk, also towed by trackers, moved upriver toward them. This junk was a conversion, a steam-powered junk. It had no sails, just the vestigial mast stumps needed for towing. The current was running eight knots or more, and few steam-powered junks could carry the fuel to fight a current of that velocity for long. At times, the current in the Gorges might reach fifteen knots. Coaling stations were still rare and wood to burn was rarer. This other junk's trackers trudged with the same "ayah-ayah!" cadence, but it appeared the steam junk was lighter than Yi's junk.

Yi began stationing men with rifles at high points each night when the towing had ended. Crewmen greased the spars used to hold his junk away from the bank and trackers were issued long knives.

The trackers, too, began looking over their shoulders. At one particularly difficult bend, the shoreline track was only the width of a single man. The junk's trackers had to choose their steps carefully.

Yi and Hobson tramped onshore behind their trackers. Yi had given all the crewmen rifles and left only the sweep oarsmen and the helmsmen aboard.

Hobson heard two or three loud thumps, and the junk swerved in the current. He couldn't tell where the shots came from, nevertheless the sound caused a slow and tragic unraveling. A half-dozen trackers dropped to their sides and attempted to dig their heels into rock that would give them firm ground. The vessel's sudden swerve had caused its cargo to shift, or perhaps the junk had hit a rock. In any event, the upriver gunwale dipped, and the junk's masts dropped to a 45-degree angle with the river's surface.

The helmsman abandoned his post and ran to the foremast, waving a great knife.

Hobson looked to Yi, and the Korean's shoulders seemed to sag. *"Seven times down, up eight."*

Yi waited only a moment, and then made a downward slicing gesture with his hand.

Seconds later, all his trackers fell forward as the junk's towing line was cut.

The boat didn't right itself, but instead swung broadside to the current and began to sink. The sweep oarsmen and the helmsmen scrambled into the sampan, and then the junk was gone.

The great *yaolu* sweep oar slowly pin-wheeled down river.

The trek back to where Yi could pay off the trackers and send them on their way was long. The Korean seemed grim yet philosophic. The tracker headman clearly thought he wouldn't be paid. The other trackers seemed to care much less. Yi promised they would get their money soon.

Hobson observed a McCollum & Spuyten steam tugboat racing up the river after their boat. He wondered what salvage work they would risk in that treacherous stretch. The currents intertwined like the braiding in a Manchu queue. The patterns of this queue changed with every rainfall.

Hobson studied the name, "Spuyten.' He remembered his fight with the merchant officer who'd bullied the jinrikisha runners in Shanghai and noticed that Yi was studying that name painted on the tug's wheelhouse. Was there a connection?

Yi, his trackers, and the junk's crew passed through one village and into a second. There, they were met by another boat. It contained a celestial in a blue gown. Yi jumped aboard and spoke with the man for an hour out of Hobson's earshot. Then the blue-gowned man paid off their trackers. Yi took hold of Hobson's elbow and pushed him toward the blue-gowned man's junk.

Onboard that boat, Hobson found the men who had first abducted him in Shanghai. They provided him with the second pile of attire, his Western professional clothes.

The Japanese had lost their gold ingots, and now Yi had lost the ingots as well. Perhaps the salvage tug could raise the junk, though it seemed unlikely. The weight of the rice buckets, the rocky bottom, and the swift currents would have broken the junk apart and scattered ingots. Hobson could only think of dead Ensign Hayes and Yi's hope to finance an insurrection.

Would Yi attempt to drive off the salvage tug and salvage the treasure himself?

CHAPTER NINETEEN

Shanghai, Hongkou District, August 1913

The US General Consulate building was an impressive ornament to the US concession. It was a brownstone, multi-arched building, albeit hardly as majestic as the British or French consulates.

Consul Jameson Hadbury gave Rear Admiral Simeon "Blue Flame" Bulkley a cigar after some small talk about the relative merits of the Perkins and Cody observation kites. Hadbury, Admiral Bulkley knew, was no scientist, no engineer, nonetheless he appreciated that if American naval power was to ever pull even with the preeminent European powers, that equity would be due to technology: kites, steel, boilers, muzzle velocity, dreadnoughts, and so on.

He held it, but did not light it.

Admiral Bulkley knew he needed to handle Hadbury with due care.

Consul Hadbury turned the conversation toward regional politics and his mood grew grave: "The Japanese have been rough in their occupation of Korea since 1910, some say brutal. They argue the Koreans are a backward people, unfit for self-government and in need of guidance and protection. I guess the Koreans are fit for forced labor since reports indicate they're burying a high number of Koreans for every mile of railroad track the Japanese lay. No telling how many are dying in the mines. Large-scale executions have taken place throughout Korea, and our missionaries are included among the dead. The Japanese are stripping the country of anything that grows or is buried in the ground."

Hadbury hadn't stopped to take a breath. Then again, he was on home ground.

Admiral Bulkley gathered his thoughts. He knew the slow climb to his present position had made him, of necessity, increasingly formal and often embarrassingly pretentious.

First, formality allowed him to move incrementally. It gave him time to think. Nothing upset the international delegations and the Navy's bureaucracy like sudden moves.

Bulkley swirled his drink in its glass.

Second, a leader in his position had to underscore his fitness for his position. In wartime, a leader's acts were easy to measure objectively. In an uneasy peace, a leader had to remind his enemies, and his subordinates, that he was knowledgeable, thoughtful, and wise.

The stern face in the painting behind Hadbury scowled Bulkley into a response.

"Without question, they've been clever in their adaptation of Western technology and tactics — whipping the Russians and Chinese — but you're right, they're getting out of hand. I wish the British, their former allies, could get them to act, well, more gentlemanly. Of course, the Navy Department is watching the Nipponese closely. The trouble is how far away they are from us. Our Asiatic Fleet can handle smaller problems, unfortunately the logistics of coal make bringing real Western force to play in the Far East nearly impossible."

Hadbury nodded and drew a small circle in the air with the unlit tip of his cigar, continuing to listen.

"And then, Washington's attention is centered on the Atlantic. We don't have a single battleship this side of the Pacific. As you know, the time is coming when we'll stand toe to toe with the Japanese. Their victories have only made them more ambitious." Admiral Bulkley ran a cigar under his nose, then snipped the end off with a pocketknife. "And the Taft-Katsura Agreement hasn't helped any."

Hadbury nodded agreement.

"Then too, we have our hands full with the Philippines."

Admiral Bulkley was familiar with the ongoing Moro rebels in the Southern Philippines who objected to American rule when Spain turned over the Philippines after the Spanish-American War.

He smiled when he thought of the Battle of Manila Bay, a highpoint of American naval history. He'd been there for that one.

"The Philippine rebels had received support from the Japanese ultra-nationalists," Bulkley added.

The admiral paused and nodded toward what lay outside the window. "Korea is just a *zakuski*, an *hors d'oeuvre*, an appetizer for Japan. They have designs on China. I keep pointing that out to Washington without success."

"A toe-to-toe circumstance may be sooner than you think," the consul said, dropping into a wingback chair that enveloped him like a giant clamshell. "I have been directed by the Department of State to investigate allegations that members of our Navy have participated in the expropriation of another government's bullion, and worse still, have had some ties to..." The consul cleared his throat. "...a sex slavery ring."

The admiral blinked a few times. "You can't be saying that!"

"Never been more serious. I've been directed to undertake an investigation."

The admiral was thoughtful, as if reminded of something. "Our navy then? Someone has been enterprising. You're familiar with naval affairs?"

"Not one iota," Hadbury replied.

Admiral Bulkley searched the consul's face for the barest hint of sarcasm. How much did he know? How much should I tell him?

Bulkley reminded himself that all naval officers were risk-takers. Who else would sail halfway around the world to confront situations where the numerical odds were against them? As a naval officer's authority grew, however, a naval officer was measured more by his ability to balance risk and benefit. Admiral Bulkley had taken a great risk to slow the Japanese juggernaut and he would continue to run that risk for his country's benefit.

"Then, sir, you will need my assistance."

"Most assuredly."

Bulkley sipped his glass of Cyrus Noble. He combed his well-trimmed beard back with his fingertips. "I'll have my flag captain *cum* chief-of-staff initiate an investigation and prepare a report with all due speed."

Hadbury had everything upside down, and what he didn't have upside down he had sideways, Bulkley observed with discomfort.

The Navy was involved right up "to its highest traditions," but he couldn't tell Hadbury because the operation was still active, and the lives of three men, "Skookum" Yi, Lieutenant Draper, and Quartermaster Hobson were still in play, and their lives at risk.

The ultimate application of that gold was uncertain and hostile organizations were converging on all sides.

Bulkley read Hadbury as a man who drew his energy from the formalities of life. He was a man best addressed through formal processes.

"Do you have any idea who is claiming these improprieties?"

"The Japanese ambassador in Washington."

"Did he explain, perchance, why Japan was shipping gold into China?" The admiral replied.

Where did they get the notion that the Navy was involved rather than some triad? Well, at least they hadn't gone through naval channels, Bulkley thought. How much did Hadbury know?

"Oh. Well, then this is serious. Gold and the sex slaves, are they connected? White-slaving or something else? I don't suppose the Japanese use the term 'white slavery?'" Hadbury shrugged indifferently.

If this man were a prizefighter, he'd be 90 percent footwork, thought the admiral, *all maneuver, and afraid to punch.*

"They don't say. They don't say much, other than to complain." The consul nodded and seemed content.

"Are the sons of Nippon alleging we have a *sub rosa* 'Belaying Pin Triad' in our midst? Perplexing."

Bulkley guessed that Hadbury hadn't understood a word of what he'd just said. A "belaying pin" was the original seagoing blunt instrument and a "triad," a Chinese criminal organization of the worst kind. The words together conjured up an image of particularly vile thuggery.

"A mystery, really," Bulkley added to allay Hadbury's concerns. "I've never taken the Japanese for fools. I'll put an officer or two on it immediately." He could afford to be gracious for the time being. Clearly, the consul hadn't a clue.

Consul Hadbury lit his cigar and soon smoke filled the room. If only he knew.

The Japanese were likely whistling in the dark, but they had blown the whistle.

Well, my patented 'Ol' Blue Flame' Bulkley bureaucratic magic will be sorely tested," Bulkley argued to himself as he watched Hadbury walk away. *I can still conjure or unconjure, or find someone on Asiatic Station who can.*

A man could be blinded with a search light.

CHAPTER TWENTY

SECRET
Commander-in-Chief, U. S. Asiatic Fleet
USS SARATOGA, Flagship
Shanghai, China
3 June 1913
To: Naval Attaché, Tokyo and Peking
Subject: Gold ingots, diversion of
Reference: Office of Naval Intelligence (L) cipher message to Commander-in-Chief, U. S. Asiatic Fleet dated 3 June 1913
    1. ONI(L) should be prepared to report in one week to the undersigned on the as-yet undetermined ultimate disposition of in excess of a million dollars in gold ingots recently shipped to Shanghai by the Imperial Japanese Navy and operations to divert said shipment.
    2. ONI(L) should be prepared to assess Imperial Japanese Navy intentions with respect to said ingot shipment and destabilization of China.
    3. ONI(L) should be prepared to counsel the undersigned on any and all potential for negative consequences to the national interest or to this command on operations initiated pursuant ref (a).
    By Direction,
    J. Payson
    SECRET

US Embassy Annex, Tokyo, June 1913

Stuyvesant Draper crumpled the letter, his vision rippling with waves of frustration.

Then he reconsidered.

The letter to his immediate senior, the naval attaché for Tokyo and Peking, was signed by flag captain Payson by direction of Admiral Bulkley. Strange, thought Draper, since Bulkley knew a good deal about the Japanese ingot affair, almost as much as Draper did. Was this some rarified incidence of bureaucratic amnesia?

He placed it on his blotter and attempted to smooth it flat with his hand.

The chief question in Draper's mind was: Where were the Japanese gold ingots now, and if they had reached their destination would they stay there? The flag captain wanted to know. Draper wanted to know. *Everyone wanted to know.*

He was exaggerating, as "everyone" was a small number of people within the Asiatic Fleet. Two ship's crews knew there'd been an irregular night operation, of their number only Hobson knew about the gold. A dozen members of the admiral's staff understood gold was involved. At the moment, Draper speculated, only Yi and Hobson knew the present whereabouts of the gold.

Where was Hobson? Heaven only knew. Draper assumed Hobson was with the gold.

Why would anyone, other than Admiral Bulkley, ask Draper? That was an easier question to answer. When the topic came to information on the Far East, Draper had been designated the fount of all useful local knowledge. After all, the Office of Naval Intelligence came under the Bureau of Navigation.

The Navy had hordes of trained men to watch and chart hazards to navigation offshore. However, when the issue came to the restive masses ashore in the Far East, all information funneled through a single uniformed junior officer — Draper. The United States Navy, presently consumed by such things as steel technology and fuel consumption afloat, had little time to appreciate that many of the greatest monsters that threatened it rested both hind legs on terra firma.

Draper began churning the files and erecting two pillars: one pillar for incineration in the embassy's furnace and one pillar related to the Japanese gold ingot operation. Red-Crowned Crane was all about ingots, not bullion, not nuggets, not dust. It was about gold, not silver, diamonds, or sapphires. Ingots were easier to slip into circulation. Ingots, unlike bullion, could be carried in a pouch, and wouldn't blow or wash away like gold dust. This second pillar, the Japanese ingot files, contained reports going back two decades.

"Sir, do you need some help?" Marine Corporal Carnahan, standing at the door, was looking anything, but polite. Draper had been slapping around files and hurling them on the floor like Zeus dropping thunderbolts. Apparently, someone downstairs, "below," he corrected himself, had complained, and a Marine had been dispatched to enforce good order and discipline upon the peculiar naval recluse in the garret who wore a rumpled uniform, and who appeared to be under a great strain.

Draper tried to reassure the corporal. "Everything's well in hand. Carry on, carry on."

"You're sure, Professor?" The Marine, Draper saw, wasn't satisfied with his explanation.

"Well, you could get me some kerosene and we could burn one stack of all this in situ." Draper had considered dressing the corporal down for not addressing him as "Mr. Draper," as naval custom dictated, but thought an incendiary allusion more efficacious.

Carnahan backed away, clearly viewing junior officers as a particularly treacherous and unpredictable subspecies. He hoped, Draper thought, that a temporary tactical withdrawal might soon catch Lieutenant (Junior Grade) Draper with the kerosene in hand.

However this Marine was borderline insubordinate, and couldn't contain himself. "Would you need a fiddle to go with that kerosene? I've heard tell that good fiddle music makes great fires burn better…sir."

Why had the admiral directed him in writing to investigate an operation he'd helped plan and execute? He was giving the admiral reports on developments almost daily. He was new to Asiatic Station, notwithstanding this made no sense.

Whereupon, Corporal Carnahan disappeared and Draper pondered how to address the easier of his two new problems.

For now, the Kempeitai, Japan's military secret police, Draper suspected, kept his dance card full with nubile *Japonaises*.

All his present girlfriends had Kempeitai connections. He knew they were all quizzed weekly by curious military officers. As a foreign naval officer, Draper was carefully watched. The best he could hope for was a girlfriend who was only an informant, and not on some other more dangerous Japanese organization's payroll, inclined to inviting him over for home-cooked meals.

Keiko was the granddaughter of a daimyo, a pre-Meiji samurai warlord. Yumiko ran a *ryokan,* a boardinghouse for Westerners. Hanako taught English.

From time to time, Draper divulged information, like steel-making developments in Pittsburgh might have a marked effect on naval armor, or was it, gun barrels? The answer didn't matter; steel-making was coming out with new techniques in yearly spurts, so any raw speculation was close to the truth. He was feeding them unclassified information as "secrets." At some point, he would be ready to follow with misinformation.

Any visit by a senior officer required the visited junior officer be inspection-ready. Draper had never done all that well where uniforms and shiny objects were concerned. He knew himself to be a major Irish pennant in human form from the regular Navy viewpoint.

Draper knew he should look upon this new requirement as a diversion, an exercise to keep his mind off the actual risks of an undertaking still in play. He feared a bad outcome. Men and women had died already and many more would die if this effort failed.

Should the plan dubbed "Red-Crowned Crane" come to light, the uproar would be disastrous.

If only Quartermaster Third Class Hobson hadn't been away. Draper had last seen him in Shanghai. Hobson's street, or more properly, waterfront, savvy had provided a welcome counterbalance to Draper's academic skills.

Draper now brushed aside a tangle of folders leaning against an oak cabinet and made an exclamation, in Greek to his professional embarrassment since he was now officially an Oriental-language-dedicated linguist. Spilling over the far edge of his oak campaign desk rested a binder labeled "Red-Crowned Crane tasking."

Draper skipped down three flights of stairs to the Marine corporal's guard station and looked through the embassy window to the sidewalk outside.

"Did you find your kerosene, sir?" Corporal Carnahan asked impassively. "Or fiddle?"

"Decided I didn't need them. I've got some 'Strike anywhere' matches topside,'" Draper said, nodding to his firetrap office above. "However, I might know a naval petty officer with a ukulele."

Outside on the sidewalk, he saw no familiar faces, although one Japanese male waited in the same place as a succession of gray Japanese watchers had for weeks. This fellow, too, wore no facial hair, a hat, and glasses, and appeared to be of military age.

Draper pondered the resolution to his newest problem, not a big problem, and happily unrelated to the operation.

True line officers in their reports had the luxury of a chronological approach. They were always establishing written "plans."

As an intelligence officer, Draper was called upon to synthesize a mass of information stretching across twelve time zones, a decade-and-a-half, and four countries into regular reports to keep an inspecting officer "without any loss of steerage and in the channel." No one controlled the organization of "situations." Situations evolved as snarls of conscious and unconscious competing interests.

Draper untied the ribbon on one folder and examined a faded photograph of a ship, *USS Rainbow*, sandwiched between folders. When had the phrase "Red-Crowned Crane" first come to the attention of the US Navy? He thumbed through the file. It contained documents addressing the tragic Yi 1893 tribute incident in Tientsin, the man's grueling Klondike adventure in 1897-1898, and his wretched first contact with Hobson at Woosung in 1911.

Lieutenant Randolph, Draper's predecessor, had collected the Tientsin and Klondike folders as part of a serendipitous discard file exchange with British naval intelligence. The Woosung folder was the product of an internal survivor debriefing. The survivor had been Hobson.

Draper's assignment here in the Far East had been troubling from the outset. Only when he'd arrived in Tokyo had Draper learned about his predecessor.

"Corporal Carnahan, have you ever heard of datura?" Draper yelled into the hall. He knew Carnahan was out there.

Draper had observed that Carnahan regarded naval officers as little more than bureaucrats. Carnahan tried not to be disrespectful, even so he probably wondered why naval officers even wore uniforms.

"No, sir can't say that I have."

"Particularly nasty poison. My predecessor, Lieutenant Randolph was carted off in a straitjacket. He's in Manila now. They say there's hope for recovery. Randolph spoke Italian. When Japanese is rendered into our alphabet, it is done using Italian rules of pronunciation."

The word "poison" seemed to puzzle Carnahan. It had perhaps never occurred to him that naval intelligence was in any way connected with physical danger.

"There's a mnemonic for datura, 'hot as a hare, blind as a bat, dry as a bone, red as a beet, and mad as a hatter.' When they found Randolph, he had registered nearly all those symptoms. Dry, hot skin — dilatation of pupils along with loss of accommodation — dryness of the mouth and throat, unquenchable thirst — dilatation of cutaneous blood vessels — difficulty in talking — drunken gait — delirium and drowsiness. Essentially, you could say…"

Draper smiled. "…he succumbed to the onslaught of symptoms beginning with the letter 'D'."

Carnahan had probably also assumed that the chief tool in naval intelligence was a set of binoculars applied from a sedate vantage point, unlikely to be more dangerous than a harbor cafe.

"Corporal, you're looking a bit red in the face. You have my permission to unbutton your collar, er, the stock on your blouse. Would you like a drink of water?"

"No, sir." Carnahan coughed.

"In Randolph's case, I was told, there was no death due to respiratory or cardiac failure, though I haven't really read anything official, just scuttlebutt. Someone had slipped powdered datura into his rice. Intelligence officers tend to eat on the economy when gathering information. It takes about 160 ground-up datura seeds to kill a man of average height."

Draper studied Carnahan. Carnahan was blinking like a lighthouse. "Are you sure you wouldn't like a drink of water?" Carnahan shook his head.

Carnahan was now demonstrating the same reaction to that

lecture that Draper had shown upon reporting aboard at the Tokyo Embassy. "Sympathetic symptoms." Draper had been concerned for some time that he had reacted so viscerally. He took comfort in Carnahan's present show of growing discomfort.

"A senior embassy officer told me, 'If you're going to work here, you must inspect what you eat carefully, or eat very slowly so you won't ingest enough to kill you.'"

Carnahan, now beet red, nodded.

"You're probably asking yourself if an antidote or perhaps some preventative procedure might be available? I asked if I might build an immunity by taking datura in progressively larger increments in the same way one could development an immunity to arsenic."

Draper began sorting documents again. He had made three bundles. He stopped to thoughtfully thumb through the Randolph's pillow book collection.

Carnahan, still attempting to clear his throat, looked ready to explode.

"*Sir, and wha-a-at did they say?*" the man finally wheezed.

"The embassy staff was, just laughed."

"For months, I examined all my food carefully, looking for dark pepper-like flecks, and ate slowly so one of two symptoms would take hold sufficiently to preclude any further advance toward the ultimate symptom, respiratory or cardiac failure," Draper concluded with a sigh. "Essentially, naval intelligence is a steady diet of stress and circumspection."

Carnahan, now regarded the "professor" as something special, a dead man walking. He would now show Draper a new deference.

The datura story was true, and it haunted Draper.

Satisfied with resolving the problem of the importune Carnahan, he realized the flag captain's report would require him to establish a more permanent presence in Shanghai.

What amount of twisting and stress made men able to bear a great strain, and what amount destroyed them?

He was being consumed by the urgent need for Japanese warship technology, a concern over the whereabouts of three tons of Japanese gold, and a demand for a Kafkaesque report for the flag captain. Heaven help him if he forgot or overlooked one critical detail.

CHAPTER TWENTY-ONE

American Consulate Annex, Hongkou District, Shanghai, June 1913

The three-story building, part of the American consular complex, was impressive, though hardly as impressive as the Astor House, Shanghai's foremost Western hotel, just a few buildings away. Draper sensed that the consul held court in another, more expansive building closer to the flag pole.

Upon arrival, Draper scanned the consulate annex's ground floor, which was rimmed with offices. His eyes were led upward to an atrium surrounded by balcony halls on the first and second floors with wrought-iron railings.

An impressive spiral staircase rose out of the spacious lobby at the rear of the atrium. The staircase was constructed of finely worked wrought iron and cast-iron plate. It spun upward, clockwise like the staircase in a castle's keep. This stairway was the only way up or down. Desks and bulky furniture had to be hoisted up with block and tackle. The Boxer Rebellion of 1900 had influenced this architecture, Draper concluded. Heaven help them all in case of fire.

"And who might you be?" called a woman looking over the handcart and boxes as Draper and another man entered the lobby and attempted to explain their business to the Chinese security guards.

Her chignon hovered atop her like a thunderhead, surmounted by a bun pierced by pens and pencils. The storm didn't stop there.

"You, of course, have identification?"

She wore an immaculate white shirtwaist blouse with cameo at the throat of its high collar, a Swiss-waist dark skirt, and cream-colored practical lace-up shoes. She matched the hourglass ideal in vogue with admirable symmetry. The ax-like severity of her Roman nose and her thin lips, however, gave Draper pause.

"Lieutenant Junior Grade Stuyvesant Draper, Bureau of Navigation. The gentleman next to me, Lieutenant Fields, is a naval courier." Draper pointed to the thin man beside him. "These are our orders."

He flicked a wad of papers toward Field's holstered sidearm and then slapped the papers on a nearby ornate table. "Where's your strong-room? This will be a temporary situation, even so it is necessary."

"Who will be responsible for these boxes of documents?"

"You will be, ma'am. For now, only I will need access."

"Will I be able to review them?"

"Absolutely not. You have no need to know." Draper suspected this was not a chance interception.

She bristled slightly, but contained her rising ire.

"Well, Mr. Draper, I'm sure that will prove cumbersome. Maintaining and protecting records with an understood purpose is easier. Once on a dare, I rode a toboggan blindfolded over a small cliff near the Androscoggin River. Is this going to be like that?"

She frowned at Draper through large tortoise-shell glasses whose arms ran back precisely from the nine and three o'clock positions on the lenses. The lenses reminded him of the burner plates on a cast-iron stove. A gold chain cascaded from her temples, securing the glasses around her neck. She waited silently.

When he didn't respond, she pecked at each of the sealed boxes with the nib of her pen, jotting down numbers and comparing them with the list of boxes Draper had provided. She unleashed a flurry of questions, each with the pace and impact of drops in a driving rain.

Most of her questions Draper declined to answer.

"More like a sleigh ride behind a team of four under a fox-pelt blanket, I would suggest," Draper eventually responded.

"I see, sir, we are at an impasse." She drew breath into her ample bosom, and released a sigh of resignation. "The Bureau of Navigation? They need classified storage ashore? I find that difficult to credit."

She held out her hand, and Draper caught the fragrance of lilacs. He estimated she was just over twenty years old.

"These boxes will be gone in a few weeks," Draper offered.

The look she gave him suggested he would be the one needing a warm blanket.

"I'm Franconia Knapp, the deputy consul's second secretary, and records custodian here. The strong room is on the top floor. This is Shanghai, you know," she said, as if that answered everything.

As Draper turned away, the corners of his mouth curled upward subtly.

He admired her spunk and dedication, though he doubted his duties would allow time for him to get to know her. He feared the stress and urgency of the project would make him poor company, if it hadn't already made him seem starchy.

He could allow himself no diversions, and he realized he was growing increasingly disagreeable to those around him. He was beset by distractions and had to put a distance between himself and those around him if he was to obtain mental clarity. So much had occurred and too much remained to transpire.

I will not be overwhelmed, Draper told himself, rubbing the bridge of his nose beneath his half-glasses and sighing.

Draper could remember advice from Petty Officer Hobson, who was fond of allegory, during an earlier visit to Shanghai. "Buoyage, Mr. Draper, markers. Set your course and hem in your efforts to concentrate on your desired destination. Channel your efforts. Guide those alongside you with *evidence and persuasion*, since you're in a staff position, and do so before they can blunder onto a reef. Provide coordinates for wreckage and other hazards to navigation. Cover range and bearings to flotsam and jetsam, and most importantly unknown vessels approaching on a constant bearing."

He would say all this while arranging his whipcord sailor's physique around any convenient piece of furniture and briefly flashing his self-effacing, high-cheek-boned smile.

Hobson had no real standing with Naval Intelligence. The Navy had better things to do with a quartermaster third. Translators could be hired, however qualified sailors were not to be frittered away reading the personal correspondence of others. The Navy was as yet unsure that gathering of intelligence was an honorable or productive naval enterprise.

Hobson was a sailor, aggressive and rough around the edges, but Draper knew when to exercise tact. He just didn't have the patience to sustain any such efforts. In any event, in this matter no one had called for him to do so.

The significance of the usage "Red-Crowned Crane" would not be readily apparent to the flag captain, though Hobson's significance as one of the fleet's natural linguists was known to "Ol' Blue Flame" Bulkley and the flag captain, Payson. Hobson didn't have Draper's knowledge of Japanese and Korean characters, but he spoke those languages with far greater fluency.

The characters were images, stylized drawings that long ago had been quick merged symbols that stood for words and syllables.

If only Japanese language materials were the limit of Draper's investigations. He was now acquiring piles of Chinese documents in Shanghai. The Chinese used pictograph characters primarily, but with exceptions, such as phonetics. Many of those Chinese characters had been borrowed by the Japanese and the Koreans. The characters represented the same meaning, but a different word with the same meaning in Japanese or Korean.

Piled against the wall were bundles of documents collected by Draper's agent in the Reverence to Lettered Paper Society and Randolph's pillow books.

In China, inscribed paper could only be destroyed in particular ways. For centuries the Chinese had accorded special respect to the written word. This esteem hearkened back to the days when groups worshipped a god of literature, among others, and only increased with the Mandarin emphasis on scholarship. A special respect for written communication was ingrained, and written communications could only be destroyed in a reverent manner.

Consistent with local practice, the agent's chapter of the Reverence to Lettered Paper Society — one of many in Shanghai — collected inscribed paper, burned it, and deposited the ashes ceremoniously in the Huangpu River.

The bundles stacked like fortifications around his small roll-top desk were the cast-off invoices and memos of the Japanese consulate, its vendors and suppliers, and several Japanese banks and manufacturers. They were more than Draper could ever translate, so he'd hired a few trusted American expatriates to sift through them. Draper could handle Japanese, but Shanghai's Wu dialect required him to hire translators.

He was confident the Japanese burned their most sensitive discarded documents, even so routine documents often left small clues.

A final bundle of pillow books, explicitly illustrated manuals for new brides, had been left by Lieutenant Randolph. Perhaps this was how Randolph soothed his nerves.

The idea occurred to Draper that perhaps the best way to relate the Red-Crowned Crane plan to Flag Captain Payson was through the Tientsin, Klondike, and Woosung folders. He'd follow with his verbal account of the cutting-out expedition.

He could proceed no further without hearing from Hobson, or Yi.

It then occurred to him there was a strong possibility he might never hear from them again.

CHAPTER TWENTY-TWO

American Consulate Annex, Hongkou District, July 1913

Miss Knapp caught Draper dripping on the American consulate annex's first floor staircase landing, not 24 hours later.

The phrase, "Rain outside and heavy weather is in her eyes," occurred to Draper and he sighed inwardly.

"This will not do, Mr. Draper. It simply will not do. Your office and the strong-room already smell of buckwheat noodles and exotic sauces. Complaints have been made. When I say 'buckwheat noodles and exotic sauces,' I'm doing my best to be inoffensive. They smell of garbage and…"

"You're right, it will not do, and candidly garbage is where they come from. I was hoping to find an answer to this problem, sadly my imagination isn't up to the task."

She gave Draper a sharp look, searching for any sign of disrespect.

Still on the verge of exploding, she began again, "The people bringing in these bundles of paper don't provide identification and are reluctant to talk to anyone, except perhaps you."

"Miss Knapp, you're completely correct. I could see something like this coming, regrettably I've been presented with a short schedule and an impossible list of things to accomplish. I'd hope for some revelation, a sign from above, but sadly all I've seen this morning is rain. Could we find a place around here where we might have some privacy and a pot of tea?"

"Fair warning — don't play smart with me, Mr. Draper," she said wheeling about and heading for the street doors.

Draper realized he must fall in behind, and did.

He had too many things to do, and Hobson was still missing. Right now, he was stuck with a story without an ending, a report without a conclusion.

They settled into a noisy half-Eastern and half-Western establishment that was a maze of beaded curtains, curios, and tiny private tables.

Each alcove was an explosion of color. Casual establishments in Shanghai never used a single color when several would do.

He looked at Miss Knapp and decided to take a risk. "What I'm about to tell you must be kept a secret to the greatest degree possible. I suppose you'll have to tell the consulate staff something, but just say as little as possible. We want to avoid an international incident."

She peered at her tea through her large glasses. "Is that true?"

"Yes, you'll be helping me with part of a larger challenge."

Something had changed in her demeanor. Was she leaning toward him?

"I suppose no confidence man would start his pitch with anything as disagreeable as garbage. Trifle with me, and you'll rue the day. You'll be booted out of the consulate annex and whatever you have in our strong-room will be turned over to higher naval authority with a stoutly worded complaint."

Her glasses were down and resting on their chain. Her large, dark eyes had a brightness to them that he hadn't noticed before.

He described the Society and its origins and the problems with processing the papers, especially why the processing must not draw attention. He explained the gleaners and interpreters must not meet each other.

"Why?" she asked.

"Because then someone could start working their way down the processing line to this consulate."

He stressed that he must find a way of disposing of the valueless papers as well as recovering the valuable paper.

"Why again?" she interposed.

"Troublemakers can deduce what we find valuable by knowing what we don't find valuable."

"Bridge House Print Shop where the consulate does all its printing has a large warehouse," Knapp stated confidently. "They have a discreet way of discarding extras of written consulate materials. The consulate has similar problems, just not as sensitive as yours. We'll have someone we trust destroy your documents, using their facilities"

After she asked a few more questions and made a few more suggestions, he considered the problem solved.

She suggested the Bureau of Navigation rent a small shop next to the consulate. That would keep him in the consulate annex, and with proper procedures, keep strange odors and disruptive strangers out.

Knapp had ingeniously resolved the problem and made the system more efficient.

"There now, I've helped you," she said. "Now, you're going to help me. I want you to promenade me."

"You want a prom, a coming out? You want to be a debutante?" Draper wondered if the price was too high.

"Don't be silly. I'm a schoolmarm, and dairyman-trapper's daughter. I milked my father's cows, drove his team of draft horses, and tended his trap lines. I'm not sure I want to attract the attention of polite society in a grand way just yet, however I wish to have options. By 'promenade,' I mean be taken on long leisurely walks once a week. That's something my beaus and I did for entertainment at the Farmington State Normal School in Maine." She gave him a meaningful look.

"Shanghai is both exotic and daunting. Unescorted women get bundled off the street on a daily basis. I'm unattached, unchaperoned, and frequently unescorted. Unescorted women — even during the day — are not viewed as ladies. Westerners are kidnapped for ransom every day. I wish to see Shanghai, on the other hand I need someone who knows something about the culture to help me see it."

"I can appreciate why you'd feel like that," he interjected. "So many strange and beautiful things to see. In many respects, their way of thinking is different, yet they arrive at conclusions we can understand."

"I've been here six months and my time has been a matter of slogging through every working day at the consulate annex and returning every night to a ladies residence hotel. My life is presently confined to twenty blocks in the Hongkou District. That can't continue. I was told what to expect when I came here. This is my great adventure. This is the way I've decide to adapt."

Draper appreciated a woman who knew her mind, however he wasn't going to get ahead of himself.

"You must introduce me to everyone we meet, male and female, the short and the tall, rich and poor, lame and halt, quick and dead."

"I will keep introductions to the dead to a minimum," Draper said. Was there mischief in this farmer's daughter?

"I wish to see parks," Knapp continued, "curios, the Great Tow Path..."

"...the Bund?" Draper attempted to clarify.

"Yes, if that's what it is called, the Old Chinese City, the French Quarter, the shops boulevard..."

"Nanking Road? Bubbling Well Road?" he suggested.

"I can't really say. Ordinary Chinese life, plus a rugby game, a music hall, a horse racing track..."

Draper realized she'd had the idea of these explorations bottled up too long.

"The Race Club?"

"Er, yes, the Race Club. I understand monetary wagering may take place there. I will make no monetary wagers myself, of course. I adhere to the view expressed in the parable of the talents. That which comes into our hands should only be placed at risk for a larger purpose than ourselves. The sheer excitement would be enough." She raised her chin, indicating conclusion.

"I understand, ma'am. I'm Dutch Reform, myself," he assured her.

"Then you appreciate my position. And my list may include a few places where genteel women are not generally expected."

He had never been to many of these places on her "promenade" list, even so her demand appeared achievable, even inviting.

A waiter hurried by, setting in motion one of the many glass wind chimes. Draper could hear others in the distance. Here at least, they would have no surprise interruptions.

"I would think, though, that you lost your bargaining advantage when you provided me with a full-blown plan prior to setting this particular consideration. You must consider me either a fair man, or a man who enjoys the company of adventurous women."

"I'm given to understand that naval officers are capable of both." Knapp tapped her fingertips on her saucer for a moment, then added, "You have introduced doubt to this negotiation. Perhaps I should take heed and simply consider you 'an interesting man.' Is that acceptable?"

Draper hesitated.

"Upon reflection, I will insist upon one other condition. I assume you have more than one uniform. When you work at the consulate annex, kindly present yourself with a freshly starched uniform daily. When we promenade, you must be appropriately resplendent."

So, his reputation for dishevelment had preceded him. He understood and accepted. He did wonder how to interpret "appropriately resplendent" when coupled with the phrase 'in a few places where genteel women are not generally expected.'"

CHAPTER TWENTY-THREE

American Consulate Annex, Hongkou District, June, 1913

"Would you like to visit Nanking Road, the retail district?" Draper asked.

"By the Old Lord Harry, that's an excellent idea. The consulate annex is closed to the public on Wednesday afternoons. Will that be the extent of it, shopping? Will I be seeing China?" Knapp gave him a sidelong look.

"Yes. Well, one of its infinite parts. As for the extent, shopping in Shanghai, that could consume a whole week, not just an afternoon. The population of Shanghai is one million people. Many will have something they want to sell you."

Draper was growing more comfortable.

"Clearly larger than Boston or Portland," Knapp acknowledged. "An afternoon should work just right. I've been putting off some purchases since I arrived. I propose to dress practically. Will that do?"

"Assuredly. Shanghai has two seasons, wet and dry. This is the dry season, though you must always allow for humidity."

He'd reminded himself to turn over a set of dress whites to the stewards on *USS Saratoga* with ample time and directed the stewards to lay out his civvies.

Draper's knowledge of women was uneven, ultimately he was convinced they as a sex thought strategically. The first of her promenades had to address logistics. If this was a campaign that entailed adventure and meeting people, then walks to parks, the French Concession, the Old City, and the track could wait. She must address the proper attire, and accoutrements to achieve her professional and personal aspirations. She needed new armor for a new battlefield.

"You didn't wear your uniform? I must say you look quite dashing in your uniform these days. You also didn't wear your sword? Shall I be safe?" she asked with false severity. "Is that a 'Panama' hat like the one Teddy Roosevelt wears?"

Draper wore a *pongee* Norfolk jacket with bellows pockets and off-white trousers. He decided not to tell her he'd worn a bowtie, rather than a long tie, because Hobson had once observed that in a brawl anything that dangled low from the neck could become a potential noose.

"You have a parasol and a cape. If local Algerine pirates do threaten, I will ask to borrow them both. As for you, you put Camille Clifford to shame."

Clifford had won a contest for her personification of illustrator Gibson's ideal. Draper swept the back of his hand to indicate her garments from the top of her beflowered, high-crowned straw hat to her "practical" shoes.

Draper was pleased Knapp wore a walking dress that didn't brush the ground as some "fashionable" women did. He wasn't sure about the color of her ensemble, though he had heard the term "dusty rose" once, and he guessed it applied here in variations. He detected no evidence of whalebone or wire stays; her silhouette was a natural one. With that thought barely contained, he offered her his arm.

"This is an umbrella, not a parasol, sir. I've seen enough of the wet season to know about the importance of an umbrella. This is a cotton shoulder cape, I crocheted it myself." She spun and it flared nearly horizontal.

Draper bowed. "As an officer, I'm allowed to wear civilian clothes in off-hours under certain circumstances."

The large volume of her hat matched the volume of her hair. She wasn't going to lose that hat. The low heel on her shoes ensured she possessed the ability to make the most of the afternoon.

"I've once walked twelve miles in hip-deep snow," she said, catching Draper's glimpse at her shoes. "As I've said, I'm no powder-puff debutante."

"And how shall I address you?" Draper asked.

"'Miss Knapp' will do." Her words were stern. "Our promenades are strictly a business undertaking, a matter of mutual contractual benefit. They shall constitute nothing more."

"Well then, naval officers below the rank of commander are traditionally addressed as 'mister.' I'm a lieutenant junior grade and fall into the category. Perhaps at some point you will feel comfortable addressing me — my friends do — as 'Van,' the first syllable of my middle name."

"We shall see," she muttered, and she said no more.

The walk from her hotel in Hongkou to the Astor House Hotel was short. There, they boarded the British tram that crossed the Garden Bridge to where the Bund intersected Nanking Road.

The Garden Bridge was a barricaded checkpoint and several barricades and checkpoints could be found throughout the city. Shanghai was on a near-wartime footing in the midst of the Second Chinese Revolution.

Nanking Road was the primary retail district in Shanghai. At the Bund end, Nanking Road offered premier foreign shops and department stores. Moving west, Chinese shops became more plentiful.

General Shih-kai Yuan had been a Qing general. When he saw he had no future with the Qing Dynasty, even if he defeated the Nationalists, he maneuvered the abdication of the child emperor, and switched sides in 1911. Overnight, he became a Nationalist general. The Nationalists didn't take long to realize that Yuan didn't really support Nationalist principles, simply the Yuan cause, and by that time Yuan was the Nationalists' most powerful leader and a dictator with an army at his disposal.

Yuan's forces now held the Woosung forts and arsenal, and General Ch'i-mei Chen's Anti-Nationalist forces were just days from attacking the Woosung Forts, and perhaps Shanghai.

"May I suggest we get off here, take a quick look at the European stores, but do not purchase," Draper said. "As we go down the road, I'm told we may find Chinese products with good workmanship at considerably better prices. We'll be coming back this way in any event. Many of the shops, both European and Chinese, deliver."

He was not indispensable. She could find the way back to Nanking Road on her own. The weight of the Red-Crown Crane plan made this diversion all the more welcome. He needed to think. The consulate annex walls had already started closing in on him.

"Oh look, I made this!" she said, pulling what appeared to be something like a menu from her purse with a giggle. "I forgot to mention it. I cut out the advertisements for all the likely Nanking Road shops I could find in yesterday's *North China Herald* and arranged them by intersecting street. They won't fall off. I used mucilage."

Today, she wore smaller, rimless glasses. Her eyes were shining with expectation of the walk, he concluded, not necessarily his "contractual" participation.

Draper pointed out the many warships in the roadstead off the Bund: French, Italian, German, Austro-Hungarian, Russian, Japanese, British (which contributed the largest number), a few Chinese, and, of course, American. "This is where the East and West truly meet."

Draper explained the ship types and their purposes. Miss Knapp's questions showed surprising interest, even excitement.

"I've seen many ships from the consulate annex. Now that I know what they are and who they are, I can imagine their crews sitting down to dinner, sending flag signals, doing their laundry, or firing their great guns."

They turned up Nanking Road into a confused palette of color and humanity.

"The raiments, the raiments," she cried. "I've never seen so much silk in daylight! Oh, how do all these women dress on Sundays?"

"I'm not sure 'Sunday-best' means as much here in Shanghai," Draper suggested. "At least, to the Chinese."

Miss Knapp put her fingers to her lips. "I suppose I'm still a farmer's daughter, but I shall not apologize. My quiet background makes this all so much more wonderful to me."

He wasn't surprised that she was overwhelmed by the clothes, banners, signs, and ribbons. They saw Easterners in Western clothing, Westerners in Eastern clothing, and many mixtures of both. The sidewalks couldn't hold the throngs. Pedestrians on both sides of the street established an unofficial right-of-way, a second side-walk's width into the street. As a consequence, Nanking Street was jammed with jinrikishas, sedan chairs, and trams. The turbaned Sikh store guards, doormen, and policemen all looked dangerous and seven feet tall.

Draper smiled. This woman was a pistol. Fortunately, the stores along Nanking were numbered in the Western style.

"Well, you have a plan. Press on, press on, though kindly slow down when you see a men's shoe and boot store. Or a book store."

Draper hastened to keep up, as Miss Knapp teeter-tottered between the dictates of dignity and her inclination to skip through the crowd.

Americans were easy to identify by appearance and most times confirmed by attire, Draper was quick to introduce Miss Knapp.

The crowd now was packed cheek by jowl and Draper habitually checked reflections in the shop windows. If they were being followed, their stalker would have to remain close. As a gentleman, he was hindered by the necessity to walk on her street side, away from the shop windows. Her frequent stops, on the other hand, gave him the opportunity to make a casual partial-pivot and scan the crowd. He had no cause to anticipate undue attention, despite the fact each of the countries commanding all those warships in the roadstead were looking for an edge to dominating the sea-lanes of the Pacific.

He kept her on his right side for another reason. He had his military .45 tucked in his left-hip jacket pocket in a right-grip suede pocket-holster. That had required his tailor to reinforce the jacket and sew a few extra buttons into the bottoms of his hip pockets. The Colt 1911 was bulky and heavy, but it had proved itself in the Philippines. Once or twice he had tried a shoulder holster, though Shanghai in the summer was an open-air Turkish bath.

The day should have been a happier one. The sun was out, and the sky was clear. He had a lady lively and attractive on his arm — but he couldn't shake free of the questions that hung over him like a Sword of Damocles.

Where was Hobson? Where was Yi? Where were the Japanese ingots? Where were the two missing ingots? If the Red-Crowned Crane plan was a failure, what would the retribution be and where would it come from?

Draper wasn't allowed in Miss Genevieve's Foundations. So, he found a jinrikisha, and gave its owner a coin to rent his street-side seat. The jinrikisha-man looked at the coin doubtfully. "No pull?"

"No pull. I sit. I watch. I think."

"Ah, think." He chained the wheels. "I be back by'n'by, not long. Here newspaper."

Draper looked at the newspaper, yet his mind was elsewhere.

Miss Knapp swirled out of the undergarment shop with undiminished energy. "Wake up, dear man. I will not let you spend this fine afternoon dozing in the street. Ah, Miss Genevieve's Foundations was such a successful enterprise.

They were now well up Nanking Road. They walked down a man-made canyon bracketed by peaked, mansard, and pagoda curl roof lines and clock towers. On either side flowed story-high banners emblazoned with bright characters. The road surface was a Western blend of severely horizontal and severely vertical stones, cement, and tram rails, yet above, the architecture was all whimsical curls and flourishes.

Draper gestured his companion into a small dumpling shop with a three-bladed fan airing out the smell of chives, shellfish, and sandalwood. "I don't see any Western utensils. Can you show me how to operate those?" Knapp said, pointing to chopsticks and smiling enthusiastically.

Draper asked the waiter for some twine and paper and he improvised tweezers by folding the paper into a wad and then tying the wad two-thirds up the chopsticks as a fulcrum.

"There, these are training chopsticks. Eventually you won't need the wad of paper and the twine."

Draper explained the assortment of dumplings, and they ordered several varieties. When the waiter brought their order, Draper inspected it carefully.

"Sometimes they mis-hear us and serve us something other than we ordered, "Draper explained apologetically before he let her eat.

Miss Knapp admired his attention to detail. He ate slowly, she remarked, for a man she had judged to be sprightly and otherwise determined in his actions. He had decided beforehand not to mention his datura concerns.

"Those were delicious, and that was elegant," Knapp volunteered as they left. Draper bought her a set of cinnabar chopsticks as they were leaving.

While they worked their way to the west, the crowds thinned.

After a few more stops, Draper sensed they were being shadowed.

"Miss Knapp, I believe I know of an interesting curio shop on the side street to our right."

He diverted her. After going up to the side street a few yards, he came to a stop. "I guess I was wrong. This is the wrong street. We should return to Nanking Road."

He turned about face to see three Chinese men seemingly unconnected, one in traditional workman's attire with a bandana around his forehead, one in Western dress wearing a newsboy hat, and a third in a mixture of both and wearing a straw boater. They were oriented in different directions, and each was consumed by inspecting an item in his hand that was better inspected remaining stationary. One inspected a sales flyer, the other inspected something on flimsy note paper, and the third was wiping something off his hand with a rag. They had been caught flatfooted. Now the object was to look ordinary and bored.

"Yes, let's find a good curio shop. Perhaps I can discover something that will amuse Uncle Hiram," she said.

He decided not to tell her they had company. He'd look hopelessly dramatic if he were wrong.

He located several curio shops before she found one with something appropriate for her relative, an elaborate spinning whirligig carved in ivory. "Uncle Hiram likes various gadgets as well. That's what people Down East do in the winter, make gadgets or play with them. I'll find something else for him eventually."

They were nearly at the junction of Bubbling Well Road and Nanking Road when Draper spotted Lieutenant Commander Wheelwright, captain of the collier, *USS Pluto*.

Wheelwright's square jaw reminded Draper of a Leyendecker illustration in a shirt advertisement, and it was too late to divert Knapp's attention. Wheelwright was every woman's heartthrob and every mother's ideal son-in-law.

"Wheelwright, has our prodigal sailor returned?" asked Draper, determined to draw something of value from the meeting.

"Draper, how are you? Do you mean Hobson? No, we haven't heard from him. He seems overdue, but he is Admiral Bulkley's representative, great responsibility there. I'm worried about him. *USS Pluto* needs him."

He turned to Knapp and touched the visor of his pith helmet. "Now who is this exceptional representative of the fairer sex?"

"Miss Knapp's from the American consulate."

She glowed, acknowledged the compliment, and offered her hand, vertically not horizontally.

Wheelwright was in civvies, too. He wore a hound's-tooth linen jacket, a striped shirt with a celluloid collar and long tie, and white duck trousers.

"Out for a stroll? The professor is the perfect guide for Shanghai's nooks and crannies. He can decipher all those brush-stroked notices the Chinese put over their doors and in their front windows."

"The professor?" She looked sidelong. "I guess he's been holding back. A naval officer and professor, both?" She gave a brief laugh. "I've noticed his ability to guide is well above the average, sir, and he looks upon shop signs with deep understanding. Had he been born earlier, he might have prevented the confusion of tongues and saved the Tower of Babel," she said, squeezing Draper's forearm.

"I don't think I'm ready to address the confusion of tongues just yet. I have confusion enough to address here in Shanghai," Draper offered. "Nor would I ever attempt to elicit sympathy from a naval ship captain. For at best that would only encourage them to inventory their own tribulations."

Knapp had appreciated the cleverness of Wheelwright's initial jibe, but hoped Wheelwright would move on.

Wheelwright looked at his pocket watch and shook his head. "I have a meeting and need to catch the next steam launch to *Pluto*. Draper, these days, I expect your alarums and excursions are on a higher order than mine, though I trust you'll handle them with style."

Knapp nodded as if to confirm the compliment. She was tiring of all this courtliness.

Draper wanted to scan the street.

Had they lost their shadows or had they just gathered more?

CHAPTER TWENTY-FOUR

Nanking Road, International Settlement, Shanghai, June 1913

Upon reaching Bubbling Well Road, Draper and Knapp agreed to head back. They crossed to Nanking's opposite side and located the next designated tram stop. Draper paused to find a shop window. Discovering one, he searched the reflections behind him — in this section many of the shops were open-air — and shortly spotted the three men he had noticed before. They were spaced out, and seemingly unconnected. Contrarily, now they had reversed direction too.

"Miss Knapp, mounting and departing Shanghai trams is hazardous. Why don't we do a little training drill? It'll be a lark."

"Mr. Draper, I've ridden trolleys in Portland and Boston. I'm not sure how the different name they use for trolleys makes the hazard any greater, but if you say we should do some skylarking, I'll take the bait."

Draper didn't like her metaphor.

When the tram came up, Draper saw the first man, the day-laborer in a headscarf, move swiftly past them, probably to the next tram stop down the line. The second man, a clerk with prospects, in a jacket, tie, and newsboy's cap, waited behind Draper and Knapp. The third man, dressed in an ankle-length tunic and straw-boater stayed behind and waited for the next tram. Draper committed them to memory: "Headscarf," "Newsboy," and "Strawboater."

The trams moved slowly. A man walking at a brisk pace could keep up with a tram.

Just as Knapp was about to board, Draper pulled her elbow and let the second tail board first. "I'm sorry, do you have a few wen?"

he said to Ms. Knapp, naming China's coin of smallest denomination. "I don't think I have any pocket change."

As soon as Newsboy climbed aboard ahead of them, Draper released her arm. "Never mind. I have some change after all. We can't hold everyone up."

Knapp looked at him strangely.

They boarded the tram from the front sidewalk side — about five feet from the curb — and gave their money to the trainman who sat on a stool on the tram's "front balcony." The tram had four exits, on the right and left at the extreme front, and on the right and left of the extreme rear. Bench seats ran the length of the tram. If Newsboy was intent on shadowing them closely, he would do so preferably from behind, unnoticed, but Draper had reversed their positions by fumbling for change. Now, Newsboy had to pick a position about midway down the tram so he could watch all the exits.

Draper led Knapp to a location right in front of the rear street-side exit. Just after they made the next stop, he took hold of her arm, whisked her onto the rear balcony, and out the tram's rear street-side door.

"Mr. Draper, I fear this is going to be an expensive game, and we're going to be hit by a handcart, carriage, jinrikisha, or a coach and four."

"No, I don't need any more wen," he said. "We need to take a different tram. No worry, we can go on doing this forever."

She rolled her eyes.

They were now standing in the middle of the street and they had given the Newsboy the slip. They walked back to the stop as their tram departed and waited. They didn't have to wait long.

They boarded this time from the rear. Straw-boater appeared to be napping about two thirds up the sidewalk-side bench.

"We're going to have to do it again. That's one of the three men who are following us."

"Following us? Now you're being silly. I'm not sure I'm enjoying this at all."

"Next stop, we're going out the front street-side door," he said, trying to make it all sound routine.

"We've gone only two stops and exited twice. This isn't making sense."

"Consider it a formality. Everyone watches everyone in Shang-hai." Yes, he thought, when three tons in Japanese gold ingots have gone astray.

She gave him a look and his hopes for the day vanished into the ether.

"Okay, the next stop is right up here."

He started tugging her up the car, when he stopped abruptly, and she found herself tugging him in the same direction.

Strawboater's traditional tunic was buttoned diagonally from the neck under the right arm. Surprisingly he had an isolated pearl-shaped button midway between where his belly button would be and where the top of the inverted U that shaped where the top of his rib cage would be.

Draper didn't touch the out-of-place button, but Strawboater's body swayed, and his hat tumbled to the floor and began to roll. What Draper saw was not an out-of-place button, but the decorative end of a hatpin. The sharp end of that hatpin had pierced the man's heart.

"That's him, the second follower. He's dead." He said it, and then wished he hadn't said anything at all.

Several of the passengers stood up, encircled the still-seated body, and began to argue. Knapp yelped as a man in a long white tunic and a blue frogged vest pulled off her shoulder cape and rushed to the front street-side door. He paused, and then vaulted out of the slowing tram.

She took off after him. "That's my cape you've glommed, you plagued gorby bird! I want it back!"

Draper couldn't locate Knapp, nor could he see the man who had stolen her cape. His mouth was dry, and he knew the afternoon was not going to end well. He dog-trotted forward, not sure which way the thief and murderer, or Knapp, had gone.

Dodging donkey carts, street touts, pedestrians, and jinrikishas, he suddenly spotted a red and black fully-enclosed sedan chair going in the opposite direction. Two burly porters carried their colorful lacquered box aloft on two poles. Normally, sedan chairs this ornate carried an affluent or influential passenger. Some sedan chairs were longer vertically, so the occupant could sit up. This one was longer horizontally, so the occupant could recline like Cleopatra.

As the first porter approached him, Draper focused on the chair's front door. The door was one-piece and hinged at the top, not two-piece and hinged both sides, opening at the middle as he had seen before. The door wasn't fully closed and a folded segment of *Franconia's* shoulder cape protruded from the bottom. Kidnapping, in broad daylight off busy Shanghai streets, was common.

Draper had no way of telling who was in the sedan box as it didn't have curtains or windows. This sedan chair only had louvers, and the louvers were shut. Draper felt sweat trickling down his spine.

He knew she couldn't have gone far.

Draper reached into his pocket, pulled out his .45 caliber handgun, and pistol-whipped the first porter. The front end of the sedan chair went down on its front poles. He pulled at the cape and the door popped upward.

Knapp wasn't inside, but a huge celestial — a wrestler perhaps — clamped onto Draper's free hand and tried to put a wet rag over his face. He was attempting to yank the naval officer into the sedan car enclosure. The image of a dentist's chair whipped through Draper's mind, and he realized he could smell ether. The scent of ether and the rag were connected.

When had he started thinking of her as "Franconia"?

The pistol-whipped porter was now up. He grabbed Draper from behind and started pushing him into the sedan box.

Draper turned, dropped to one knee, and fired upward into the first porter. Then lifting the door again, he poked his head into the box, and fired at the huge man who smelled of ether. The contained space amplified the shot and the flash from his Colt ignited the traces of ether.

The bullet must have gone right through the massive man in the enclosure and into the second porter because the red and black sedan chair toppled onto Draper. The huge man, floating dead in a harness above him, was dripped blood onto his pongee jacket. The harness wasn't there for comfort; it was for leverage.

Both his ears were ringing. Nanking Road was always loud and fractious, still now Draper could hear screams of fear and roars of anger. Somehow, all the noises sounded as if they were generated through a xylophone.

"A red-hair has attacked a bridal procession," a street tout yelled.

"'Red-hair' was one of the names the Chinese reserved for Europeans.

Two Sikh policemen in turbans, khaki uniforms, and Sam Brown belts pulled Draper out by the legs and began beating him with lathi.

"I'm am an officer in the United States Navy. A lady and I, we've, we've, we've been the subject of a kidnapping attempt. Stop beating me. Stop!"

"Being still, being quiet, sahib, we pummel you fiercely now, or the crowd will tear you apart. Perhaps kill you."

Draper lifted his arm to parry the blows from the lathi. "Navy, Navy. Nava…" he mumbled.

He glimpsed Knapp rushing in his direction. She'd stopped running at some point.

And then all was quiet.

The Minotaur Cafe, International Settlement, Shanghai, June 1913

"Mr. Draper, Mr. Draper, dear man, no, no dozing please, this is the second time today," a woman pleaded despondently.

Draper tried to open his eyes, but they were just slits. He touched the bandage round his head. His head felt swollen, and he couldn't open his eyes completely.

"What happened? Where am I? What's all that ringing and background noise?"

The woman spoke to a man, and someone was raising Draper's head and putting something soft under his head. Her voice sounded familiar.

"Where are we, sergeant?" the woman asked.

"We're in a back room in the Minotaur Cafe near the French Concession. I'm Sergeant William Ewart Fairbairn of the Shanghai Municipal Police. My Sikhs and a couple of His Majesties' tars thought we ought to pull you both off Nanking Street, and out of sight, despite the fact this man was giving as well as he got."

Is he under arrest?" she asked.

"Certainly not. With two shots he killed three of the Green

Gang's most dangerous members, including a lieutenant and a no-torious enforcer. Did me a great favor, he did. The latter two, he took out with a single shot."

As an afterthought, he added, "I'm glad he took care not to wound any of our city's honest citizens."

Draper realized the woman was Knapp. His eyes wouldn't focus.

"Miss Knapp here tells me you're a serving officer in the Yank Navy, so I don't have to be concerned that you're carrying a firearm with all that goes on around the Woosung Arsenal these days."

Draper found he could identify the outline of the burly police sergeant addressing him.

"He's with the Bureau of Navigation," Knapp said, speaking again. She was alive. She was safe.

"Oh, yes, but of course. He was taking soundings on Nanking Road."

The room smelled of rum, coffee, fried eggs, and mildew. Draper's eyes were beginning to focus. He sensed they were in a walk-down establishment.

"He is." Draper realized she was at a loss what else to say.

"I am with the Bureau of Navigation." Draper felt he had to take control of this conversation.

"We haven't had many attempted abductions of cartographers this year. That's what you are, a cartographer? Or a chronicler of tides and currents?"

Draper studied the nautical bric-a-brac tacked up on the walls slowly coming into focus. Knot display boards and framed post-cards of British warships were everywhere.

"I'm a linguist."

Draper had been unceremoniously laid out on a table. His arms crisscrossed his chest and his bloodied Panama hat had been placed where they intersected.

Knapp and Fairbairn were at his feet. He could see her clearly now. He realized her shoulder cape was under his head.

"Ah, perhaps you're worth something to them?" Sergeant Fairbairn observed. "A ransom? Nothing criminal, no opium dealing, no white-slaving?"

"No, absolutely not," Draper croaked.

"A fourth man on a Nanking Road eastbound tram was expertly dispatched with a hatpin…" Fairbairn hadn't stated it as a question, though it was. He followed with: "Miss Knapp, did you or Mr. Draper have anything to do with that?"

Draper was still trying to understand his location. "Minotaur" was the name of a famous warship. Was that the origin of the name, or did it come from the establishment's labyrinthine layout. He could feel his attention drifting.

"By the Old Lord Harry, we did not." She looked concerned. Draper was glad to be alive, despite the fact his every bone ached and his head ached twice as much as the rest of him.

He was trying to remember the trams and the sedan chair. "Two others were involved. All three were taking turns following us. We tried to elude them. I had no idea what they were up to. Never saw the other two after the fellow in the straw boater displayed a pearl button a few inches above the belly button."

"No loss. The lad was a member of the Three Harmonies Society. Very well-known in the wrong circles. Another favor I'll have to repay some day. Your hearing off? Carry a Colt 1911 myself. Wouldn't give tuppence for a Webley. Great stopping power, but in a closed space it will make the ears ring, don't it?"

"What's that noise? Is that music?" Draper realized he had difficulty ordering his thoughts. His ears were ringing and every sound had a tonal quality.

"Some call it that. It's that raggedy-timing music. If I'm not mistaken His Majesty's tars in the bar have just toasted you, and in homage the piano player is playing a tune I believe is called the 'Ragtime Cowboy Joe.' Two of 'em helped bring you in, I think they have a little ceremony planned. Royal Navy full of ceremonies. I did a hitch in the Jollies, the Royal Marines, me-self," Fairbairn clarified.

"I don't know how these two triads are going to take this. It looks like they were competin' for something," Fairbairn added.

"Perhaps my shoulder cape?" Miss Knapp snipped. She looked as if she were floating down the rabbit hole and not enjoying it. She rearranged the cape beneath Draper's head.

Knapp was moist eyed. "My shoulder cape was bait for a trap. The whole thing was a simple box-drop trap. Something you'd use to trap a small animal. The minute you jiggled the cape, they sprung the trap." She apparently knew whereof she spoke.

"They ignored me watching it all. I never saw the man in the frogged blue vest again." She held up the blue vest on the tip of her umbrella. "He left this behind on the street. I went to pick it up, and he, Mr. Draper, went right by me, searching for that man and my shoulder cape."

Draper thought the man in the blue vest had likely discarded his long tunic also. Readiness to change his appearance was part of his plan. Knapp began to shiver.

"It all worked out for the better, Miss. They're not going to try a second time without reinforcements. Mr. Draper, you'll need a few stitches and perhaps a cast or two. We can take you to a facility of your choice, English or American. I'll generate a police report with your name badly misspelled — so the press can't find you, but which you can provide to your superiors for verification — indicating you stopped a kidnapping, though I won't point out it was your own.

Fairbairn continued, "When they put in the stitches, ask them not to do the stitches too tight. A good scar or two will have great value in future donnybrooks."

He held up his palms and then displayed his forearms, which were latticed with scars. "I'd recommend, once you get out of hospital, you stick to three locations for the next fortnight, *USS Saratoga*, the naval launch to the consulate, and the consulate compound."

Draper assumed Franconia had told Fairbairn he shared his time between the consulate and the flagship.

Then he added kindly, "If you're not in a hurry, the layabout tars in the bar would like to toast you in person. Now it's going to be like a wake and you on the table will be sort of like a talking corpse. A rare honor, I'd say."

"Just so the piano player doesn't play 'Grandpa's Ailments,'" Draper quipped.

CHAPTER TWENTY-FIVE

Knapp sat in a fan-backed rattan chair with her hands clinched tightly together. She looked confused, chagrined, and upset. Draper assumed he had destroyed any chance of reciprocal interest. An afternoon involving theft, murder, assault, and kidnapping, was no one's runaway success.

"The shoulder cape meant nothing to me, though I think I know why you did what you did. All of it. I'm sorry." Knapp gave Draper a glum look.

Seven white-uniformed tars filed in and assumed a rigid, but occasionally weaving, oval formation around the table. Each carried a tot of rum in his left hand. They were led by a diminutive white-haired salt of indeterminate age with a neatly trimmed white beard. His words were clipped and fierce. His face battered, scarred, and puckered like old leather. He wore crossed-anchors on his sleeve. These men were followed by several other more casual, and also uniformed, tars.

"Miller's senior," someone said and they all looked toward the bearded white-haired salt.

"Matelots, uncover," the old salt barked.

They clutched their white flat-hats to the center of their chests.

"Eu-lorgies, report," he demanded looking straight ahead.

Draper heard the phrases "un-wake" and "almost wake" several times. What followed he took to be premature eulogies. He couldn't understand more than a smattering of the words. Rum, slang, and widely varying syllable emphasis, made the eulogies difficult to decipher, and he realized, the onset of delirium on his part didn't help. He picked up references, he believed, to "Jones the Pirate," "George Washington," "Davy Crockett," "Admiral Dewey," "Hector," and even "Beowulf."

"Present arms," Miller barked again.

They held out the enameled cups.

"To the 'Yank cowboy,'" Miller growled. "To a fellow warrior. Matelots, up spirits!"

One by one, the tars in the room toasted firmly, "to the Yank," and downed his tot of rum, then slammed his cup on the table where Draper lay immobile.

"Was that an old ceremony?" Draper sounded out each syllable carefully.

"Name's Miller," the old man muttered. "Can't say, not really official, init? Did one for a mate what cleared a taverna in Crete with a broom handle when the Greeks and Turks got into it in '97. Unarmed he was, 'cept for that broom handle an' I don't mean a Mauser pistol. Mean a real broom handle."

"Trouble there were they established a temp'ry truce between 'em, the Greeks and Turks, an' they went after him personal. We had to haul 'im to safety unconscious, too."

He paused for a moment. "No rum that time. We had to settle for ouzo. He weren't never the same. Great bloke, but never the same." He frowned in remembrance.

"Seemed this were a time to do it ag'in, even it being a Yank what done it. Valor's valor, bein' what I always say. Savin' a fair damsel's noble-like. Pardon, my sayin' so, if bein' a damsel ain't the same as bein' a lady."

Either Miller, or Miss Knapp, was snuffling. Draper's head was back on the table and he was gazing at the stamped-tin ceiling.

He had been gallant, though he now realized that he had been the more likely subject of surveillance, and clear kidnapping target. Draper didn't know where the gold was going, but he knew a good deal about the heist.

"I'll see Miss Knapp gets back to her residence hotel safely," Fairbairn said, and offered Knapp his arm. "Sergeant Fairbairn, at your service. Meeting you has been a honor, Lieutenant Stuyvesant Draper. An honor, sir."

Draper drifted in and out of consciousness, thinking it a rare honor indeed to be recognized by comrades-in-arms and the possible lamentations of a woman. The pain was considerable, yet he speculated the honor was one of those best appreciated in retrospect.

The tars broke off the legs of the table, hoisted the table top with him on it to shoulder-height. They carried him to the French hospital, St. Mary's, because "them Frog nurses were 'deevie,'" which he assumed meant "divine." Fairbairn hadn't shared Draper's geographical limitations with the Royal Navy.

Sailors — officers, and men alike — took great comfort in traditions, Draper could appreciate — even those they made up.

The sky was dark and forbidding when the left the café. By the time they'd reached the French Concession, they were enjoying a monsoon deluge.

Miller's tars only dropped him once.

St. Mary's Hospital, French Concession, Shanghai, June 1913

He had hoped their light-hearted "promenade" might lead to something more, yet in the space of seconds it had degenerated into something both grisly and ominous.

He had joined the Navy to avoid killing one man, and now had killed three. Draper anticipated despondently that Knapp would keep future contacts strictly professional.

What disturbed him most was the unthinking speed of his reflexes when the matter came to aiming and firing.

At the hospital, he began preparing the timeline of Hobson's service after the Woosung landing party and his foiling the robbery of the Red-Knight's-Pawnshop courier. Draper had never put those matters to paper. He didn't want to go back to USS Saratoga, not yet. Here at last he could collect his thoughts. A courier brought him files and stayed with him as long as he had the files.

The hospital was a riot of shades of immaculate white. The French nurses fluttered in their Sphinx-like head scarves. Since neither he, nor they, could maintain a conversation in the other's language, he gloried in the quiet.

His injuries allowed him to delay his report to the flag captain. Hobson hadn't returned, and Draper's hospitalization offered the perfect excuse.

"Asperities and obliquities," he muttered aloud. He was talking to himself more and more these days.

"*Qu'est-ce que vous dites?*" the nurse asked, fluffing up his pillow and inspecting the new cast on his left wrist. He guessed she was asking what he'd said or something like that.

"Nothing, nothing," he felt compelled to respond. He waved his palm, dismissing concern.

Draper realized he desperately needed Hobson's cultural insights and practical advice.

Hobson's parents had been circuit-riding lay missionaries in the Far East and been "schooner-schooled." In his late teens, he was sent back to San Francisco to finish his education under the supervision of his aunt. Then some years after the Japanese takeover of Korea, Hobson's parents disappeared.

Hobson, who had seen the Great White Fleet arrive in San Francisco in 1908, realized he had only one way to go back to the Far East. He signed papers in San Francisco and was soon on a warship headed east.

On arrival in Manila Bay, Hobson had been drafted to the distillery and troopship *USS Rainbow*. A year or so later, when his language skills became better known, Draper had suggested that the skipper of the experimental collier *USS Pluto* claim him. As part of the Naval Auxiliary Service under the Bureau of Navigation, colliers had a merchant seaman component to their crew, however not *USS Pluto*. She was an experiment in efficiency, an all-Navy collier. *USS Pluto* was, like all colliers, despised by the spotless regular Navy.

The flag captain was known as "the Seagull." Draper reminded himself to investigate the origins of the flag captain's nickname.

He noticed several nurses, disciples of Pasteur, searching the rooms for microorganisms and attacking them with chlorine.

From the window, he recognized a lean Chinaman in Western attire waiting outside on the sidewalk. Kempeitai? Three Harmonies Society? Green Gang? Those were the best bets.

Or the man was simply a member of a patient's family.

CHAPTER TWENTY-SIX

The Yellow Sea, July 1913

Hobson, urged by the tall Korean to change into the Western businessman's outfit, was also given a revolver with an impressively tooled belt and holster. He knew he was not a prisoner, still he also knew he had better keep close to Yi as the second junk sped Hobson and Yi to a steamship headed for Chinnamp'o.

Hobson watched as they loaded new cargo aboard a tired Chinese side-wheeler that then wheezed itself across the Yellow Sea. The side-wheeler struggled against the powerful tidal currents, and soon Hobson found himself staring at Korea's rugged mountain profile. Something not quite right about the scene gnawed at the back of his mind.

"What am I going to tell Admiral Bulkley? That we allowed the gold to be dumped in the Yangtze?" Hobson asked.

"When you return to Shanghai, you'll know what to say," Yi answered.

Hobson recalled that an ancient Korean proverb observed, "When whales fight, shrimp get nervous." Korea had always been the shrimp and China, Russia, and Japan the whales. Japan defeated China in 1895 and Russia in 1905. Japan was the only whale left in the game to swallow Korea, and that whale was a mean one.

To Hobson, Korea was defined by the familiar smells of charcoal, garlic, and night soil. Shanghai sent forth no pervasive smell of garlic. Moreover, Shanghai smelled of burning coal, not charcoal. The odor of night soil, though present, was not as pervasive.

Korea, he knew, was part of him.

The fact that Korea was under the heel of Japan tore at his gut. He had lived in Japan, too, and regarded the Japanese and the Koreans as cousins. He enjoyed aspects of both cultures, yet in the here and now of Korea, he knew he couldn't be proud of his knowledge of the Japanese language and culture.

Observing the current situation was like watching favorite relatives' fight. As an American sailor, he was aware of his country's unease with Japan and its ambitions. That only increased his inner turmoil. Korea was the place he most regarded as home, and the distant mountains that drew his eyes reminded him of black crepe bunting. He flicked his shoulders and braced himself

At Chinnamp'o, the steamship had off-loaded a great number of crates marked in English "Heavy Equipment." Hobson observed, measured, and recorded mentally. The crates were transferred to the schooners of an American gold mining company.

The schooners carried the crates, plus Hobson, Yi, and his men, to Anju on the Chongchon River. There, the crates were transferred to flat-bottomed barges, which were worked upriver to Unsan.

Hobson had never heard of Unsan, but realized it was a place of significance when a wagon train with an armed guard consisting of Americans and Chinese met them at the pier. After Japan's actual occupation of Korea in 1910, Koreans couldn't legally own guns.

In the distance, Hobson saw the smokestacks of smelting furnaces.

Hobson caught Yi alone, watching the loading of the barges.

"Yi, where do you hide gold?" Hobson said, though clearly, he didn't need an answer.

Yi smiled for once.

"You hide gold where gold goes unnoticed, where it is nothing special, with more gold." Hobson answered his own question.

Koreans manhandled the crates onto the wagons. Hobson repeatedly heard the word *nodaji* said in a questioning manner. It sounded Korean, however he knew it wasn't.

"*They can't read the words,*" Yi explained, standing beside Hobson on the pier. "They've simply been told over and over, 'No touchee' the contents of heavy crates. 'Nodaji' outbound normally means gold." That pidgin English phrase had become the local Hangugo word "for gold"

Yi looked as though he had something else to say, then thought better of it.

"I'm home," Yi said. He waved one thankful hand expansively toward the rising mountains.

"I am, too, even so we can't stay, can we?"

The country surrounding the Unsan gold mines was exponentially more rugged than the mountains that surrounded the Yangtze Gorges.

The Korean miners couldn't see what was in the crates, though context told them it had great value.

"The Unsan mines were first worked by your countrymen in 1898, when I was seeking gold in the Klondike. Americans still run these mines, but only with Japanese permission now that Japan controls Korea."

Yi calmly proceeded to explain to the guide that the crates contained important mining equipment. This made sense, since returning gold to its source would be nonsensical. Hobson noticed that Yi's men were as well armed as the mining company's guards.

The mule-team drawn wagons took the trail to the mill, yet then turned off on a side road. The mining company guards lost interest, and eventually Yi had only one guide to where he was going.

By nightfall, Yi's party had reached a dormant mineshaft and a set of outbuildings well beyond the sounds of the mining company's engineering building.

Hobson kept scanning the mountain peaks.

The lone guide, a redhead with a drooping mustache and a soft Virginia accent, cleared his throat and asked Hobson, "You the engineer for this sub-leasing? You from that new syndicate?"

Hobson glanced at Yi, who seemed preoccupied. Then answered, "Not me, I handle the practical end of things. Name's Havilah Perkins."

Hobson had been coached for this moment, though he hadn't been brought into the full plan. If things went wrong, he didn't have much to tell anyone at this point.

"Just here to drop off equipment and look the shaft over," Hobson resumed. "Pumps are the key, they say. I leave the techni-loco folderol to the gallons-per-minute college boys and their slide-rules.

I'm just good at puttin' machinery in the right place and keeping it goin'."

The Virginian nodded. "I'd tend to agree. From what I've seen, maybe the 49ers could get by with a pan and a sluice box, but not around here. That shaft has flooded so many times the fellows with the celluloid collars have just given up. Hope you-all have better luck. Hope someone knows what he's doing. You've hauled some pretty heavy equipment a mighty long way if you can't un-flood this shaft. A mighty long way."

The guide looked thoughtful. "The fellows you have with you look pretty sturdy. Iffen they're looking for work, we're always looking for miners," he said. "We treat our workers better than the Nips do. Our workers live to spend their pay. Plus, we value a rugged Korean," the guard said. "An' he can earn real money. Heck, they even save money on work clothes' wear an' tear."

Hobson looked at the Virginian questioningly.

In response, the Virginian chuckled. "Heh, with the dust and humidity and close quarters, the local miners work naked as jaybirds in the mines. We don't want them collecting gold dust in their clothes."

Yi simply looked at the tin roofs of the buildings that covered the mineshafts, silently, without expression. Access to the mineshafts was controlled, even dormant shafts. Miners and mining crews couldn't come and go at will.

The Virginian left.

By kerosene lantern, Yi's men hastily erected sheerlegs from the materials they had with them and began lowering capped *hanmul*, small rice buckets of Japanese gold ingots into the flooded shaft.

Hobson watched, realizing the buckets were going 60 to 80 feet down the flooded shaft before arriving at the bottom. In these conditions, the depth, the darkness, in the midst of a well-secured mining field, under the boot of the Imperial Japanese Empire, it would be no mean feat to retrieve this gold. Assuming anyone other than Yi and the admiral's representative knew it was there.

The next morning, Hobson looked out on the river valley. The mine's numerous shafts were tucked between the spurs of the Nangnim Range, which rose ever higher to the east. "Spurs" was an apt term, for its jagged, granite-topped ridges were as daunting as a mouth full of broken teeth. Pines attempted to cover the mountains like a series of shimmering emerald fringes, and steep rock outcroppings poked between the infinite quilt edges. Hobson realized they were only a few hundred miles from the Chinese border. Korea's many ranges, seen from China, looked like the onslaught of successive lines of wave crests in a heavy sea. Rugged Koreans and those steep, jagged waves had foiled Chinese army after Chinese army for centuries.

Later, Hobson checked and counted each hanmul of ingots. He knew the exact number of hanmuls they'd filled from the Imperial Japanese Navy casks. All the gold ingot hanmuls held the same number of ingots except one. The last hanmul was two gold ingots short. The remaining hanmuls were in excess of the number of casks taken during the cutting out expedition and inexplicably contained silver.

There are too many rice buckets. Hobson could think of no way to raise the issue obliquely.

The junk that sank in the Yangtze had been a diversion. The junk cruise had been an elaborate hoax. Yi's junk had likely carried a cargo of rocks, yet gratifyingly the Kempeitai would expend months of salvage time before they'd realize they'd been had. By then the trail would have run cold.

Yi turned to Hobson with a half-smile. "Yes, too much. Too much is better than too little."

"But why?"

"We have the Japanese gold, and also taels of silver. I've been saving this silver all my life — replacement silver. I'm paying debt. The principal is the silver. I was a courier once for a payment of tael to China, a courier from the king of Korea to the empress of China. Through my carelessness, the Japanese were able to steal that shipment. As I see it, the Japanese borrowed the silver from Korea. The gold is an interest payment on the silver. This is all about finance, you savvy?"

Yi had a look of serenity on his face. "I needed a long time to gather the principal. It is paid in the same form it was sent to China, in fifty-tael sycee. I started earning it back with the help of a good man in the Yukon, the ends of the earth, but sadly, much of it was acquired by bad deeds to bad men. Each bad deed brought me closer to Korea. Does a bad deed done to bad men become a good deed? Strangely, my destiny has been to smuggle precious metals in chaotic times, chaotic for Korea, chaotic for China." He smiled.

"That tugboat that showed up right after the junk sank is owned by Spuyten & McCollum. The Spuytens do bad deeds to good men. And I have done bad deeds to the Spuytens. I believe they work with the Japanese or a triad."

Hobson remembered crossing paths with one of the Spuytens in Shanghai.

"I can't be impulsive. When a man shows up to withdraw money from a bank, he must show the bank that he has a right to that money. My dead friend in the Klondike liked puzzles. I have constructed a puzzle.

"When men come here to withdraw this treasure from this flooded mine shaft, they must show they have the initiative, and the technical and organizational skills to exercise the right to that treasure. If they take it intelligently, they are capable of spending it intelligently, and then they will free Korea," Yi observed.

"First knock to test the soundness of a bridge before crossing, even one constructed of stone," Hobson summarized with a Korean proverb. *Always test first.*

Hobson was amazed by the explanation. "You don't believe just giving the insurrectionists money directly is enough. Tens of thousands of lives could be lost in an ill-conceived uprising, and you will have done more harm than good. You want proof of will and competence. You want assurance that the insurrection will have a chance of success."

Yi seemed satisfied.

Hobson soon found himself hustled back to Chinnamp'o and then to Shanghai.

He realized he had completed his work as the admiral's representative, even so he feared the Red-Crown Crane tasking wasn't over.

Hadn't Yi observed that precious metals were linked to chaotic times?

PART V

DUNGAREE LIBERTY

Men need harbors almost as much as
they need the gods.
—Hilaire Belloc

CHAPTER TWENTY-SEVEN

USS Pluto, Huangpu Moorings, Shanghai, August 1913

Hobson returned to Shanghai by barge and side-wheeler. Yi, he believed, had one or two more diversions to implement, but was on his way to Shanghai, too.

A week later, Hobson was back aboard *USS Pluto* and standing in line for the evening meal.

"That be the p-p-prodigal quartermaster?" Washboard observed aloud.

"Aye," Harp responded with a glance at Hobson "That be the culprit, in the flesh. Surprised he's not in confinement, and they're letting him eat food that's got nourishment. Thought he'd be on bread and water for the near future." He and Washboard projected a genteel air of indifference.

Washboard yawned. "No, defaulters don't go on bread and water until they're sentenced, and mostly deserters get sentenced to a lot worse than bread and water and confinement."

Washboard's father was a judge, so his observations held sway on such subjects on the ship's small mess deck. "Deserters habitually rate a long drop on a short rope," he continued. "Especially when they desert in the face of the enemy and especially when they abscond to foreign parts."

Hobson crossed his arms. "Can you get permission to desert? Hey, shipmates, I had 'Ratified Special Emergency Leave' just for the purpose of planting burrs under a net-load of certain lazy, barnacle-encrusted backsides."

"Boatswain's Mate Harp, did you hear anything?"

"Why no, Yeoman Washboard, nothing of significance. You know the prodigal quartermaster didn't make it back from liberty some weeks ago. I say again, weeks ago."

"I hear the captain of our fair ship called out the shore patrol to retrieve the prodigal," Harp said.

"Aye."

Harp and Washboard were tormenting him and this was not an impulsive hazing.

"In my exalted station as yeoman, I heard the admiral notified the Shanghai Municipals."

"Aye, the call went out to the Shanghai Volunteer Corps, who I understand specialize in kidnappings and the sort," Harp said.

"Do tell. Were their horses shown pictures of the prodigal quartermaster?"

"The horses, they were duly shown," Harp agreed.

"Strange, that ragbag naval militia officer over t'embassary or consulation came aboard and informed the captain of this fair ship that the prodigal quartermaster was on extended leave with no precise expiration date," Washboard confided. "The leave was admiral-approved leave, mind you. No expiration date, legal desertion."

"Didn't the admiral notify the Shanghai Municipals and the Shanghai Volunteer Corps that the prodigal quartermaster was missing? Was the admiral forgetful?"

"Mistake, the search for the quartermaster was all a mistake. The admiral's aide had misplaced the papers that the admiral had executed." Washboard shook his head. "Hard to believe the admiral made a mistake. My experience has been that admirals never make mistakes, "Boatswain's Mate Harp."

"Aye, hard to believe indeed," Washboard responded. Harp adjusted himself to address a distant mess table.

The chiefs ate on the same mess deck as the others. *USS Pluto* did not have the room for a separate chiefs' mess. The chiefs simply had a separate table with a fancy tablecloth.

In stentorian tones, Harp directed a question to the chiefs' mess, "Chief Phipps, in all your years of service, did you ever hear of in all your born days an admiral-approved extended leave for a quartermaster third? Ever, ever since you signed on with Noah?"

So, this was a shipwide concern, Hobson concluded. *They want me to explain what's been happening or why. I can't tell them.*

Harp and Washboard were shoveling in food while wearing their dress whites with piped blue cuffs and collars. Khaki leggings, and khaki pistol belts without pistols, topped the whole rig off. At their sides were nightsticks. They were shortly to go ashore, not on liberty however, for special duty.

Hobson seethed silently. He now realized the wardens of the lower decks viewed him fair game.

"Wasn't no authority higher than Noah hisself in those early days, and he was only a commodore,' said Chief Phipps. "Heck, we didn't even get around to admirals at all 'til my umpteenth hitch during the Civil War. Admiral-approved leave for collier-deserters? Never heard the like." The chief petty officer rubbed his chin thoughtfully. "Colliers are as low as tarnation and precious far removed from admirals upon high. Colliers and admirals are as far apart as the heavens and the abyss."

"Chief, this exceeds even my legal grasp of naval custom," Washboard continued. "Can they hang you for desertion for taking admiral-approved leave?"

"They can punish anyone for anything they take a mind to punish," Chief Phipps said. "All the rest of us have been confined to the ship for the past few weeks for no reason at all as far as I can tell. No one sayin' why. I guess they can hang a deserter on admiral-approved leave, if they please, however they may have to get permission from the admiral in question."

Harp's face was contorted as he considered this complex problem. "Chief, think there's a connection between us not being able to go ashore to visit our loved ones and a lowlife prodigal quartermaster?"

"Aye, some mighty suspicious-ness goin' on."

Hobson squirmed, but bit his lip.

"Bread and water!" chimed in several members of the crew, whipping away Hobson's plate and substituting a single slice of bread.

Hobson expected to get "the treatment" for some weeks to come. He couldn't say a thing in his defense. That the crew remained confined to the ship for the foreseeable future didn't help.

That evening, after Harp and Washboard had gone ashore on their detail, Hobson found a roost on the fantail bitts, plucking the strings on his inlaid ukulele and avoiding everyone. These days, he kept the ukulele hidden in the charthouse.

The rest found perches on chocks or bitts or reclined on caulking mats. Others simply sat on the steel deck and leaned against stanchions. Hobson eventually pulled out his canvas caulking mat and slept on deck with the rest of the crew. Hammocks below-decks in an enclosed space, in hot weather, were insufferable.

His shipmates stayed angry with him.

Day and night on the Huangpu, junks and sampans moved up and down, from bank to bank and back. They likely covered every square foot in any 24-hour period. Deep into the night, Hobson was studying constellations, attempting to judge the time by Cassiopeia's rotation around the sky. The trouble was, the Bund's three-decade-old streetlights and the river traffic lights flooded out all but the brightest lights in the sky.

The result was as if *USS Pluto* had been reduced to the size of a toy and dropped in the middle of one of the shooting galleries by the fantan tables in an amusement center on Tibet Road. The silhouettes were boats that ran repeating loops in opposing directions. The shooting galleries' targets were framed by riverbanks comprised of warrens of finger piers.

The processions of junks and sampans — primarily sampans — filed by as if they had someplace to go, still Hobson wondered if many were just avoiding the cost of tying up. Some sampans were little more than coracles carrying a single standing fisherman, while others were essentially multifamily houseboats.

All Shanghai knew the crews of *USS Pluto* and *USS Rainbow* had been confined to ship, and the bumboats were circling the ships like a wake of vultures. Every half-hour a different bumboat would tie off on a rope ladder off the stern to peddle its wares. One of the petty officers on watch kept a constant lookout, and only two crew members could set foot on a bumboat at a time. The bumboats served as floating five-and-dime stores. They carried candy, postcards, newspapers, souvenirs, silk fabric, and sundries. The rule with bumboats was no alcohol could be sold, though no one could be sure how well that rule was kept.

Generally, one or two men handled the boat and one or two women handled sales. As Hobson gazed down at a bumboat that had pulled up, he saw that one woman onboard had a bright smile and a husky silhouette similar to that of Clementine.

Hobson realized he missed Clementine. He liked her. He wondered if he liked her for her intelligence and spunk, or was it her availability?

For a woman in China, the institution of prostitution presented a bad array of demeaning possibilities, however the circumstances didn't have to be a dead end. A woman could work her way out of its confines. Yet frequently, the vocation itself was all the woman had in order to work her way out of a bad situation in a culture that offered women few options to begin with. For an American sailor, it was one of the few institutions that offered the prospect of feminine contact. Hobson realized his thoughts were drifting in a circular eddy that he couldn't himself work his way out of. Here he was a quartermaster, a sailor responsible for knowing where he and his ship were at all times, and he was now much adrift.

Off to his left — by the light of a hurricane lantern — was a group of men playing acey-deucey, a seagoing variation on backgammon. Hobson could hear the clicking of tossed dice and the banter of competition. To his right was a quieter, more thoughtful group generating pipe smoke. From somewhere forward, he heard a harmonica and the twang of a jaw harp. Hobson recognized Chief Bydecker's tenor voice singing one of the tunes he had heard on Madam Guan's mechanical Polyphon.

Hobson was unhappy. Yes, the Yangtze diversion had been a success. He had been impressed by the lengths Yi had gone to. The Red Crane ingots – all but two — were safely tucked in a mineshaft so far underwater only hardhat divers could recover them, and that was unlikely.

Now, however, his shipmates believed he had broken faith with them. He had disappeared, and they were confined to the ship. They suspected cause and effect.

They blame me and want an explanation. I can't do that.

"Time's up, bumboat away," shouted the watch's petty officer, pointing at the battered hourglass in his hand.

Two Pluto crew members on the bumboat lunged for Jacobs

ladder and pulled themselves up to the main deck — barely using their feet — with their new acquisitions, candy, dime novels, and a jingling brass wind chime for a mother or sister, tucked in their pockets or in the backs of their waistbands.

A new bumboat jockeyed into position. The process began anew. The sailors waiting in the bumboat line began roughhousing, while two of the forward crew members, satisfied that the next boat behind it wouldn't offer a better selection, descended the ladder.

As a group, they weren't exactly on a desert island, though their proximity to a bustling waterfront made their isolated plight as painful as if they had been.

Hobson carried the added discomfort of believing the isolation was somehow his fault.

The next bumboat had several paper lanterns.

Hobson watched it while listening to the acey-deucey game.

Something white and just below the water's surface moved by the bumboat. The crew was dressed in their denim work uniforms, and bumboat Chinese rarely wore white. Koreans often wore white.

The white oval drifted slowly with the current. Hobson stared at it. It had a dark, vaguely familiar square cut-out that pointed down-current.

"Can I borrow someone's lantern for a minute? Something's in the water by the bumboat."

The request triggered movement by several coalpassers new to *Pluto* who saw themselves as a formidable alliance with a political future.

"Look, Hobson," said their thick-necked spokesman through a cheek swollen with tobacco. "It's been one continuous field day around here for us since you went shoreside on that stovepipe leave of your'n. You were shuffled off *USS Rainbow* and we're thinking maybe you should get shuffled off *USS Pluto* to something suitable. I don't know, a spitkit, maybe."

The other two coalpassers, one short and wide who carried himself like a wrestler, and the other, simply wide and quiet, guffawed. Hobson couldn't see their eyes in the darkness that didn't matter. He watched their hands.

Expecting a push or a sucker punch, Hobson rose from the bitts, attempting to also keep an eye on the Huangpu.

"Why don't you three just pipe down?" Hobson asked. "Since when does a third-class quartermaster control liberty on any ship in Uncle Sam's Navy? You think of that? If it were up to my exalted authority, we'd make liberty real easy to take. Maybe give it to anyone who could spell Mississippi, recognize a quarantine flag, and be able to eat cornmeal mush."

The coalpassers shifted their weight to the balls of their feet, and Hobson readied for the onslaught, talking a mile a minute. "You swing a scoop shovel a little and get a tad dusty and think you get a say 'round here? You wait, you put in your time and you wait. Coal dust isn't the only thing that takes the measure of a member of this man's navy."

He dared not turn to see if that white oval was still there.

"'Man the drag' with a landing party when a screaming horde cascades over you like lumps of coal down a chute," Hobson said, his temperature rising. "Then maybe, just maybe, you get to talk sassy to a petty officer. All in all, save it, sleeves, 'cause I don't scare one darn."

Hobson thought he could still see the white oval off one of the stern bitts.

Chief Phipps growled from somewhere in the darkness amidships, "Look, you uppity quartermaster. Coalpassers don't need to know that folderol. They are the heart and lungs of this here collier, and they have mighty concerns for the welfare of all and sundry.

"I know for a fact that quartermasters can't restrict coalpassers or any other enlisted naval personnel to their ships in port," Chief Phipps continued. "I talked about it with the skipper just yesterday, and he agreed with me. I do know I can arrange to restrict enlisted naval personnel to this ship once the present restriction expires, should they attempt to hold an unscheduled boxing smoker on the fantail without proper permission."

No one was sure whose side Phipps was on.

"And I know these three wouldn't know what a quarantine flag looked like, if anyone asked them. Not sure they could spell Mississippi either."

The coalpassers found something else to do with their evening. Blackgang rates rarely had much opportunity to look at flags, for instance.

"Hobson, you are a real pain." Chief Phipps said, handing him a kerosene lantern. "Haven't you caused enough trouble yet?" Then he whispered, "I'd keep my head down hereabouts."

The penumbra of the lantern was enough. Hobson saw stripes. His sense of familiarity made it clear. He was looking at the navy-blue collar on a dress white jumper.

He shone his lantern and pointed. "Man overboard, man overboard. Five yards, two points abaft the larboard quarter."

Two men jumped from the fantail and a third tossed them a line and a barrel buoy.

"Hobson, if he's *Pluto* crew, you're just plumb bad luck for everyone," a sailor called from the darkness. Hobson concluded that was unlikely; the uniform for crew that evening had been denim. He'd been aboard *Pluto* for a few hours, and he only had to look around to know the uniform prescribed by the plan of the day.

The body laid out on the fantail was a sailor, an American sailor.

"No use tryin' to res-pie-rate him," pronounced one of the acey-deucey players.

The corpse wore dress whites with their piped blue cuffs and collar, and khaki leggings.

CHAPTER TWENTY-EIGHT

"Ain't that Culper? Ike Culper, the hospital apprentice on *Rainbow*?" Chief Phipps called out. Others recognized him, but Hobson knew this wasn't the time to be first to show familiarity with a dead man.

Hobson worked his way through the small huddle of gabbing sailors.

"Yeah, I served with Culper when I was on *Rainbow*. Let me see. Yeah, now I remember his pure sun-shiny personality."

"Perfect for *Rainbow*," one of the young coalpassers said with equal sarcasm.

Hobson remembered Culper well. Hobson had barely survived the ill-fated landing party action at Woosung. Culper had pulled him and his fifty-tael sycee into the steam launch. Culper had turned the sycee over to *USS Rainbow's* paymaster, and a few months later Hobson had been transferred to *USS Pluto*.

Hobson looked at the sailor's lifeless face, white as his uniform. His neck was distorted. He studied the corner of Culper's jaw and ran his fingers lightly below it down to Culper's Adam's apple. He found two diagonal openings, two bloodless slashes, on the right side of his neck.

"Didn't drown. Someone cut his throat. I thought you fellows said *USS Rainbow's* crew was confined to ship, too. What's he doin' in his liberty rig?" Hobson asked.

"Hobson, you sleeve, look. He's wearing leggings. He was on a detail." Another of the young coalpassers had found his tongue.

"Doesn't make sense. *Rainbow's* on the Pudong side of the river upstream from the Fleet Landing. If someone ashore carved him and dropped him in the river, he'd be on his way to the Yangtze or out to sea," Hobson questioned.

"Harp and Washboard got provost duty," Chief Phipps commented. "They're on shore patrol tonight. I hope we don't see them washing up someplace."

Hobson hadn't seen Harp or Washboard since the noon meal. If he had been low-spirited before, he felt like crawling across the deck now.

The officer of the deck, an ensign, broke the huddle and started taking notes.

Hobson noticed the ensign made sure not to touch the body.

The ace-deucey game took a while to restart. Several players had lost interest.

Neither Harp nor Washboard returned that night and were listed as missing. No more talk of unauthorized absence or desertion ensued. Life aboard USS *Pluto* was growing stranger, ever darker.

The next afternoon, Hobson was assigned to courier duty and handed a dispatch case and a Colt .45 semi-automatic pistol, new to the fleet. A black coalpasser from Charleston, called Olmstead, was to accompany him. Both had been shaken by Culper's inexplicable end and the mysterious disappearance of Harp and Washboard.

As Hobson donned his dress whites, pistol belt, and leggings he tucked Yi's Owl Head pistol in its money belt-style holster under his jumper.

"Olmstead, you mind if we take what you might call a detour on our way to the consulate? I think I know where Harp and Washboard might be overstaying their welcome."

"Madam Guan's?"

"You're too smart to be a coalpasser. Ever think of striking for quartermaster?"

"Not enough exercise. I'm thinking if I stop stoking coal it might ruin my stylish line when I a-go ballroom a-dancin'."

Hobson and Olmstead moved briskly though the alleys until they came to the Lane of Lingering Joy, always a prime reference point. From there, they moved past the opium den and finally to the Lesser

Shanghai "Indian Club & Garter Society." At the building, surprisingly enough, they saw no sign of life. No movement whatsoever. Hobson jingled the massive front door. It opened. He called out yet received no response. The furniture was gone. Hobson bounded up to Clementine's old room, taking two steps at a time, leaving Olmstead to stand watch in what had been the parlor.

Her room was empty.

Hobson heard footsteps in the hall. He whirled to see Cornelius Spuyten and two burly seamen filing through the doorway.

Spuyten held a straight razor; the others brandished lengths of pipe.

"Tackline Spuyten, you just backwater! Be quick about it." Hobson's words were as fast as they were futile. He pulled his newly-issued .45 and slipped the safety. Tackline cocked his arm. Instinctively, Hobson raised the dispatch case in his left hand and began firing with his right.

They'd been waiting for American sailors.

The lighting wasn't good, consequently Hobson concentrated on the razor. He emptied his magazine in the direction of Tackline and the others. The roar of the .45 in a small room was deafening. He stepped over two inert bodies, Cornelius Spuyten and a celestial. A third man was badly wounded and his mouth was moving. Hobson guessed he was swearing, but he couldn't hear because his ears were still ringing. The man couldn't stand and Hobson kicked him out of the doorway. Below, he felt percussions through his feet.

Others were downstairs with Olmstead. Hobson loaded his second and last magazine. The third man clutched at Hobson's ankles. Hobson kicked him again and he lay quiet.

Hobson ran down the stairs. "Olmstead, it's me," he bellowed before turning the corner into the parlor.

Olmstead was on the floor, moaning. Before him lay two dead men who'd broken his femur trying to take him alive. Six altogether had been on the attack, four Western merchant sailors and two Chinese. The sixth and final attacker, seeing Hobson, was shuffling out the door.

Olmstead gazed up at Hobson with a look of disorientation. "Heh. Guess Harp and Washboard ain't here." He coughed, and his body slackened.

Hobson looked around. They hadn't taken all the furniture. The massive Polyphon was still there. Polyphons were expensive and rated special handling. He kneeled to run his hand along its ornately-carved legs. The base cabinet had a small latch. He undid the latch and the player opened like a flour bin. Tucked between the dividers — just out of sight — was a shore patrol baton. Hobson studied it carefully and noticed two letters crudely carved into the hilt of the black baton. The two letters, "AC," were short for "auxiliary, collier" in the USN's identification system. Harp or Washboard had carried that baton and had intentionally stashed it out of sight. The message was "we were here."

It hadn't landed there unintentionally. Harp and Washboard had come to pay a call on their old girlfriends, practice billiards, and hear a tune or two on the Polyphon.

Alerted by gunfire upstairs, the second trio had approached Olmstead with razors and brass knuckles.

Apparently, Spuyten and his men hoped to abduct unsuspecting patrons, and the arrival of Hobson and Olmstead — armed — had been an unexpected development. Sailors on liberty didn't normally carry guns. Sailors on shore patrol only carried truncheons. Sailors on courier duty, however, always carried guns.

Shanghai never slept and its byways teemed with those rushing here and there, contrarily few people were visible at this moment and the streets were quiet around Madam Guan's empty establishment.

Hobson pulled aside a curtain and looked down the street. The day was warm and humid, but no one was out on their outside balconies, which was unusual. Hobson saw no one in an open window, but he thought he detected movement behind a few louvered shutters.

On the right, fifty yards down the street, he observed a small cluster of men, Western men. He wished he had his binoculars. Within that cluster, the men all seemed to focus on one of their number wearing a lightweight gray-blue frock coat. The central figure was older, and his neck seemed to fold into his rounded shoulders, still his level of animation made him almost appear to be dancing. Around him were his followers, and he was working to convey his message that he didn't have a care in the world and they needn't worry either.

The cluster began to move toward Madam Guan's and Hobson studied the gait of the man in the gray-blue frock coat.

The group moved down the alley. They were physical men, men who worked at physical trades — that much Hobson could tell from their necks and shoulders. They didn't swing their arms, even so he thought he caught the glint of hardware in their hands.

Two Sikhs in turbans, khaki shorts, and Sam Brown belts came running down the street blowing whistles, clearly bound for Madam Guan's.

The cluster reversed direction.

The left foot of the man in the blue-gray frock coat didn't roll properly. This impediment was brought on by some mild discomfort, barely perceptible. Hobson knew that momentary check of movement occurred when a man carried a folding straight razor in the arch of his shoe.

The gait was always a matter of mechanics, or "machineration," as Washboard would say.

Several Sikhs from the Shanghai Municipal Police escorted Hobson to the consulate and a few Shanghai Volunteers took Olmstead to the Shanghai General Hospital.

Madam Guan and her girls were missing. Clementine was missing. The house on the Lane of Lingering Joy was out of business and had been converted to a trap for former patrons.

The Spuytens had somehow identified a point of vulnerability. If the matter hadn't approached that level before, it was now personal.

Would others be joining this fracas alongside the Spuytens?

CHAPTER TWENTY-NINE

American Consulate Annex, Hongkou District, Shanghai,
September 1913

Draper was two days back from the hospital in the French concession. The bruises on his head and shoulders were now only an eggplant blend of green and purple, but he did wear a cast on his left wrist.

Lieutenant Commander Wheelwright had visited him in the hospital. Franconia Knapp had not.

"Are you keeping company with Miss Knapp?" Wheelwright had inquired at the hospital. "Don't want to intrude on a work-in-progress."

Draper had given the question some thought. "I have no claim on her. She has no expectations of me."

Not after the Nanking Street promenade, he thought.

Some men just didn't know how to show a girl a good time.

She had wanted to get out and meet people. She could accomplish that better with Wheelwright. He had no right to cordon her off.

Franconia Knapp had been distant on his return. No talk of further promenades had ensued. She had difficulty making eye contact. He kept to his office on the second floor, and she kept to her office, the strong-room, on the third floor. He remembered that she had stopped him on the staircase earlier that day. "Found some items in the Japanese consulate's written trash," she had said in tones so controlled they bordered upon bland. "I'll send someone by to your office with them."

Though he knew Hobson was back from his mission as the admiral's representative, Draper hadn't yet arranged to debrief him. Draper did a quick review of the contemporaneous Shanghai Municipal Police Reports. The Shanghai municipal authorities weren't happy that Hobson had been bundled off by American Consulate officials. Two sailors in a bordello popping holes through a half-dozen of Hellfire's bullyboys didn't seem to rate the umbrella of "diplomacy." Fortunately, a clever consular official pointed out that Hobson was a courier carrying dispatches, not a rowdy sailor on liberty. At that point, the city officials knew they were licked.

Draper hadn't wanted to use his Sergeant Fairbairn card this soon.

In part, Draper was pleased because he saw the attack on Hobson as an act of desperation. He saw it as an indication that circumstances were reaching a crescendo, and hopefully culmination. That perception was tempered by his fears for the missing sailors and Madam Guan's girls.

Now, unexpectedly, Draper found Hobson, accompanied by Wheelwright, thrust into his annex office by a brace of Marines.

The civilian functionaries on the floor quickly withdrew — with much deferential nodding — to less stressful surroundings. Draper noticed that Hobson's eye focused on the fifty-tael sycee that Draper inappropriately used for a paperweight. The sycee was barely visible amid peaks of books and files that Draper mused might remind Hobson of some stretches of Chinese, and Korean, coastline.

"Admiral Bulkley is waiting in the conference room next door," Draper said.

Wheelwright's eyebrows lifted in surprise. "Well, I've run the interference needed to get you here, Hobson. No need for me to become immersed in matters of greater sensitivity. Good luck. I'll have the mess cooks hold aside some chow for you in case the admiral or Draper don't invite you to dinner." Wheelwright gave Hobson a wink.

Wheelwright turned to Draper. "Took Miss Knapp to dinner the night before last. Thanks for the clear course."

Wheelwright then gave Draper a wink.

Draper clutched the door latch unsteadily and realized he had still not recovered from the incident on Nanking Road.

The deputy consul's eyes were wild. "Look, this man has just been wrested out of the hands of the Shanghai Municipal Police. He's connected with the shooting of six men, that shooting occurring on some alarum or excursion...for all we know, some frolic. He should have been on his way over here directly. Tell me why we shouldn't turn him over to the local authorities. What have you to say for yourself? What's your name?"

Draper had expected only Admiral Bulkley and perhaps his flag lieutenant, however he should have anticipated the consul or the deputy consul would be ranging around their own piece of Shanghai.

The admiral gave Draper a meaningful glance, then chimed in. "Deputy Consul, would you excuse us for a moment, sir? You are quite right. This is a question of naval discipline."

The deputy consul glared at everyone in the room in uniform and turned just as he took the door latch. His mouth began to move, but then he apparently thought better of it and left with a forceful door slamming.

"One of the good things about uniforms is they achieve a uniform appearance," mused Draper to Hobson. "In a few days, the deputy consul won't be able to identify a clean-shaven Hobson. To civilians, all naval officers look alike, and better yet in your case, all sailors look alike. The Shanghai consulate is a busy one, and this matter will merge into the general blur of naval activity."

The room now only contained Hobson, Admiral Bulkley, and Draper.

Hobson related that the ingots were in a flooded mine in Korea.

Ol' Blue Flame began, "So the gold is at the bottom of a flooded mineshaft in Korea, a mineshaft controlled by an American company and guarded by an American security force accustomed to guarding gold. I suppose we should be satisfied. Mr. Draper, what do you make of it?"

This was the admiral's first salvo, and Draper realized it was aimed at him.

Draper looked at Hobson with the knowledge that the quartermaster's time was coming and wondering how long he would be able to keep up with the admiral's desperate need for reassuring information.

As Draper had foreseen, the admiral's approach then took a different turn. "Let's look at this from a Navy Department perspective. Hobson, as I see it, you've just violated several provisions of The Rocks & Shoals, your recent work for Naval Intelligence notwithstanding. Dereliction of duty? What have you to say for yourself? Have you engaged the Asiatic Fleet in some personal war? If so, shoveling coal may be a pleasant memory compared to your future assignments. I don't see I'll fare any better if the Navy Department comes after me."

Draper knew it was time to intervene. He pushed his half-glasses up the bridge of his nose, looked the admiral square in the eye, counted to fifteen, and said soothingly, "Hobson, what's going on here? Have we been had?"

The past three weeks had taken their toll. Hobson's eyelids were leaden and his shoulders seemed ready to drop away from his spine.

Hobson started slowly, largely, no doubt, because he wasn't quite sure of what was happening either.

On the floor below, they could hear the deputy consul giving the admiral's flag lieutenant all seven bells. The cadence of distant conversation was akin to the sound of a typewriter. The deputy consul's recriminations came like the clicking of keys, the flag lieutenant's short response like hitting "return." After a brief pause, the deputy consul would start up again.

"Please excuse me, sirs, but my head's a-whirling like a free running sheave in a single-whip tackle." Hobson pronounced tackle "TAY-kul."

"This is partly 'cause I've just shot three men and have an unconscious shipmate in a civilian hospital. I believe two other shipmates and the entire staff of Madam Guan's bordello have been kidnapped, and this all relates to the ingots. I know they're prostitutes, but well, the crew of *USS Pluto* is sort of partial to some of them. Oh yes, and last night on *USS Pluto* we pulled Hospital Apprentice Culper of *USS Rainbow* out of the Huangpu. Dead."

The admiral raised an eyebrow and then suddenly bellowed down the hall for his flag lieutenant. "Mr. Vail, get three shore patrol over to Shanghai General Hospital — yes, over by Suzhou

Creek — and put a guard on Coalpasser Olmstead. Also send over our senior corpsman to make sure they are taking proper care of that sailor. Under no circumstances is Olmstead to be interviewed by anyone. I may have to put him on report to keep him isolated in that hospital, however we'll address that later."

"By the way, what's happened to your face?" the admiral asked, giving Draper a full inspection. "And your wrist."

Draper had kept his own incident on the down-low and realized that hadn't been such a good idea.

Hobson gave Draper an odd look, and Draper realized Hobson didn't know either.

"Someone tried to kidnap me on Nanking Street," Draper reported.

"Starting to see a pattern here. And you didn't see fit to inform me?" Admiral Bulkley tapped a sheaf of papers on the conference room table. "And now some men have just tried to either abduct or kill Hobson." The admiral looked deadly serious.

"Are the Japanese taking prisoners or hostages or someone else?" he wanted to know, casting a gimlet eye.

"Wasn't clear regarding a connection. No direct Japanese involvement. I don't know, sir, who's involved other than some triad thugs," Draper responded.

The deputy consul's typewriter-cadence conversation had gone silent though Draper could still imagine the "return" ringing at even interludes.

Draper watched Hobson sway and struggle to take hold of himself. "One of the men I shot today was Cornelius Spuyten, and he was wavin' a straight razor. Culper had his throat cut, and it looked like the work of a straight razor. The tugboat that chased Yi's junk up the Yangtze had 'S & McC' on its stack and 'Spuyten & McCollum' painted on its wheelhouse."

Draper walked back to his office, reached for the fifty-tael sycee on his desk and brought it back to the conference room table. "I'm acquainted with the name "Spuyten," though not McCollum."

Hobson observed the sycee with some interest. The Chinese character looked as if it had been drawn by a child with a pencil. Asian characters, Chinese, Japanese, Korean, were most commonly written as if they had been applied with a brush. An engraved character normally mimicked the direction and sequence of brush strokes of a painted character. This character was a poor counterfeit. It wasn't the character for "courage."

"Tugboat? Yangtze?" The admiral looked puzzled.

Draper struggled to explain. "Sir, that's why I had Hobson come over here today. I debriefed Yi, but I thought you'd want to hear Hobson's story. I didn't know that we'd be converging several operational currents."

Draper had Hobson recount his Yangtze Gorge journey and the situation at Unsan. He had also heard the story from Yi, even so an additional set of eyes always provided a different perspective and a more complete picture overall.

The admiral listened with widening eyes. "You were shadowed by a Spuyten & McCollum tug?"

Admiral Bulkley, Draper figured, could deal with the Japanese; he knew his authority. The political influence of the merchant shipping industry was always an unknown quantity.

Hobson could contain himself no longer, and turned to Draper. "Where did this sycee come from? Last time I saw one of these, Culper had it, and I assumed he was going to turn it over to *USS Rainbow*'s paymaster to safeguard as a ship's battle memento. The one I turned over to Culper was genuine. This is a fake."

Draper's turn to look uncomfortable had come.

Ol' Blue Flame was trying hard to grasp these seemingly unrelated threads. "If you know, tell him."

"It's been on my desk, figuratively, for six months. My regular station is our Tokyo embassy. As you know, I'm sort of a circuit rider, and as part of the Office of Naval Intelligence under the Bureau of Navigation, I'm also called in to investigate criminal activity. I try to cover all my responsibilities, still I'm better at intelligence. It was in Tokyo and now it's sitting here because *USS Rainbow* is here."

Hobson had picked up the sycee and kept rolling it over in his hand.

"The present captain of *USS Rainbow* brought it to my attention. Apparently, the previous skipper had arranged for a jeweler to look at it. The jeweler determined the original fifty-tael sycee that Hobson brought back from Woosung was genuine silver and was inscribed with a Chinese character, as is the custom — in this case the character for 'courage.'"

Draper took the object in question from Hobson and handed it to the admiral.

"This is lead painted to look like tarnished silver. The 'character' is incomprehensible," Draper pronounced. "It is clearly the work of one illiterate in Chinese. Someone took the real fifty-tael sycee. What USS Rainbow's new paymaster discovered in Rainbow's trophy locker was this counterfeit. The real fifty-tael sycee was in the custody of USS Rainbow's then-paymaster. That earlier paymaster was promoted and is now the fleet's paymaster, Commander McCorkran."

Draper and Hobson both cleared their throats. Hobson wrinkled his nose.

The admiral bellowed once again for the flag lieutenant and stepped out to provide detailed instructions. "Get a competent paymaster in from Manila to audit USS Rainbow's ship's books." His words thundered through the walls. "While he's at it, he will need to audit those of the Asiatic Station staff here. In the meantime, have the senior Marine officer on my flagship place the paymaster under arrest, and no visitors!"

Hobson had never heard any officer achieve that volume level without a loud hailer.

Draper could hear the flag lieutenant hurtling down several flights of stairs two at a time. "Yess-i-i-i-rrrr" trailed the fading words behind him.

"Better give me that service pistol they issued you, and…" Draper whispered to Hobson—tapping the bulge under Hobson's jumper. "…and make sure you keep that hammerless under your jumper out of the admiral's sight."

Hobson might well have wondered how Draper knew it was a hammerless. He brushed the edges of his jumper down thoughtfully and no doubt was glad he wasn't responsible for reading the barrage of light signals the admiral had just initiated. USS Rainbow's yardarm signal lights would be blinking like a love-struck seaman third class.

Hobson passed Draper the Colt under the green baize table, while noting Ol' Blue Flame was working up a full head of steam.

CHAPTER THIRTY

Qilin Cathay, Shanghai Coaling Depot, August 1913

On *Qilin Cathay*, the Western freighter tied up at the coaling quay Weng, a triad member was weighing his options. He knew what had happened to the women of the Lesser Shanghai Indian Club & Garter Society.

"Pockmarked Weng" wasn't his name nor was it a name he would have picked for himself. However, the moniker had its uses. It indicated that he was less than handsome. Pockmarked had been beaten frequently during his childhood, by neighborhood bullies, by strangers, by family members. His immediate family members were petty criminals who were used to being roughed up, to the extent it was almost their primary form of communication. Surely, a beating was the cost of doing business. If he had kept scientific records, he might have come up with the theory that the damage he incurred was directly proportional to the closeness of each relationship.

Pockmarked's battered face was his fortune. The pockmarks of disease were an afterthought. As he grew into manhood, the scars on his face made him look fierce, rather than victim-like. He became feared, perhaps respected. Moreover, he was connected by blood to the Shanghai criminal class, which led to his induction into a triad, the Three Harmonies Society. He was skilled labor, for by now he could dish it out as well as take it. Hailing from North China, he was taller than most South Chinese. When he wasn't applying muscle at the direction of the Three Harmonies Society, he maintained decorum at Madam Guan's skivvy house as its doorman.

Like his father, and his mother, he could throw a punch.

Pockmarked Weng had never been on a Western ship before, and he hated it. The fact was, Pockmarked didn't like many things, and he didn't like Persimmon Ma, the man, more than most.

He was in the bowels of the merchant steamship, *Qilin Cathay.*

First, Pockmarked was uneasy with the ship's name. A *qilin* was part dragon, part fish, and all nightmare.

Three of their kidnapped captives had been separated from the twenty-two shackled in the hold, and were now held in two near-empty bunkers of the ship's otherwise topped-off coal bunkers.

Second, the tomb-like bunkers were ominously humid, and the coal grit that lined them gave Pockmarked the sense he had entered the mythical Chinese underworld.

Finally, the sounds — voices, machinery, engines, bells, whistles — were all just beyond identification, and distantly haunting.

Persimmon Ma had called on Pockmarked to inflict pain on a Chinese woman and two American sailors in order to get answers to questions that Persimmon put to the Chinese woman in the Wu dialect. Questions to the two American sailors were shouted at them by a cranky merchant captain, whose presence there he couldn't explain. The questions were about Japanese gold.

Persimmon would tell Pockmarked that "Captain Hellfire" wanted Pockmarked to hit the woman and the two men hard. Pockmarked thought foreigners had odd names, yet that name, "Hellfire," was particularly strange and unlucky. Pockmarked could understand a little English, though he couldn't speak too much beyond basic pidgin.

Why wasn't one of the Three Harmonies Society bosses around? Wasn't Madam Guan's establishment under Three Harmonies protection? Why wasn't a boss present? Persimmon was just a lieutenant. Normally a boss was present when foreigners were "pressured."

Pockmarked knew Persimmon was going about this interrogation all wrong. Persimmon and the captain did their questioning separately, though Pockmarked was applying beatings to all three. Beating the woman in one coal bunker was as close as he got to women for the most part, other than working as a doorman-bouncer at a brothel, and he found it unsatisfying.

The American sailors in the other coal bunker were a challenge. They were big and strong, spitefully so. Pockmarked thought beating the woman in front of the men would get the men to talk more quickly. He had worked with other interrogators far more skillful than Persimmon. Pockmarked sighed. He was a blunt instrument, and he was at the disposal of Persimmon and the captain. Triad discipline was strict.

Effectiveness, however, didn't really matter. Pockmarked concluded quite early that none of the three had much useful to say, and that they had already said what little they did know. He didn't like the coal bunkers. They were too confining. He could hear women, different women, somewhere nearby, whispering. They became quiet every time the Chinese woman screamed. They were Chinese women, too, he suspected. He wished Persimmon would lose interest and that this would all be over. He wore leather gloves, but his hands were still starting to hurt.

The case seemed to be that the two American sailors had helped steal the gold and had taken a couple of ingots for themselves. They hadn't taken the two ingots back to their ship, but stashed them with their girlfriends at a local brothel, Madam Guan's. Persimmon didn't know Pockmarked had worked as a doorman at Guan's.

Pockmarked Weng didn't volunteer any information on Guan's. That was a different job, where he knew the patrons better than he knew the girls. He had been surprised to learn the establishment had closed down, however hadn't been told why. He'd hoped the closure was a temporary matter.

The two Americans called "Harp" and "Washboard" had returned to the brothel for the ingots some nights before, then changed those ingots into spending money at a local place, the Red-Knight's Pawnshop. Their girlfriends, however, hadn't been as closed-mouthed as they should have been. The Chinese woman they addressed as "Clementine," also a prostitute, or as she said, a former prostitute, had reported information about the gold to the Nationalists. She, too, was a Nationalist, and thought the gold should go to the Nationalists, rather than back to the over-reaching Japanese.

Pockmarked used his fists, although he had learned to be an observer also. He kicked a stray lump of coal with his foot and waited.

The woman Clementine felt an affinity for the American sailors, and an even stronger loyalty to the Nationalists. An ex-prostitute with ideas and ambitions, she had chosen to support the Nationalist's third-ranking officer, Chiao-jen Sung, one of its rising stars. She had little to contribute, but what information about Westerners came her way might be useful to the cause. That, thought Pockmarked, was completely understandable. Pockmarked Weng had heard Sung's name before.

"Sung mobilized the gentry and merchants for the Nationalists," Pockmarked's mother had told him.

She knew about these things.

"He helped the Nationalists win the 1912 National Assembly election and push in constitutional parliamentary democracy," she had said. "He was an idealistic fool."

She had smacked her son open-handed on the head to drive the point home.

"The new National Assembly's president, Shih-kai Yuan, is also a Nationalist," Pockmarked's mother had said. "Yuan is trouble, and the triads know that. He is shrewd. Yuan had been one of the empress dowager's generals and he swapped allegiances as often as women change undergarments," Pockmarked's mother said.

Yuan had ignored the new parliament and the constitution and made himself a generalissimo. He understood power.

She had brought her cane down on the table inches from Pockmarked's knuckles.

"Watch and learn. Yuan is no fool. Yuan arranged Sung's assassination."

So, the woman Clementine, Pockmarked concluded, had backed the wrong horse and Yuan's supporters had betrayed her to Persimmon Ma.

Clementine cried out unintelligibly.

Clementine knew of the ingots in the brothel and nothing more.

Pockmarked gathered that the Yuan Nationalists would be willing to split the Japanese "finder's fee" for the ingots with the Three Harmonies Society, the idea being that the hooker and the two sailors could lead them to the gold. He was now convinced that wasn't true. Pockmarked wondered if the Chinese woman had meant to betray the American sailors. All this treachery gave Pockmarked a headache. Simple brutality was more his line. Hadn't Confucius said, "Life is simple, but we insist on making it complicated?"

"Leave the woman alone," one sailor yelled. "She don't know a thing about the two lousy ingots w-w-w-we snagged." One of the sailors yelled unclearly. Pockmarked realized he had broken the jaw of that sailor. The larger sailor was missing some teeth.

Pockmarked hated this ship. It sweated with anxiety like a living thing as rivulets of condensation trickled down the blackened sides of the bunker.

He realized the rivulets were a sign they were below water level. It was unnatural. He could live in the close proximity with anyone, but not here. He wanted to be back on the firm soil of the Celestial Kingdom.

One other thing bothered Pockmarked as he struggled to breathe.

The absence of a Three Harmonies boss made him wonder if a triad boss had authorized this interrogation. A month back, the order had come down that one American sailor was not to be touched by any member of the Three Harmonies Society under any circumstances. Pockmarked couldn't recall the sailor's name. He hoped Persimmon wasn't attempting to work around the bosses, and involving him.

Pockmarked knew about the sadistic merchant captain. The Three Harmonies Society sold him opium, which he distributed throughout the Pacific, even in the United States. The cranky merchant was simply a triad customer, or so Pockmarked had thought. Why was this merchant captain giving triad members orders?

Pockmarked Weng watched Persimmon Ma and the ornery merchant captain step out of the bunker to confer.

He hurriedly jammed chloral hydrate pills down the throats of both the American sailors and then washed the tablets down with a pail of water. He had used chloral hydrate frequently at Madam Guan's to quiet unruly customers. That approach was easier than using his fists. He always kept a pail or two of water around for interrogations. Sometimes interviewees had to be revived. Frequently the interview area needed to be cleaned.

One of the sailors, dazed, coughed up the pill and so Pockmarked repeated the process with another pill.

In the Shanghai dialect, Pockmarked reported to Persimmon, "They are both out cold. Not getting any more out of them tonight."

Persimmon too was tired and realized the questioning of the sailors and the woman was a waste of time. He looked over at Hellfire.

The captain lacked patience. He groused, notwithstanding even he could understand the futility of beating unconscious victims.

He, both Pockmarked and Persimmon realized, drew energy from the pain of others.

After leaving the *Qilin Cathay* that night, Pockmarked checked in with his triad contacts. The sailor with special status was called "Hobson," which was not the name of either of Persimmon's American sailors. Discreet inquiries had their limits, at length he was satisfied his triad was indeed looking for the Japanese ingot gold, yet knew nothing about Persimmon and a foreign customer's particular hunt for that gold. Persimmon was acting on his own.

Pockmarked didn't return to the *Qilin Cathay* the next day.

CHAPTER THIRTY-ONE

Shanghai Consulate Annex, Hongkou District, August 1913

Only four men occupied the conference room. Sensing a pending eruption, Draper wished there were more.

Ol' Blue Flame had composed himself for the moment and returned with his flag lieutenant. He studied Draper and Hobson as he spoke, "Let's get to the important part. The gold's in a flooded mineshaft. If Yi betrays us, or we see it's going to fall into the wrong hands, we could get some of our own hardhat salvage divers to recover it."

"Well, yes, not openly, but masquerading as American mining engineers," Draper replied. "The Japanese watch that concession carefully. They contend that all gold that comes out of that mine is theirs. I suppose one of the ironies is that a layer of security for those Japanese ingots is the unknowing Japanese."

The admiral turned to Hobson. "You saw the ingots go into the mineshaft? Personally?"

"Rice bucket after rice bucket," Hobson reported. "The tops were removed and replaced. I took inventory of the gold only. I counted out the contents of each hanmul, each rice bucket. They all matched, except one bucket, which was two ingots short. That was something that we'd learned in Woosung."

"Two ingots missing? How'd that happen?"

"There was mention of a broken rice bucket. It seems unlikely that it was intentional, though maybe one of our men recognized their value and swept them up."

Hobson was reliable, and forthright in any naval context. Draper always drew comfort from his steadfast character.

"Then Yi deposited his own supplementary contribution of rice buckets filled with Mexican silver dollars and tael. That was something personal, I think."

The admiral rubbed his chin. "Difficult for us, however near impossible for Korean insurgents, wouldn't you think? Yi does this all for them and then makes accessing the aid impossible for his own people. Why?"

Draper studied the admiral, suspecting old Blue Flame had already drawn his own conclusion and was testing him.

"Hobson, I don't suppose Yi reads Greek, does he?" Draper interposed.

"Never came up in any conversation. No, not as I recall." Hobson was uneasy.

"I've spoken with him about Confucius, about the Eastern ancients, still and all I don't know much about our Western ancients. Can't remember him indicating that he did." Hobson shifted on his stool.

The conference room was knee deep in paper and files. No doubt Hobson wasn't used to being in such close quarters with any officers, let alone an admiral.

Draper twisted a *netsuke* carving of an ox in his pocket. He'd found it in the market before the Nanking Road promenade, scouting promenade locations. He intended to have the button like ivory figure worked into a watch fob. Perhaps it would bring him luck. After all, this was 1913, the Year of the Ox.

"Why the mineshaft?" the admiral asked. "Shouldn't Yi have converted the ingots to coin? And then spread it around in some less conspicuous form that the individual insurgents could get their hands on, and spend easily?"

Hobson probably knew that Draper was slipping into his professorial persona, a persona that rarely got good results in naval circles.

Draper could think of no other way of explaining Yi's "test."

"Admiral, the ancient Greeks found themselves in a similar situation and it ended badly," Draper began. "The Ionian Revolt, and the siege of Miletos, is analogous to any Korean insurrection. The Ionian Revolt is what Yi wants to avoid. Yi wants to be careful about what he sets in motion. He wants Korea to be free of Japanese oppression, still he's not sure what demons a revolt will summon. In the time of Cyrus the Great…"

The three men stopped to identify the shrieks welling up from the floor below. The shrieks were feminine, shortened and controlled. Then came the sound of breaking glass. Glasses were being thrown into a fireplace situated on the ground floor of the atrium.

They had overstayed working hours in the consulate annex. This was "after hours."

The admiral's eyes looked thoughtfully at the vaulted ceiling. "Yes, yes, Cyrus the Great…"

Draper continued. "The Greeks had settlements on the Turkish coast under nominal Persian rule. The Athenians encouraged the Ionians to revolt, but sadly the revolt was a disaster. At the end of the siege of Miletos, all the Greek settlers, the Ionians, were massacred." He paused. "The Koreans are the subject of a military occupation, and their oppressors are less than a day's sail away."

Draper paused and rolled the ox netsuke in the palm of his clinched hand.

"No one among the Greeks actually took the time to assess if those settlements had the right leaders, and those leaders had the skills to lead a revolt. You can't just blindly encourage revolt. You must be sure that revolt has a chance of success, or you may simply make a bad situation worse."

Draper looked around at the others.

Hobson pretended to make a note on a mess chit form he'd found.

"This may have been all for nothing? How I hate engaging the foe without immediate result!" Admiral Bulkley struck the conference table for emphasis, and a small geyser erupted from the nearest inkwell.

All three men flinched. Each wore dress whites. When it came to stains on dress whites, each would have preferred blood to ink. Ink stains would be immediate, humiliating, and clerical in nature. Bloodstains on the other hand, somewhere in the distant future, were honorable, and warrior-like.

A floor below them, several feminine voices joined in song.

"The Navy has tests for everything," Draper argued. "Why can't Yi have a test for insurrectional competence?"

The flag lieutenant brought in a pot of coffee, and the three men lunged for it.

"Sir, we have had an immediate result," Draper argued. "We have foiled a Japanese attempt to undermine the Chinese economy. Remember, we have reduced Japan's ability to create mischief by three million dollars. Remember our escapade has caused great embarrassment to its intelligence service."

Hobson scrubbed at a small ink spot on his trousers with crumpled paper from a wastepaper basket.

Draper tapped his index finger on the conference table keeping clear of inkwells. "A Korean insurgency must be organized and competent. If they have the leadership and cohesion to recover the gold, they may have the leadership and cohesion to apply it toward undermining the Japanese occupation."

The admiral rarely sat so still for long. Draper realized he had held the man's attention.

"The Koreans may never be ready. The very fact they are on their own makes the situation worse. We can't help them. Logistically, we can't come halfway around the world to beat a naval power like Japan in its own backyard, not yet. A coal-burning ship has a short cruising radius. And we have the Philippines to worry about."

The room became quiet. They were all talked out.

Admiral Bulkley rose, indicating the meeting was over.

"It's done. Yi upheld his end. We upheld our end. I understand his thinking. He gave us an opportunity, and he's bought us time. I believe The United States Navy is going to lock horns with the Japanese eventually, though probably not on our watch."

CHAPTER THIRTY-TWO

USS Saratoga, Flagship of US Asiatic Fleet, Huangpu River,
August 1913

The next morning, Draper and Hobson took the steam launch from the consular compound to *USS Saratoga*. A morning meeting had just concluded, and several captain's gigs were pulling away from the warship. The quarterdeck was bustling with salutes, side boys, and whistling boatswains' pipes.

Draper and Hobson, barely noticed, gave the mandatory salutes to the national ensign and the quarterdeck, and were then peremptorily waved aboard.

After Draper's time in a hospital and in the consulate annex, he found *Saratoga*'s narrow passageways, low ceilings or "overheads," and steel ladders, cramped and over-utilitarian.

To Hobson, after life on *USS Pluto*, a Chinese junk, and a side-wheeler, the spit and polish, and the somewhat larger living spaces of the flagship, made *Saratoga* feel like a palace.

Admiral Bulkley saw them immediately. The fact that he met them alone gave them both a feeling of significance. The flag conference room was half the size of the consulate annex conference room.

"Sir, can I ask a question?" Hobson was seated, his back as straight as a jack staff. Somewhere in the small office a clock was ticking under a pile of files.

Admiral Bulkley and Draper exchanged glances.

Hobson asked, "Why are the crews of *Pluto* and *Rainbow* confined to their ships?"

Draper cleared his throat. "Three weeks ago, after the ingot heist, after you and Yi left on your journey, two ingots showed up at the Red-Knight's Pawnshop. The clerk at the shop notified me, to my disappointment he could only describe the two men who sold the ingots as 'American sailors.' You remember one cask had been damaged, and we had concluded an ingot or two might be missing. We guessed those two sailors came from either *Pluto* or *Rainbow*.

"We cancelled all liberty. We couldn't risk anyone in Shanghai connecting the concept of gold ingots with American sailors. We planned to move our ships in Shanghai to Cavite and hoped we'd put the matter to an end."

Draper removed his half-glasses and rubbed the bridge of his nose. "A little over a week ago, an attempt was made to kidnap me and possibly a member of the consul's staff. Recently, we've had reports from friends of the fleet in China that a triad offered a reward for any two or three American sailors from the *USS Pluto* or *USS Rainbow*. The reward is five hundred Mex per sailor. Someone is coming close, and they think they can get the information from crewmembers of those ships."

Hobson shook his head and whistled. "Not good. Someone's connected the missing ingots with the US Navy. Worse still, to those two ships."

"Yes, in particular because those were the two crews we used for the Red-Crowned Crane plan," Draper mused.

Hobson wondered if Persimmon Ma, the thug with one droopy eyelid who had confronted him during his first meal with Yi, was still trying to impress his boss, or maybe his boss's boss, or merely engaging in a personal vendetta. Perhaps Yi's influence with Three Harmonies Society had waned. Hobson would need to be doubly careful. Two of the six men killed at Madam Guan's had been Chinese. And one had been a Spuyten.

Draper ruffled through some papers, giving the admiral time to stop the conversation if he wished. The admiral nodded ambiguously.

"So, we decided not to give them the opportunity to strong-arm information from sailors on liberty," Draper added. "We don't think they'll be gentle."

The admiral interjected, "We'll all be coaling shortly, and then it's off to Cavite."

Draper resumed. "We're not sure which triad, though I think it might be the Three Harmonies Society or the Green Gang."

Hobson inhaled audibly. "I had a run-in with those thugs, although Yi smoothed it over. At least I think he did."

Draper looked Hobson in the eye. Hobson's girlfriend and two best friends were missing. He'd shot three men and been taken into custody. "Well, the bounty might explain why Hellfire's thugs were lying in wait at Madam Guan's establishment. The two best places to intersect sailors of those crews are the fleet landing and Guan's. The fleet landing is really too public and too open for an ambuscade. The other ships' crews have their own favorite skivvy-houses."

"I wonder how Hospital Apprentice Culper's cut throat has anything to do with the rest," offered Hobson. "He had no marks on him indicating interrogation."

They others made no response.

"Five US Navy ships are on moorings in Shanghai right now." Draper's mind was processing quickly. "The single thing our two have in common, which excludes the others, is they were directly involved in hijacking the gold. How would the triads know that? They're attempting to pick up the trail of the gold. That tugboat at the gorge was one effort — this is another. I think Yi trailed his shirt a bit on the Yangtze. After all, the scuttling of the junk was a diversion."

Hobson nodded. "That's what I thought, too, that he wanted to attract his serious pursuers. That fifty-tael sycee reminds me of another thing those two ships have in common. They both have crew members who participated in the Woosung landings two years ago. Culper was at Woosung and so was I."

Hobson inhaled slowly. He looked as though he needed more oxygen. He was probably exhausted. The gunfight at Madam Guan's must have taken its toll. "The fifty-tael sycee may be what brought Culper and Paymaster McCorkran together. Clearly Culper turned it in and *USS Rainbow*'s paymaster would have taken responsibility for its safekeeping. Yet I always took Culper for a fellow who'd collect what he could on the shady side of the street."

"The beginnings of an alliance perhaps. Where did that fifty-tael sycee come from?" asked the admiral.

"The mud underneath the Jinsen Steam Navigation Wharf in Woosung." Hobson offered. "Yi's warehouse in Woosung."

"Yi's wharf?"

"That's how I figure it," Hobson responded. "He was defending his silver. Yi's warehouse moved silver sycee. Those flooded mines in Korea are filled with rice buckets of Yi's silver sycee, as well as Japan's gold ingots. Yi has put a fortune of his own, mostly in fifty-tael sycee, into those mines on top of the Japanese ingots.

"Paymaster McCorkran deals in silver," Hobson continued. "Every month he issues pay in Mexican dollars."

"Hobson, did you know Yi was once a Korean tribute courier?" Draper asked. "I have a Japanese file that I received in exchange for some intelligence with the British. Yi was responsible for bringing tributary tael, those boat-shaped silver ingots, to China. He was robbed once and had to flee. A few years later, he ended up in the Klondike. He was also in San Francisco, and eventually came back here and to Korea after the substitute assassination of Korea's Queen Min."

Draper then thought for a moment. "For Yi, this has been a matter of retribution against the Japanese and redemption for failing Korea, his homeland."

Hobson reached into his jumper and pulled out a coin. It was a tailor-made uniform and had a small inside pocket. Most China hands, Draper knew, wore tailor-mades.

"This is all I have until my next payday, one Mexican dollar," Hobson said. "This is one of the Mexican dollars we get paid once a month. Do they really come from reputable banks, or even Mexico? We only have Paymaster McCorkran's word for that."

"Are you saying McCorkran's playing the silver exchange with government money?" Admiral Bulkley snapped.

"He converts US dollars into Mexican dollars," Hobson suggested. "A clever operator can always find a way to grift a percentage in a conversion like that. My guess is the paymaster's been working different ways to divert naval funds and sailors' paydays both up and down the line. He took a big risk to get his hands on a bit of stray silver, my piddling fifty-tael sycee. I think he's used to taking those kinds of risks. That one probably didn't make him miss a heartbeat."

Draper smacked his right fist into his left hand, forgetful that his left wrist was encased in plaster. "I've been so preoccupied with that report for the flag captain, Hobson, I never thought to show you the related files. Maybe you ought to look at my two files from British intelligence on Yi. That name Spuyten keeps showing up. Pretty sure it's Dutch. Nectar and ambrosia, I ought to know. How many Spuytens can there be?"

"I follow," Hobson said. "I wonder now when we hear Spuyten, whether the name McCorkran will come up."

Hobson could hear rapid steps headed up the stairs. Mr. Vail, the flag lieutenant, had signaled USS Rainbow, the station ship, troop-ship, and now station ship again. An inaudible, but animated discussion took place in the corridor between Mr. Vail and Admiral Bulkley.

Admiral Bulkley stormed back into the conference room. "The minute we summoned Paymaster McCorkran, he filed a chit for a request mast."

It was as if the ship's magazine had exploded. Even Admiral Bulkley seemed angry and dazed. In the Navy, the term "mast" was associated with discipline, though not always. Any sailor charged with major wrongdoing had the option of requesting a court-martial, or a mast. A court-martial was conducted like a trial before a jury of sailors from other ships or units of roughly the same grade. A 'mast' was a less formal hearing before the accused sailor's commanding officer or a unit commander farther up that sailor's chain of command. In either case, court-martial or mast, a determination of guilt or innocence was made, and a sentence, when appropriate, was handed down.

That was the more common mast, the disciplinary mast.

The other mast was the "request mast," essentially a sailor's request for a hearing. Often, the inquiry had nothing to do with a disciplinary offense at all. It was simply an official request to be heard. Theoretically, the application could go to a commanding officer. If rejected, it could be appealed to that commanding officer's superior and so forth.

Paymaster McCorkran apparently felt he had something to say. As a member of the admiral's staff, his commanding officer was the admiral.

"He's got gall. I give him that," roared Ol' Blue Flame.

Draper and Hobson stood motionless with their covers on. Admiral Bulkley stood behind a portable podium that a steward had brought and mounted on the conference table.

Paymaster Commander McCorkran was marched in. On his right was a Marine lieutenant colonel.

"You may uncover," Ol' Blue Flame began. Each man removed his cover, and tucked it under his left arm. "And you may stand at ease."

"Sir, I have a plan," Paymaster McCorkran said.

The admiral glowered at the paymaster. "I'm sure you do. It was someone's plan, perhaps your own, that has brought you before me."

The paymaster didn't blink.

The Marine officer shifted his weight from his left foot to this right foot and back again.

"Admiral, sir, I request this mast be heard before you alone," McCorkran added.

Hobson imagined Admiral Bulkley suspected the paymaster would try to bribe him if he could get him alone. Ol' Blue Flame, he believed, didn't plan to take a single step down that road.

"Request denied. Your escort, the lieutenant colonel, has my confidence and I have no inclination to listen to you outside the hearing of others. This petty officer is going to take notes."

"I have a plan, sir, to get the Navy's money back."

Hobson concluded the man was as brazen as a grappling hook.

"What money? And in return for that plan, what do you get?"

"You put me ashore in Manila, and I disappear."

The admiral hesitated. Brazen McCorkran might be, yet Hobson noticed his hands were shaking like palm fronds before an erupting volcano. "I was expecting something like that. You know the money we have in mind?"

Hobson believed Ol' Blue Flame wasn't aware that the Navy had any missing money, though if anyone in the Asiatic Fleet would know, the paymaster would know. Admiral Bulkley was not going to admit ignorance.

The admiral studied the paymaster.

"Perhaps you should first tell me why I should listen to your request at all. Normally if a paymaster allows Navy money to disappear, that paymaster gets a stateroom at Portsmouth Naval Prison. The winters are cold there. The blankets itch, and the Marines have bad dispositions. I don't know if they still use painted lines to delineate cell boundaries. I know there's been agitation toward the more conventional steel bars. Sounds like coddling to me."

Though the paymaster was standing at attention, his knees seemed about to buckle. "I can get a lot of money back for you, with interest at the very least."

"Well, you can favor us with your proposal tomorrow. This mast is continued until tomorrow. Furthermore, consider yourself under investigation for misappropriation of naval funds and government property. You are confined to quarters. A Marine will be stationed at your stateroom door, and the chief steward will see that your food is brought to you."

Draper talked to *USS Saratoga*'s chief quartermaster, and that chief petty officer found him some reading space in the pilothouse, a razor, and a set of undress whites.

Studying the papers Draper had given him, Hobson recognized the young tribute courier in those old reports. Yi was a patriot, a descendant of the warrior aristocracy. He was a man bred to loyalty and to defend Korea. Japan had its samurai and Korea had its muban. As a Korean, Yi was every bit as guided by Confucian wisdom and filial piety as any Chinese warrior, sometimes more so.

Yi valued loyalty, and he understood the concept of honor. He had gone to great effort to repay a debt and to return a missing fortune to Korea. That fortune had been intended to secure China's protection of Korea from aggressors. Had the tribute found its way to the Chinese empress as intended, perhaps Korea could have retained its sovereignty. Who could say otherwise? Certainly, Yi could not have allowed himself to think otherwise.

Hobson leaned back and suddenly noticed something. In the margin of the first page of the first British file, someone had penned in "Liqin," just two Chinese characters. Her name didn't appear in file once, but Hobson recognized it as a courtesan-style "entertainer" name. Had she been a Japanese agent working as a British double-agent against the Japanese?

Hobson sighed. He couldn't argue Yi out of his sense of guilt, his sense of debt. This was a debt of honor to the ancestors. The loss had been a matter of trustworthiness, and loyalty to the Hermit Kingdom. Eastern philosophy put a high value on harmony, yet not as high a value as debts of honor.

The second British file concentrated on the stolen tribute and Coffin's murder. Hobson hadn't known about Coffin, still if the Alaskan Spuytens were the Shanghai Spuytens, Yi was going to feel a strong call to action. In Alaska, Ephraim Coffin had served as Yi's older brother in the Korean meaning of that phrase. The Alaska story went beyond cultural standards, being more universal. If Yi were now to become aware of the intervention of the Spuytens, nothing could stop him from repaying the second debt, the Alaska debt, at any cost.

Paymaster McCorkran's request mast entered its second day in the admiral's conference room aboard *USS Saratoga*.

"What do you have to say that's worth hearing?" Admiral Bulkley started.

McCorkran didn't look well.

"I changed my name from 'McCollum' to "McCorkran" when I entered the Navy as an enlisted man," Paymaster McCorkran said. "I wanted no confusion with my San Francisco cousins. The Navy quickly appreciated my bookkeeping skills. I became a warrant officer in no time. Eventually, I gained a commission and rose over time to my present status."

A commander who was in charge of the pay and business matters of a station was addressed as "paymaster." In addition to handling pay disbursements, the paymaster supervised the purchase of all provisions and supplies for his command. In the Far East, fortunes could be made on the potential kickbacks to buyers. The admiral had reviewed the records before scheduling the mast. Paymaster McCorkran had been watched and audited for years without a single blemish or accusation on his record.

"And then Spuyten & McCollum established themselves in Shanghai and Yokohama. The 'McCollum' in that partnership name belongs to my cousins, who started their lives of intimidation and graft on San Francisco's Barbary Coast.

"Spuyten & McCollum ship normal cargos, though they primarily make their money in opium and the sex slave trade along the rims of the Pacific. Recently, they've positioned themselves to be useful to the Japanese. To conduct that sort of business, it's helpful to have a sponsor, and the Japanese have become their sponsor.

"My cousins are predators, and as predators are drawn to predators. They connected with Hellfire Spuyten and his five sons on the Frisco waterfront. You don't want to get on the bad side of my cousins. Many a sailor who has crossed a Spuyten has succumbed to the kiss of a straight razor. Hellfire, in a rage, has been known to push crewmen up to the rail and then tip them over into the sea. With my cousins or the Spuytens, better never turn your back, and watch your front, too."

Hobson sat rigidly in his chair, not at all knowing where this story was going.

"Culper made that mistake, and to some extent that was my fault. Sailors can be tough, naval or merchant, and Spuyten & McCollum are madman-sailor tough, an unholy convergence."

The admiral sat quietly, moving his fountain pen back and forth across his desk blotter.

The paymaster continued. "First thing, they intimidated me into using waterfront suppliers they selected and deposited kickback money into my personal account with the *huaqi yinhang*, the "colorful flag" bank. Initially the deposits were made without my knowledge. I expected kickbacks in cash, instead the Three Harmonies Society had a clerk who handled the forged deposits."

The paymaster used the nickname shared by Americans and Chinese for the oldest American bank in Shanghai. "The colorful flag" was the American flag. This was the bank that had received Qing dynasty reparations made to the United States after the Boxer Rebellion.

"Later, I learned these waterfront suppliers were under triad protection, the Three Harmonies Society. Once they put money into my personal account, they blackmailed me based on that malfeasance, wanting me to give them quick turnaround loans using Navy funds.

"They always repaid, so no one noticed, and by then I was hooked. I could see no way out. The loans went into a Spuyten &

McCollum account at the same bank. As far as I know, the kickback money is still there."

The admiral, Hobson realized, had never liked the paymaster. No one did. On the other hand, no one had ever uttered a word against him when it came to performance of his duties.

"The combined key to all this is the Mann Act and the fact that I signed deposits into their accounts in the Colorful Flag Bank," the paymaster observed.

"The Mann Act? Doesn't that have to do with the interstate transportation of women across state lines for..." The admiral fished for a word appropriate to his station, "...immoral purposes? Isn't the Mann Act what they're using on Jack Johnson, that fellow who hired Gunboat as a sparring partner?"

Gunboat Smyth had been heavyweight champion of the Pacific Fleet and a legend. Hobson knew the admiral wished Gunboat had stayed in the Navy.

"The law also includes the words 'transport in foreign commerce' which means 'brought across our borders,'" the paymaster pointed out. "Spuyten & McCollum is allied with the Three Harmonies Society. That's where they get their opium and their girls."

"They're kissing up to the Japanese Kempeitai to expand their distribution network. Japan has introduced opium into Korea to keep the riff-raff docile and increase the flow of shadowy information from that country.

"I guess it gives them a direct line into folks who are pliable and a way to blackmail the Korean criminal element into doing their bidding," McCorkran continued. "I have no idea how Japan enters into the Chinese opium trade, yet they're using opium to open cracks all over Asia. The British first introduced the trade by bringing opium from India to pay for tea, though these days, with the collapse of the Qing dynasty, the sources are hard to trace."

The admiral shook his head, as if to clear it. "You're talking about American civilians, Chinese civilians, and Japanese intelligence. How's the Mann Act going to get the United States Navy leverage over those groups?" No doubt the admiral's head was throbbing. He surely wasn't getting enough sleep. Hobson knew no one was getting enough sleep. "This story is going to explain the death of Hospital Apprentice Culper eventually?"

Paymaster McCorkran looked hurt. "Sir, I apologize. This story is complicated. I will get to Culper."

"Proceed," Ol' Blue Flame said wearily.

"In any event, the loss of the gold ignited a powder trail that snakes through this end of the world like a river dragon. A Yuan Nationalist had tipped off the Japanese that the United States Navy was involved."

Hobson realized Clementine had Nationalist inclinations, but so did many others in China.

Paymaster McCorkran slowed his delivery a bit. "I might have told them the ships involved were USS Pluto and USS Rainbow. Didn't do any harm, did it?"

Hobson realized McCorkran didn't know Harp and Washboard were missing.

"When no one could grab a US sailor or two to extract information, Spuyten & McCollum decided to go for secondary sources and turn a profit along the way. They bought out Madam Guan's. The Three Harmonies Society had the largest interest. The girls all had contracts, and theoretically those contracts survive the buy-out. The contracts still hold. The girls now belong to Spuyten & McCollum. They'll be squeezed for information and eventually sold soon as 'a complete and exotic collection' to a house somewhere outside of China."

The paymaster exhaled. "I'd be willing to sign a set of affidavits confirming my misdeeds, and confirming the money in my account belongs to the US Department of War. I'm willing to sign a set of affidavits confirming the money in the Spuyten & McCollum account is the illicit gains from shipping women to San Francisco for illicit purposes."

"But you don't know they're going to San Francisco?" the admiral said, his brows knitting like the convective clouds of a gathering typhoon. "How do we prove that?"

"We'll get one of the women to say that was where they were being taken," McCorkran offered glibly.

"What's the legal phrase I'm looking for, Mr. Draper? You're good with languages, even English." Ol' Blue Flame cracked his knuckles.

"Suborning perjury?" Draper responded.

"Hmmmm" was the admiral's uneasy acknowledgement. "As if their captors would give them the slightest hint where they were going." He rubbed his head, seeming to be in constant pain.

"Sir, I will cooperate fully with seizing all Spuyten & McCollum and my assets in the Colorful Flag Bank in the next few weeks when you get wind of a shipment and identify the ships. I'll sign the affidavits. You'll have a need for my deposition here in Shanghai since as a member of the United States Navy I 'might not be available for testimony in the future.' Then, just put me ashore in Manila with a set of civvies and a week's pay and you'll never hear from, or better yet, of me again."

"Yes, Paymaster. I only wish the conclusion of this business could be as easy as that. How much of all this do you expect me to believe without verification?"

"Most of it will be easily provable. Just don't let Spuyten & McCollum give you the slip. Take their ships in tow with girls aboard and the crews will sing in four-part harmony. You won't much need me after that."

Hobson realized McCorkran knew nothing about Harp, Washboard, or Clementine.

The admiral raised his voice. "What about Hospital Apprentice Culper? How does he, and that chunk of Chinese silver, figure into all this? From what I've heard, that's what got all this started. You seem inclined to have seized the initiative. Pray show me where the McCorkran initiative was exercised there?"

"Culper desired to turn a buck here and there," Paymaster McCorkran responded. "He'd run errands for me. Collect the messages from the suppliers. He came up with the idea of lending his shipmates money at a high interest rate — what do you call it, a 'usurious rate.' Who's going to cross a medico? It could cost you your health. I'll tell you; I'd never play cards with him."

Hobson agreed; that sounded like the Culper he knew.

"He always had an eye for an opportunity," the paymaster added with admiration. "That's why it surprised me when he balked about getting involved with the local grifts, with a triad. He wanted nothing to do with them, and nothing to do with McC & S. He didn't want any partner he didn't see on a daily basis. We never did any physical stuff. No rough stuff, docking sailors' pay and moving that money elsewhere. We simply made up some paperwork to pull it out of the deadbeats' pay when they wouldn't repay willingly."

"Of course, Culper is dead and has no way of defending himself," Admiral Bulkley interrupted.

"I'm sorry. You're right, Admiral. No way at all," McCorkran said in comforting tones. "Anyway, Hellfire Spuyten, he says he'll have one of his boys sweet talk him, Culper that is, into the organization. All I have to do is have one of Spuyten's boys talk with him, right on *USS Rainbow*. Culper wasn't going to get skittish about a visit to a naval warship. On Culper's turf, for gosh sake." The paymaster shook his head.

"Culper was right," he said. "You can't be a partner with the devil. I left them alone on the fantail. Culper was on his way to a shore patrol assignment. The Spuyten boy, he just comes back and smiles, just a how-do-you-do smile, and says the partnership problem is all cleared up.

"The truth, the truth is, I swear it, that I didn't know what Diderick Spuyten was up to. He goes by 'Diddler.' I don't know why. He must have put Culper right to the rail and cut his throat. Had him over the side in a heartbeat. I hear that was what the old man did. I'll bet he taught his young'uns. 'Spuyten' must mean a tangle of snakes in some lingo or t'other. Maybe I can guess why they call Diderick, 'Diddler.'

"Anyhow, Culper never left the ship to go ashore," the paymaster added. *"I don't want to go ashore in Shanghai ever again."*

"And Hobson, how does he figure in all this? Didn't Hobson give you that fifty-sycee tael off Woosung?"

"Hobson?" The paymaster was grasping for leverage and probably wondered how he could play Hobson, despite realizing the admiral was asking questions too fast for him to start improvising.

"Never actually met Hobson. Hobson was nothing, other than he found the fifty-tael sycee through dumb luck. We got him transferred to that darned collier, *Pluto*. Couldn't have him around to identify the fifty-tael sycee. Heck, he had already had a reputation. And double heck, I heard when the guy was recruited, he was already Asiatic. He speaks Japanese and Korean, still and all not the local lingo. That's not much good. Not much good at all. Can't trust a fellow like that."

Hobson realized he hadn't been introduced by name. Now McCorkran was taking credit for his transfer to *USS Pluto*. Perhaps he'd tried, but that was Draper's work.

McCorkran's eyes suddenly brightened with comprehension. "Huh, with the Japanese looking for their gold, maybe then I could have used him. If I knew where the gold was, or knew somebody who did. I suppose I missed a bet there."

Hobson sat quietly. He knew McCorkran hadn't determined who he was.

Why had Admiral Bulkley thrown in the Hobson question? Hobson speculated it could have meant the admiral trusted him a great deal or very little. He suspected the question was a test. Like his relatives, McCorkran's internal compass was reversed. Anyone McCorkran felt comfortable with was crooked and anyone he distrusted was reliable.

So far, Hobson, though central to the Red-Crowned Crane plan, knew he had gone completely unnoticed by two Chinese political factions, two Shanghai triads, and the intelligence service of arguably the most powerful naval power in the Far East.

Hobson congratulated himself. If "gone Asiatic" meant cultivating a low profile, demonstrating great intelligence, exemplifying integrity, and maintaining a scrappy disposition, he decided he'd elect to have his inconspicuous Asiatic medal be awarded him by an outrigger canoe filled with be-flowered wahines at the next harbor he visited. McCorkran, Hobson mused, had provided helpful information, even so his plan constructed upon his own priorities, was flawed.

CHAPTER THIRTY-THREE

Charthouse, USS Saratoga, Huangpu River, Shanghai, August 1913

Hobson sat up in the charthouse, staring at the file he'd placed in the middle of a chart table, when Draper arrived.

Too many open questions.

We need to take action, Hobson thought, but what action? It was time to go on the offensive, but how?

"Mr. Draper, we have to find Harp and Washboard." Hobson climbed partway up the ladder to the deck above them to see the sky. "Guan's girls, too. They have value in several ways, on the other hand I think they'll feel Harp and Washboard's worth will end after interrogation."

Hobson had lost all track of time. It was early evening, that he knew. The horizon was dark, despite a peppering of gaslights and paper lanterns. No help there. Shanghai didn't sleep. Then he heard the ship's bell chime, eight o'clock, end of the watch.

"That was the admiral's word to me," Draper said. "They have first priority, albeit Shanghai's a rabbit warren, a labyrinth."

Hobson nearly stumbled as he returned to his chair. "My brain's a mass of gun cotton, a spongy mess about to explode. The paymaster says Guan's is shut down, and the girls will be going to Frisco. Tell me, what's the opposition's first priority?" Hobson asked.

"Let's assume they know the US Navy is connected with the disappearance of the Japanese ingots. They want to talk to the fellows they think diverted the gold to its final place of concealment," Draper responded. "They're not available. They're confined to their ships."

Hobson interjected, "If you're the Kempeitai or the Three Harmonies Society, who are you going to question? The women, our girlfriends from Madam Guan's. If that doesn't work, who are you going to hold for ransom for information? Those same women."

He waited a beat and then continued.

"Who are you going to watch like a bunch of tethered goats? If you think sailors stole some gold and you can't get at the sailors, you lock up their women. You wait, and one way or other, that's going to get your information.

"The women haven't left for San Francisco yet," Hobson continued. "They're still useful until our ships leave. That is, assuming McCorkran is right and not spinning a yarn to get him off the hook. Now the admiral's announced we're leaving their value as leverage disappears. We need to do something to save the women, perhaps Harp and Washboard, and end Japan's economic subversion plan conclusively."

Draper studied Hobson, and shook his head.

"The warm-hearted girls of Madam Guan's are the key to US national security in the Far East?" Draper asked.

"No offense, but my gal, Clementine, can tell you more about warship arrivals and departures than any intelligence officer in the dozen or so navies that visit Shanghai."

"No offense is taken."

Hobson was leaning forward and resting his arms on the chart table while Draper scratched at the skin at the edges of his cast. These were social realities Hobson understood, and Draper no doubt was only beginning to appreciate.

Draper threw his palms upward. "The women are a source of information, though I'm sure they've divulged whatever they knew which wasn't much — mostly, now they're just leverage. They're also bait. Who wants the gold?"

"Everyone. Anyone who knows about it," Hobson opined. He remembered the Spuytens especially, though said nothing. This particular national security matter was becoming personal.

"The Kempeitai can't keep this all to themselves because they want to recover that gold. They're going to ask discreet questions and offer discreet rewards. How about a triad or two? How about the paymaster? And are the Yuan Nationalists and Anti-Yuan

Nationalists going to get wind of all this? Well, we've narrowed that down to pretty much all of Shanghai. I suppose we need to find the girls," said Draper. "When we take the people holding them, we're going to get a good sense of who we're up against. And McCorkran's plan allows us to hold them."

"They're here in Shanghai still, I know it," said Hobson. "They're held in a warehouse or wharf or somewhere isolated from the public."

"We can't seize Japanese merchant ships without verifying that the women are aboard unwillingly. Now if Harp and Washboard are being held, that gets even more ticklish." Draper looked as though he was beginning to lose heart, to think the factors against them were insurmountable. "You stay here on *Saratoga* for the night. I've fallen behind in review of the Japanese consulate trash courtesy of the Reverence to Lettered Paper Society. I'll probably be in the consulate annex reading half the night and then trying to catch forty winks on a cot for the remainder."

"The Reverence to what?" Hobson gave Draper a dubious look.

"Never mind. You know your Shanghai and I know mine."

Consulate Annex, Hongkou District, International Settlement, Shanghai, September 1913

In the late afternoon, Draper caught a glimpse of Miss Knapp as he headed to his office on the second floor of the consulate annex. She was swirling across the balcony walkway on the third floor. The entire atrium reminded him of a birdcage. He was sure she'd been avoiding him.

"Have I missed something here, Miss Knapp?" he called out. He was thinking about the promenades, still made the question appropriately vague so that it might apply to consular matters.

She walked a few more steps away from him, stopped, seemed to consider, and finally faced him. "Our garbage processing program may have turned up some irregular activity."

She put her fingers to her lips, and gestured "stop" with her free hand. She bustled across the balcony and down the spiral staircase.

"The Japanese consulate has been pretty circumspect, however I have noticed a flurry of invoices to a Western shipping firm. I'm going through the translations now."

"Have you been avoiding me?" Draper blurted out. She didn't want to hear this question, even so he needed to know where he stood.

She flashed him a look of fear. He'd asked the question she apparently wanted to avoid at all costs.

"You're an interesting man. Very interesting — too-o-o interesting. You may not survive the interest you generate."

Her look of discomfort was intense.

"As for me, I'm not sure 'interesting' is enough to base any long-range decisions on. Interesting is a superficial thing, really, don't you think?" She made a moue, studying his reaction.

Draper stood still for several minutes. "I don't know."

"I don't know either," she said with finality.

By early evening, Hobson realized he couldn't relax. He had to go ashore. He wasted no time finding his dress whites, slipping onto the fleet launch, and finding Draper at the consulate annex.

"I'm going to find Clementine, Guan's girls, Harp, and Washboard, sir. That slipknot McCorkran set me thinking."

Draper seemed to consider that. Given the events of the day, no doubt, Draper seemed sympathetic. "How are you going to do that?"

"I'm going back to Madam Guan's," Hobson said, leaving no room for argument.

"Alone?"

"Alone."

"Hmm, that didn't work so well this last time. Remember two of you went together that time. And you're the precise source they're trying to get their hands on, though they don't know it. Officially, I forbid it."

Hobson looked Draper up and down.

"Not sure they know your role in all this. Don't get taken," Draper added.

"I'll bear that in mind if I'm asked. I think the Spuyten boys have probably decided to adopt some new plan. As I recall, my reception committee wasn't purely delegates from Spuyten & McCollum. I also wonder if I can't unearth someone in the neighborhood who saw, heard, or knows something useful."

"Well, being the Bureau of Navigation's representative for the Asiatic Fleet, I can think of a few people I should speak to also," Draper said. "Affairs are drawing to a head. I suspect someone in the opposition has set a time limit for results." He gave Hobson a serious look.

"Now, I've lost track," Draper resumed. "Did you have any trouble getting off *Saratoga*? I don't think you're confined to stay anywhere. I guess you're still the admiral's representative, and my thoughts are simply advisory."

Hobson raised an eyebrow. "Can't remember the admiral providing any guidance on that subject. I guess I'm still the admiral's representative when it comes to the Red-Crowned Crane matters."

Their eyes locked.

Draper seemed frustrated, unready to suggest the flag captain take a swim in the Huangpu. "You're going to need a dispatch case of Mex dollars. I think Harp and Washboard are worth it, don't you? Moreover, it's going to be dark soon. Those whites are going to be easy to spot."

Draper probably could remember taking back Hobson's government-issue Colt, perhaps he couldn't remember asking for the hammerless pistol. In view of recent events, he might dismiss the idea of recovering a weapon that didn't officially exist.

Hobson didn't want to be captured and tortured. In view of recent events, he might rescue Clementine, Harp, and Washboard.

Mandarin and the Wu dialect weren't Hobson's languages. He spoke Japanese and Korean, on the other hand he hadn't grown up in China's linguistic maze. He had picked up a couple dozen phrases, yet now he needed something more than rote idioms. What he needed was a street tout. As a regular at Madam Guan's, he had fallen out of the habit of dealing with touts. Now, he walked from the consulate annex down to the fleet landing, looking for a familiar face.

As he left the fleet landing, he came across Miller, the British tar who'd explained the Polyphon.

"Know any reliable street touts?"

"Sure, I know a bloke name o' Sunny. Well-liked feller," Miller said, scratching his white beard.

"Yes, I know him. Where can I find him?"

Miller gave Hobson directions, then asked, "You know a Yank officer named Draper? Hazy headed notwit'standin' a ruddy, blazin' 'ero he is. We had a grand ceremony for 'im."

"I know the name, though can't say I know him."

"Well, good luck with Sun, Yank. Just remember the Royal Navy put this port in commission. Don't damage 'er."

Miller briefly doffed his cover and was gone.

A half-hour later, Hobson recognized Sun — a well-known tout — from the back. Sun faced the Huangpu. Sun wore a perennial smile like a mask. He was slight and non-threatening, the ideal tout. No one ever saw the whites of his eyes because the flesh around them curved in permanent, tight, inverted U's.

"You long-time China sailor, but Sun can help. Madam Guan place no more. I find you new place, first class, savvy?"

"Yes, I know that. What happened? Where's Madam Guan and where are her girls?"

"Madam Guan sold out. Gone back to Tientsin. Girls go someplace else. All together."

Hobson jingled the coins in the dispatch case and pulled out a Mexican silver dollar. "I need to find out where the girls went."

He placed several Mexican dollars in Sun's hand. "We need to find out where the girls went," repeated the American sailor.

Sun looked thoughtful. "You need to talk to people. I take you talk to people. I paid to steer gobs to new place now. I get no money to send gobs to Madam Guan's anymore. No never mind. I like you. I help you."

"Don't worry, Sun, you'll be compensated."

The jingle of coins caused several other touts to close in.

Hobson turned to the crowd of touts. "Sun and I have an agreement, gentlemen. If it doesn't work out, well, I'll be back to visit with each of you."

One corner of Sun's mouth curled ever so slightly downward, yet otherwise he beamed beatifically.

Hobson and Sun went directly to Madam Guan's abandoned building. The neighbors told Sun the building had been vacated. The neighbors, a young couple, an old woman with two small children, and a teenager became agitated when they described the recent shootout and looked at Hobson strangely. The old woman stated that the brothel had been disruptive at times, otherwise had generated business for the neighborhood.

Sun and Hobson tried the flower-smoke-room across the street, and no one knew where Guan's girls had gone. "They go home, all, maybe" was the comment offered by one ethereal flower-smoke girl. The opium den's manager realized Sun and Hobson were not prospective patrons and shooed them away.

Sun looked at Hobson's dispatch case.

"You only interested in talking to parlor-house girls, right? Madam Guan's girls only?"

"I'm interested in the girls, however I'm interested in anyone who knows where they went." Hobson smiled because he could follow Sun's thought process. "Ask about other staff members, like the maids, the bar mistress, the doorman?"

The gaslights were on now, and Hobson could feel time running through his fingers.

Sun spoke to a young boy on the opium den's stoop, a runner. They held a heated discussion; which Sun didn't translate. The boy got up and beckoned.

They followed.

"Boy knows. Not girls he knows, but doorman." Sun seemed pleased. "Man has holes in face. Broken face. Name is Weng. Not a good man, but doorman."

Hobson read "doorman" to mean "bouncer."

They could barely keep up with the boy, who eventually brought them to the north gate of the Old Chinese City beyond the gaslights.

Months earlier, Hobson, Harp, and Washboard had often wandered the Old Chinese City maze. Washboard's father, the judge, had sent his son the book *Gulliver's Travels*. Washboard had shared the book with Hobson. Reading was a matter of finding a place and finding the time. As a quartermaster, Hobson could sit in the charthouse and catch a free minute or two to read. He had been brought up on traveler's tales of different sorts. Without question, he found Lemuel Gulliver's chronicles the funniest of the lot. Whenever he entered the Old Chinese City, he thought of Gulliver.

No one knew why American sailors were considered to be the tallest sailors in China. Was the cause the fact that the United States Navy had begun to recruit the corn-fed farm boys from the interior states? Or had the recruiters determined that tall men could stoke coal better? Or naval management believed tall sailors would fare better in another Valpariaso street riot?

The Lilliputians, one-twelfth the size of Gulliver, looked up at Gulliver. Hobson knew of no race of men one-twelfth the size of a Westerner. In many ways, Hobson knew, the Chinese looked down on Hobson and all Westerners. Many Chinese were taller than their Japanese and Korean counterparts. China was a more confusing cultural jumble than anything Gulliver could describe. What Hobson did feel was that though human proportions did not vary that much between the US and China, the matter of space did.

In the Old Chinese City, proportions changed. The alleys were far narrower than anything on the Bund, or Bubbling Springs Road, or around Suzhou Creek. In the Old Chinese City, people routinely came closer to each other than anywhere else Hobson had ever been, including Japan and China. Doors and windows were smaller. More people were packed into each room. More stood shoulder to shoulder in the alleys and ignored each other than in any other country he had visited.

A Westerner walking through the Old Chinese City always felt the buildings were packed too tightly together. People seemed to carry more, on their heads, on their backs, with yokes. A Westerner always kept one eye oriented toward daylight. Little light poked through the shuttered windows. A few wealthier men carried glass-enclosed candle lanterns suspended from short sticks by a chain. Down an alley, Hobson could see the glow of dying embers in an untended brazier.

Hobson had mentioned Gulliver once to Washboard during an exploratory trip to the Old Chinese City. "N-n-no use traveling halfway 'round the world to see folks just like you, is it?" Washboard had responded. "We go places and see things. Olmstead's got some photographs he took just last month of thieves being beheaded with swords. Ever see any of their acrobats? Sometimes I eat food here, and I don't know what I'm eating. It's just so much

dee-lightful chaos. Where there's chaos, my friend, there's opportunity."

"For what?"

"Heck if I know. It's the prospect for opportunity that feeds my
fires. Me, I'll have stories to tell, like that fella Kipling."

Hobson had grown up on travelers' tales, however in the Old
Chinese City, sometimes he thought he had traveled perhaps too
far.

The boy slowed and signaled them into an alley. He gestured
to Sun.

"Doorman, man with holes in face, pockmarks, will be through
here by-an'-by. Name is Pockmarked Weng. Give boy money. Not
too much. Not much danger him, little danger, maybe more money,
then little more danger. So not much money."

Sun's smile had an empty look. He looked at the dispatch case
and appeared to wonder if what was to come was worth it.

"Hey, sailor-boy. I think I know this story. Sun know many,
many stories. Sailors, Shanghai, all my business. My business to
know all stories. I give top-drawer business. This story interest
you? Women gone. Shootout. Navy sailors disappear. Later sail-
or shot bang. You look too muchee for girls, maybe not good. You
navy sailor. Maybe you shot bang by someone. Pockmarked Weng
is bad man, but not carry gun. He use fists."

Sun's speech was racing. "Maybe you should not talk to Pockmarked Weng face-face. Pockmarked Weng maybe problem man.
How much money in case? Only Sun should talk to Pockmarked
Weng. Everyone like Sun. Not everyone like United States sailor-boy."

Sun was right. Who knew where Pockmarked Weng stood on
the matter of two American sailors and Madam Guan's girls? Trust-
ing a street tout with significant Mex dollars was questionable, too.

Sun was becoming bossy, "You walk away, little bit. I meet you
at North Gate, Chinese City. Give me hundred Mex. Maybe I give
some Pockmarked Weng."

With a couple years' experience in China, Hobson understood
pidgin better than most. Sun was asking that he, Hobson, trust him.

Hobson wasn't about to go all in. "No, fifty Mex now, fifty Mex
later."

Sun shrugged his shoulders. "Everyone likes Sun."

"You give me 'nother more fifty Mex." Sun wore his empty-smile look again. They had quickly gone back to the original hundred Mex.

Hobson wished Harp was with him. Harp was the only sailor he knew who got energy from negotiating with land sharks. Harp positively enjoyed it. He would hum "Casey Jones" and accept each haggling as another step along the route followed by Jay Gould, J. P. Morgan, and Diamond Jim Brady.

Hobson pulled himself back to reality. Harp couldn't help today. He was the objective of help, not the source.

"Pockmarked Weng took all money. Pockmarked, me, Sun, we talk. Long time talk. Pockmarked Weng talk. He mad at Persimmon Ma. Persimmon Ma tricked Pockmarked Weng into doing work. Pockmarked say no more. Chinee girl and American sailors, on ship *Gorgon* today. Also, ship's name *Qilin Cathay*. *Qilin Cathay* and other same family ship, *Gorgon*, are at coaling depot. Other girls on *Qilin Cathay*, maybe *Gorgon*, too. Leave one, two days for Land of Shining Mountain, state-side"

"How many girls were there?" Hobson was afraid he'd forget to ask something important.

"Weng no say. He not know. Ship held Chinee women. He know Guan girls, but he no see muchee."

In an instant, Hobson formed his plan.

"Sun, if Pockmarked's information is good, I give you a bonus fifty Mex tomorrow."

Sun gave Hobson a sour look. "Sun not know Pockmarked Weng say true? Who know? Weng lie? Sun not get bonus. Sun did good job. You give bonus."

"You get bonus by'm'by, Sun." Hobson gave him a hearty handshake.

Hobson looked for a sturdy jinrikisha man. He had hoped to set a record on going from the Old Chinese City to the American consulate annex, yet he couldn't locate a jinrikisha.

The walk was a long one in the dark. He changed direction several times and doubled back, several times. He now had a spring in this step, a pistol tucked under his jumper, and the inklings of a plan. He had a small window of time and a very unconventional plan. Could he sell it?

As they walked away, a man pulled aside a plain bamboo-beaded curtain. He was of slightly above average height and otherwise unremarkable, but for the texture of the skin on his face.

CHAPTER THIRTY-FOUR

Consulate Annex, Hongkou District, International Settlement, Shanghai, September 1913

Draper awakened, suddenly realizing he'd fallen asleep at this desk. He was in his office in the consulate annex, and it was night. He checked his pocket watch: 3:00 a.m.

The resonance of an explosion hung in the air.

Gas main? Had a gas main exploded?

He sniffed the air. The scent of a week-old sheaf of Society pickings was strong. That wasn't what he smelled. The smell was familiar, yet no, it wasn't gas, it was a sweet smell…dynamite.

With sudden realization, Draper grabbed his, and Hobson's, issue Colts, left his office and locked the door behind him. He dropped to the floor of the interior balcony walkway. Crawling along the balcony walkway, he caught zoetropic glimpses through the ornate railings of men fanning across the atrium below. He couldn't get air into his lungs fast enough. He needed to find his way to the spiral staircase.

The walkways on all three floors were filigreed with wrought-iron railings, ten-inch cast-iron diamond kickplates, and steel-plate stairs. The staircase matched that motif. He slowed, inching to the stairs, taking care to remain unseen beneath the cast-iron diamond kickplates.

Draper peeked through the railings and saw three men ascending the stairs. Someone had dimmed the gaslight sconces. Miss Knapp? Could she be in the building at this hour? In the past she'd been known to go through Society bundles through the night.

No time to find her.

Below, he could see more than a dozen men in straw-colored uniforms wearing Anti-Yuan Nationalist armbands, all armed with Broomhandle Mauser pistols. Several were staggering. Draper concluded that the assault party had been too close to the satchel charge that had splintered the heavy oak front doors.

He could hear three men puffing up the circular staircase. Another man with the shoulder devices of a captain was yelling orders excitedly from the main floor. It would take the Marines assigned to the consulate time to identify the threat and prepare to engage. These men couldn't waste time.

Draper could hide, or fight to keep them on the ground floor. He had no idea who else was involved and where else they'd attack.

They were likely after the files in his office, the files in the strong-room, or him. A few bits and pieces of intelligence, and they could recover the gold ingots. He realized he didn't have a choice.

He peered over the top step and fired two shots downward. The three ascending men tumbled into each other and were still.

Three men with two shots. Was that going to be inscribed on his epitaph? He'd had similar success with the sedan chair.

Draper found himself in the middle of a lead nor'easter. A dozen Mauser pistols emptied into the short iron bridge between the balcony and the circular staircase. Draper could feel iron spalling off the back of the kickplate like hard, horizontal rain. Each Mauser round caused a piece of iron to break off from the back of the kickplate. Occasionally, a round would squeeze through the little ornamental diamonds cut into the kickplate, though fortunately their trajectories arched over him and their velocity was diminished.

Their captain called his men to cease fire. Draper willed himself not to move a muscle, blink, or breathe. He knew they wanted to take him alive, or at least, mostly alive. He was the only USN intelligence officer in Shanghai. Apparently, someone had concluded that the key to the whereabouts of the Japanese gold ingots lay in the consulate annex.

The captain barked orders in the Wu dialect. Draper could translate Wu spoken at a conversational rate, not in bursts heavily peppered with invective. Draper inched to one of the diamond holes and looked down. Six celestials lay on the floor. How had he done that? Were three of them the ones he knew he'd hit?

The captain bellowed something about a reward.

He looked at the captain and recognized him. He was the hat-pin assassin from the tram. The invaders wore uniforms, but he was sure they were Green Gang men. Were they working independent-ly, or for Yuan Nationalists, the Anti-Yuan Nationalists, or directly for the Japanese? The factions were increasing like Jason's sown dragon's teeth in Greek mythology, breaking apart, and reforming as new alliances daily. Draper decided to take this attack at face value. The Green Gang was working with Shih-kai's Nationalists. They were pretend Nationalists.

Draper felt fresh footfall vibrations on the staircase.

One man this time scaled the staircase as fast as his legs would move.

Draper eased up to the top stair from the left this time and fired.

Again, a fusillade of pistol fire peppered him with bits of disin-tegrating kickplate in response. His neck and back felt as if they'd been attacked by a swarm of wasps. He placed a second magazine where he could reach it, and still watch the staircase.

He felt eyes above him. He looked up.

There on the balcony on the next floor, slightly to the right, be-hind a support post, was Miss Knapp. She was standing on some-thing, a chair perhaps, so she would have been difficult to see from the ground floor.

"Artemis the Huntress, an exciting apparition indeed," Draper whispered to himself. He never saw her look so lovely, or so strange. She had "fried egg eyes," excited eyes with the white showing all around. He was sure his eyes looked every bit the same. In her right hand she flipped a Winchester repeating rifle forward, levering a round into the chamber.

Her dress was hiked up in the front and locked in place by a hol-stered .44 single-action revolver. She wore the revolver high upon her thigh over some French lace frippery. Draper realized normally that pistol would have been concealed under her skirt. Had she worn it on Nanking Road? Now the front of her dress was hooked over the substantial backing of her unconcealed holster, allowing her greater freedom of movement. All this armament was kept aloft above two comely blue-stockinged legs.

Draper recognized that the rifle and the pistol grouping allowed their possessor to use the same Winchester .44 center fire round. It was an efficient combination.

At her feet, he guessed, would be a small crate of ammunition and another .44 revolver.

"Hell, Hull, or Halifax, can't say where that explosion intended to place us. Draper, what manner of fury have you brought down upon us this time?" she bellowed.

He realized she was addressing him. She was angry, killing angry, even so not at him. She was angrily supporting him.

The Green Gang assault party pivoted in her direction and Draper realized that was his cue.

He stood up and began firing with his, and then Hobson's, Colts.

The captain went down and several of those closest to him. Miss Knapp was good for another six Green Gang pretend Anti-Yuan Nationalist casualties.

The survivors scuttled to the wrecked oak doors where they ran into the Marines who didn't have the luxury of taking prisoners when American — consular — soil was under siege by an unknown number of assailants. The Boxer Rebellion was still fresh in their memory.

Afterward, Draper had the Marine detachment establish a perimeter around the building. They draped an old tent across the damaged oak doors. He sent a runner to a place where Yi was known. Yi was to photograph and dispose of the bodies discretely. Eventually, the photos would go to Fairbairn, but this was an American matter now.

For all Green Gang leadership knew, their attack had been successful, unfortunately the assault party decided they wanted the gold ingots for themselves and were now pursuing their own ends.

Knapp plucked at the front of her dress, which was pulled up around her rounded hips and blushed. "Bloomers don't work well in this humid climate. My mother's side of the family is French Canadian and I have access to the least cumbersome undergarments in vogue."

A moment of silence ensued. Then she swooned and he rushed to catch her. Her glasses slipped from her nose, retained only by their chain.

Both her eyes were closed, then one eye alone opened.

"Did I do that right?" she asked brightly.

"I wasn't raised in the woods to be scared by owls," she added matter-of-factly. "I put the Winchester and two Colt revolvers in the budget. Uncle Hiram had recommended this arrangement. The rounds match."

"Uncle Hiram of Sayreville?" Draper suggested, testing his memory. "The one interested in gadgets."

"Now Sir Hiram Maxim. He helped me get this job. Not easy for an American woman to finagle a job with an American employer in a foreign country. I came with an education, administrative experience, and first rate sharp-shooting skills."

"Your uncle's the famous American inventor? The one knighted by Queen Victoria?" Draper asked, unable to conceal his surprise.

A dead-shot, well-formed adventuress-heiress had swooned into his arms, quite self-consciously it seemed.

"Yes, Uncle Hiram," she said, flicking the fingertips of her right hand, as if to dismiss the thought.

Yi's men took care of the bodies, and the Marines had established a perimeter, Draper grabbed the cot from his office and took it into the strong-room. Knapp found some candles.

"Cyrus Noble bourbon or Japanese plum wine?" she offered.

"May I pour?" he asked.

She voiced her preference, and he watched her begin to drink. Then he said a silent prayer and began to sip the bourbon. It was a moment he knew he'd remember forever.

He needed to abandon that train of thought.

He smiled with continuing relief.

"Were you wearing that revolver when we visited Nanking Road?" Draper asked tentatively.

"Of course, you gallant fool, this is Shanghai."

He had an opportunity to study the fastener-engineering of a derringer in a concealed, mauve, suede holster, and several other items of feminine apparel. The other items engaged most of his time, and he took direction well. The modern twentieth century woman was smothered in more protective layers than a jeweled codex in storage.

"I didn't know what to do about you after the Nanking Road incident. Everything was happening so fast. I needed time to think. I wasn't sure I'd fit in with your assassins-at-every-turn lifestyle." She took another hefty wallop of the wine.

"Tonight, I couldn't see you after the explosion. I didn't know, if in protecting the consulate annex and its strong-room, I could also divert my attention to protecting a live naval officer or perhaps a well-uniformed corpse. I'm glad I decided you and it were equally important, and you weren't already a corpse."

She stretched kittenishly. "You may approach." She then lunged at him, nearly knocking him over onto her campaign cot as he attempted to decide again between bourbon and wine. He held the bottles high and saved both bottles.

He found himself pinned and graciously capitulated. Not long afterward, they reversed positions. It occurred to him that the strong-room had come to resemble a lace fabric stall torn asunder.

"Did we just experience a typhoon?" Draper asked. "Would have thought we'd be safer in a strong-room three stories up. And by the way, why were you here at all?"

"The Society and the invoices."

Though he would long regard that strong-room cot with fondness, Draper resolved to take a private room with a four-poster and interior plumbing somewhere in this God-forsaken city. He'd settled for a strong-room once, though the ventilation had been poor and a lavatory at the end of the hall was awkward.

He pondered the stimulating effect of a near-death experience upon man-woman relations, and decided not to mention the subject as it might be considered unromantic.

He knew he was inclined to overanalyze, but what had just happened in the strong-room stemmed from more than the sheer joy of mutual survival.

"You may call me, Frankie," she offered in the early dawn. She hummed an unidentifiable tune as she fussed with her hair. "There's no accounting for tastes, I suppose. For no good reason I can explain, I'm favorably disposed to interesting men who are incorrigibly gallant idiots. I came to Shanghai because I wished to experience some excitement. I will be more cautious with my wishes in the future," she concluded.

She began to brush the particles of cast iron off his white uniform.

"You look like one of those Himalayan snow leopards," she said. "I will expect to be promenaded regularly as before for altogether different reasons."

She stood back and gave him a measured look. "You should consider replacing this uniform."

Draper found his new status as marked territory to be the one bright spot in a bad month.

Promenaded? How many secretive Far Eastern factions and societies had placed a bounty on him? Given recent events, for now all his thoughts were going to be short term.

"We are winning, right?" she asked, her voice trailing off. "Will all this begin to diminish in ferocity? The events have been exhilarating, certainly, nonetheless even Shanghai can't keep up this fast a drum-beat, can it?"

This wasn't going to end any time soon, he mused, straining to keep his face absolutely expressionless.

"Oh, I almost forgot," she said. "I didn't want to say anything earlier in the atrium, too public. I did notice something strange in the last Reverence to Lettered Paper Society bundle. A shipping company, 'Spuyten & McCollum,' dunned the Japanese Embassy for supplies delivered to the *Gorgon* and *Qilin Cathay*. We have two invoices with different dates for the same supplies,"

She watched Draper carefully.

"Prompt payment must be a matter of some urgency," she pointed out. "Why would the Japanese be using a non-Japanese shipping line at all? Don't they have several of their own?"

"As it turns out, Spuyten & McCollum these days is a Japanese registry shipping line," Draper told her

"Oh, sorry, that's what caught my eye, the Western name. Guess it wasn't important after all."

"What kind of supplies?" Draper collapsed onto the cot and held his head in his hands.

"Foodstuffs and twenty mattresses? Could that be important?"

He suspected her intuition told her it was.

"There's a notation 'twenty passengers.'"

Draper's neck tensed.

"Yes, *Gorgon* and *Qilin Cathay* are readying for sea. The invoice heading was 'San Francisco transport.'"

"Castor and Pollux," Draper exclaimed, to himself.

Which ship to which location, or would they be sailing together? Draper thought he knew. The name Spuyten rang too many alarm bells; this was no coincidence.

He couldn't tell her about the gold ingots, the Spuytens, or Yi, even though she was now deeply involved as well, too involved.

"I also found a third demand for reimbursement with the name 'Spuyten' on it, 'D. Spuyten,'" she added, sensing his excitement.

"Diderick Spuyten," Draper said, reaching for his clothes.

"He was seeking money expended for twenty sets of manacles, and forty I-bolts."

"Proof, proof of transport for the purpose of prostitution." Draper realized this was what he had most needed. With just a modicum of supporting evidence, it provided proof of the girls' unwilling transport. "Forcing women to leave their homeland in chains is explosive imagery. And mislabeling them indicates conscious deception. By squeezing the Japanese for pennies, Diderick Spuyten has given us what we've needed."

The downside to this welcome information was that he wouldn't put it past the Spuytens to sink their ships and the manacled women with them, to escape prosecution. They'd simply float innocently upon the surface in lifeboats and play victims.

However, with these documents, the Asiatic Fleet had something to hang their hats on under the Mann Act or several standing orders that equated slave trading with piracy and allowed captains great latitude in protecting lives.

The next morning, Admiral Bulkley and Draper carefully wended their way through the debris and filed into the consulate annex's conference room.

Hobson shuffled in red eyed and needing a shave. "Admiral, *Pluto* and *Rainbow* must come into the coaling depot at dawn tomorrow morning," Hobson said, beginning the meeting.

Draper knew the admiral wasn't used to petty officers taking this tone, however Hobson had first talked to him, and he had given the admiral a brief outline in advance.

The captains of *USS Pluto* and *USS Rainbow*, and a chaplain were later summoned to *USS Saratoga* where Admiral Bulkley hosted a planning session.

"I ask that you listen carefully to Quartermaster Hobson. Yes, normally a briefing like this would be given by an officer, but this is Asiatic Station. We coined the phrase, 'gone Asiatic,' and I supposed we must live by it."

Hobson stood up slowly. Hobson couldn't remember when he had enjoyed a good night's sleep. Last night he'd taken a risk, bordering on reckless.

"Originally we'd considered boarding *Qilin Cathay* and *Gorgon* at sea," Hobson started. "One reason we can't board at sea is because *USS Pluto* and USS *Rainbow* are too big and slow. We have no other ships available. *USS Saratoga* is a station ship and rarely leaves Shanghai. The other three ships that were on the Huangpu just last week are doing training well offshore and can't be recalled in time. All the Spuyten & McCollum ships are built for the opium trade. Don't let their fine lines fool you, gentlemen. They're smugglers.

"The other reason dates back to a problem that plagued the Navy's African Trade Patrol in the first half of the last century. Often slave-trading ships covertly tossed chained slaves over the side when pursued. We've learned Spuyten & McCollum has purchased manacles in preparation for their cruise to San Francisco.

"We may capture those two ships at sea, except we may never recover Madam Guan's girls if *Gorgon* and *Qilin Cathay* see us coming, or get word what we're up to. We're not going to take that risk. We're going to break a little piece of the Rocks & Shoals, to enforce the spirit of several laws."

Hobson laid out his plan. He addressed the difficulty of an American attack upon Japanese registry ships within the foreign concessions in a country without a stable government.

An undercurrent of dissension ran through the room.

Admiral Bulkley spoke up in full voice from the back of the room. "This plan is not just irregular, it is extremely irregular, and stands to undermine good order in the Asiatic Fleet."

"We could seize both ships officially, waiving documents whose legality will have us in the courts for months. By then Quan's girls will have 'disappeared,' and we'd risk a dust-up, an international incident at the highest levels. Moreover, it might bring attention to our recent activities on the Huangpu.

"Hobson has suggested a bold plan of blatant illegality, but which has the potential to achieve success more quickly and conclusively. It is far less likely to draw international attention. It's all damned irregular, but hasn't the Asiatic Fleet been irregular from the outset? This plan has all the imagination of our Tripoli heroes Preble and Decatur."

He waved off questions.

Draper added, "*Qilin Cathay* and *Gorgon* are Japanese registry vessels. According to the harbormaster, they're scheduled to leave Shanghai on Monday, the day after tomorrow. I talked to Sergeant Fairbairn, and the Shanghai Municipal Police can't search a foreign ship on that short a notice, and sailors and *femmes de nuits* are not a high priority for them."

Hobson continued. "We have confirmation that a large group of women are embarked on *Gorgon* and *Qilin Cathay*. I'm not going to explain how, still and all we have invoices from Spuyten & McCollum covering payment for passengers to San Francisco by a bureau in the Japanese consulate. The passengers are not identified by name or origin, though that in a way is further confirmation, because we think they are Chinese women who can't enter the US under the Chinese Exclusion Act of 1882. And then the Mann Act also protects them."

Hobson was uncomfortable using any idea that originated with Paymaster McCorkran, but it was the kernel around which he had built his plan. He sat down, and the room was silent as the grave.

Admiral Bulkley searched the faces in front of him for a challenge. "Yes," pronounced the admiral, re-establishing his authority. "Monkey drill for all hands, prior to evening meal."

Hobson groaned and chuckled simultaneously. Monkey drill was calisthenics, and normally performed before breakfast. Aboard a collier, it was universally despised and hardly necessary.

Ol' Blue Flame was warming to the idea, Hobson thought. "Monkey and single-stick drill shall be followed by a demonstration of cutlass manual-at-arms by the senior master-at-arms of the two ships." Single sticks were long wooden dowels, cutlass-length nightsticks, used for cutlass drills.

"You can tell your crews that they should be expecting boarding party action in the near future."

Hobson thought that would put the crews in the proper frame of mind. The admiral knew a thing or two.

"This operation tops that last one for irregularity, but we need to protect the whole Red-Crowned Crane plan, and I think Hobson's supplementary plan will do just that. Our young quartermaster third seems to have an aptitude for navigation, both maritime and multicultural. And he knows naval culture pretty well, too. His abilities might just keep him out of the brig this tour," the admiral proclaimed. "And *Pluto* and *Rainbow* will get a chance to fight for their womenfolk.

"Divine Service will be early in the forenoon watch," he continued. "The prescribed uniform will be denim work uniforms. Worship will be a combined service, *Rainbow* and *Pluto*. *Rainbow*'s crew will bring folding chairs. The chaplain and *Pluto*'s duty officer will be briefed on their responsibilities."

Divine Service meant Sunday church services aboard ship.

"Will Olmstead be out of Shanghai hospital?" Admiral Bulkley asked.

Draper checked his notes. "Olmstead is already aboard *Pluto*, sir, in her sickbay, such as it is. Hobson needs to go ashore briefly. He still has a few more things to arrange. Then he'll be returning to *Pluto*."

"Good, then all our fire-eating Reuben Jameses will be in the fray. Indirectly, the United States Navy got these girls into this fix," Admiral Bulkley concluded, "I don't think they had too much say in choosing their line of work. I'd say implicit in Madam Guan's contract with them was the obligation to protect them. Now the United States Navy is going to get them out of this predicament. We rescue them and they'll have a say. Dammit."

Draper nodded his head, "Wheresoever you go, go with all your heart!"

Several chairs creaked and the chaplain looked puzzled. Bulkley gave Draper an odd look. "Odysseus? Penelope?"

"Confucius," he offered deadpan. Other cultures understood the concept of a romantic quest.

Hobson left *USS Saratoga* by the fleet launch and hiked to the Red-Knight's Pawnshop. Yi wasn't there, so 'Gold-tooth' sent out a runner.

Shortly, Yi arrived with two Korean men. Hobson and Yi exchanged information at one of the back counters. Hobson laid out his plan. Yi stiffened on hearing the name "Spuyten."

"I knew they were here somewhere, and no good would come of it. That family torments or corrupts everyone and everything in their path." Yi paused and clearly struggled to control his feelings. "They're powerful in their own way, I told myself. Be patient you have other things to do first."

Yi went on, "I want your Mr. Draper to send these three communications by couriers in no way connected with Americans and to make absolutely sure they get to the appropriate parties."

Hobson's eyes widened when he read the addressees. "I don't think that will be a problem."

Yi added, "I have a strong-room in a warehouse on the road to Yangshupu. *If we time this right, we will end all further interest in the missing Japanese ingots for a decade.*"

Hobson immediately recognized the value of this one last move.

Hobson observed a change in Yi, who said, "Yes, I hope this will work. This action may settle a longstanding debt for me. I'll be there tomorrow." Yi's weathered squint made him appear impassive, yet his demeanor signaled exhilaration and perhaps a sense of resolution.

"You only need to arrange this other matter for me tomorrow. No need to be present personally, really," Hobson suggested.

Yi had done too much already, he felt.

"Yes, need." Yi's firm statement didn't invite a response. "Retribution, redemption. I had an adopted 'older brother' named 'Ephraim Coffin whom I addressed as hyungnim. The Spuytens murdered him. I honor my debts."

Hobson had in the past addressed Yi, using a similar honorific, "seonbae," in the Korean manner. He understood the Asian view of debt and obligation.

Yi was a gambler, a banker, and a warrior. Hobson doubted even Yi knew which trait dominated.

Hobson lingered in the pawnshop. Looking at curios relaxed him.

As he was about to leave, he was confronted by a Chinese girl in a long shirtwaist dress with a tie and a tightly wrapped umbrella in her hand.

"Can I use the mirror in here, sir?"

His eye fixed on the long, flowing Western-style dress. For a moment he had mistaken her for Clementine — the same husky build, the same self-assuredness, the intelligent brown eyes, the same interest in strange Western ways. No, this wasn't the time to be thinking of almond parfaits.

"Scoot, Yankee sailorman, get away from me," she said making double-grip swatting motions with her umbrella.

He was angry with himself for the error. It seemed disloyal somehow. He desperately needed sleep, even though there would be no time for sleep.

CHAPTER THIRTY-FIVE

Coaling Depot, Shanghai, August 1913

As the *USS Rainbow* sailors filed aboard with collapsible oak chairs, several *Pluto* crewmembers focused their attention on the two civilian ships, *Gorgon* and *Qilin Cathay*, on the opposite side of the quay.

Two *USS Pluto* members of the blackgang, blinking unaccustomedly in the sunlight, looked on idly. Out of habit, they kept to the shadowy areas of the main deck. Blackgang work was dirty. Normally blackgang members couldn't come on deck in their work clothes when the ship's boilers were lit. Today the ship was nearly "cold iron," all but one of its boiler fires having been extinguished. The two men were for once virtually as clean as when they went ashore.

"Those two ships maintain quite a topside watch. More than most man-o'-wars. What kind of uniform is that — over there on the steam yacht, on *Gorgon*?" the first blackgang member asked.

"Livery. It's livery." The second blackgang member behind him, explained while cleaning his fingernails.

"Only livery I know has to do with horses."

"Not too far off. You ride for the owner of a horse; you wear his livery — his special style and color clothes. Ain't you ever been to the track?"

"Those guys look almost naval," the first member stated with a hint of irritation.

"They're wearin' steam-yacht livery. The ones wearing jumpers got no black neckerchief. No Navy striped blue collars or cuffs. No stars on collars either. Just an S & McC on the left pocket. Pretty sure they're legal. Hot today. Most of them are wearin' striped shirts."

"Yeah, 'Spuyten & McCollum,'" the second member said. "*Gorgon's* crew looks flashy, big 'make-see pidgin,' though the crew on *Qilin Cathay* looks run of the mill. The officers wear uniforms, and the crew wear hit or miss. Some of their guys show up at Madam Guan's when they come into port. They're a surly bunch. S & McC is big on driver captains and bucko mates. Captain ain't happy, nobody's happy. I reckon 'happy' ain't the word of the day with them. I think 'mean' might be the right word. If they're legal, it's only in the way of uniformery — get it?"

Minutes later, the two men heard the notes of a boatswain's call and the announcement, "Divine Service will be held on the main deck aft. The smoking lamp is out. Knock off all unnecessary work. Maintain quiet about the decks during Divine Service. This church call is mandatory for all hands. No dress whites. Dungarees mandatory."

Draper occupied one of the oak folding chairs arranged in orderly lines on the main deck. Part of Draper's worldview, and his scholarly discipline, made him think in terms of footnotes. Understanding why things came to pass and how the name ascribed to a fabric became associated with a particular type of anarchy was important to him.

In 1855, Charles Nordhoff in *Man-o'-War Life* described work naval uniforms fashioned from a material called "dungaree" occasionally authorized by skippers. The word derived from Dongari or Dungri, a section of Bombay. The cloth was commonly dyed indigo, a color that derived its name from the Greek word for India.

By the early twentieth century, that cloth was the important component in blue work clothes associated with manual labor.

Dungarees were a work uniform, normally comprised of a smock or jumper and straight leg trousers. Sailors weren't normally allowed to wear them ashore. They were tattered, often stained, and most importantly, didn't indicate the wearer's origins, his ship or his navy.

On occasion, sailors would slip ashore in dungarees without authorization. The practice was known as "dungaree liberty." Often it resulted in an organized, yet forbidden, gang fight. Invariably, that fight occurred between sailors who were ashore unofficially and those who had wronged sailors there.

Draper knew the conventional wardroom wisdom was that no good could come of a dungaree liberty. Moreover, dungaree liberty violated several Navy regulations and was a court-martial offense.

Hobson watched sweat bead on the young chaplain's temples as he rose to take his place behind the makeshift pulpit, a breadboard that bridged two chair backs. *USS Pluto* was shaped like a plump gravy boat, and the pulpit was placed smack in the middle of the highest full deck. "Today's sermon, 'Saving the Jezebels,' will address both Old Testament and New Testament themes of evil and salvation," he announced.

"This should be good," Chief Phipps confided to those around him. Chief Phipps, Hobson had learned, was inclined to interpret scripture to the inhabitants of the lower decks since his great-grandfather had been a successful circuit riding preacher until it had become known he had two wives — unacquainted with each other — on his circuit. "Ain't never heard no good words for Jezebel, though I always found her kind of interesting. Was she ever headstrong and womanlike! Is he gonna throw in Herodias and Salome, too? Maybe next Sunday, Eve and Delilah. And Lilith, she gets no credit at all. Why does no one remember Lilith?"

The chaplain spelled it out. Jezebel was a strong and assertive woman, who was — some said — unfairly attacked after being led astray by evil men. She had been their captive and she should have been rescued. The chaplain talked of the heathen religion, Baal. He then somehow slipped into a description of another heathen idol, the Chinese *qilin*, a creature with the head of a dragon, the antlers of a deer, the skin and scales of a fish, the hooves of an ox and tail of a lion.

Hobson watched several sailors look over *Qilin Cathay* and study her figurehead.

The chaplain described Jezebel's charms in unchaplain-like terms that left the main deck as quiet as it had ever been. He included references to "soiled doves" and "lost lambs."

Disjointedly, he switched from one mythical creature, the qilin, to another mythical creature, a female creature with snakes for hair, a *gorgon*.

That creature's appearance would turn a man to stone. Sermons discussing the salvation of fallen women were rare, and no *Rainbow* nor *Pluto* crewman had ever heard a sermon connecting Jezebel with Chinese and Greek monsters.

"We can save the Jezebels, yes! They must be separated from the craven idols."

Church call was rarely mandatory and seldom did a real chaplain lead services on a collier. The novelty of the occasion and the subject matter left the two crews spellbound.

"Little stiff, yet this chaplain has potential," whispered a *Rainbow* yeoman in the second row. Yeomen were very literary. "Just wish he didn't sound like he was reading his sermon for the first time. Snakes for hair, now that-there has the makings of an absolutely first-rate tattoo."

"Quiet," bellowed the master-at-arms, who'd had an awkward moment with a sea snake once.

Before reaching for a glass of water, the chaplain emphasized that the words "rescue" and "saving" and "salvation" carried the same meaning. He traced his finger down the program and announced with trepidation that the hymn would be "The Battle Hymn of the Republic." The crews of *Rainbow* and *Pluto* enjoyed the selection. It was a fiery hymn, much to their liking.

"Sir, I'd like to say a prayer." The speaker was Olmstead — on crutches — who had positioned himself against the quay-side rail. Olmstead held his white hat tightly in one hand and self-consciously tamped down his cowlick with the other. "Them girls over there ain't truly Jezebels. They just had few options in life and always have the hope of buying their contracts out – with a little grubstake to boot like Clementine did. They've been good to us, all of us."

The chaplain apparently wanted to end the service, however he had his orders. He wiped his forehead with his handkerchief and fumbled with the handwritten program that he'd found so hard to read.

"Lord, thank you for giving us a chaplain who will spin a sermon that can stoke our fires," Olmstead said. "That dern sermon — excuse me, chaplain — that inspirin' sermon had meaning, deep meaning, for all of us.

"I'd like to pray for the salvation of the soiled doves, the girls being held below decks on *Qilin Cathay* for sure, and *Gorgon* maybe, over there. Girls you an' me all know, the girls of the Lesser Shanghai Indian Club & Garter Society, Madam Guan's girls. They're bein' shipped to Frisco and I know they don't like it. They are never going to see any of us or their mommas, again."

"No-o-o-o," was the responsive chorus.

Olmstead lifted one of his crutches and pointed. "We need to know what to do, sky pilot, sir. It just makes me mad. It makes us all mad. We need a sign."

"Sky pilot" was the naval usage for a clergyman, especially a chaplain. "Pilot," to sailors, meant "guide."

At that moment, the duty officer bellowed, "Attention on deck, quarterdeck watch and all officers, jack staff...face. Salute."

Hobson had never heard that command. In some ways it seemed appropriate. Tradition dictated the Star Spangled Jack be flown on the jack staff on Sundays. The jack staff was on the stem, away from *Qilin Cathay* and *Gorgon*. The quarterdeck watch came to attention and turned, the chaplain did an about-face, and all the officers faced the jack staff and saluted. Management had their backs to the crew. They held their salutes and held their salutes.

"Dungaree liberty!" someone yelled unseen, though later no one could remember just who exactly. "Salvation and Jezebels, ho! Save the soiled doves!" The voice had the deep timbre of authority. Many thought they recognized it as Chief Phipps, but Hobson was never sure.

At that point, Hobson noted, at the completion of Divine Service, all hell erupted on the depot's lone coaling quay.

Pluto's deck was soon littered with abandoned "Fighting Bob Evans" white hats, the last vestige of identification that might link men in denim with the United States Navy.

So began what was later to be known as the "Great Coaling Quay Riot."

Shanghai Coaling Depot, August 1913

Chaos and conflict? Gian Singh of the Shanghai Municipal Police had seen it all. On three occasions in his native India, he had heard the 48-hour, uninterrupted recitation of the Sikh holy scripture — a reading called the Akhand Paath — and prepared for death. Today, from his position in a windowed sentry box far from his native country, he realized he hadn't seen this level of chaos in years and wished he were as well-prepared as he had been on those three earlier occasions. He felt a familiar tightness in his chest. Time seemed to be slowing down.

Singh stood seven feet tall from the heels of his boots to the crest of his red turban, the model of a retired *havildar* of the 14th Sikhs. His burly frame, accented by his waxed moustache and full beard, were in keeping with his ethnic heritage of steadfastness. An employee of the British colonial power that reigned here, Singh would not be moved from his post. He had never faltered as an infantryman on India's North-West Frontier, or during the Boxer Rebellion, or as a policeman holding the line against rioting Chinese.

His post was the Shanghai coaling depot where the river met the railhead.

About a hundred men in denim were cascading over the sides of two American naval ships, the troopship and distillery, *USS Rainbow*, and a collier, *USS Pluto*. They carried coal shovels and improvised blackjacks, socks filled with coins or rivets. The American sailors were rushing an equal number of Spuyten & McCollum crewmen of assorted origins, aboard the steam yacht, *Gorgon*, and the freighter, *Qilin Cathay*. The Americans moved in a great wave that split and flowed around Singh's box toward the civilian ships. Singh could not divine the exact words in the American dialect, though the exchanges between the two factions carried the discordant tones of vengeance.

Rocks rattled against the side of his sentry box. Singh blew the whistle code for assistance though he doubted another policeman was within earshot.

Several men apparently in authority on the *Gorgon* and *Qilin Cathay* carried firearms. This time, shots, not explosions, echoed through the steel-hulled vessels. Numbers of the men onboard and many of those rioting would not outlive this day. Singh believed that some of those men would be good men. The sentry saw several Americans tumble between the ships and piers. "

The crews of the civilian ships counter-surged down their brows or gangways, hurling a half-dozen American sailors onto the pier timbers. The defeated lay like crumpled rags below, having either fallen or been pushed or been coldcocked.

Most of *Gorgon*'s crew wore livery-striped shirts. The crew of *Qilin Cathay* wore flat caps and bib overalls, and some carried long-shoreman's hooks.

A gray truck arrived with US Navy sailors and a few officers in white uniforms with khaki belts and leggings. Some carried truncheons. Singh breathed a sigh of relief. That would bring order to the American sailors in working uniforms. During a pause, the crews of *Gorgon* and *Qilin Cathay* seemed to open a way. At first, the truckload detail of shore patrolmen seemed to be clearing away the American sailor vanguard, yet then the new arrivals suddenly swung up the gangway. The shore patrol detail seemed to ignore the men in denim altogether and instead proceeded to board *Qilin Cathay*. The intervening peacekeepers were a ruse.

A Spuyten & McCollum ship's officer stood blocking the gangway, brandishing a Webley. A crisply uniformed naval officer shot him with one of those new boxlike American pistols they used in the Philippines. Singh noted he wore a cast on his wrist. *We can find no help there*, he thought.

The shore patrol detail stepped aside, and Singh heard the chant, "Bluejackets forward!" The American sailors began clearing the civilian ships' topsides with shovels and sock-blackjacks. The Spuyten & McCollum's hefty crewmen were being thrown or pushed into the fetid harbor waters. At a distance, the action looked like simple roughhousing, but Singh knew many cracked skulls and broken necks would result on both sides.

Singh had heard rumors, one about gold ingots and another about women. The rumors had something to do with the American Navy. He wished he could remember the details.

The explosions continued, and Singh realized he could expect no assistance. He couldn't see the explosions, just hear them, and they sounded distant, perhaps down by the warehouses beyond the rail connection. Whatever was to happen was going to happen with little intercession on his part.

Frustrated, Singh blew his whistle one more time.

"You many *badmash*. Stop. I am saying stop right now. The

Shanghai Municipal Police is demanding it." He was angry and defiantly shook his lathi toward the ships. Even now, without the prior recitation of the Akband Paath, he was prepared to die if duty required it, while the explosions continued, and the waves of seamen broke against each other like confused harbor chop against pilings. He doubted anyone could even hear his shouting. Many of the men below would today meet death and begin the cycle of reincarnation unprepared. Sadly they would likely be unbelievers.

Singh sighed, and the tightness in his chest subsided.

The wave of American sailors in work uniforms had passed him. Restive, he climbed down from his sentry box and walked to the edge of the pier.

Tangled in the lines of a floating paint stage were three bodies. Two men in white uniforms with blue collars and cuffs — Americans. The third body belonged to an attractive Chinese woman in silk pajamas the color of lychee fruit. The pallor of their skins was a clear indication they were beyond further assistance. Singh noted two dark nicks on the side of one man's neck.

He walked back to his sentry box before sounding his whistle for the third time. He didn't know if these bodies were the cause of the riot, byproducts of the riot, or wholly independent of the riot. For the moment, he dared not draw attention to the bodies and further fan the flames.

He had heard the Europeans repeat the "Sodom and Gomorrah" analogy to Shanghai many times. The Sikh knew this Chinese port city teemed with wickedness.

Singh believed Shanghai itself was at the root of all this mayhem, with its gold, its silver, its corruption, and its women. Looking around him, Singh wondered how long such a wicked city could survive.

Hobson watched several men search for single sticks, but they found the sticks had been padlocked. He then sprinted halfway down the portable gangplank referred to as "the brow" and vaulted the rail. Three crewmen in succession did the same before they were enveloped by the remainder of *Pluto* and *Rainbow*'s crews.

"Jezebels and salvation!" echoed between their steel hulls.

Above the din, Hobson could hear shots inland and to the north and talk of the Anti-Yuan Nationalists attacking Shanghai soon was making the rounds. The shots weren't coming from *Qilin Cathay* or *Gorgon*, although potential shooting from those ships was a concern.

A Sikh police officer faced the sailors with his lathi, and then watched the mob simply part like a river current around a rock.

Aboard *Qilin Cathay* and *Gorgon*, some watch-standers realized their ships were the simultaneous objectives.

"Bluejackets, don't let them pull up the brows! Don't let them get to their fire hoses!" Hobson heard a half-dozen familiar voices shout.

Already, the crews aboard *Qilin Cathay* and *Gorgon* were running to their gangplanks and attempting to push the boarders down onto the pier. A dozen denim-clad sailors sprinted up the gangways, throwing forearms into the merchant watch-standers. The merchant crew defenders were using brass knuckles and leather blackjacks.

A second wave of boarders clinched control of the gangplanks, and a sea of denim broke across the main decks of both ships.

Hobson was alarmed when Yi came from out of nowhere, following the denim-clad sailors up *Qilin Cathay's* gangplank with two personal bodyguards.

None of the American sailors knew Yi, and the S & McC crews were of mixed origin. Anyone not wearing denim was the enemy. Yi knew merchant ships, having been in the Steward's Friendship Society out of San Francisco. His eyes swept the superstructure and he saw what he was looking for and pointed. *Qilin Cathay's* duty officer had a Webley.

Yi moved for him first, unaware his bodyguards were gone, mistakenly tossed over the sides by the American sailors, along with a significant number of *Qilin Cathay's* crew. "He's on our side," Hobson yelled as several hands reached for Yi.

Hobson saw a gray truck filled with shore patrol petty officers roll onto the pier. Lieutenant Draper burst out of the back of the truck with a truncheon in one hand and a Colt in the cast-wrapped other. Draper raced up the brow and *Qilin Cathay's* duty officer, 'a gargantuan specimen,' as Draper might have described him, with 'a cauliflower ear,' raised his revolver. A loud report, and Hobson saw Draper standing over the dead duty officer. He'd dropped the duty officer as casually as dousing a flag hoist.

Hobson struggled to keep himself upright as the two naval crews fought to gain control of *Qilin Cathay*'s main deck. *Qilin Cathay*'s crew hosed down the main deck, making footing difficult. The defending merchant sailors were soon retreating to the bow.

Hobson saw that Yi had found a firefighting ax. As an officer of the tribute guard, Yi must know how to use a spear and a halberd. The ax seemed too short for his liking, however it would do. He swept horizontally and drove it deep into the chest of a large man who'd assumed a position of leadership among the ship's defenders. The ax stopped there as he pulled it free, and he began swinging it in figure eights as he advanced to meet Hobson.

Many of *Qilin Cathay*'s remaining crew sought the sailor's refuge over the side. Some plunged into the harbor, others made a pier-head jump, and some not fast enough to choose, met a grisly, blood-splattered death.

Hobson was pushed to the rail and saw the merchant sailors flow over the side like rainwater out of the scuppers.

He looked farther from the side and saw three bodies floating, barely held afloat by discarded dunnage, or perhaps, an abandoned painter's stage.

Hobson felt queasy. He dropped to his knees and began to vomit.

He'd been to war more than once, several times in China and the Philippines. He'd seen the violence of the Japanese occupation of Korea. He had endured official naval discipline and the occasional unofficial below-decks bullying.

This was different.

He wanted to hold her, and comfort his friends, even though he knew they were all beyond the warmth of human contact.

There could be no mistaking them: two coal-smudged white uniforms — Harp and Washboard — and an Asian woman in pale burgundy pajamas — Clementine. They were draped across the timbers like swab strands and were pale as enameled white buckets. He couldn't see the two men's throats, still something was odd about their necks. A wave tossed one head, and Hobson again tasted bile. Two parallel cuts slashed diagonally across Harp's neck, and he assumed the others would display the same workmanship. Someone had determined they were of no further use, but were impediments.

They had been executed sometime during the night, and the bodies had been tossed overboard during the dungaree assault. They had become liabilities.

He was torn between going to them, and confronting their killers. His head told him one thing — his heart another.

They had to be dead.

Diving to their aid would be pointless. Yi needed watching.

"Ships an' trains, ships' an' trains, one or t'other, will carry your remains," Hobson whispered to Harp, who was quite dead.

"You were chewed up in the 'machineration,' Washboard," he choked out.

"Clementine…" Hobson resisted releasing a sob by keeping his voice low, yet the words wouldn't emerge. "Emancipation released you from too much, too fast."

What had happened to him? Shanghai was to be just another port-of-call during the Asiatic Fleet's seasonal rotations between the Philippines and China. He had seen the locals bustling about… He had been a transient with no connection. That had changed.

He was a "defender," and now that categorization was no longer limited to wartime engagements between big steel ships at sea. The definition of engagement had enlarged to more subtle, but no less ugly, unsanctioned back-alley battles among cultures in collision.

Chief Gillingham, Harp, Washboard, Clementine — where had they gone, and for what? He had answers, of course, but right now those weren't satisfying. He would prefer to be back manning a Gatling gun, yet that wasn't among his current options.

Some of USS Pluto's crew referred to him as the "third-class petty officer who'd gone Asiatic." Yes, and he'd had a head start on that. In his own way, he believed he would reconcile his conflicting feelings and would make being trapped between cultures work for him.

Unsteadily, he whipped his head back and forth — forcibly blinked his eyes — and began to rise. Unconsciously, he sucked air into his lungs, and then realized he was wailing. His knees nearly buckled.

He shook his head once more, and drew himself up to his full height. He executed an unsteady about-face.

Then he patted the hammerless Owl Head pistol in its pouch under his denim jumper.

CHAPTER THIRTY-SIX

From the main deck of the *Qilin Cathay*, Hobson looked forward at the steam yacht, *Gorgon*. She was getting up steam and he noticed a single older man in merchant officer *uniform* expressing his wishes by manhandling members of *Gorgon's* crew and pointing at *Gorgon's* stack. Hobson looked up at *Qilin Cathay's* stack. *Qilin Cathay* was attempting to get steam up, also.

"Don't let either ship cast off lines," he yelled, realizing instantly that he had heard the same command from others, moments earlier.

A third surge of American sailors kept most of the freighter's sailors from making their way below decks to her armory. Still aboard *Qilin Cathay*, Hobson ducked down a ladder and saw three merchant officers scrambling forward and down. Each of them resembled Tackline. These were the remaining Spuyten boys. The old man, Hellfire Spuyten, was bullying the crew on *Gorgon*. His sons still aboard *Qilin Cathay* were an equally serious threat.

Steel ships were mazes. *Qilin Cathay* was large enough to hold several dozen women. *Gorgon* was not. Above, Hobson could hear the crews of *Rainbow* and *Pluto* lifting the hatches off the holds and reactive screams from Madam Guan's girls. Below decks, the passageways circled the holds and led to the engine room, berthing spaces, heads, and galley, and on this ship, likely the armory. The hanging catwalks were intertwined with labeled pipes, most either red or white, and truncated by compartmentalization nowhere as extensive as on a warship, there nevertheless.

Draper was down there and Yi with him. Hobson found them. They, too, knew the dungaree navy's present advantage could reverse if *Qilin* Cathay's officers, the Spuyten sons, reached the ship's armory.

Yi was moving with such intensity of purpose his wet body-guards had not been able to catch up with him.

Yi, Hobson, and Draper came upon a watertight door, slightly ajar, with the symbol of a small flaming grenade stenciled above it.

Still carrying his ax, Yi pushed the door open. Three shots, like a volley from a firing squad, stopped his entry. Draper made to reopen the door. On the other side were Diderick, Bram, and Elias, if his count were right, and perhaps others.

"No!" Hobson yelled, and he brushed Draper away. He pulled back the inert Yi and pulled the Owl Head pistol from its peculiar money-belt holster under his jumper.

He opened the heavy steel door a few inches and could hear the breathing on the other side. Hobson had guessed that Draper intended to open the door to get a clear shot, except that would have been foolhardy. Draper didn't know ships the way Hobson knew ships. Hobson took aim and fired one shot upward and to the right, at an exposed, insulated pipe.

A roar and ungodly screaming sounded in his ears as Hobson pulled Yi free and slammed the watertight door.

The screaming voices were distracting, though they didn't last long.

"Down seven times, up seven times only, this time." Yi was limp and wheezing. He could hardly be heard above the roar of escaping steam. "I think the ancestors are chuckling, nephew. They look down the long, straight line of the Yi family and see one great deviation. Perhaps Ephraim Coffin will put in good word for me. Well, the ancestors have awaited the opportunity to sit in judgment so long, they needed a laugh."

His eye movements were quick and disoriented, Hobson noted.

"What entertainment I have given them! Have I won back my honor? Perhaps, or perhaps not."

No one spoke. Hobson held the Korean, and could see no balancing of the scales. For a moment, Hobson saw Chief Gillingham's image. *Uncle Billy's Last Stand.* He decided Yi's death was going to turn out better than Gillingham's death. Hobson was tired of brave, wise old men dying ingloriously

Remembering three floating bodies, he realized he owed his fatigue to broader origins: corruption and injustice.

More shore patrol members began to collect around *Qilin Cathay*'s armory. Yi could do nothing more, still Hobson knew it wasn't over.

For a moment, Hobson had to remind himself of the significance of the hissing steam. As intended, his shot had punctured a steam pipe. The stream of released steam was capable of cutting a man in half. If it didn't do that, it would at least easily scald the men on the other side of the door to death. The Spuyten sons were dead. Only Hellfire Spuyten, the last of the Spuyten clan, remained.

Gian Singh of the Shanghai Municipal Police, supported now by two additional Sikhs stormed down the passageway carrying lathi as several sailors traced out the valves controlling the escaping steam. He took note of Draper's shoulder devices and shore patrol belt and leggings.

"Being too, too, hot down here. You are senior man here?"

Draper nodded, wiping his glasses. "Lieutenant Junior Grade, New York Naval Militia at your service."

"What happened? That man, who is he?"

Draper pointed down at Yi. "He's not US Navy. Apparently, some men in there shot at him as he opened the door. The steam pipe's broken. I've asked my men to shut off the steam."

The area suddenly became quiet. One sailor opened the armory door slowly with rags wrapped around his hands and groaned. "Criminy, they look like one big lobster bake, all fiery-red lobsters, size extra-large. Hoo-ee."

The three Spuyten boys no longer looked human. The air inside was too hot to enter the armory.

"Your pistol. May I see your pistol?"

Draper looked surprised for a moment, and then realized the delicacy of the situation. An officer of the foreign military turning over his weapon might be misconstrued.

The Sikh immediately understood the implications. "The pistol. I will return it. I wish to know if it has been recently discharged."

Draper handed it over. The Sikh waved its barrel under his nose. "No recent discharge." Singh returned it with the faintest hint of a bow. "Therefore, I am not needing to take it."

Draper was momentarily puzzled. He had recently discharged it, though not below decks. Singh had with a few deft statements and observations, simplified the situation in his and the Navy's favor.

"One might think these men were executed, but who can guess why?" Singh mused out loud as the pipes kept banging as they cooled down. Execution by cooking, er, steaming was unusual. "And this man..." He pointed at Yi. "He might have been executed also, like a firing squad." He raised his hand and dropped it as if signaling an invisible firing squad.

"Officer Singh?" Draper asked. "A group of women is here someplace. They're being held against their will as, well...as slaves."

"Women? Perhaps these men needed shooting," Singh said. "Well, we'll attend to that. Your men. I'll need the name of each of your men involved in this riot, and immediately."

"Oh yes, very soon." Draper agreed.

"Riot?" Draper continued, changing the subject. "Well, some men were involved in a ruckus to rescue the women, really, and other men also came to our aid to get it all under control. I really can't say who was who. We just arrived to preserve order. They all look pretty much alike, clean-shaven and denim uniforms without insignia. I assure you the wrongdoers will be identified and punished by the United States Navy."

"Make it so," Singh said, clicking his heels. He and his men stormed off to attend to the kidnapped women.

Something in Singh's eyes made Draper think the Sikh policeman believed not a word of it.

CHAPTER THIRTY- SEVEN

Hobson reached the main deck just in time to see Persimmon Ma and a powerfully built old man in a gray-blue frock coat spill down one of *Gorgon*'s mooring lines. Hobson remembered Hellfire Spuyten from Hobson's last visit to the Lane of Lingering Joy. The absence of tin-cone-shaped rat guards on the mooring lines confirmed Hobson's fear that the ships had been preparing to set sail.

Hellfire followed the gangster, almost skipping, yet with a slight rolling of his left ankle. Hobson could see the man loved the pain and commotion he created.

Hobson pursued Persimmon and Hellfire as they rushed off the coaling quay through the adjoining shipyard and into the Japanese section of the International Settlement. Shanghai was already in a state of high alert. Police, soldiers, reporters, gawkers, and even a fire wagon, were now streaming over the coaling quay.

Charging into the International Settlement, Hobson nearly bowled over an elegant Asian woman and her maid or companion, both dressed in European finery. They had been watching the Spuyten ships with their wrists crossed and their hands into the cuffs of their unbuttoned sleeves.

"Excuse me, ladies." He said on impulse in Hangugo.

The older woman's eyes flared in happy recognition of her language, and then cooled with indifference. Hobson had used too informal a form of address for a woman of her station.

Stuffing hands into opposite sleeves was very Asian. In one sleeve of each woman shirt, he suspected there'd be either a dagger or a lady's pistol.

"Bossman Yi, where?" She demanded. It was at that moment, he recognized her as the nurse on the Jinsen Steam Navigation wharf in Woosung and the owner's representative on the river tug during the gold heist, but this was not the time to trace connections, exchange niceties, or offer condolences.

She recognized him simply as an American sailor.

Her interest here was not casual.

Hobson studied her face, then pointed and yelled over his shoulder, "*Qilin Cathay*' and sprinted off.

Had to overtake Hellfire, had to.

He couldn't unceremoniously just tell her Yi was near death, not if she was the Japanese-Korean changsan, could he? Had Yi forgiven and reunited with Liqin to confound the Japanese despite her betrayal? Had *she* uncovered the Japanese plot behind the gold?

The last question made him reduce his stride.

Had he seen a tear on her cheek?

He had to overtake Persimmon and Hellfire.

Hobson could hear shots, though couldn't tell where they were coming from. Did they come from *Gorgon*, *Qilin Cathay*, or from inland?

At first, he struggled to keep the two men in sight. Outside the shipyard, the crowds began to thin. Eventually, the streets were unpopulated, yet the sound of gunfire grew more intense. He was so wrung by emotion, and spent by lack of sleep, that it was all he could do to focus his eyes.

Persimmon was no doubt out of his element in the Japanese Concession.

He ducked into a blind alley, and then had to backtrack. Spotting Hobson, the gangster obviously realized he was within range. Persimmon fired his revolver at Hobson, and missed.

Behind Persimmon, Hellfire assumed a taunting stance. Hobson saw Hellfire's eyes, like holes burnt in canvas.

His adrenaline was accelerating his senses to a degree Shanghai around him slowed.

Hobson braced his wrist against a window sill. He rested his pistol with the other hand on that wrist and focused on the rear sight.

When Persimmon devolved into a blurred human with arms and legs, he fired.

Persimmon's leg buckled. Favoring his good leg, he ran to Hellfire, grabbed the madman's shoulder, and spun him around.

Hellfire's reaction was quick. He went for the razor in his left shoe, still Persimmon wouldn't let him bend down. Instead, he put the barrel of his pistol to Hellfire's thigh and fired.

With a roar of pain, Hellfire collapsed onto one knee.

Persimmon Ma hesitated for a moment and nodded in Hobson's direction. That one droopy eyelid held Hobson's attention and Hobson understood the message: *There, you have what I think you want. Forget me.*

He backed away from Spuyten.

Hobson was taken aback. He only had three bullets left, and didn't want to strike a deal with Persimmon. The matter was personal with Persimmon, too.

A moment later a peripheral movement coalesced into a shape, the shape of a man whose height was slightly greater than that of the average Chinaman. His head down, his arms held away from his body, and the fingers on his hands strangely splayed. That man was heading straight for Hobson.

The man raised his head. His nose was unnaturally flat and his face pitted. Without question, the new arrival was Pockmarked Weng.

Persimmon wasn't as sure of Pockmarked's objective as Hobson, and began to raise his gun.

Then Pockmarked was on Persimmon, parrying the pistol with the knuckles of one hand, and following with another punch. That explained the splayed appearance of his relaxed fingers earlier; he was wearing brass knuckles, dull surfaced and green with age.

Persimmon's pistol dropped to the paving stones far beyond Hellfire's reach.

Perhaps for Hobson and Spuyten's benefit, Pockmark addressed Persimmon in English. "You lie me. Job not approved by Three Harmonies. My boss mad. Three Harmonies mad."

Pockmarked unleashed an expert combination of punches leaving Persimmons seated against a half-smashed hogshead.

Not far away, Hellfire was hoisting himself upright.

"You leave Shanghai forever, maybe two days. If no do, you dead. You need me more convince?"

Persimmon waved with open palms. Hobson guessed his jaw was broken.

"Two Yankee sailors, one woman in river. My job to change minds. Who kill them? Can't change minds when they dead. Who destroyed my project by killing?"

Persimmon pivoted and pointed to Hellfire.

Pockmarked looked to Hellfire unsurprised. "You kill two sail-or-boys and Chinee women?"

By now, Hellfire has risen to his full height and holding his straight razor aloft too eloquently. Persimmon scuttled off to an alley to the west leaving his pistol with Pockmarked.

"You killed. Not necessary. You in Shanghai, not necessary. Maybe Hellfire anywhere, not necessary no more."

"Come an' get it, celestial," were Hellfire's first words. Hobson was surprised he'd been quiet so long. Hellfire began to laugh.

Pockmarked punched Hellfire in the ribs and his extended hand came down. Pockmarked Pocketmarked smashed his wrist and sent the razor flying.

The Chinaman stopped to remove his brass knuckles. He wrapped them, the pistol and the straight razor, in his tunic. He placed the bundle on the street in the middle of the road.

"Now, I beat you only as much as I beat each Yankee sailor on *Qilin Cathay*. I beat woman not so much. Maybe you learn something from experience."

Hellfire kicked. He tried to bite Pockmarked and tried, unsuccessfully, to go for the bundle. He tried to jab the Chinaman with staves from the hogshead. He went for Pockmarked's eyes. All to no avail.

Finally, Hellfire collapsed and he was still.

Pockmarked nudged his body, and examined him expertly.

"He learn something from this experience, no one else could make him learn..."

Pockmarked slapped off the dust on his tunic and put it on.

"...that he had bad heart," he skoffed with finality.

The last Spuyten was dead.

Behind him, Hobson heard the clatter of horses' hooves.

"Okay, Yank, that's as far as you get. This ain't the American West an' we ain't the bleedin' cavalry."

He couldn't identify the accent — Cockney? Australian? Hobson wasn't sure, though he recognized the uniforms. One rider, with a face like a hatchet, and two stripes on his sleeve, was talking, but not smiling. Two other horsemen whirled around Hobson. Now he recognized them. They were all riders from the Shanghai Volunteer Corps.

After the riders had drawn their service revolvers, Hatchet-face said, "See, we only recognize organized groups with guns, this bein' the East. Individuals don't count for much. That's Nationalist territory – which faction I can't say — now, there up ahead. Been that way for a half-hour. They've run up against the Japanese and maybe a triad or two. Anyway, they're playing it like a high-stakes shootout for some reason. You show up in that eye-catching white uniform, alone, and you're going to need more ammunition than I think you're carrying."

Hatchet-face gestured with the barrel of his Webley. "We're preventative, that's what we are. No kidnappings for ransom. My brief doesn't say anything about reenacting the Battle of Balaclava. So just turn around and head back to your ruddy boat, barge, yacht, punt, coracle, or what-have-you. Any shootout between the Yuan Nationalists and the Anti-Yuan Nationalists, the Japanese naval infantry, and the organized sinners of Shanghai, may have a net pacifying effect. It's all about makin' our bleedin' work a trifle easier, isn't it?"

Hobson turned and broke the cylinder of his hammerless. With one bullet, he had scalded three men to death. With the other bullet he'd wounded one man who'd deserved it, who had in turn wounded another equally deserving man, who was now dead.

He doubted he could do better with the remaining three bullets.

One Shanghai Volunteer Corps trooper was examining Hellfire Spuyten's body.

The leading trooper looked at Hobson.

"Don't think this gob did that. Look at that man's face and at his temple. That geezer may have taken a shot in the leg, but he was beaten to death."

"Yank, your hands look pretty clean and you have only that pistol and not many bullets. Go home, or your ship, or wherever sailors go."

A half-hour later, Hobson tossed the Owl Head hammerless off the coaling station quay when no one was looking and approached *USS Pluto*.

Draper pitched his issue .45 pistol into the Huangpu that night.

Since the gun was Navy property, he filed a form for an operational loss and it was quickly replaced.

He reached into his pocket and found the ox netsuke still there. This was the Year of the Ox, he remembered.

As he recalled, oxen were associated with persistence.

CHAPTER THIRTY- EIGHT

Consulate Annex, Hongkou District, September 1913

Flag Captain Payson entered the space like a dark cloud and looked at Draper severely.

"Are you getting over a case of the measles?"

Draper realized Payson was looking at the scabbed-over spots on the back of his hands and neck.

We're off to a fine start, Draper thought.

"No, sir, this is what you might call a case of secondary shrapnel."

"I noticed coming in, the doors here had been damaged. Something about an attack by the competing Nationalist factions? Bullet holes everywhere. Were you the Horatio at the Bridge I've heard about?"

Draper was uncomfortable. "Well, I was fired upon and I returned fire with the support of a consular employee, Miss Knapp."

"That cast on your wrist, was it the result of this battle?"

"No, sir, an altercation with the Green Gang on Nanking Road a week or two back."

Captain Payson scratched his head. "Why isn't a fire-eater like you in the sea-going navy?"

"Sir, I was recruited for my language skills. Intelligence is where I'm most useful to the Navy. On the other hand, as a naval officer, I'm not disposed to giving ground, sea room, or the weather gauge."

The flag captain seemed thoughtful.

"Mr. Draper, I want you to listen to me with great care. Can you do that?"

"Yes, sir."

"I'm going to ask you two questions, and I want you to answer those questions only. You strike me as an academic in a staff position who is unfamiliar with the traditions of the operational Navy. I want no side trips, no frolics or excursions, no addenda, no footnotes in your answers. Is that absolutely clear?"

"Yes, sir."

"After thorough investigation, do you conclude that the Asiatic Fleet, in any way or form, currently possesses, or did it at any time attempt to possess for itself, gold belonging to the Empire of Japan?"

"No, sir."

"After thorough investigation, do you conclude that the Asiatic Fleet did at any time attempt to place women of any race or nationality into bondage for sexual purposes?"

"No, sir."

"I accept your extensive report as exemplary. Thank you, Mr. Draper."

Captain Payson picked up his dispatch case and departed.

Seagulls were known to fly in quickly, land with a disruptive flapping of wings, squawk loudly in many directions, and leave voluminous deposits. It was then their practice to fly off with equal haste.

The Seagull had arrived, Draper observed, squawked cautionary words, run excrement down his neck, and quickly departed.

At last, Draper understood the origin of Payson's nickname.

Draper was gratified to note that behind the flag captain's performance was a purpose.

USS Pluto, Shanghai, September 1913

Draper caught Hobson's elbow as he was about to climb the ladder to *Pluto*'s bridge.

"I'm heading back to Tokyo. My work here in Shanghai is done."

Draper opened a square, velvet-lined box that held a set of Zeiss binoculars. On their strap was a note with a chop mark. *"To a man who sees far and what none others see. May he continue to share that gift with his countrymen, in the Realm of the Golden Dragon."*

"Yi holds you in high regard," Draper added. "He left me a handsel, too."

Draper opened a long box of the same quality, which held a sword. Tied to the gold knot that intertwined its handle was a note with a chop depicting a Red-Crown Crane, which read: *"To a scholar who studies the wisdom of the ancestors, may you continue to apply that wisdom."* The sword was engraved to *'Lieutenant Lincoln De Groot Moss, NYNM.'* Draper guessed it had belonged to a naval militia officer during the Spanish-American War. "NYNM" stood for "New York Naval Militia." Now that officer's legacy carried on through Draper.

Yi had grown tired of silver and gold, Draper thought. Utility, and an adopted ancestor, had more meaning.

"You may not be aware of all Yi set in motion," Draper began. "He manipulated a three-way train wreck. During *Pluto*'s Divine Service, Yi had provided information anonymously — perhaps with a tiny bit of help from me — that the gold was in a Hongkou District warehouse and was about to be moved. He provided that information to the Three Harmonies Society, then the Kempeitai, and finally the Yuan Nationalists. He didn't bother with the Anti-Yuan Nationalists who were already in disarray, as was the Green Gang.

"Yi staggered the release of that rumor. The Three Harmonies Society showed up first, to find the warehouse doors were welded shut. By the time they had broken down the doors, the Japanese Kempeitai showed up and started shooting at the Three Harmonies Society men, who fired back. Then a company of Yuan Nationalist soldiers and intelligence agents showed up and the fracas became a three-way gun battle.

"Each successive group was larger than the previous group. We can expect these factions won't be sharing information in the next decade, perhaps next generation. Many of those supposedly in the know died, and much of what they knew is now irretrievably lost. That protects us all. Yi, you, and me. Our trail has now officially run cold." Draper smiled wanly.

"Deception and predation," he added. "Those are the heart of this last coup. Deception was always a required skill for tribute couriers. Yi learned predation in a hard school and reluctantly, but

I think that's why he became so skillful in their application against evil."

Draper paused. He knew a classical education would be no help in addressing what must come next.

"I'm sorry about Clementine," Draper offered, removing his glasses. "You helped her buy herself out of her contract at Madam Guan's. You liberated her and she wanted to pass on the favor on a larger scale by helping to liberate China. The trouble was she hitched her wagon to a doomed, rising Nationalist star.

"She needed something to contribute, and she needed to show her commitment to the cause. How was she to know that divulging a few confidences about foreigners was going to turn out the way it did? How was she to know that she was at the convergence of two Chinese triads, a pathological American family, and the national interests of three countries? The Nationalists started off with good intentions, but Shih-kai Yuan wants to be emperor. I can only hope the right Nationalists find their way back."

Hobson seemed not to hear.

"You gave her freedom and hope," Draper continued, and Hobson did seem to hear those words. "She wasn't untrue to you, or us. She was simply true to something that doesn't exist quite yet."

USS Rainbow, Shanghai, Huangpu River, September 1913

Draper watched as the crews of USS *Rainbow* and USS *Pluto* were paraded on the main deck of USS *Rainbow*.

"Toe the line," the master-at-arms bellowed, and the men fell into several ranks along chalked lines on USS *Rainbow's* expansive decks, facing Ol' Blue Flame. The toes of each of their feet touched a line.

Before Ol' Blue Flame stood the crews of USS *Rainbow* and USS *Pluto*, resplendent in their service dress white uniforms. Each man was attired in a blue-cuffed and collared jumper, a Fighting Bob Evans hat, a loose neckerchief secured by a reef knot, and billowing trousers with inverted creases on the seams. As a group, they were immaculate, uniformed to the letter of the *Bluejacket's Manual*, so tense the backs of their necks ached. Behind them stood their chief petty officers in double-breasted white jackets and navy-blue bowties.

Draper noted trepidation among the chief petty officers especially. Many had earned three consecutive good conduct awards and had won the right to wear gold thread service stripes and chevrons. Non-judicial punishment would scotch a successive good-conduct award and force the proud wearer to replace his gold stripes with blue ones.

Everyone was being brought up for mast. This was an honest-to-Providence admiral's *disciplinary* mast for all who wore dungarees aboard *Pluto* and *Rainbow*. Word was the paymaster hadn't been seen since his admiral's request mast. Request masts were boringly benign. No one could remember an en masse admiral's disciplinary mast. Few had ever stood before an admiral's disciplinary mast. Now captain's masts were common and involved one or two crewmen, seldom more than a dozen, but an admiral's mast was as rare as honor among soiled doves. Rarer still were admiral's disciplinary masts that encompassed the entire crews of two separate ships. If the number of defaulters was of an unheard-of magnitude, what might the magnitude of the punishments be? The Navy didn't have a brig in the Pacific large enough to hold them all, and that meant Ol' Blue Flame might get creative.

Admiral Bulkley was harder than number nine coal, and hard men in the Navy were known for unhealthy creativity.

The master-at-arms called the formation to attention, and Ol' Blue Flame lit into them with a rare fury. The Asiatic Fleet had its standards. The eyes of the world were on the American fighting man. This was the new global United States Navy and its new status would not be sullied. In Brooklyn, back in the state of New York, laws had been passed so that no American sailor could be denied entry into a bar, tavern, or hotel. The United States was now recruiting sailors from inland states, and sailors with high school educations.

Admiral Dewey, the hero of the Battle of Manila Bay, had been considered for the Presidency. The hero of the Battle of Santiago Bay, a fellow name "Hobson," not *USS Pluto*'s Hobson, was a member of Congress, a senator. All these things should have inspired the men of the Asiatic Fleet, but instead they had acted as undisciplined ruffians, hooligans in dungarees. Ol' Blue Flame had a mind to...

After his comments, the admiral paused.

"Master-at-Arms, read the charges."

The master-at-arms read the charges: "Irreverent or unbecoming behavior during Divine Service. Scandalous conduct tending to the destruction of good morals. Absent from station or duty without leave. Unlawful destruction of public property not at the time in possession of an enemy, pirate or rebel. And while ashore, plundering, abusing, or maltreating any inhabitant or injuring that inhabitant's property in any way."

He didn't read the names of the accused. They knew who they were; they were everyone.

"Master-at-Arms, witnesses?"

"Sir, we have no witnesses."

"None?"

"None, sir. None apart from the accused and, Admiral, sir, you said you'd offer no leniency to those who testified against their shipmates. It would hurt crew cohesion."

"So, I did. So, I did. How strange. Who was the investigating officer? Do we have no one who would provide testimony without an offer of leniency?"

"Mr. Draper, that shore-bound naval militia officer who used to wear rumpled uniforms, sir," the master-at-arms retorted.

"That would explain it." Ol' Blue Flame looked at Draper severely and reflected for several minutes.

Draper attempted to look contrite.

"All charges dismissed," the admiral stated, then paused. "Seeing that they're all in dress white and a wonder to behold, pass the word that overnight liberty has been granted for all hands until midnight tomorrow. Officers shall stand all in-port watches alone during that period."

No outsider would ever know what had happened in the past few months.

Men had died on his watch.

He regretted that, but through the years, even in peacetime, and this was 'peacetime," men had died on his watch, regardless, with regularity.

At times, he had set his fleet in motion in ways that affected hundreds, sometimes thousands of lives. Men in ships were vulnerable to the forces of nature, and the unknown, in faraway places.

No, they'd pulled it off. *If he, Ol' Blue Flame, wasn't to be remembered by his country for his deeds on its behalf,* he smiled ironically, *he'd be remembered by his men for his eccentricity.*

They were his men and he loved them for their energy, guided and misguided, and their grit.

Once again, they – and he — had taken a risk and the benefit had exceeded the risk. Their trade assured each one of them a shot at destiny.

The Empire of Japan was a developing country. It did not have much gold to back its currency. In attempting to use it as a weapon, it had squandered a significant portion that gold.

Japan's subversive machinations in China had been dealt a severe blow.

As Draper watched, a great white cotton duck amoeba flowed off *USS Rainbow* onto the coaling quay and surged and flexed until gravity drew it to Rue Chu Pao-san, or what would soon be known the world over as "Blood Alley." Some of the girls in the French Concession were drawn to the men who roamed Rue Chu Pao-san, by their crisp uniforms, virility and Mexican silver. A larger than usual detail of shore patrolmen from other ships tried to contain the women's enthusiasm for the next twenty-four hours, even so the battle was a losing one.

Singh of the Shanghai Municipal Police watched the commotion with patience. Sergeant Fairbairn had told him triad activity was down.

Singh wouldn't have admitted it, but he most likely hoped, as did all afloat and ashore, that someone would fill the market vacuum left by the demise of Madam Guan's establishment.

In the end, Draper thought, the admiral's generosity at disciplinary mast only triggered innumerable captains' disciplinary masts further down the line. Discipline among sailors was always a close-run thing.

The great white cotton duck amoeba settled down, at last, when it found an establishment — Draper learned later — with a Polyphon.

USS Pluto, Huangpu, Shanghai, September 1913

Hobson barely believed it, yet word had come that Yi was alive and in hiding. He had taken several ricochets off a watertight door and lived. Hobson knew better than to look for him. The Three Harmonies Society, the Kempeitai, and the Yuan Nationalists each had long, unforgiving institutional memories, and the uniformed American sailors who had been Yi's allies were too easy to follow, so he severed the connection for the foreseeable future.

USS Pluto strained at the lines that secured it to the coaling quay. The greased rat guards on those lines swayed hypnotically.

It was an hour before taps. The bumboats made their passes and the discordant noises and bright lights of life ashore made a stark contrast with the darkness and harmonies of the ship. On the fantail, someone was playing an English concertina.

Not everyone had taken overnight liberty. Though he claimed to be all oak, iron bound, and sound as a barrel, Olmstead realized any more excitement might tear his stitches. He had poleaxed one of the crew of *Gorgon* with his crutch with painful consequences to himself.

Chief Phipps, with nearly 30 years' service, was saving money for a farm, pool hall, or coal delivery service. In recent years he'd only gone ashore for tattoos. Recently, he determined he had used up all reasonable skin surface and viewed that discovery as an ominous revelation.

Hobson's reason for staying aboard was less practical. He sat on a caulking mat, and plucked at his ukulele.

"I dunno. Are the people we protect worth the people it costs to the protect them?" he asked, looking at Chief Phipps' silhouette.

Phipps tapped his pipe against a stanchion and appeared to wonder if the question required an answer.

"Who do we actually protect, Hobson, do you know? Do I know? Heck, the admiral doesn't know. We try. I want you to walk all the way forward. Take a look right on our cutwater. You'll see the red, white, and blue shield of the Department of War. I never heard anything said about who gets to benefit from that shield…or whether whoever gets that benefit really needs to be worthy or not. How would you go about telling? Tests or something? How often they attend Divine Services? How much they have in the bank?"

Hobson was surprised by Phipp's unexpected fervor.

"We hold up the shield. Those who elect to take refuge behind it are not exactly ours to choose until someone comes up with a special rating for mind readers, fortunetellers, and crystal ball smiths. That's someone else's call and maybe that's the glory to us that we fight to protect without paying too much attention to the likes of who we're protecting. As long as that shield is part of our her-old-dree, we just kind of gotta take it all on faith that most of the folks we're protectin' are worth protectin'. If they ain't, well, maybe their cause is."

Chief Phipps saw the tobacco was low in the bowl of his pipe and apparently realized he needed to locate his other pouch. He rose. "It is all like a game of horseshoes. Close is good enough. I can't say a six-pound gun can cure all evil, but you'd be surprised how much evil it can cure, properly applied."

Hobson kicked at the base of the stanchion.

"And of course, we do get paid fer doin' it," Phipps added as he ascended the ladder to the bridge. "As long as they keep paying us, somebody must think it's all worthwhile. You get three squares, a place to sleep, and somewhere to strum that a-cursed ukulele."

Phipps pronounced the word "a-cursed" with three syllables.

Consulate Annex, Hongkou District, Shanghai, September 1913

Some members of the white cotton duck amoeba had carried Draper on their shoulders off to the main Consulate, new used sword and all. He returned to the consulate annex and was greeted by Miss Knapp who examined the condition of his uniform with approval. She'd taken to keeping extra sets of his whites in the strong-room.

He required some time to get changed.

She ran her hand affectionately along the sleeve of his fresh uniform. "Admiral Bulkley's wife and I have found homes and missions that'll take in Guan's girls." They'll have time to decide on their new lives."

"I think I'll be traveling between Tokyo and Shanghai frequently," he said with a smile. "Tokyo's the best place to track Japan's war hardware. It's my view that Shanghai's the best place to keep an eye on Japan's operations in Asia."

"Oh, and you can tell Hobson the Mex he owes Mr. Sunshine is here ready for delivery," Miss Knapp added.

"Almost forgot. I've spoken with Sergeant Fairbairn," Franconia interjected, all efficiency again. "He'd like someone to identify the bodies found in the water near *Qilin Cathay*.

"There seems to be a discrepancy," she said scanning her notes.

"The bodies of Yeoman Striker Harte and Boatswain's Mate Second Class O'Grady have been recovered and are being prepared for burial," Miss Knapp reported.

"The body of the woman, Huiwen "Clementine" Zhong, could not be found. A woman matching her description was reported to have been picked up by a bumboat off the coaling quay – no date was given. She was alive, although badly beaten. She was deposited on the Pudong docks, though has since disappeared.

"Speculation is: she's in the care of the Anti-Yuan Nationalists."

HISTORICAL NOTES

In olden times, when tigers smoked long stem pipes...
— Traditional opening to Korean folk stories

When the US occupation forces landed in Japan post-surrender, they were surprised to discover large stocks of ceramic incendiary grenades. These stocks had been collected for distribution to the civilian population during the anticipated last ditch battle for the home islands. Perhaps the idea had been triggered by the memory of the difficult Captain Yi, or someone like him.

My thanks to CDR Arthur McCormick, NYNM, who allowed me to use his artifact, the Lincoln De Groot Moss presentation sword, as a participant in this yarn. Naval Lieutenant Lincoln De Groot Moss was a Columbia University engineering professor who served aboard the *USS Yankee* during the Spanish-American War. McCormick, Moss, and Crossland share ties to the New York Naval Militia and Columbia.

In 1913, Shanghai was just beginning to develop a frontier-town reputation for decadence and crime, but it was already a frontrunner when it came to vice, loose women, and bare-knuckle capitalism. The city brought together the best and worst of East and West, assuring it legendary status. Shanghai, however, was more than that: It was China's entry point for new ideas such as nationalism, democracy, and the equality of women.

Skagway and Shanghai were not as far apart historically as the reader might think, especially where the US Navy was concerned. A rice bucket resembled nothing Western more than a firkin. Popular as the firkin was as a bulk butter container, it imparted an unfortunate woody flavor. The discovery of gold in the Yukon triggered a stampede of an unusual grade of hopeful miners. The Yukon Gold Rush stampeders were, as a group, the best educated and most affluent of any group of miners of the period. Affluent miners were willing to pay any price in order to satisfy their taste for perishable animal protein. (One of Jack London's best-remembered tales, "The One Thousand Dozen," addressed the willingness of miners to pay any price for eggs.)

Perishable foods were unknown delicacies in the Arctic. Butter was one of these perishables. Suppliers in the United States working on the problem found that butter sealed in vacuum cans was still fresh months later. Consequently, the discovery of gold in Alaska gave impetus to canning butter in tin containers, a practice that was later followed for expeditions and cruises to remote and unknown regions such as, well, Shanghai.

By 1912, the US Navy was settling into its role as the arm of a global power and it became interested in this method of packing American butter all over the world. The Dairy Division of the Department of Agriculture was impressed by the Navy's effort and suggested canned butter be put on the commercial market. This was done successfully, to the great satisfaction of the dairy states.

Desperate, cut-throat merchant captains drove sailing ships, and there crews, to their limits. The economics of the first two decades of the twentieth century allowed sailing ships one more respite before they flared nova-like and expired. Historians of sail, like Alan Villiers, owed their opportunity to document the majesty of sail to this brief resurgence, but at a terrible cost particularly during World War I, when tired ships with minimal crews were put back into commission carrying urgently needed cargoes.

The Seamen's Act of 1915 made merchant officers and ship owners accountable for brutalizing their crews. Diederik Cornelius "Hellfire" Pedersen was one of the first captains tried under the act. Hellfire Pedersen routinely intimidated his crews by tossing men over the side as a warning to the others. Apparently, Pedersen believed his license title, "master," was without limitation.

His misdeeds caught up with him in 1918 aboard the barkentine *Pauko*. That barkentine's owners directed him to take a cargo of lumber from Vancouver to Capetown. World War I had created a cargo shipping crisis and many tired sailing ships — and third-rate merchant officers — were being recalled to service. As captain, Hellfire made a practice of shackling and then beating *Pauko*'s men, sometimes crippling them for life, or locking them into a confined space and subjecting them to the "water cure."

Pedersen sailed with his two sons, tutoring them in this peculiar leadership style. When the *Pauko* arrived in Capetown with two of its twelve crew members missing, the complaints of the crew triggered an inquest and trial. Pedersen was tried and convicted under the Seaman's Act and sentenced to six concurrent eighteen-month terms. Surprisingly, Pedersen was able to renew his license in 1922. Pedersen's first mate served five years at hard labor for his contributions to making *Pauko* a hell-ship. This case was one of the first stands taken against such brutality, yet the sentences were trivial when measured against murder and mayhem.

Ukuleles and the Navy were connected. "Ukulele" is purportedly Hawaiian for "jumping flea." The instrument was invented by the Portuguese, and Portuguese sailors introduced it to the islands of the Pacific. No one is sure whether the term "jumping flea" applies to the disposition of the instrument's players or to how the instrument is played. Its first wave of popularity came when it was introduced to the US mainland at the 1915 Panama Pacific International Exposition, and it gained wide acceptance among jazz musicians. Its second wave of popularity came with early TV pioneer Arthur Godfrey's great popularity. He learned to play the ukulele as a Navy radio operator on destroyers during World War I.

The ukulele owes its association with sailors to its simplicity, portability, and durability. The best ones are fashioned from Hawaiian koa.

Red-crowned cranes and economic warfare were connected. The red-crowned crane is known in Asia as a symbol of luck, longevity, fidelity, and nobility. It breeds in Mongolia and migrates to China, Korea, and Japan. In Chinese mythology, a mortal who has gained immortality rides off on a red-crowned crane. In Japanese mythology, a red-crowned crane lives a thousand years life. The imagery continues, for red-crowned cranes are currently on the face of the Japanese one-thousand yen note.

Sailors of the Asiatic Fleet had the opportunity to observe war through currency. Imperial Japan did attempt to undermine China's currency. During the time period 1938-1940, the Japanese worked to strategically devalue the Chinese yuan, not by a show of gold backing, instead by offering an artificially favorable exchange rate. American missionaries in Korea increased the value of their meager paychecks by converting US dollars to Chinese yuan, then converting yuan to Japanese yen, and in the process trebled their buying power.

Sun Tzu noted in his fourth century B.C. work, *The Art of War*, that "to subdue the enemy without fighting is the acme of skill." Economic warfare is one of the components of modern grand strategy, and the Japanese applied economic warfare against post-Qing dynasty China. We know all too well the costs of economic instability. One of the chief features of the Post-WW II Bretton Woods system was to adopt a monetary policy that maintained the exchange rate of its currency within a fixed range in terms of gold and the ability of the International Monetary Fund to bridge temporary imbalances of payments. The Bretton Woods system, however, could not achieve its objective of global stability. The United States abandoned the Bretton Woods System in 1971.

The Mann Act had a history of misapplication. Jack Johnson, the first African-American world heavyweight boxing champion, was charged with, and convicted of, a Mann Act violation in 1912, for taking his girlfriend across state lines. Johnson's prosecution was racially motivated and derailed his career. Johnson's most famous sparring partner was Edward "Gunboat Smith" Smyth, former Pacific Fleet boxing champ. Some years later, "Gunboat" held the title of world heavyweight champion himself. The admiral was probably thinking of Johnson's May 1913 conviction, and Smyth, when he considered use of the Mann Act. The admiral's creative application of the Mann Act, however, better reflected the statute's original intention. On May 24, 2018, Jack Johnson received a posthumous Presidential pardon for a century-old criminal conviction under the Mann Act. The conviction was motivated by racial malice.

To stickler historians, I confess occasional application of dramatic license. The collier, *USS Pluto*, didn't exist, though a captured Spanish ship became the US Navy collier *USS Saturn*. Colliers never had all-Navy crews, though such crews were being considered just at the time the Navy decided to switch over to oil. Colliers were administered by the Bureau of Navigation, as was the Office of Naval Intelligence. *USS Rainbow* served as a distillation ship, a flagship, a troopship, and station ship in China, during the time period portrayed.

Exercising dramatic license, I moved the story's climactic coaling depot scene up the Huangpu River from Woosung to Shanghai.

The gold mines of Unsan did, and likely still, exist. In the early Twentieth century, Korea had several Western mining communities spread mainly throughout the northern part of the peninsula. Although many of these mining communities were quite small, with only a handful of Westerners and a couple hundred Korean, Chinese, and Japanese workers, others were huge, with several thousand employees. The largest was the Oriental Consolidated Mining Company's concession at Unsan. Oriental Consolidated Mining received the concession to mine gold in Unsan Province in 1897 from King Kojong.

The Unsan mines developed a problem. Though tons of gold were mined successfully, constant flooding left a good deal of gold submerged. The Americans were the only ones in the world capable of handling the mines and were left alone to do so until 1938. In 1938, Japan realized it needed to seize or control all gold possible, and by 1939, the American-owned Oriented Consolidated Mining Company was forced out of Korea. At that point, Americans lost access to the mines.

Despite their technological acumen, Japanese didn't fare as well as the Americans, and the mines fell into disrepair and several shafts collapsed. Increasingly sophisticated pumps helped to some extent, though ultimately the Japanese, and then the North Koreans, couldn't master the flooding problems. During the Korean War, the Battle of the Chongchon River caused further damage to the mines.

Unsan falls above the 38th parallel, about 150 kilometers north of Pyongyang, North Korea's capital. In 1902, Japan suggested dividing Korea along that latitude with Russia, but nothing came of it, and eventually Japan took control of all Korea. At the end of WWII, Korea was divided along that latitude, forming North and South Korea. Unsan became part of North Korea. If the Japanese didn't have the technology to successfully exploit the decaying mines at Unsan, the North Koreans surely did not. And they weren't about to acknowledge the need for Western help.

The chances of a successful Korean insurrection during the Japanese occupation, without the aid of a third country, were slim. On April 10, 1919, several Korean refugees met in Shanghai and established the Provisional Korean Government. Between 1910 and 1940, "anyone who was anybody" in Korean culture, arts, and politics spent at least some time of their life in Shanghai.

After the Manchurian incident in 1931, staged by Japan as a pretext for the invasion of northeastern China, the Provisional Government moved to Nanjing, and later to Chongqing. The Japanese occupation was too brutal and too effective for the Provisional Korean Government to fight. Moreover, the Provisional Korean Government had minimal financial support. The Japanese didn't withdraw from Korea until their defeat at the end of WWII.

That guerrilla war would have dislodged the Japanese from Korea is unlikely. Guerrilla war is most effective when it has a steady source of outside support. Only after four decades of Japanese occupation of Korea, a major conventional war, one million WWII American dead and wounded, and the detonation of two nuclear bombs, did Japan reconsider its designs in the Far East and elsewhere.

If Yi's rice buckets of gold and silver did come to rest in Unsan's flooded mineshafts, they lie there still for a future generation of Koreans to secure after a long-awaited unification.

Yi's efforts would have come so near, yet so far.

GLOSSARY

The reader has been dropped into a foreign, tumultuous, and disorienting time and place with its own strange cultural and professional vocabulary.

He or she might want to become familiar with the below glossary and additional aids to survive the experience and achieve maximum enjoyment.

Akband Paath – (Punjabi) the Sikh practice of continuous recitation, without break, of sacred religious texts

ambrosia – the food of the gods

Artemis – "Greek goddess of the hunt

back water all – a coxswain's command to a crew under oars "to back up"

badmash – (Hindi) a rogue, ruffian, bad person, criminal, naughty one

beam – the maximum width of a ship's hull

bighted bowline – bowline with a double loop used for rescues by employing one loop under the arms and one loop under the buttocks

billet – organizational workplace assignment

bitts – a post or pair of posts mounted on a ship for fastening ropes or cables

blouse – jacket of a uniform

bluejacket – nickname for a sailor of the United States Navy

blue lighting – smuggling

boatswain's mate – a deck force petty officer who specializes in seamanship

box the compass – to count off all 32 points of a compass in order, to spin around completely, to spin 360 degrees

breeches buoy – a lifebuoy with canvas breeches attached that, when suspended from a rope raised with sheerlegs (see sheerlegs), is used to transfer a person from a ship to safety ashore bucko mate – a brutal, abusive ship's officer

Bund, the – ancient boat towing path along Shanghai's Huangpu River that evolved into China's most famous commercial district

Castor and Pollux – constellations of the Zodiac, they are both half-brothers and twins in Greek mythology

caulking mat – a canvas mat original designed for crewmen caulking wooden ships on their backs, but eventually used by crewmen aboard steel warships when sleeping on deck

celestial – a subject of the Celestial Empire (China), a Chinaman

changsan – (Chinese) Chinese courtesans and entertainers who frequented gambling houses

cheechako – Alaskan tenderfoot

Chemulp'o – *McCune-Reischauer*, Incheon, Korea; renamed Jinsen under the Japanese, *Revised Romanization of Korean* Jemulpo

Chilkoot – Alaskan Indian tribe of the Tlingit Nation

Chinnamp'o – *McCune-Reischauer* Pyongyang, Korea, *Revised Romanization of Korean* Jinnampo

chop – a colored – frequently red – seal or stamp of authority

coalpasser – a special naval rate that entitled those within that rate to draw extra pay due to its strenuous demands, a stoker

cold iron – all boilers and machinery have been shut down, or rendered inoperable

confused chop – waves coming from a variety of directions, an inconsistent or "sloppy" sea

cover – hat or headgear

coxswain – the steersman of a ship's boat

cutting-out – a boarding operation, frequently employing small boats, to "cut out" or seize an enemy ship in harbor by employing stealth and speed

cutwater – the forward edge of a ship's prow

datura – a common poison derived from most of the parts of nine species of vespertine flowering plants also used as an herbal medicine and a hallucinogenic

Dagu Forts – Imperial Chinese forts at the mouth of the Hai River that protected the seaward approaches to Tientsin and Peking, *Wade-Giles* Taku Forts

Diana – Roman goddess of the hunt

double-time – to run

dog – to fasten or close a hatch or door

drag – two parallel lines attached to the tongue of the Gatling gun carriage

dreadnaught – an armored warship introduced in the early 20th century, larger and faster than its predecessors and equipped entirely with large-caliber guns

driver captain – a brutal, abusive ship's master

dunnage – pieces of wood, matting, or similar material used to keep a cargo in position in a ship's hold

fantail – the overhanging rear deck on a naval ship

fid – a conical tool traditionally made of wood or bone used to work with rope and canvas; (naval slang) the male reproductive organ resembling that tool

filibuster – freebooter, adventurer, mercenary

Fighting Bob Evans hat – The white hat worn today originated in the 1880s as a low, rolled-brim, high-domed item made of wedge-shaped pieces of canvas popularly associated with Admiral Robley "Fighting Bob" Evans, who initially commanded the Great White Fleet

flag captain – commanding officer of a flagship, frequently an officer of some presence in his own right

flag lieutenant – an officer on an admiral's staff who acts as his personal aide

flotsam – the wreckage of a ship or its cargo found floating on or washed up by the sea

freeboard – the distance from the waterline to the lowest exposed deck

gabion – a basket, cage, cylinder, or box filled with rocks, and sometimes sand and soil, normally used to construct fortifications

Gatling gun – one of the best-known early rapid-fire weapons, an American-invented forerunner of the modern machine gun

gibun – (Korean) harmony

godown – (Eastern Asian) a warehouse

Gorgon – each of three sisters with snakes for hair, able to turn anyone who looked at them into stone

Great White Fleet – the nickname for the USN battle fleet that circumnavigated the world 1907-1909

Hai River – river connecting Tientsin to the Yellow Sea and is the only waterway from Peking to the sea (*Wade-Giles* Peiho River)

Hangugo – (Korean) the Korean language

hanmul – (Korean) a rice bucket, the standard measure of rice

haragei – (Japanese) repression of emotion for the greater good, a concept also practiced by Koreans

havildar – (Hindi) a noncommissioned officer in the Indian army, equivalent in rank to sergeant

highbinder – an assassin, especially one belonging to a Chinese-American criminal organization

hospital apprentice – lowest level medical rate in the US Navy Hospital Corps. Hospital corps' rating roughly equivalent to seaman or fireman

Hongkou – Shanghai district at the confluence of the Huangpu River and Suzhou Creek, part of International Settlement (*Giles-Wade* Hongkew)

Hotchkiss gun – any of several American-invented, French-manufactured machine, field, or mountain guns

Huangpu River – major river running through Shanghai (*Giles-Wade* Whangpoo)

hubae – (Korean) a junior, an underclassman, a mentee

hyung or hyungnim – (Korean) older brother, also boss

Irish pennant – a loose or untidy end of a line or other part of a ship's rigging

Jack Tar, also "tar" – a common term for a seaman, particularly a seaman in the Royal Navy

Jason – In the quest for the Golden Fleece in Greek mythology, Jason is told to sow a gift of dragon's teeth. They sprout into fierce, fully armed warriors, causing his problems to multiply.

jetsam – unwanted material or goods that have been thrown overboard from a ship and washed ashore, especially material that has been intentionally discarded to lighten the vessel

jeyug bokgeum – (Korean) spicy barbecued pork

jige – (Korean) an A-shaped pack-frame, chige *McCune-Reischauer*

Jilseong – (Korean) the Big Dipper

Jinsen – Incheon, *McCune-Reischauer* Chemulp'o

jinrikisha – (Japanese) a small, two-wheeled, cart-like passenger vehicle with a fold-down top, pulled by one person, formerly used widely in Japan and China, purportedly invented by Rev. Jonathon Scobie, also "rickshaw"

Josun – (Korean), *McCune-Reischauer* Chosun, Korea, Land of Morning Calm, the Land on Edge, the Hermit Kingdom, sometimes McCune-Reischauer "Choson" more frequently used for the dynasty

jungin – in the Korean class system, the class below yangban

kanji, hiragana, and katagana – three primary Japanese writing systems or "alphabets"

Kempeitai - the unconventional military police arm of the Imperial Japanese Army until 1945

ladder – any piece of equipment vertical or sloping, comprised of rungs or steps, used aboard ships to move from one deck to another

lagan – anything dropped into the sea, but attached to a buoy or the like so that it may be recovered

Land of the Golden Mountain – United States of America

lathi – (Hindi) a heavy stick, often of bamboo, bound with iron used in India as a weapon, especially by police to disperse crowds or quell riots

Lesser Shanghai Indian Club & Garter Society – Shanghai brothel on the Lane of Lingering Joy, owned by Madam Guan

lighter – a large flat-bottomed barge, especially one used to deliver or unload goods to or from a cargo ship or transport goods over short distances, also to convey (cargo) in a lighter

libertymen – sailors on liberty, on authorized free time ashore

livery – a special uniform worn by a servant, employee, or official

loud hailer – a megaphone

maekgoli – (Korean) unfiltered rice wine, traditionally served hot

magazine – the compartment or compartments within a warship where ammunition and explosives are stored

make-see pidgin – a symbolic message

mansei – "(Korea will exist for) ten thousand years," loosely translated as "freedom," a famous cry of defiance in opposition to the Japanese oppression

Maxim gun – British manufactured machine gun

Mex – silver Mexican coins universally accepted in China, the economy of which had been backed by silver for centuries monkey drill – calisthenics performed "monkey see, monkey do" fashion, usually with little or no special apparatus, in the late nineteenth and early twentieth centuries. They were often performed with rifles, cutlasses, and single sticks (dowels)

muban – (Korean) a member of the yangban class, and the Korean warrior aristocracy

Nationalists – *pinyin* Guomindang or *Wade-Giles* Kuomintang, a Chinese political party/movement favoring democracy, much in disarray in 1913

netsuke – a miniature sculpture that served the practical function of a button-like toggle for a kimono

Nanjing – *Wade-Giles* Nanking

nodaji – (Korean pidgin) "no touchee," a phonetic mimicking of English phrase converted to a written warning requiring that an object not be touched

nunji – (Korean) eye measure, intuitive decision-making

observation kite – a military or naval kite capable of lifting an observer off the ground for reconnaissance purposes, technology eclipsed by the development of the airplane

paymaster – limited-duty naval officer in charge of financial matters

pao – (Chinese) the cannon piece in the Chinese version of chess

peacoat - a short, double-breasted overcoat of coarse woolen cloth

Peking – home of imperial palace of the Qing Dynasty (*pinyin* Beijing)

pince-nez glasses – a pair of eyeglasses with a nose clip instead of temple arms

pongee – light, plain-woven raw silk

Polyphon – a German-made cross between a music box, a player piano, and jukebox

Pudong – district on east side of Huangpu River (*Wade-Giles* Pootung)

quartermaster – rate specializing in navigation and related ship-handling, and during the period addressed, inter-ship communications, skills

quay - a structure built along the bank of a waterway (as a river) for use as a landing for loading and unloading boats

qilin - a creature with the head of a dragon, the antlers of a deer, the skin and scales of a fish, the hooves of an ox and tail of a lion

Qingdao – *Wade-Giles* Tsingtao

Qing dynasty – (1644-1912), also called Manchu dynasty, the last imperial dynasty of China

Realm of the Golden Dragon – the area of the Pacific Ocean west of the International Dateline

Reuben James – revered Barbary War hero and boatswain's mate who was part of a boarding party led by Stephen Decatur and who was reputed to have saved Decatur's life on that occasion

Reverence to Lettered Paper Society – the Chinese had for centuries accorded special respect to the written word, by maintaining a society that disposed of inscribed paper ceremonially

"The Rocks and Shoals" – naval slang for the Articles for Government of the United States Navy, the rules governing the USN prior to 1951, due to their perilous nature according to language in article 4, section 10

roll and stopper – a method of preparing and securing naval uniforms for personal stowage in a seabag

ryokan – (Japanese) inn

sandlotter – a member of San Francisco's Workingmen's Trade and Labor Union of San Francisco, which made use of the mobilizing slogan "The Chinamen Must Go!" Sandlotters were accustomed to gathering in the sand lots in front of the city hall

scullery – a small compartment aboard a naval ship used for washing dishes

scuttlebutt – a cask of drinking water aboard a ship; rumor or gossip gleaned when sailors gathered around the drinking water cask

sea room - sufficient navigable space to achieve a tactical advantage by maneuver, "to a willing foe and sea room (naval toast)"

seonbae – (Korean) a senior, an upperclassman, a mentor

seven bells – ships used bell time to keep their crews aware of the time and the watch. The maximum number of times the bell could ring in a watch was eight times, and that meant the watch was finished. To chime someone's bell seven times was just short of finishing him

sheerlegs – a two-legged lifting device resembling scissors or shears

shoal waters – shallow waters, a perilous zone likely to result in a shipwreck shore patrol – petty officers temporarily assigned limited law-enforcement duties with regard to USN sailors ashore, who wear khaki leggings, khaki pistol belts, and carry a baton, as their badges of office

skivvy – underpants

skivvy house – bordello, singsong house

skivvy-waving – sending semaphore messages using flags

Skookum – Chinook pidgin for "strong"

sky pilot – a pilot or guide to Heaven, a chaplain

sleeve – (naval slang) the arm of a jumper or shirt; (naval slang) the female reproductive organ resembling that portion of a shirt or jumper

slipknot – a knot of unreliable holding power; (slang) an unreliable person

sparadrapum – early adhesive bandage

spit kit – spittoon

stampeder – one of the 100,000 people who attempted to reach the Klondike gold fields at the end of the nineteenth century

stateroom – officer's sleeping compartment aboard ship

steerage – shortened form of "steerageway," a rate of motion sufficient to make a ship or boat respond to movements of the rudder

Shantou – *Wade-Giles* Swatow

stock – collar around the neck of a uniform designed to keep the posture erect

striker – seaman aspiring to a rate of his choosing

Suzhou Creek – tributary creek of Huangpu River that flows through center of Shanghai (*Wade-Giles* Soochow Creek)

tackline – a spacer in a flag hoist, six feet of blank line

tael – a unit of Chinese silver currency weighing between one and two ounces

tael sycee – silver or gold boat-shaped ingot

Taft-Katsura Agreement – a 1905 controversial secret memorandum between senior leaders of Japan and the United States regarding the positions of the two nations in greater East Asian affairs, especially regarding the status of Korea and the Philippines in the aftermath of Japan's victory in the Russo-Japanese War

tally band – band around a sailor's hat bearing the name of his ship or organization tar, see Jack Tar

three sheets – sheets are lines that control the shape of a sail, "sheets to the wind" are sheets that are not tied off or under anyone's control, a man "three sheets to the wind" is in a predicament out of his control

Tientsin – *pinyin* Tianjin, walled city on the Hai River which connects with the Yangtze River via the Grand Canal

tong – a Chinese association or secret society in the US, frequently associated with underworld criminal activity

Tongmenghui - one of the earliest Chinese secret revolutionary societies of early 20th Century led by Sun Yatsen and other notables favoring an end to the Qing Dynasty and unification with the other Chinese revolutionary groups

topside – upstairs

triad – a secret society originating in China, typically involved in organized crime

Triton – Greek god who is messenger of the sea

tumpline – a sling for carrying a load on the back, with a strap that passes around the forehead or shoulders, or both

umyong – (Korean) fortune, luck

weather gauge – the tactically advantageous upwind position held by one fighting sailing vessel relative to another

wherry – in the United States Navy, a light rowboat with two rowing stations designed to ferry passengers or light cargo to ships in a harbor

weir – an obstruction placed in tidal waters, or wholly or partially across a river, to trap, or direct the passage of, fish

Woosung – port city downriver of Shanghai at mouth of Huangpu River (*pinyin* Wusong)

yangban – (Korean) the highest class in the Korean class system, the ruling gentry and the military officers (muban)

Xiamen – *Wade-Giles* Amoy

yaolu – (Chinese) a large oar or sweep, used as a rudder or for sculling

zakuski – (Russian) any substantial Russian hors d'oeuvre, including caviar sandwiches

COMMISSIONED OFFICER RANKS
(in ascending order of seniority)

Ensign
Lieutenant (Junior Grade)
Lieutenant
Lieutenant Commander
Commander
Captain
Rear Admiral
Vice Admiral
Admiral
Admiral of the Navy

ENLISTED GRADES
(in ascending order of seniority)

Seaman or Fireman
Petty Officer Third Class
Petty Officer Second Class
Petty Officer First Class
Chief Petty Officer

CHARACTER LIST

Rear Admiral Bulkley, Simeon ("Ol' Blue Flame") – commander-in-chief, US Asiatic Fleet

General Chen, Ch'i-Mei - (non-fictional) Anti-Yuan Nationalist General

Coffee mill detail at Woosung – Gillingham, Krafts, Ryder, Weishar, Jefferson, Santos, Dellett, Ivorsen, Greenberg, Olsen, LaPierre, and Hobson

Coffin, Ephraim ("White Knight") – eccentric prospector and inventor,

Hospital Apprentice Culper, Ike – hospital apprentice serving aboard troopship *USS Rainbow*

Lieutenant (Junior Grade) Draper, Stuyvesant ("Professor") – New York Naval Militia officer assigned to Office of Naval Intelligence, US Asiatic Fleet

Sergeant Fairbairn, William – (nonfictional) sergeant, Shanghai Municipal Police, later to become hand-to-hand combat instructor to British commandos

Chief Petty Officer Gillingham, William ("Billy") – chief petty officer in charge of the coffee mill detail

Sergeant Go, Min-Ho – senior non-commissioned officer of ambushed tribute detail

Madam Guan – owner of "Lesser Shanghai Indian Club & Garter Society" a brothel, on the Lane of Lingering Joy

US Consul Hadbury, Jameson – consul to Shanghai, governmental official who requests investigation into an accusation of unseemly conduct by members unknown of the United States Navy

Seaman (yeoman striker) Harte, Benjamin ("Washboard") – shipmate of Hobson aboard *USS Pluto*

Quartermaster 3/c Hobson, Gideon – multilingual quartermaster petty officer, son of missionaries to Japan and Korea, who serves first aboard *USS Rainbow* and is then drafted to *USS Pluto*

Kang, Zeman – the Tottler's double

Klukwan – placename adopted as nickname by disgraced son of Chilkoot chief living incognito in Skagway meaning "eternal village

Knapp, Franconia – second secretary of the Shanghai Deputy Consul

Liqin – Japanese-Korean courtesan

Ma, Tingfeng ("Persimmon") – mid-level enforcer for Three Harmonies Society

Corporal Mun, Hui-je – junior non-commissioned officer of ambushed tribute detail

Paymaster Commander McCorkran, Colin – paymaster of *USS Rainbow* and subsequently paymaster of US Asiatic Fleet, cousin of the second partner named in the shipping firm of Spuyten & McCollum

Noble, Silas – lighterage boss

Boatswain's Mate 2/c O'Grady, Aloysius ("Harp") – shipmate of Hobson aboard *USS Pluto*

Coalpasser Olmstead, Vernon – shipmate of Hobson aboard *USS Pluto*

Flag Captain Payson, Phineas ("The Seagull") – senior captain on Asiatic Station and Admiral Bulkley's chief of staff

Chief Phipps, Elijah – chief petty officer aboard *USS Pluto*

Havildar Singh, Gian – native of the Punjab, retired non-commissioned officer of the 14th Sikhs, presently a police officer with the Shanghai Municipal Police

Lieutenant Randolph, Revere – lieutenant (junior grade) Draper's unfortunate predecessor

Smith, Randolph, III ("Soapy") – (nonfictional) con artist and Skagway crime boss

Spuyten, Adrianus ("Hellfire") – Spuyten patriarch, a "driving captain"

Spuyten, Bram – one of "Hellfire" Spuyten's five sons

Spuyten, Giles ("Gizzard") – one of "Hellfire" Spuyten's five sons

Spuyten, Cornelius ("Fightin' Spuyten") – 3rd mate, *Qilin Cathay*, one of "Hellfire" Spuyten's five sons

Spuyten, Diderick ("Diddler") – naval graft enforcer, one of "Hellfire" Spuyten's five sons

Spuyten, Elias – the man in the mackinaw jacket aboard the Skagway-bound side-wheeler, one of Hellfire Spuyten's five sons

Sun, Shoiming – likeable Shanghai street tout

CDR Wheelwright, Morgan – commanding officer, *USS Pluto*, regular Navy officer

Weng, Yongzheng ("Pockmarked") – doorman of Lesser Shanghai Indian Club & Garter Society, strong-arm man for Three Harmonies Society

Yi, Jung-hee ("Skookum") – disgraced Korean tribute courier and officer, smuggler and financier a/k/a "Snowfall"

Yuan, Shih-kai - (nonfictional) a generalissimo of the Chinese Imperial Army, Nationalist general, Nationalist president of the Republic of China, dictator who aspired to be China's next emperor

General Zang – treacherous warlord who attacked the Woosung Gatling gun landing party, owner of an armored Packard

Zhong, Huiwen "Clementine" – former Chinese prostitute with bluestocking aspirations

Ingram Content Group UK Ltd.
Milton Keynes UK
UKHW021322240323
419115UK00016B/109/J